He leaned close, his face only inches from hers.

"What are you doing?" she gasped.

His large hands clamped down on her shoulders, pulling her closer, and his sea green eyes began a slow study of her features. "You know," he drawled, a bold smile causing deep dimples to crease each lean cheek, "I'm almost beginning to think you regret that nothing more happened this afternoon."

"Why, you conceited oaf!"

Rath read the expression in her eyes, saw it change from anger to fear to indecision. The candlelight washed gently over her upturned face, causing the thick lashes to throw spiky shadows over high cheekbones; it glimmered across soft, rose-colored lips, parted in agitation. Without further consideration, he lowered his head and pressed his mouth firmly against hers . . .

Other Books in
THE AVON ROMANCE Series

BRITTANY *by Linda Lang Bartell*
DESPERATE DECEPTION *by Maria Greene*
FIRESTORM *by Brenda Joyce*
ROGUE'S LADY *by Victoria Thompson*
STOLEN HEART *by Barbara Dawson Smith*
WILD SPLENDOR *by Leta Tegler*
WINDSONG *by Judith E. French*

Coming Soon

FORTUNE'S BRIDE *by Cheryl Spencer*
MOONSHADOW *by Susan Wiggs*

SCOTNEY ST. JAMES

AVON BOOKS NEW YORK

BY HONOR BOUND is an original publication of Avon Books. This work has never before appeared in book form. This work is a novel. Any similarity to actual persons or events is purely coincidental.

AVON BOOKS
A division of
The Hearst Corporation
105 Madison Avenue
New York, New York 10016

Published by arrangement with the authors
Library of Congress Catalog Card Number: 88-92102
ISBN: 0-380-75602-1

First Avon Books Printing: January 1989

Printed in the U.S.A.

K-R 10 9 8 7 6 5 4 3 2 1

I've always been proud of the way my daughter deals with the modern world, so it was a surprise to see her in costume for a Renaissance faire and be convinced she *belonged* in medieval England. I really think that, in some other time, she was happy there, perhaps in a place like Middleham. Because of that belief, this book is for Tammy, with love . . .

L.V.

This book is dedicated, with love, to Debra and Lesa . . . Daughters are special, each in her own way. Thank you both for being everything a daughter should be, and for the unique friendships we share.

C.H.

Chapter 1

"So this is where you're hiding . . . I've been looking for you."

The plaintive strains of an old Welsh melody ended in a series of discordant notes as Marganna's fingers slipped on the harp strings. She stiffened in alarm as she felt warm breath stir the tendrils of hair by her right ear, followed by a burning kiss on her neck.

"The journey was overlong. I'm looking forward to sleeping in a real bed tonight, love."

Two steely arms slipped around her waist from behind and, to her horror, a pair of sun-browned hands moved upward to cup her breasts familiarly.

"Then it will be me between your pretty knees instead of that harp."

The man's quiet words were laced with a husky laugh, and again his lips moved against her neck, his teeth gently grazing the skin.

With a cry of anger, Marganna clawed at the offending hands, which dropped away immediately, the motion accompanied by a hearty curse. Leaping to her feet, she pushed the harp away, causing it to teeter dangerously, and whirled to face her assailant.

"How dare you lay hands on me in such a manner?" she declared.

The man's face was frozen in shock.

"Please stop leering at me that way," she snapped.

"Our sainted Lord, who are you?" he asked, as if the words were being dragged from him by force.

"I might ask you the same question."

As the surprised look slowly faded from his features, a sparkle came into his eyes, and he shrugged in an offhand way. "Surely you realize I thought you were someone else," he said, one corner of his mouth quirking upward. "Someone I know . . ."

"Very well, obviously," she retorted, her voice tinged with sarcasm.

He took a step toward her and she backed away, moving closer to the circle of light cast by a single candle in a wall bracket. A few minutes earlier she had enjoyed sitting in the shadows playing the harp, but now the dim corner seemed menacing.

"Ah," he said, a broad smile breaking over his lean face. "Now I see my mistake. In the dark your hair looked black, like Bronwyn's. Here in the light I see it is more brown. Or is it red?" His hand darted out and captured a long, curling lock that hung over her shoulder. She drew in a sharp breath but stood perfectly still. "Nay, 'tis neither red nor brown, but more like cinnamon spice." He lifted the tress to his face and sniffed appreciatively. "It even smells like spice," he murmured, and moved closer to her. "And it curls halfway down your back just like Bronwyn's does."

"Will you please release me?" she said through tightly clenched teeth. She gave a toss of her head, fully expecting to feel the hard tug of his hold on her hair, but he let the strands slip easily through his fingers.

"My . . . er . . . Bronwyn is one of the king's ballad singers from the north of England. So you see why I would have expected to find her seated at the harp. Please accept my apology for frightening you." He laughed softly. "I did frighten you, did I not?"

Realizing he intended to have a little sport at her expense, Marganna raised her chin and stared back at the man, determined not to be intimidated. After all, it wasn't as if they were alone. They were standing in the middle of Nottingham Castle, and there were scores of other people within these same walls. Just a call for help would bring them running . . . surely.

He looked amused, as though reading her mind, and for the moment they stood in silence, each studying the other.

He was tall—taller, she thought, than any man she knew. His shoulders, clad in somber black wool, were wide but not heavy. He seemed massive, standing there in such a way as to block her view of the room behind him, and yet she knew instinctively he would never be clumsy—that he would move with the graceful agility of an athlete.

His hair was thick and black with mahogany highlights, carelessly tumbling over a broad, unfurrowed brow. Worn somewhat shorter than the current court fashion, his hair barely brushed his collar in the back. His skin was deeply tanned and taut over angular cheekbones, straight nose, and squared chin. Marganna was intrigued to notice his eyes were deeply green and decidedly wicked.

Those disturbing eyes now moved slowly over her, starting with the dark spice-brown hair, then traveling with obvious interest across her face with its high cheekbones, brown eyes, and stubborn chin. Aware that she was uncomfortable beneath his scrutiny, he nevertheless let his gaze continue downward, taking in every detail of her body, from her rounded bosom to her slender waist, then upward once again until he met the wary look in her eyes.

"Did I frighten you?" he repeated, the corners of his mouth twitching imperceptibly.

"No, you did not," she declared, her manner somewhat less hostile than before. "But I'm hardly accustomed to being mistaken for someone's . . . paramour . . . and no one has ever dared put his hands on me."

"Then you have not been at court long," he stated, grinning as he folded his arms across his chest. "Who are you and where do you come from?"

"That is hardly your concern."

"Oh, come now . . . at least be civil."

"Civil?" Despite herself, she had to smile. "Your audacity is—"

Her statement was cut short by the sound of a new voice.

"Rath? Is that you? Lord, man, what are you doing here in the dark?"

An extremely lanky man strode forward, a quizzical expression on his freckled face. Catching sight of Marganna, he stopped short and ran an agitated hand through wispy, sand-colored hair.

"Oh, I see . . . a thousand pardons, my lady. I did not mean to disturb you."

"Please . . . this is not what you think," she assured him wryly. "I mean, you disturbed nothing."

"You'll never believe it, Will," the man called Rath was saying, "but I mistook this lass for Bronwyn."

"For Bronwyn?" The second man coughed uncertainly, and they exchanged amused glances. Displeased to be the object of their mirth, Marganna took advantage of the opportunity to brush past the two men and hurry from the room.

"Wait . . . don't go!"

She heard the dark-haired man's shout, but it only served to make her gather her skirts and break into a run, not pausing to look back.

When she was gone, Will turned to his companion. "She did not seem particularly taken with you, friend."

"Nay, she wasn't," Rath agreed, laughing ruefully. "Our first meeting was less than auspicious."

"Oh?"

"I told you, I thought she was Bronwyn. I'm afraid I made advances I shouldn't have."

"Ah, that explains it. Still, I can't see how you made such an error." Will chuckled. "She looked too ladylike and meek to be mistaken for your lusty Bronwyn."

Rath clapped a hand on his friend's shoulder. "Not meek, Will. I guarantee you, with eyes like that, the wench cannot be meek. They were the same spice brown as her hair—a color a man could warm himself by."

"Or be burned to cinders by. Now that you mention it, they were rather hot . . . with anger at you, I daresay."

"Aye, you're right about that."

"Well, that doesn't happen often," observed Will. "And, in truth, I'm glad to see not all females readily succumb to your charm." He cast a quick look at his friend's face. "She was a pretty thing, wasn't she?"

Rath nodded regretfully, rubbing his chin. "The hell of

it is, Will, I didn't even find out her name or where she comes from." His thoughtful gaze rested on the doorway through which Marganna had fled. "But I will . . . mark my word, I will."

Marganna slipped into the bedchamber and shut the door behind her, leaning against it and breathing heavily. Thirty minutes ago she had been eager to leave the confinement of the stuffy room, but now it seemed a haven to her. She did not know why she had been so stirred by the man she'd met belowstairs, but it was a distinct relief to be away from the scrutiny of those piercing green eyes.

"Is something wrong, Marganna?"

She glanced up to see the slight figure of her aunt standing before her. Quickly she decided there was no point in revealing the details of her encounter with the stranger, for her aunt would be horrified to learn of his daringly familiar actions. With an inward smile, Marganna reflected that his attitude had been far too earthy, indeed, for one as steeped in virtue as Margaret, Lady Stanley.

"No, nothing is wrong, Aunt Margaret."

"I've told you not to call me aunt while we are at court. Must I remind you yet another time?"

"I'm . . . I'm sorry . . . Lady Stanley. I seem to be having difficulty in breaking the habit. I promise to be more careful."

"Yes, you will have to be. It is necessary that your identity remain a well-guarded secret until . . . well, for the present, shall we say?"

Smoothing her skirts, Marganna stepped away from the door and willed herself to nod calmly.

She studied the older woman standing before her. Long, thin hands were clasped at her waist, and a jet rosary was entwined around one bony wrist. Dressed as she was in a white robe, its hood drawn up over her heavily grayed hair, nearly obscuring her face, Lady Stanley had the ascetic look of a nun. When Marganna had first gone to live with her aunt several years before, she wondered why the woman had not chosen to reside within a convent. It did not take Marganna long to discover there was an even greater motivating force in Lady Stanley's life than the need for self-perfection or adherence to religious ideals.

The woman was completely dedicated to her son, Henry Tudor. For his sake, she had developed an overriding interest in politics and court intrigue. A woman not suited to the intimacies of the marriage bed, she had nevertheless entered into two successive marriages after the death of her first husband, merely because the unions offered contacts that might someday prove useful to Henry. Her life's goal, Marganna had discovered, was to see her only child sitting on the throne of England.

Lady Stanley sighed heavily. "The castle is in a turmoil because of the arrival of visitors from Yorkshire. It is a source of wonder to me that the king holds these North Country men in such high regard, for they are little more than ruffians and thieves." She sniffed audibly. "Of course, that must be the attraction, taking the king's own dubious morals into consideration. And he did live among them for a number of years."

She turned away and seated herself at an oaken vanity table, facing a mirror. "Come here and comb my hair, child. You are the only one who can do it properly. The other girls were so giddy about the festivities tonight that I couldn't bear to have them in my presence a moment longer. I sent them all away so I might have some peace and solitude before the ordeal of dining with the king and his guests."

Obediently, Marganna approached the vanity, taking the ivory comb her aunt handed her.

"Besides, there is something I wish to speak to you about."

"What is that, Aunt . . . Lady Stanley?"

The older woman pushed back the hood of her dressing robe to reveal a fall of straight gray-brown hair that reached to her waist. Gently, Marganna began drawing the comb through its length.

"I doubt you would disagree that you are somewhat in my debt . . ."

The dark, heavy-lidded eyes met Marganna's startled

ones in the mirror. A faint blush tinged the younger woman's face.

"No, I could find no fault with that statement," she murmured. "It is certainly true you have done a great deal for me."

Saved my life, actually, Marganna silently reminded herself, ashamed of a fleeting feeling of resentment at the reminder. Had her aunt by marriage not taken an interest in her, she would have been condemned to remain in a Welsh nunnery, and as God was her witness, it was a stark and miserable existence. Finding herself fifteen years old before she was allowed to leave the walled enclosure of the convent for the first time, she knew there was nothing she could refuse this strange, intense woman. In truth, she owed her everything.

Residing within the household of Margaret, Lady Stanley, for the next five years had not always been easy, but there had been adequate food, warm clothing, and the means for an education. If sometimes the daily prayers were overlong or the lady's piety daunting, it seemed a small price to pay for having escaped the crushing poverty and harshly regimented life of the nunnery.

"As soon as I learned of your existence from your uncle Jasper Tudor, I knew I must do something to help you, Marganna," Lady Stanley was saying. "I was more than willing to take you out of the convent where your mother left you and place you in my home in Lancashire. These past years I have been gratified to see you grow from an awkward, uncertain girl into a lovely, accomplished woman. It has pleased me to have had a hand in your development, but now, for the first time, I find myself forced to have to ask you to aid me."

Lady Stanley waved a thin hand. "Oh, 'tis not that you do nothing for me now, child. I appreciate your daily assistances in the running of my household or in attending to my personal care. God knows your soft voice and the music you play so beautifully are the only balm that will soothe the vicious headaches I often get. But there is a more crucial request I must make of you."

"Then please do."

"Marganna, I brought you here to King Richard's court for a purpose." The older woman's eyes glowed with zealous fervor, and for once a smile hovered at the edges of her thin mouth. "It is time you commit yourself to our cause. You must do your part to put your cousin Henry on the throne of this oppressed country."

"M-my part?" Surprise made Marganna clumsy and the comb dragged painfully against her aunt's scalp. Lady Margaret's eyes again sought hers in the mirror.

"You needn't look so astonished, child. After all, you are a Tudor, and your family's cause must be your own."

The house of Tudor had its obscure beginning in the mists of early Welsh history, emerging with its share of rogues and rebels, loyalists and landowners.

Henry Tudor's grandfather had been Owen Tudor, a man who became the lover of widowed Queen Katherine of Valois. They eventually married, but their alliance was kept secret as long as possible, even through the births of four children. When the secret became known, the Protector of the Realm, acting in the name of Katherine's small son, Henry VI, sent Owen Tudor to prison and had Katherine incarcerated in a nunnery where she grew ill and died. Later pardoned, Owen lived to be an old man who, instead of dying quietly in bed, remained a rebel, fighting for the Lancastrians at the battle of Mortimer's Cross, only to be captured and executed by the victorious Yorkists.

Owen's children were treated generously by Henry VI, their royal half brother, especially the eldest son, Edmund, who was created Earl of Richmond and given a wife with powerful Lancastrian connections. The bride was Margaret Beaufort, now Lady Stanley, who, because she was descended from England's great king, Edward III, was one of the most important heiresses of the blood royal, providing the Tudors and their descendants with a claim to the English throne.

For many years there had been a prolonged dynastic struggle among the progeny of Edward III, resulting in civil war, with the two chief factions eventually divided into the houses of Lancaster and York. As of this moment, the Yorkists reigned supreme, but there were those like Margaret, Lady Stanley, mother of the Tudors' brightest hope, who sensed the downfall of the House of York was imminent—sensed it, willed it, and gloried in the prospect of it.

"You know, Marganna, that my goal in life is to see my son Henry reclaim for his family that which is rightfully ours." She swiveled around on the vanity stool to observe her niece's reaction to her words. "I don't suppose you can understand that kind of devotion, never having had it from your own mother . . ."

"Of course I can," Marganna protested. "I have always known of your dedication to my cousin. I think it is admirable."

Lady Margaret's eyes took on a faraway look, and her long fingers toyed with the jet rosary beads. "I was very young when the king arranged my marriage to Edmund Tudor. In less than a year I found myself a bride, then a widow, and, three months later, a mother. In all that change and uncertainty, there was nothing for me to grasp onto . . . until my son was born. Suddenly my life had purpose and meaning.

"I had him with me only five years, Marganna—five years! And then, may God condemn them to perdition, the Yorkists separated us and sent him to live with a *good* family of their persuasion. If they thought to wean him away from his own heritage, however, they were greatly in error. He was fourteen before his uncle could regain custody of him, but despite all the reverses in fortune, despite the fact he was forced to flee to the Continent branded a traitor, his purpose has remained clear, his resolve invincible. As has my own. I have always known that one day he would be king, and I am prepared to make any sacrifice necessary."

Marganna carefully laid the ivory comb on the oaken table. "I do not doubt it," she said quietly.

Too many times had she seen her aunt in this mood and knew the best way to avoid unpleasantness was to hear her out. Still, the hour grew late, and there was much to be done before the evening's banquet. Mentally Marganna began ticking off the list of things she had to accomplish before the dinner hour. Suddenly Lady Margaret rose to her feet and began to pace back and forth, recapturing Marganna's reluctant attention.

"There is something I want you to know, Marganna. I have been in contact with my son, and—he is planning an invasion of England!"

Marganna's indrawn breath was clearly audible in the silent bedchamber. "An invasion, Your Ladyship? But . . . won't that mean yet more war?"

"How else do you think the crown can be wrested from the grasping hands of our noble King Richard?" Lady Margaret's usually calm, dry voice fairly dripped venom. "Indeed, killing is the only thing that misbegotten spawn of Satan truly understands. He will be happy to rise to the challenge of battle . . ." She laughed harshly. "But when he does, he will find himself facing a formidable opponent. My son has spent his time in exile well, garnering aid from the French king and, in addition, when he arrives on these shores, the Welsh will rise up in his behalf . . . not to mention the many good English folk who have little love for the Usurper. Richard will find that not all of his subjects condone murder—even to gain the throne."

"I don't understand what I am to do, Lady Stanley," Marganna interjected, hoping to avoid listening to yet another lengthy tirade against the Yorkist king. "Of what help could I be?"

"It is time you took an active part in assisting the Tudors. As all England knows, Richard took the throne from his brother's son, causing the lad and his younger brother to be declared illegitimate. Although he had them imprisoned in the Tower, it has been many months now since anyone has seen either of the boys, and rumor has it they were murdered by his order."

"Surely it's no more than a rumor," Marganna put in. "What kind of monster would kill his own brother's children?"

"Living in the country, you have been shielded from much of the treachery that goes on at court. Politics is a fickle and dangerous business, I'm afraid, resulting in a constant struggle for power. If, as we fear, Richard did have the boys killed, it was because of his greed and political ambition. But until someone can prove their deaths actually took place, there will always be that faction seeking to find the lad and restore his kingdom to him. Henry does not want that threat hanging over his head. When he takes the throne, he wants to bring order to this country."

"But what if the children should actually be found alive?"

"Even then, there could be no question of young Edward ascending the throne, of course. England has never fared well under the rule of a boy king. It would be best for all concerned if Henry simply arranged to have the children taken to the Continent and raised by responsible people," Lady Stanley replied. "Once they were out of England, the risk to their safety would be minimized and, no longer valuable as political pawns, they would be given the chance to live normal lives." She shrugged. "However, knowing the way Richard's evil mind works, there is very little hope the lads have been allowed to remain alive. Henry wants proof the boys are dead, and he wants to know by whose hand they died. When he is in command, he will see to it that their deaths are not unavenged."

"But won't it be difficult to prove anything conclusively? I mean, if no one has had any information of worth in all this time . . ."

Lady Stanley's eyes narrowed. "Oh, rest assured, *someone* has knowledge of what happened to them. Someone besides the King, that is. It isn't likely he would have done the deed himself, so whoever performed the task for him knows the details. And human nature being what it is, that someone has probably told someone else—in all secrecy, of course—and that someone has spread the word even further. The rumors had to have started somewhere, Marganna. All we have to do is locate one of those people."

"But how?"

"By keeping our eyes and ears open. By discreet questioning. By—"

"But isn't that spying?" protested Marganna.

"It is a vital gathering of information—call it spying, if you like."

"It is treasonable," Marganna began.

"Treason! How can one commit treason against an . . . an ogre who should never have been placed on the throne in the first place? That man has no right to be king! And acting in the best interests of this country—moving to rid it of his noxious influence—is not treason. Don't ever let me hear you speak that word again!"

Marganna involuntarily took a step backward, away from the wrath darkening her aunt's face. "I'm . . . I'm sorry . . . I spoke without thinking."

"One of your worst habits. One that will, I fear, bring you to grief."

"I will be more careful in the future." Marganna chafed at being made to feel like a naughty child, but she realized it was the only way to calm her aunt.

"See that you do. And now, if you will let me continue without interruption, I will tell you what is expected of you."

Marganna nodded, choosing not to speak again. Her head was beginning to throb painfully.

"It has occurred to us that one way in which we might learn something of the princes' fate is through Richard's personal correspondence."

"His letters?" Catching herself, Marganna fell silent, but the look on her face clearly expressed her thoughts.

"Do you recall the time I misplaced the key to my jewel case and you picked the lock with one of those long ivory hairpins of yours?"

"Yes . . ."

"Well, that is what we want you to do for us—simply employ your small talent with locks to open Richard's letter casket and examine the contents. If there is anything of importance, bring it to me."

"Steal letters from the king?"

"Again, I do not approve your choice of words. It may be stealing to you, but the fact remains, it is necessary if we are going to do anything for those poor children."

"But how on earth could I ever get into the king's private chambers? They are too well guarded."

"Not tonight, Marganna, not tonight. As I've said, a group of Richard's beloved Yorkshiremen arrived this morning, and he has ordered a banquet held in their honor. My husband informs me the king has declared a night free of duties for most of those in the castle. He will keep only a minimal guard, allowing everyone else to join the celebration. After all, this is the first bit of festivity at court since the death of Richard's wife three months ago." A faint smile lighted Margaret's pale features, and Marganna did not know whether the woman was gloating over the unfortunate death of Queen Anne or simply relishing the thought of duping the king. "Lord Stanley tells me there will be but a single guard outside the royal bedchamber while we are belowstairs tonight. It shouldn't be difficult to deal with him. I will send a serving girl up with some ale, and in a very short while you will find you can come and go as you please. You need only be quick and efficient."

"The ale will be drugged?"

"Yes, but don't spare any sympathy for the poor fool who drinks it. He will likely suffer only a headache."

"And possibly the king's anger, should anything be discovered missing," Marganna said, a wry twist to her mouth.

"I understand your distaste for this undertaking," Lady Stanley snapped impatiently, "but it must be done, and you are the logical person to do it. Having just arrived at court, you are virtually unknown, and no one but my husband and I know of your relationship to Henry Tudor. With your charming air of innocence, who could possibly suspect you of being a spy?"

"But what will happen if . . . if I should get caught?"

"You won't."

"How . . . how can you be so certain? If someone should see me enter the chamber . . ."

"It would be through your own clumsiness . . . and I won't lie to you, Marganna—if something goes amiss, there is no way I can help you. I dare not admit to any knowledge of your activities because, as you know, Richard had me attainted after the failure of that disastrous rebellion plot with Buckingham. The fool was lenient that time, merely remitting me to my husband's custody and sending me to the country for awhile, but this time . . . no, this time he could not afford to be so generous. And I will not endanger Henry's plans for invasion should you become careless. Therefore, you must be clever and self-sufficient. I am not unduly worried—I have great trust in your abilities.''

''I wish I felt the same confidence,'' Marganna said in a half whisper.

Suddenly Lady Stanley reached out a clawlike hand and painfully clutched Marganna's shoulder. ''I am beginning to lose patience with your reluctance, Marganna. Don't you think you owe your family something? All these years you have gladly taken everything they gave you, giving nothing in return.'' Her fingers released their grip, and the hand fell away from Marganna's shoulder. ''You've always been something of a family embarrassment, you know. It was not easy for your uncles to accept the enormity of your mother's sin—how thankful I have been that my husband did not live to see how she made a mockery of the Tudor name.''

''Lady Stanley . . .'' Marganna began wearily.

''Don't you think you owe it to them? To me? Didn't you ever once consider doing something to repay our kindnesses or to make up for the scandal your mother caused?''

''I'll do whatever you want,'' Marganna said stiffly. Her mother was seldom mentioned, but experience had long ago taught Marganna she did not care to discuss her with Lady Stanley.

Marganna's mother was the last-born of Katherine and Owen Tudor's children. When the family had been broken up, she was sent to a Welsh convent to be raised. She remained there, acknowledged but unclaimed by her brothers, and her life was quiet and uneventful. Uneventful, that is, until the year she turned thirty. Suddenly and unexpectedly, she entered into a clandestine relationship with a man whose identity she took to her grave. The details of the affair were never known, but the result of the union was evident.

She kept her pregnancy secret for as long as possible, and by the time news of it reached her brothers' ears, it was too late for them to prevent the birth of her child, a daughter born in the autumn and christened Marganna Tudor. Two years later, Marganna's mother died, and in the time before her uncle Jasper and his sister-in-law, Lady Margaret, decided to become responsible for her welfare, Marganna experienced enough of life in the convent to understand and sympathize with her mother's actions, scandalous though they might have been. Perhaps she had awakened one day to find herself growing old, alone and isolated, desperate for a chance at a normal life. Marganna, instead of casting blame, spent hours imagining the man her father had been, and the object of her daydreams ranged from a romantic, lost traveler seeking shelter for the night to a fallen priest, oblivious to fears of eternal damnation for indulgence in sins of the flesh.

In her present frame of mind, she knew she could not bring herself to listen to another righteous sermon about her mother's lack of morality. The best way to avoid it, she decided, was simply to agree with Lady Stanley's demands.

"Of course I want to do what I can to repay you in some small measure for everything you have given me. I will do anything you want." She chose to ignore the look of satisfaction that lighted Lady Stanley's usually impassive face. "Now, may I please be excused to ready myself for the banquet?"

"Certainly. Oh, one more thing—I must advise you to wear something plain and dark this evening. There is no sense in drawing any undue attention to yourself."

"No, my lady, of course not."

Alone again in her own room, Marganna stared at the bright hues of the neatly folded dresses in the wooden chest before her. With a disappointed sigh she ignored them and reached for one of her older gowns, a plain, dark brown worsted.

There would be plenty of time to wear her new wardrobe later, she told herself. After all, she had only been at court a few days. Her aunt was right—it would be foolish to wear something colorful and eye-catching for what she had to do this evening.

My Lord in Heaven, she thought, I am nothing more than a spy . . . a traitor!

Dropping the gown on her bed, she walked to the open window and, resting her aching forehead against the window frame, gazed out. Below her, in one of Nottingham Castle's three courtyards, people were hurrying to and fro, calling out to each other, no doubt excited by the prospect of the evening's festivities. Her stomach tightened in dread, and she quickly raised her eyes to avoid the feverish activity. In the near distance she could see the shining waters of the River Leen, and away to the north, the billowing green treetops of Sherwood Forest. How she wished she could be there, walking through the cool, shaded woods . . .

It was no use. Wishing was not going to make reality disappear. She had given her promise, and now all she could do was to go through with it. And if she were caught?

Well, she reminded herself, straightening her shoulders and thrusting her stubborn chin into the air, her grandfather had been a proud old rebel, hadn't he? He hadn't balked at the thought of danger or death, and neither would she.

In one of the trunks in the room behind her lay a small Welsh harp that had belonged to Owen Tudor. Found among her mother's possessions and kept by the nuns until Marganna was old enough to appreciate it, the harp was cherished by her as her only inheritance. Now she wondered if she had inherited something of her grandfather's rebellious nature as well.

She prayed it was so, for she might need it before this night was through.

Chapter 2

Marganna did not enjoy her first formal meal at court. Unexpectedly, since her aunt did not wish to acknowledge their relationship just yet, she found herself seated far "below the salt," with those who were little more than servants. The people around her were strangers who chatted among themselves and, except for an occasional appraising glance in her direction, ignored her.

Though his association with Richard had been weakened by recent rumors of disloyalty, Thomas Stanley still retained his position as Lord High Constable, and he and his wife, Lady Margaret, were placed at the king's table in the front of the hall. Marganna could barely see them down the length of the crowded room. She had caught only a glimpse of the king when he arrived, for he had entered without fanfare and was quietly seated before anyone knew he was there. Marganna was vaguely surprised at his lack of stature and his somber dress. Most of the noblemen were more richly dressed and possessed a far more royal manner than he.

The meal was elaborate, with courses that seemed to go on and on. With nothing to distract her, Marganna's thoughts centered on the task ahead, and nervousness caused her to eat very little. She was almost relieved when the fruit, nuts, and cheese that comprised the final course were served. As little as she relished the thought of what she had to do, she disliked the waiting even more.

She slipped one hand into the deep pocket of her dress, and her fingers closed around the ivory hairpins hidden there. With a start, she realized someone was watching her. She raised her eyes and began a casual sweeping survey of the crowded hall. Suddenly she encountered the gaze of a blond-haired man and, before she could look away, he smiled. Without thinking, Marganna smiled back.

She had seen the man before—he had been lounging with some friends in the great hall when she arrived at Nottingham—but she had not spoken to him and did not know his name. That he was of the wealthy nobility was obvious from his self-assured manner and style of dress. Marganna stole another quick look, only to find he was still staring at her.

She thought he was handsome in a modish way. He wore his gold hair long, in the current fashion, and it lay in shining waves against shoulders clad in rich, ruby velvet. As the woman seated next to him said something and he turned toward her, Marganna saw the sparkle of a diamond earring in his left ear. As flirtatious as his dinner partner seemed to be, his attention was still fastened on Marganna, and when he reached for his goblet, he raised it in a silent toast to her. His fingers were laden with rings, and even that small movement sent colorful fire radiating.

Embarrassed to be caught staring, Marganna turned away with a faint blush. Immediately her eyes came into contact with another familiar face—that of the man who had mistaken her for his lover earlier in the day. Her blush deepened as he dipped his head in an insolent bow, then flashed her a knowing smile. Trying to summon her previous indignation at his familiarity, she tilted her nose upward and angled her body in the chair, turning her back on him as effectively as circumstances allowed. In so doing, her gaze swiveled in the opposite direction, locking with that of the courtier once again. This time she smiled first and to her surprise, he rose from his chair and started walking toward her.

He was, she noticed, a little taller than average, with a lithe, finely muscled physique. He was dressed in the daring and, some said, indecent fashion lately adopted by young men of the court, a style that left nothing to the imagination. His doublet, worn over a white satin shirt, was extremely short, ending just below the waist and clearly displaying that very masculine article of clothing, the codpiece. His lean hips and long, finely shaped legs were encased in clinging burgundy-red hose.

Realizing he was dressed far more elegantly than she, Marganna glanced down at her own old-fashioned brown kirtle with its russet surcoat. If only she could have worn one of the pretty new gowns she had brought to court with her. As it was, she felt like a plain brown wren.

The servants had begun to clear the board in preparation for the evening's entertainment, and in the confusion she momentarily lost sight of the courtier's approaching figure. She got to her own feet and in that instant heard Lady Margaret's low voice behind her.

"It might be a good idea for you to take advantage of this pandemonium and slip upstairs, Marganna," her aunt was saying. "I've already sent a serving girl up with the ale, so you should have no problem with the sentry."

Marganna threw a swift look over her shoulder but did not yet see the courtier. "But what if I go up too quickly and the guard is not yet affected by the ale?" she asked.

"Simply find a place where you can wait unnoticed," Lady Margaret said impatiently. "It won't take long, I assure you."

"If I should find anything of value?"

"Don't come back to the hall with it. Go to your chamber and wait for me. I will come up as soon as possible. Remember, Marganna, this is vitally important, so you must not fail us. Now, go . . . quickly!"

Reluctantly Marganna nodded, then slipped from the room as unobtrusively as she could. As much as she would have liked to meet the handsome young man who was searching for her, she knew it would be easier to disappear suddenly than to answer his questions.

Since she had not thought to bring a candle with her, Marganna found the upper hallways of the castle dark and forbidding. At intervals there were torches set high on the walls, but their light was uncertain, flaring briefly, then nearly flickering out. Sometimes frenzied shadows loomed up unexpectedly. At one turning Marganna shrank back, gasping in fright, before she realized the specter towering over her was her own shadow.

Even in the soft slippers she wore, her footsteps seemed to echo loudly on the stones beneath her feet, mocking the nervous thump of her heart. Her mind was frantically recounting the directions Lady Margaret had given her, trying to determine whether or not she had taken a wrong turning.

As she approached an intersection in the corridor, she saw the bulky figure of a man in the king's livery. He was about halfway down the hall, pacing back and forth in front of a well-lighted door. At that moment, fortunately, his broad back was turned to her, giving her an opportunity to step into the deep shadows before he turned and started toward her. She pressed against the wall and prayed he would not notice her.

With relief she saw that the man was distracted, his manner agitated. As he was again walking away from her, he came to an abrupt halt, glanced both ways, then strode off down the hall and disappeared around a corner.

Not pausing to analyze his actions, Marganna dashed from the corner where she had been hiding and slipped through the now-unguarded door. The man's walk had been somewhat unsteady as he moved away—she had little doubt he was already feeling the effects of the ale. Most likely, he wouldn't even make it back to his post before unconsciousness claimed him.

Quietly she closed the door behind her and looked around the king's outer chamber. It was a large room, richly furnished with carved woodwork, elegant tapestries, and a long table where the king dined in state. A series of cushioned benches lined two walls, for it was here in the privy chambers that ambassadors or petitioners waited for an audience with His Grace.

After a swift backward glance at the door, Marganna took one of the lighted candles from the table and crossed the room to the doorway that led into the inner chamber.

This room, smaller than the privy chamber, was also less formal. This was where the king retreated for a bit of privacy, where he might meet with his advisors or dictate letters to his secretary, or where he could settle himself before the fire for a game of chess. Across the room a door stood ajar and, curious, Marganna moved toward it. She raised the candle high and, seeing a huge, curtained bed, knew this was the innermost sanctuary, the king's bedchamber, a room few private citizens ever viewed.

Reluctantly, she turned back to the privy chamber. As much as she would have liked to explore further, she knew she did not dare. At most, she could allow herself only a few minutes to accomplish her mission.

Standing on the threshold, she let her gaze move slowly around the room until it fell on a desk and the object she sought—a letter casket. The casket had been carved from a dark and exotic wood, with mother-of-pearl inlaid on the top and an ornate gold handle at either end. The lock gleamed in the dim candlelight as though challenging her. She took a deep breath and hurried across the room toward it.

Placing the candle on the desktop, Marganna reached into her pocket and drew forth one of the ivory hairpins. With another furtive glance around the shadowy room, she inserted the hairpin into the lock and twisted. With a snap that sounded loud in the silence, the pin broke apart in her hand. The ivory was too brittle to force the lock; she would have to be more gentle.

She carefully retrieved the broken pieces and returned them to her pocket, pulling out another hairpin. This time she moved more slowly, inserting the sliver of ivory and jiggling it lightly. With the tiniest of clicks, the lock sprang open, and Marganna breathed a sigh of relief. Dropping the hairpin back into her pocket, she raised the lid of the casket.

There were several letters lying in the top drawer of the casket, and Marganna assumed these must be the most recent correspondence, for everything else was neatly organized, two of the stacks even tied with blue silk ribbons. As much as her feminine curiosity nagged at her to open one of those bundles, the more practical part of her mind was urging her to be sensible, to hurry. She seized the sheaf of loose letters and scanned them quickly. The first two were concerned with matters that had recently been brought before Richard's Council of the North, and she dropped them back into the chest. The third letter, dated just a few days before, caused her heart to leap into her throat and stay there, fluttering wildly.

"With fond greetings to my uncle, King Richard," she read. "There is not much news, Uncle, as the weather here in Yorkshire has been abominable. I am not allowed to go outdoors for fear the dampness will affect my health. Dickon and I have been unable to do much but sit by the fire. . ."

There was a slight noise in the next room, and Marganna whirled to face the door. For a long moment she stood, frozen, expecting the worst. But no one appeared in the doorway to challenge her, and eventually her breathing slowed to a more normal pace. Still, she could not afford to linger much longer.

Skimming to the bottom of the letter she held, her eyes widened as she read the youthfully scrawled signature: "Respectfully, your nephew, Edward Plantagenet."

That had to mean the princes were alive! They were alive—and in her hand was irrefutable proof of it.

With shaking fingers, she sorted through the rest of the papers but found nothing else she thought would be of interest to her aunt. Carefully, after replacing everything but the letter she held, she closed the lid of the casket and snapped the lock shut. Then she folded the correspondence from young Edward and thrust it deep inside the low-cut neckline of her gown. With one last look, to assure herself that everything in the chamber was just as she had found it, she crossed the floor and stepped into the outer room.

Quietly, she closed the door behind her and moved toward the long dining table to replace the candle she carried. Now her only worry was the guard outside the door . . .

"What in the blazing hell do you think you are doing?"

At the sound of the angry masculine voice, Marganna

stiffened in shock, shrinking back against the edge of the table. Thank God she was in the outer chamber! Thank God she had not been caught bending over the king's desk! Just a few seconds earlier and there could have been no doubt what she was doing. Swiftly, she pressed one hand to her bodice and was reassured to hear the faint crackle of paper.

The man who was just entering the room from the hallway came toward her, stopping only when he was close enough to tower over her. Putting his hands on his hips, his face a mask of fury, he again demanded, "What are you doing here?" His words were slow, his tone dangerous. "Surely you know this is the king's private chamber?"

"No, I . . . I . . ." Summoning her courage, Marganna faced the man who had accosted her earlier in the day when she had been playing the harp. "Saints protect me," she stammered, frantically wondering what line of defense she should take, "I didn't realize. I . . . I only ducked in here to . . . to avoid someone."

She raised innocent eyes to meet his distinctly suspicious ones and saw that he recognized her.

"It would seem you spend a great deal of time avoiding people," he commented dryly.

Ignoring his statement, she attempted a small attack of her own. "I don't believe this is the king's chamber. If it is, why weren't there sentries at the door?"

His eyes narrowed. "That's exactly what I am wondering. And what I intend to find out. Now, who were you trying to avoid?"

"What? Oh . . . yes. . ." His abrupt question caught her off guard, and she had to struggle to keep her voice calm. Unless she could convince this very large and very irate man of her innocence, he might report her presence in the king's bedchamber to someone in authority. She had to make him think she had simply made a mistake.

"Well, I . . . I'm not certain who it was. I think he must have followed me from the dining hall. He accosted me in a darkened corridor and frightened me rather badly. I had intended to go up to my room, but I got confused and lost my way. I arrived at Nottingham only a few days ago, and I am not at all familiar with the castle."

"I see." He eyed her speculatively. "And this man—you say he attacked you?"

"No, I did not say he attacked me. I said he accosted me . . . there is a difference, you know."

"Perhaps you would care to explain the difference to me," he said, crossing his arms and assuming a more casual stance.

"I suspect you are well aware of the difference," she replied coolly. "An attack is when someone forces his disgusting and unwanted attentions on you." She had intended her words to be ironic, but unexpectedly she was remembering the way his hands had felt on her body. She took a deep breath. "This man did not . . . touch me. It was just his manner that was offensive. Alone and in the dark, I was afraid."

"Did you ever consider the possibility that if you did not spend so much time lurking in dark, lonely corners you would not be so frequently approached by strangers?"

Her eyes flared angrily. "Are you insinuating that it was my fault?"

"I am saying that you could improve matters by keeping to places where you are supposed to be."

"I cannot believe your arrogance in thinking I *invited* these unwanted attentions!"

"Persist in twisting my words if you wish, but tell me, had you ever seen this man before?"

"I think I noticed him belowstairs, during the banquet."

"Describe him."

"He was . . . oh, what does it matter? It seems I have eluded him."

"I think the king will want to look into the matter. He would not like knowing that a lady is unsafe in one of his castles."

Marganna swallowed deeply. The last thing she wanted was to be brought to the king's notice. "I insist we drop the matter. Nothing actually happened, and I would not want to bother anyone over something so inconsequential."

He grinned suddenly. "Are you certain you didn't know the man? It couldn't have been the very elegant Donal FitzClinton, could it?"

"I'm afraid I don't know Donal FitzClinton."

"The handsome courtier so richly dressed in scarlet velvet? Come now, you must know the man. I saw the two of you exchanging glances over your meal. In fact, madam, I saw you casting several enticing looks his way just before you disappeared from the hall. And the last I saw of FitzClinton, he was on his feet. Could it possibly be that you lured the man into a dark corner and then panicked when he showed signs of becoming too . . . passionate, shall we say?"

"How dare you even hint at such a thing," she stormed, suddenly starting past him. "I will not remain here and listen to this insulting drivel."

He caught her arm and spun her around. "Drivel? Then you deny it?"

"Of course I deny it."

"All right. Who was the man?"

She jerked her arm from his grip. "I don't know, I tell you! He was . . . he was dressed entirely in black and . . . Oh yes, he spoke strangely, with a rustic, twanging sort of accent . . . I think he must be one of those rough men who recently arrived from Yorkshire." She tossed her head. "Yes, I'm sure of it. He was exceedingly crude and coarse, with manners learned in a pigsty."

She knew the man standing before her was most likely from the north, and though she received momentary satisfaction from the look of anger that flickered across his face, she quickly cursed herself for the spate of temper that made her bait him in such a way. Her situation was altogether too precarious without her needlessly making it worse.

"I'd prefer to forget the whole unfortunate incident," she said contritely.

"Oh, but I wouldn't." His tone was very quiet. "You

see, if he is from the north, he is one of my men. I will not condone such behavior."

Her scornful laugh rang through the room before she could control it. "*You* don't condone it—after the way you behaved this afternoon? I find that extremely amusing!"

"That was a mistake, and you know it."

"I refuse to believe—"

He leaned close, his face only inches from hers. "Once and for all, listen to me."

"What are you doing?" she gasped, leaning away.

He clamped his large hands down on her shoulders, pulling her closer, and his sea-green eyes began a slow study of her features. "You know," he drawled, a bold smile causing deep dimples to crease each lean cheek, "I'm almost beginning to think you regret that nothing more happened this afternoon."

"Why, you conceited oaf!" Her voice was nearly strangled with fright. If she screamed for help, it would summon people who might be very interested to learn what she was doing in the king's private rooms, but if she let him do what he obviously meant to do . . .

The man read the expression in her eyes, saw it change from anger to fear to indecision. The candlelight washed gently over her upturned face, causing her thick lashes to throw spiky shadows over high cheekbones; it glimmered across soft, rose-colored lips, parted in agitation. Without further consideration, he lowered his head and laid his mouth firmly against hers.

Marganna gave a violent start and slammed the heels of her hands into his chest. As his ruthless mouth shaped itself to hers, determined to continue its assault, she twisted her face aside, feeling the heat of his lips trail across her cheek to her ear. She kicked out, striking his shin, and was pleased to hear his grunt of pain.

She had just bent her knee to further defend herself when the outer door was flung open and a gruff voice shouted, "Here now, what's this!" It was the large, burly man in livery. He had stepped into the room, sword drawn, and was eyeing them with shock. "How did you get in here?"

"We simply walked in, Wilkes, because there was no guard at the door." The tall man released Marganna and turned his piercing gaze on the surprised sentry.

"Oh, 'tis you, Lord Rathburn," the man stuttered. "I didn't recognize you at first."

"Where were you, Wilkes?"

"Well, sir, to tell you the truth, I had to . . . to . . ."

"Well?"

The guard cast a quick look at Marganna; then, looking back at Rathburn's forbidding expression, shrugged and rushed on. "I had to relieve myself—must have been the ale I drank—and I thought it would be all right if I slipped away for a few minutes. After all, a man can't just pi—er, relieve himself against the wall of the king's chamber," he said defiantly.

To Marganna's surprise, Rathburn laughed. "No, that sort of thing would be frowned upon, I've no doubt. But isn't it customary for other guards to be here with you?"

"Yes sir, but you see, what with you men arriving from the north this morning, King Richard allowed us some time off to attend the banquet and hear the music afterward. He said it would be all right for us to stand guard duty one at a time. I swear, 'tis the first there has been any sort of merriment at court since poor Queen Anne passed away."

"Yes, I know. Well, no harm done, Wilkes—just don't leave your post again." He turned to Marganna. "Come along, my lady."

"Come along where?"

"Down to the great hall. I want to determine just which one of my men insulted you. I can promise he will be reprimanded."

He took her arm and ushered her through the door, giving her no time to protest. The guard watched with ill-concealed amusement.

Once they were in the hallway, she pulled her arm free and hissed, "Don't touch me again! I insist upon retiring to my chamber."

"And I insist that we return to the hall."

"Why should your men be punished for something they no doubt see you do all the time?"

"Guard your tongue. I doubt very much that you would like seeing me truly angry."

"I'm certain you are correct. I like you little enough as it is."

She was nearly running, trying to stay far enough in advance so that he could not take her arm again. He followed relentlessly, as close as a wary sheepdog, herding her along the halls to the stairs. When she hesitated at the top step, his large body bumped into her from behind, and one strong arm shot out to curl around her waist and keep her from falling forward.

"Oh!" She twisted around to deliver a scathing remark, but his lips, framed by those maddening dimples, were entirely too close. "Oh," she exclaimed again, pushing his arm away and flouncing down the stairs.

Their reappearance in the noisy great hall went unnoticed by all but one person. Marganna paled as she met the flat obsidian gaze of Lady Margaret. Clearly it was not going to be easy explaining why she had deliberately disobeyed her aunt's order to wait in her room. Hopefully, Lady Margaret would be so gratified by the news Marganna had to tell her that she would not be angry for long. That she was angry now, seeing Marganna not only return to the hall but also in the company of a stranger, was plain to see.

Taking her elbow, Rathburn steered her through the group of people standing before them. "Do you see him anywhere?" he asked, bending to speak in her ear.

Marganna pretended to study the faces on either side of them, then turned back to him. "No, I. . ."

"Shh!" an elderly man standing nearby hissed at them. "Silence! The king's ballad singer is performing."

A circle had been cleared by the huge fireplace at the end of the room, and there the minstrels and musicians were gathered. In their midst stood one of the loveliest women Marganna had ever seen. She was plucking a small harp, her fingers darting back and forth over the strings, drawing out a strange, disturbing melody. A hush fell over the room as she raised her head and began to sing. Her voice was low and harsh, with an edge to it that rasped on Marganna's nerves and sent shivers along the back of her neck. It was beautiful in an oddly compelling way, well suited to the tragic ballad she had chosen to sing.

The woman raised huge, dark eyes and looked across the room, directly into the eyes of the man beside Marganna. His answering expression was intense, making it evident there was a strong emotion between them. There could be no doubt that this was Bronwyn, his courtesan.

Marganna regarded the woman with renewed interest. The ballad singer had an untamed look about her, as though she would be more at home roaming the misted hills and moors than standing in the king's parlor entertaining his guests. Her black hair hung to her waist in a wild tangle of curls, and her eyes were restless, searching, challenging. Her olive skin glowed in the dim light, contrasting with a mouth the color of dark red roses. She was dressed in a plain black gown, cut daringly low over full breasts, girdled at the hips by a gold chain. She wore a jeweled dagger in a leather sheath, bringing to mind stories Marganna had heard of the northern ballad singers, fierce women who traveled the country, earning their living by singing or, when necessary, selling their bodies. Strong minded and independent, they had even been known to follow their men into battle. Bronwyn was the first such woman Marganna had ever seen.

Marganna glanced back at Rathburn. Like his mistress, he was garbed entirely in black, the color relieved only by the rich glow of gold jewelry, and, again like her, he stood out in the crowd because he made no concession to fashion. Obviously, they were well matched.

The ballad singer's voice was a melancholy cry in the echoing room, binding the listeners in her spell. As the last notes of the song faded away, the chamber exploded with wild applause.

Bronwyn nodded once; then, fastening the harp to her

girdle, she crossed the hall to stand directly in front of Rathburn, her eyes never leaving his.

"Who is she?"

Marganna was so startled by the woman's question that she instinctively glanced at the man beside her. A muscle was working in his jaw, and he looked irritated.

"We will have this discussion later, Bronwyn."

"I want to hear your answer now," the dark-haired woman said, tilting her head sideways.

"It is none of your concern."

"Why won't you tell me who she is?"

"I'm telling you, she is not important."

Marganna's head jerked up, sparks glinting in her eyes. "If I am so unimportant," she snapped, "why did you persist in bringing me belowstairs again? Why didn't you just leave me alone?"

Bronwyn's gleaming black eyes moved from Rathburn's face to Marganna's, then back again. "Yes, why didn't you leave her alone?"

The man shrugged. "If you must know, this squeamish little virgin claims to have been . . . accosted by one of my men. I thought it best to resolve the matter. We can't have innocent womanhood placed in jeopardy, can we?"

Bronwyn shook back her snarled hair and laughed, a low, melodious sound. "No, my lord, we cannot have that. There are few enough virgins left in this world. We must do what we can to protect them." She leaned close to him, looking up into his face, one hand coming up to stroke his arm. "However, I would much prefer you find someone else to champion her."

Her anger at her lover seemed to have suddenly dissipated, leaving Marganna with the unpleasant feeling they were now united against her.

"I must go," she murmured, gathering her skirts for flight. As she turned, she came face to face with her aunt and was dismayed to see the unpleasant scowl on the other woman's face.

"Marganna, what is going on here?" demanded Lady Margaret. "Your association with these people is creating a scene that has caught the king's attention."

"The king?"

"He has called for another song and wants to know why this"—she turned to rake Bronwyn with a contemptuous gaze—"woman does not comply."

Bronwyn smiled coldly. "I am parched. I must have something cool to drink before I am able to sing again."

"Even if the king commands it?" Lady Margaret folded her hands before her, a smug expression on her long face.

"King Richard is aware of the toll creative talent can exact," the singer replied. "He will respect my wish to rest awhile before performing again. Perhaps I will sing later."

With those words, she walked away without a backward glance, leaving Lady Stanley staring after her in consternation.

"That impertinent, ill-mannered strumpet! What am I to tell the king?"

"Simply find someone else to perform, madam," suggested Rathburn, a faint smile playing about his mouth. "That should not be too difficult."

"And whom do you suggest?" Lady Margaret's voice was icy.

"This young woman—I believe you addressed her as Marganna—seems to be in your employ. Is she not a harper?"

Marganna's eyes grew wide. "No, please! I don't want to play before all these people."

"Is your talent so slight then?"

"I do not have to defend my ability to you, sir."

"Marganna, enough of this unladylike behavior," admonished Lady Stanley. "I brought you to court because of your musical abilities, and though I had not intended to present you just yet, your actions have made it necessary. You will attract less notice, I think, if you simply borrow a harp from the musicians and play something for the king. He grows weary of waiting."

"But, Au— I mean, Your Ladyship, I . . . I don't even know what songs the king favors."

Rathburn smiled nastily. "His Grace likes a lively tune," he said. "Play something that will cheer him and make him laugh. Why do I think your playing and singing will make him laugh, I wonder?''

An arrow of pure anger shot through her.

''You . . . you. . .'' She glanced at the chain he wore, from which dangled King Richard's emblem fashioned in enameled gold. ''It is most fitting you wear the king's white boar. It suits you perfectly.''

She strode boldly across the floor and made a request to borrow the harp. Her mind was busy trying to contrive a method of getting even with the man called Rathburn—easily, she decided, the most horrid man she had ever met!

One of the musicians brought a wooden stool for her, and she sat down, bracing the harp against her knee. Her fingers idly stroked the short, curved neck of the instrument as she considered what to sing. There was one ballad . . . if only she dared. No, it was far too bawdy to sing in this company, and she knew her aunt would be sorely distressed . . .

She had learned the song years ago from the convent gardener, the only person she'd ever known to recognize and foster a latent spark of rebelliousness within her. He'd surreptitiously taught her to pick locks and to rob beehives and to release rabbits from the snares set by the convent cook. She hadn't thought of the old fellow for a long time . . .

She glanced up, and Rathburn favored her with a slow, insolent smile. Another tide of resentment washed over her, and suddenly her fingers were sliding across the strings, picking out the first notes of the song.

Her voice was not haunting in the way the ballad singer's had been, but it was pleasantly clear and strong, and as she started to sing, those in the chamber fell silent.

> *''Once I was courted by a North Country man,*
> *His kisses fair put me to sleep.''*

A few feminine titters sounded from the crowd and she smiled to herself.

"His manners were crass, for he brayed like an ass,
And I swear, he smelled just like a sheep!"

A wave of raucous laughter swept the room, and Marganna's hands fairly danced over the harp strings as she sang the refrain.

"Oh, all ye young lassies pay heed to my song,
The North Country man in a stable belongs.
To win a fair maiden, he'd have to use force,
No wonder he always beds down with his horse.
Hey, nonny! Hey, nonny! Hey, nonny ho!"

Her audience roared again, stamping their feet and calling for more. She dared one rapid glance at Rathburn and was delighted to see a discomfited expression on his face. It would seem he did not like her choice of ballads. Good!

She smiled brightly at the circle of listeners closest to her and launched herself into the second verse.

"He wooed me with passion so fierce and so wild,
With terror my poor heart was smote."

She deliberately let her eyes linger on Rathburn as she sang the next lines.

"Forsooth he did brag he was much like a stag,
But methinks him a randy old goat!"

The refrain was nearly drowned out by the shouts of laughter, and more than a few heads turned to follow her gaze, reveling in the challenge she had apparently thrown the dark lord. The man called Will who had interrupted them in the great hall that morning had stepped up to Rathburn's side and laid a restraining hand on the taller man's shoulder. His features were contorted with the effort he was making to look stern and serious, but when he spoke to his friend, he could not completely deny a smile.

Marganna leaned over the harp, her red-brown hair swinging forward to hide her own smile.

"Oh, all ye young lassies pay heed to my song,
The North Country man in a stable belongs.
To win a fair maiden he'd have to use force,
No wonder he always beds down with his horse.
Hey, nonny! Hey, nonny! Hey, nonny ho!"

"Rath! For God's sake, man, 'tis only a joke!"

When she heard Will's anxious cry, Marganna looked up to see Lord Rathburn pushing his way through the assembly to stand in front of her. She had expected furious anger and was not prepared for the sardonic humor glinting from his eyes.

"Your . . . talent overwhelms me, my lady," he said in loud, ringing tones. "I'm certain you won't take offense if I join your little song."

Marganna smirked. "Not at all," she murmured.

Rathburn turned to face his audience, only to find them pressing closer, their expressions avid. That this barbed exchange was providing superb entertainment there could be little doubt.

He placed one foot on a wooden stool and rested an elbow on his bent knee, then began to sing in a surprisingly good baritone voice that reached every corner of the room.

"I came down from the north to spend time at court,
I was seeking my sweetheart fair.
The lady, in truth, I found long in the tooth,
And hard-ridden as my old gray mare!"

The crowd cheered in glee, and Marganna's fingers stumbled over the strings as she caught the meaning of his words. A burning blush crept up her neck and she lowered her face, refusing to look at anyone.

"Oh, all ye young laddies pay heed to my song,
My lady from court in a stable belongs.

To woo me and win me, she'd have to use force,
Methinks I would rather bed down with my horse."

Marganna's hands stiffened, then dropped away from the harp, leaving him to sing the rest of the refrain without accompaniment.

"Hey, nonny! Hey, nonny! Hey, nonny ho!"

Rathburn leveled a leering glance at her, one black eyebrow cocked high. She tossed her head and looked away, but somewhere behind her, a second harpist took up the tune and the song went on.

"She was bony and swaybacked with flanks like sticks,
Her withers had started to sag."

It seemed to Marganna that rude laughter and even ruder catcalls bounced off the very walls.

"I couldn't tarry, she wanted to marry,
And harness me to an old nag!"

Exuding an inordinate amount of self-satisfaction, Rathburn again rendered the refrain, and by the time he was finished, Marganna was on her feet, to the unbridled delight of the bystanders.

"I believe it is my turn," she announced, and though she sounded very much as if she would like to swing the harp she held against his head, there was a telltale sparkle in her eyes.

He bowed mockingly. "By all means."

She smiled sweetly.

"Oh, the man of the moors, no lover was he,
His ancestry numbered some swine—"

"Wait, you two," exclaimed Will, pushing his way between them. "Rath, the king wishes to speak to you."

"To me? For what reason?"

"I . . . I'm not certain. You had best find that out for yourself."

"I expect you are right."

Without looking at Marganna, he strode off across the room, disappearing in the midst of the milling onlookers, each one of whom was straining to observe the meeting between Rathburn and his king. Marganna could see nothing but their collective backs and was just considering climbing onto the stool for a better view when the people before her moved aside to let Rathburn approach.

There was a determined look on his face as he made a low bow and reached for her hand. She tried to pull away, but he held her fingers so tightly she thought the bones would break.

"The king tells me he enjoyed our little song very much, but he feels our exchange is growing a bit heated. He thinks we should demonstrate that it was all in the spirit of fun by dancing together."

"Dancing? With you?" she sputtered, hearing the music begin behind her. "But I meant every word I sang."

"As did I. But he is the king, and he has issued a command. And if you would bother to look, you will see he is watching us carefully."

Marganna followed his gaze and there, across the suddenly still chamber, was the dark-clad figure of the king. He nodded encouragingly, and she bobbed an embarrassed curtsey. Immediately, the musicians struck up a tune, and when Rath grasped her waist with one strong hand, she made no further protest, allowing him to swing her into the circle being formed for the roundelay.

The tune was lively, and for a few minutes she struggled with the intricate dance steps. Her upbringing had afforded few opportunities for dancing, and she was ashamed of her clumsiness. Despite his size, her partner was light on his feet, executing the movements with ease.

As she was momentarily passed to another partner, she found herself looking into the eyes of the man Rathburn had quizzed her about earlier—Donal FitzClinton.

"Where did you disappear to, milady? I had hoped to make your acquaintance." His smile was gently chiding.

"I'm sorry . . . I was sent on an errand by my mistress."

"The dour Lady Stanley?"

She nodded.

"Then I cannot fault you for obeying so promptly. Perhaps we—"

She was suddenly reclaimed by Rathburn, who swung her away, giving FitzClinton no chance to finish his suggestion. Irritated by Rath's calculated rudeness and sensing the other's puzzled stare, she ignored them both and concentrated on the dance steps, presently mastering them sufficiently to allow herself to relax somewhat.

She dared a quick look at her partner's face and found he was watching her with an appraising smile. Her chin rose haughtily. She had never known anyone who issued such a blatant challenge . . . and she was still dazed by her own willingness to rise to that challenge. If she forced herself to admit it, she'd actually enjoyed their musical exchange.

The ladies stepped to the center of the circle, curtsied to the men, and danced back to their partners, who spun them about. As Rath reached for Marganna, she noticed his eyes lingering on the low-cut neck of her gown. Self-consciously, one hand crept upward to shield her bared flesh from his scrutiny. How crude he was!

"Must you stare so?" she demanded harshly.

Rath stopped short, throwing the other dancers into confusion. He reached out to close ruthless fingers around Marganna's wrist, slowly pulling her protective arm away from her bosom.

"What do you think you're doing?" she gasped in a half whisper, glancing around her in embarrassment.

Still he did not speak, and it seemed as though his eyes would blister her skin. Suddenly filled with dread, she, too, looked down. A folded corner of parchment had worked its way upward and was now visible in the cleft between her breasts.

She closed her eyes as she felt Rath's other hand plunge into the neck of her gown. When she reopened them, he was unfolding the letter she had hidden there earlier.

Quickly, he scanned the letter's contents, and when he raised his eyes to her face, she quailed before the look in them. Dimly she heard someone behind them ask what was wrong and realized the music had slowly faded. Over Rath's shoulder she caught a glimpse of her aunt's set, tight face and thought her knees would buckle in fear.

Rath's first words were so low she could barely hear them. "You little bitch! You lying little bitch!"

She wet her dry lips and attempted to speak, but his next words were shouted so loudly they drowned out her feeble explanation.

"Guards! Arrest this woman—she's committed an act of treason!"

The room was instantly filled with an ear-splitting din. It seemed to Marganna the word *traitor* was being spoken on all sides of her. She took a step backward and found herself hemmed in by a line of armed men wearing the king's colors. She whirled about, only to come once again, face to face with Rathburn, looking as if he would like to strike her.

"I should have known you were a spy," he snarled. "No woman is as innocent as you pretended to be."

"But I—"

"Silence! You can make your excuses to the king."

Two of the guards roughly seized her arms. She began to struggle, but her strength was no match for theirs, and they easily dragged her across the floor. She cast one last terrified look over her shoulder, trying in vain to catch Lady Margaret's eye.

"My God, what a shame," she heard one man saying as he watched her being taken past. "Seems a pity to see such a comely wench beheaded for treason."

"Aye, ye'd think Richard could find a better use for one such as her."

"I'd be happy to punish her for him," spoke up another.

Marganna was carried out of the hall and into a wide corridor beyond. Suddenly the men holding her stopped, giving her a shove that propelled her forward onto the floor. Slowly Marganna raised her eyes and observed soft black boots nearly concealed by the hem of a black brocaded gown. Looking higher, she saw the gleam of gold and knew she was lying prostrate at the feet of the king of England.

"Well, well," she heard him say, his voice tinged with amusement, "what have we here? What, indeed?"

Chapter 3

Through the confusion that rocked the hall, Marganna heard King Richard's calm voice ordering the guards to take her upstairs to the privacy of his chambers. There, as though to seal her fate, they found further proof of her guilt—the sentry, Wilkes, was sprawled in the corridor outside the king's rooms, unconscious and snoring loudly.

"She must have drugged him," said Rathburn's friend Will, who had accompanied the small procession up the stairs.

"And misjudged the dosage," added Rath. "The poor fool was still on his feet when we left the chamber earlier." He knelt beside the unmoving man. "Well, he's down like a felled ox now. We'll have to have someone carry him to his quarters."

Marganna was taken into the outer chamber and, at the king's gesture, seated on one of the long benches. Richard eyed the small group of men surrounding him.

"I want two guards outside this door. The rest of you may go back to the dancing. Rath, Will, I want to speak to you in the next room."

"What about her?" Rath asked, inclining his head toward Marganna without looking at her.

"She can wait here until I am ready to speak with her," the king replied. "Don't look so disapproving, Rath. Where do you expect her to go with two men outside the door?"

With a shrug Rathburn reluctantly followed the others into the next room, banging the door shut behind him.

Marganna breathed a sigh of relief . . . at least the confrontation had been momentarily postponed. She huddled on the bench, knees drawn up, head resting on them. She was surprised she had not been thrown immediately into the dungeon or, at the very least, chained and manacled.

She caught snatches of words from the inner chamber and distinctly heard Rath describing her as "vicious" and "deceitful."

She would have expected him to think little else. Considering his loyalty to the Plantagenet king, he could only view her action as the most unpardonable treason.

She dared not think about what would happen to her now. She would simply have to trust Lady Margaret to intervene, despite her vow that she could not and would not come to Marganna's aid.

Hearing more heated words from the inner room, she shuddered and closed her eyes tightly. Something told her Lord Rathburn would be a formidable enemy.

"Surely you can't think the girl was acting on her own," Richard said, settling himself on the chair before his desk. The letter casket remained open after a hasty search to ascertain what other correspondence might be missing, and now he idly toyed with one of the bundles of letters tied in silk ribbons.

"No, there must be others involved," Rath agreed. "We must find out whom she knows here at court."

"I asked belowstairs," Will stated, "but could find no one who knew even her name, much less anything about her."

"She's employed by that Stanley witch—there's the best place to start questioning," Rath said. "That woman has been involved in treason before."

"I remember it well," Richard said dryly. "And, I must point out, that incident was a great deal more serious than this seems to be."

Rath flung out his hands in frustration. "For God's sake, Richard, this *is* serious. The fact that she took only the letter from Edward indicates she was specifically searching for information about the princes. Not only did the little tart find proof of the boys' existence, she even knows they are somewhere in Yorkshire. Just how long do you think she intends to keep that news quiet?''

''Yes, and I am aware of just whom you think might consider it important. You think Tudor is behind this, don't you?''

''Who else could it be? Who has better cause than Tudor and his conniving mother, whose presence, for some unknown reason, you suffer here in your court? You know as well as I do that they would like nothing better than for those boys to be dead. They hope you have done the dirty work for them, but if not, the next best thing would be to locate the princes and have their own agents murder them. Now, somehow, this girl has gotten the very information they seek.''

''Do you think she has told anyone yet?'' asked Will, looking from one man to the other.

''It is my guess that she has not. I walked in on her while she was still in the outer chamber and remained at her side throughout the rest of the evening. I don't think she had the opportunity to tell anyone else what she found.''

''Then all we have to do is keep her from seeing or talking to her accomplices.''

''There's only one way to do that effectively, Will.''

''You can't mean she should be executed!'' The sandy-haired man seemed shocked by the suggestion, but Rath merely nodded.

''If she were a man, there'd be no question of what to do with her. What difference should it make that she is a beau—a woman?''

''Are you certain her crime warrants such severe punishment?'' the king asked quietly.

''She is a spy! She deliberately drugged Wilkes, sneaked in here, and somehow gained access to your private correspondence. In so doing, she laid hands on information that could put young Edward and Dickon in serious danger.''

''They've been safe enough this past year.''

''But you yourself have said the situation is changing. What if Tudor is finally making his move? Perhaps he needs to know where those boys are in order to destroy them."

Richard shut the lid of the letter casket and sighed. "Be that as it may, we are dealing with the question of the girl, not Henry Tudor. Were that bastard here, I would know exactly what to do with him."

"It should be no different with the girl," Rath reminded him.

"I disagree. After all, Tudor himself is experienced in treachery—he has been raised to it. But that girl can only be acting on someone else's orders. I doubt she even knew the significance of that stolen letter."

"Damn it, Richard, you are too trusting!"

"Rath . . ." Will said, warningly.

Richard smiled. "It's all right, Will. I won't take offense and toss our friend into the dungeon. Here in privacy he is free to speak his mind . . . and remember, he has had a trying night. Which makes me think, Rath—how did you happen to discover the girl in my chambers?"

"Strictly a coincidence."

Will grinned. "Don't expect us to believe that, old friend." He turned to Richard. "You see, Rath and the girl met under strained conditions earlier in the day. My guess is he followed her from the hall thinking to rectify that unfortunate beginning."

"Did anyone ever tell you that you gabble on like an old woman, Will?" growled Rath. "I did not follow the girl intentionally. I was merely in the same corridor on my way to my rooms when I saw the unguarded door. It struck me as strange and I decided to investigate."

"And I assume the girl had a plausible story to tell you," commented Richard. "Considering your suspicious mind, she must have been convincing, or you'd never have permitted her to return to the hall. Which brings me to another question—why did it seem you enjoyed such an intimate relationship with this girl if, as Will claims, you only met this afternoon?"

Rath scowled. "Intimate? I'd hardly say it was that."

"Believe me when I tell you it *seemed* fairly intimate,

the way the two of you stood up and sang your ballad, with eyes only for each other."

"For Christ's sake, I don't believe this! The woman insulted me, and I answered in kind. What is so intimate about that?"

"Didn't you get the impression they were doing more than merely entertaining the crowd with a song, Will?"

The freckled face looked alarmed. "Oh, now, leave me out of this, please, sire I . . . I. . ." He cast a swift look at Rath, then suddenly burst into laughter. "I'm sorry, friend, but when she started singing, you should have seen your face. You couldn't have looked any more surprised had she run you through with a sword."

"And, Rath, though you swear it was all innocent, I believe you should give thanks that Bronwyn had already left the hall. The imagination boggles at what she would have made of your exchange with the lovely young woman."

"Well, I'm certainly glad I have provided the two of you with such amusement for this evening," snapped Rathburn, "but do you suppose we could get back to the real reason for this discussion? What is to be done about the spy?"

"First we will question her," Richard said with a sigh, "though I doubt she will give us much information." He raised a hand. "Don't say it, Rath. I will not employ torture. I don't believe she knows that much in any case. And because she was accused so publicly, there is no way we can use her to set a trap. She was only important to the conspirators as long as she remained undetected. Now they will conveniently forget about her and busy themselves with some alternate plan."

"But you won't just release her, will you?" asked Will.

"No. I agree with Rath. We must prevent her from telling anyone that the princes are hidden in Yorkshire."

"And there is no way to do that except to execute her," Rath insisted. "You can't afford to take any chances, Richard."

"The Tower?" suggested Will.

"She'd come into contact with too many people there,"

replied Rathburn. "We can't be certain every jailor is reliable."

"Rath is right about that, Will. We've got to place her in the keeping of someone we trust without reservation, someone who can be counted on to guard the lady's movements night and day."

"There is no such person."

"Oh, but there is one I would trust above all others. Especially in the matter of keeping a mere woman in hand."

"Oh, my God," breathed Will, dropping onto a bench.

Rath looked at Will, a question in his eyes, then shifted his gaze to the king's amused face. Suddenly his own was drained of all color.

"No! Christ Almighty and all the saints! Surely you must be joking . . . Are you truly thinking of . . . No! I won't do it."

"You refuse your sovereign?" Richard was still smiling.

"How could you ask this of me? I can't be a nursemaid to that . . . that female."

"No one is asking you to be a nursemaid, Rath. You must be the stern jailor. Your only task is to prevent her from spreading the information she has."

"Impossible."

"Oh, come now, it's not impossible. You are a very resourceful fellow. I have no doubt you will be able to find effective ways of keeping her silent and occupied."

"The only effective way is execution, I tell you."

"Rath, I hardly know what has happened to you," Richard said, shaking his dark head. "There was a time when you would have relished such an assignment. Your creativity would have been challenged, and you'd have thought of several interesting ways in which to keep the lady busy."

"Perhaps his affair with Bronwyn has unnerved him," suggested Will. "Mayhap he has no stomach for the scene she will cause when she finds out about this arrangement."

"Leave Bronwyn out of this," Rath retorted. "It has

nothing to do with her. I just don't understand why a spy doesn't receive a spy's punishment."

"I daresay she'll think she's being adequately punished," said Richard, chuckling.

"Aye, she'll think being constantly in Rath's company is worse than death." Will laughed.

"I'm glad you both find this so bloody funny. I hope you don't stop laughing someday to find we are all up to our necks in serious trouble!"

Rath stalked to the door, tossing the next words back over his shoulder. "I think it's time the prisoner was questioned." With that, he slammed the door behind him.

Will looked uneasy. "I've never seen Rath so upset. You know he's not ordinarily rude."

"I know, Will. That's one of the reasons I think he may have finally met his match. God, I'd give anything to be able to watch what will transpire between the two of them in the next few weeks. They think they hate each other, but I'm of a different opinion. What do you think?"

"To be honest, I'm not sure. I suppose the girl intrigued our friend because she resisted his charm from the first and he saw her as a challenge. Now, with this spying business, he has to view her as an enemy, and I don't think he knows how to deal with being attracted to someone he feels he should despise."

"You know, Will," Richard said, suddenly looking more tired and strained than his thirty-two years warranted, "tonight was the first time I have laughed since . . . since Anne died. The first time I have felt any sort of emotion at all. There was something so intense, so intriguing about those two standing up in front of the whole castle, oblivious to everyone but themselves. I'd like to think we were all privy to something special."

"A splendid thought. However, if you are thinking this will lead to anything serious, I believe it is safe to say you can forget the notion. I've known Rath long enough to be convinced there is no woman alive who can claim his full attention for any length of time."

"Wouldn't want to make a small wager, would you, Will?" The king started toward the door, then stopped short. "From what I witnessed in the hall tonight, I think this girl might be the very one to tame our friend Lord Rathburn. In fact, I'm so certain, I'll put up this castle, Westminster, and the Tower of London against your estates in the north."

Smiling, he made his exit, leaving Will standing alone, a perplexed and disbelieving look on his thin, freckled face.

"For the last time, who sent you to spy on the king?"

Rath paced up and down in front of the girl, frustration tempting him to put his hands around her slender throat and strangle her. Once again, she opened wide her spice-colored eyes and shook her head.

"I don't know what you mean. I'm no spy. I merely lost my way."

"Spare us from having to hear that story again." He swung about to face her. "Look, you've been caught with evidence on your person. Don't you think it would go better for you if you told us everything you know?"

"But I know nothing!"

"You're lying. . ."

"What is your name?" Will asked. Gratefully, she turned toward him. At least he was calm, exhibiting none of the murderous rage that goaded his friend.

"Marganna," she answered.

"And your last name?"

"I have none."

"I see."

"Oh, damnation, surely you don't believe her?" Rath burst out.

"Calm down, old man," Will cautioned. "It makes little difference anyway."

"Then why are we wasting time asking these questions? Why not just let her go on about her business? Why not open the damned letter chest and let her look to her heart's content? Tomorrow she can sit at the council meeting! Christ, what is wrong with you both?"

There was a discreet knock at the door, and the king

nodded at Will to open it. "I've asked the guards to summon Lady Stanley—that will be her."

The door opened to reveal the slight figure of Marganna's aunt, looking more than ever like a nun in a plain black houppelande gown that fell from her narrow shoulders to the floor in precise folds. Her hands were folded at her waist, again bare except for a plain gold wedding band and the rosary wrapped around one wrist. She knelt stiffly before King Richard until he extended a hand to raise her to her feet.

"Lady Stanley, I want to ask you a few questions about this girl."

The woman's black eyes were expressionless as she flicked them to Marganna, then back to the king.

"Very well."

"She is in your employ, is she not?"

"Yes, she is."

"In what capacity?"

"She is a musician."

"That is her only duty?"

"Sometimes she acts as a lady's maid, though she has little experience in that area."

"And you have never asked her to perform any other . . . duties for you?"

"What do you mean?"

"You must realize that this young woman has been arrested for treason. We want to know who gave her her orders."

"Surely you do not think it was I?"

"There is every reason to believe you had something to do with it," Rath put in. "After all, it wouldn't be the first time you have acted against your king."

Margaret Stanley's eyes glittered dangerously, but she answered in a serene voice. "I assure you, I know nothing of this girl's activities. I found her in Lancashire and brought her to court because she has superior musical ability. What she has been up to since her arrival here, I do not know."

"Have you seen her in the company of others?" the king asked.

"No. To my knowledge, she has kept to her chamber."

"Do you think of anything you might have to tell us that could aid in the solution of this matter?"

"No, sire, I do not."

"Very well."

"What is to be done with the girl?" Lady Margaret asked.

"I have not yet decided," Richard replied gravely. "For the moment, I am putting her into the custody of Lord Rathburn. He will hold her as a prisoner in the north until we have had a chance to delve into this a bit further."

"No!" Marganna cried, leaping to her feet. "I won't go with him!"

"I'm afraid you have no choice in the matter," Richard stated. "You should be glad we are not going to execute you forthwith."

"Perhaps it would be preferable," she said faintly.

"My sentiments exactly," snapped Rathburn. "I suggest we discuss it at greater length."

"My mind is made up, Rath, and you know it. Now, Lady Stanley, that will be all. Thank you for your . . . cooperation."

With a slight obeisance, Lady Margaret turned to go, pausing in front of her niece.

"You are a stupid little slut to let yourself get involved in something like this. I should have left you where I found you!"

Trying to think of some way to convey her news to Lady Margaret, Marganna did not see the blow coming. She was taken by surprise as her aunt's hand flashed out, striking her cheek with a resounding slap. The rosary beads wrapped around the bony wrist struck Marganna's skin and left it stinging.

Marganna cried out, recoiling from the fury she encountered as she looked into the dark eyes. For a long moment, Lady Margaret's gaze was unblinking; then she turned and walked out of the room.

"She was lying, Richard, and you know it," Rath began.

"No, I don't know it. I can only suspect it. We can do

nothing until we uncover something more about this plot. As of now, no real harm has been done."

"I hope you're right."

"The only way tonight's events can hurt our cause is if this girl is allowed to tell what she knows."

"But I don't know anything," Marganna exclaimed.

"Be quiet!" Rath muttered in a low and furious voice.

Ignoring their exchange, Richard went on. "I want you to keep her isolated until morning. Then you will return to Yorkshire, taking her with you. Hold her there—at your estate or at Middleham Castle, I don't care which—and wait until I send you further instructions."

"I'm to return to Yorkshire in the morning? But I've just arrived."

"I realize that and regret it very much. But there seems to be little else we can do right now."

"Send her with someone else."

"Nay, you are the only one I can trust with this duty, Rath. No, I'm very much afraid you are going to have to sacrifice your visit to take care of this bit of business for me."

"I don't mean to question the intelligence of your decision—"

"Then don't."

At the king's quiet words, Lord Rathburn dropped his head in apparent submission. A storm of curses and arguments raged through his mind, and it took him a few minutes to regain his self-control. At last he nodded, then announced, "With your permission, I'll go to bed now," and started from the room.

"Don't forget your prisoner."

Richard's words sounded as though he might be laughing, but when Rath's head snapped up, the king's face was composed.

"Remember, she must not be left alone."

Rath glared at Marganna, then reached out to grasp her wrist. "Then come along, damn you. And I'm warning you, don't cause me any trouble. I've had enough of that to last a lifetime."

If Marganna had discovered a lack of vindictiveness on the king's part, she soon found she could not expect a similar reaction from Lord Rathburn. After speaking a few terse words with one of the guards outside the king's quarters, he grabbed her arm and began dragging her down the hallway. Far from increasing her fear, his imperious manner served to disperse it entirely. She protested noisily, jerking her arm away each time she stumbled and he yanked her unceremoniously to her feet. By the time they arrived at his chambers, her knees were bruised, and her arm felt as though it had been wrenched from the socket. It was something of a relief to find herself dropped onto the hearth rug and told to stay there.

Her relief was short-lived, however, for when Rathburn answered a sharp rap on the door, he was met by the king's guard, who handed him a pair of iron manacles.

Grimly he fastened one metal bracelet around her wrist and attached the other to a bedpost. She huddled against the side of the bed, unable to lie down or move around because of the shortness of the chain. Her right arm was raised painfully, the metal scraping her skin every time she attempted to find a more comfortable position.

"Now," Rath was saying, pacing up and down in front of her, "let's get one thing straight. I don't like being responsible for you, and if you try to make trouble, I will take pleasure in seeing that you regret it."

"But I—"

"Silence!" he thundered. "The first thing you can learn to do is to keep quiet. If I had wanted to hear you speak, I'd have given you permission."

He stood gazing into the fire, idly kicking at a log that had rolled forward onto the hearth.

"Do you know how thrilled I am that I must travel back to Yorkshire immediately? Four days on the road through rain and mud, and then—because of you—I must retrace my footsteps without even a decent interval to rest. Do you know how furious that makes me?"

He whirled to look at her, but this time she only stared back and made no attempt to speak.

"Damn it, can't you answer me?"

"You told me to keep quiet."

"Oh, by all the saints! How can I be expected to put up with this?"

"It's your own fault," she stated stubbornly.

"My fault? My fault!"

"Yes, your fault. Had you left well enough alone . . ."

"You think I should have turned a blind eye to your spying?" He was livid.

"You might have given me a chance to explain matters."

"There could be no possible explanation to make what you were doing right. No, it couldn't be overlooked or excused—I did the right thing to expose you. The problem seems to be King Richard's demented joke of hanging you around my neck like a millstone. Damn it, you should be shivering in some dungeon right now, waiting your turn at the block."

"Only the cruelest of beasts would speak that way," she cried.

"Madam, you will find that where you are concerned, I fully intend to be the cruelest of beasts. It is no less than you deserve."

They glared at each other a long moment before Marganna dropped her eyes. It would do no good to continue in this vein. As little as she liked it, she was under his control, and it would be foolhardy to anger him further.

Presently she heard the man cross the room, and her breathing eased. But a few seconds after his footsteps died away, there was a new sound—the rustle of cloth. Her head snapped up.

"What are you doing?" she asked hesitantly.

"I'm getting undressed. What does it look like I'm doing?"

She raised her eyes to find him standing in front of her again. This time he was without his doublet, clad only in a black satin shirt, which hung open to reveal his bare chest and black tights. Quickly she averted her gaze.

"But . . . why should you undress?"

He laughed harshly. "Ah, the virgin once again fears for her innocence."

"No, it's not that," she said, bristling. "I just . . . I mean . . . well, I couldn't think of any reason you should be disrobing."

"A man usually undresses before retiring for the night."

"But under the circumstances is it entirely necessary?" She met his eyes again, wondering if he expected her to beg for his modesty.

"I do not sleep in my clothing, no matter what the circumstances."

"It would be—"

"I didn't ask for your presence in my chamber, remember. If you don't enjoy seeing unclothed men, don't look."

His hand went to the fastenings of his hose and she closed her eyes. It would seem the man did not want her to beg, after all. He truly saw nothing wrong with divesting himself of his garments and standing stark naked in front of her.

After a few minutes her self-imposed darkness seemed to grow even darker, and she realized he must have extinguished the candles burning in the room. Slowly she opened her eyes to find the bedchamber lighted only by the dim glow from the fireplace. Dim as it was, however, it provided sufficient illumination to clearly see the figure of the man standing at the foot of the bed, his back turned to her. He was staring into the darkness as though lost in thought.

As much as Marganna wanted to look away, she found she could not. A chance to study the first naked man she had ever seen was simply too compelling. She was frankly fascinated by the dance of firelight over the strong neck and shoulders, noticing how it burnished the dark hair with golden highlights and caressed the smooth muscles radiating from the indentation of his spine. She found herself enjoying the sight of tautly sinewed buttocks and powerful thighs, faintly hazed with dark hair. Never had she dreamed a naked man could be so . . . so beautiful! Ashamed of her thoughts, she forced herself to look away, and in the next instant she gave thanks she had, for the man spoke, and the sound of his voice told her he had turned toward her.

"I trust you will use this night to reflect upon your criminal behavior. Perhaps by morning you will be prepared to tell us something more of this plot against King Richard."

"There isn't anything to tell."

"Good night," he said curtly, and she fell silent. Soon she heard him settling himself in his bed, and she likewise tried to compose herself for sleep.

She strained closer to the bed, trying to ease the painful pull on her arm. Her wrist was chafed, and each movement made it feel even more raw. She sighed, knowing it would do no good to complain. The northern lord would be only too happy to find she was in pain, and she would not give him that satisfaction. She wriggled again restlessly, stretching her legs out in front of her, despite the protest of her scraped knees. She caught her breath as another sharp stab of pain seared through her wrist.

"Good Lord, what is the matter with you?" came the irritated voice of Lord Rathburn. "Do you intend to keep me awake all night with your tiresome floundering?"

"What do you expect?" she snapped. "This chain is so short I can't get comfortable."

"It was not my intention that you be comfortable."

Mentally Marganna shrugged. She had expected no other answer from the brute.

"Oh, hellfire!" He suddenly appeared in front of her, his lower body swathed in the sheet he had snatched up from the bed. "If I don't do something, neither one of us will have any rest tonight. And, thanks to you, we have a long journey ahead of us."

He held a key with which he unlocked the manacle bracelet from the bedpost.

"Get up," he ordered.

Obediently Marganna scrambled to her feet. She looked around the darkened room, wondering where he might now expect her to spend the night. Suddenly she heard the snap of metal and, looking down, saw that he had fastened the bracelet around his own wrist.

"You can't do that," she cried.

"I've done it," he stated. As he started walking back

around the bed, she was forced to follow, the metal biting sharply. "Now get into bed, and for God's sake be silent."

"You expect me to . . . to sleep with you?"

"Spare me any maidenly arguments, if you please. The only thing you have to fear from me is making me angry enough to use this chain to strangle you. Now get into the damned bed!"

His last words were uttered so forcefully that she decided it would be wisest simply to do his bidding. At least, she thought, he would be beneath the covers and she would be on top of them, fully clothed.

Rath followed her into the bed, loosening the sheet he wore and tossing it carelessly over himself. As his head struck the pillow he emitted a gusty sigh, and Marganna knew he must, indeed, be nearing the end of his patience.

Serves him right, she thought, easing her head onto a pillow and closing her eyes.

Exhaustion washed over her in gentle but inexorable waves, though just as she surrendered to sleep, she heard the sound of the chamber door creaking open. She knew someone had come into the room and was approaching the bed. Carefully she eased one eye open and peered through the feeble light.

Bronwyn stood at the foot of the bed dressed in a white linen smock, covered by a loose brocade dressing robe.

"Rath?" she whispered. "Are you asleep? Surely you were expecting me." She moved to the side of the bed and reached out to caress the sleeping man's naked chest. He came awake with a start; as he raised to a sitting position, Marganna's arm was yanked forward and she sat up in the bed also.

"You!" exclaimed the singer. "What are you doing here? What is *she* doing here, Rath?"

"Calm down, Bronwyn," he cautioned. "There's no need to rouse the entire castle."

"I want to know why she is in your bed!"

"Because she is my prisoner, and I am not to let her out of my sight. Surely you can see for yourself this is no lovers' tryst."

The woman put her hands on her hips, thrusting her full breasts forward, her black eyes wickedly angry. "What I can see is that you are stark naked and in bed with another woman."

"Who is fully clothed," he reminded her. "Look, Bronwyn, I didn't think to warn you about this. In fact, I forgot you were to join me."

A low scream issued from the woman's throat. "You forgot? Blast you to Hades, how can a man forget he has invited a woman to his bedchamber?"

Rath threw out his arms in exasperation, causing Marganna to crash against his side.

She was jolted by the impact with his warm flesh; her naturally high spirits suddenly returned, and she began to see the humor in the situation. Some perversity, perhaps sheer exhilaration at escaping a death sentence, made her dare to prolong Rathburn's dilemma. She raised her free hand to his chest as though her balance was threatened, letting her fingers splay against the springing black hair. She heard the other woman's angry gasp and nestled closer.

Rathburn gave her a withering look, then returned to Bronwyn. "This has been an incredibly strange night, and I find myself with unexpected and unwanted duties. The king has commanded me to stand guard over our spy here—how could I refuse his orders?"

"Couldn't you have chained me in the hallway?" Marganna asked innocently. She loved seeing the autocratic lord being taken to task by his irate paramour!

"I can't risk letting you speak to anyone else."

"But why does she have to sleep in your bed?" Bronwyn's tone was dubious.

"It's certainly not by choice," Marganna murmured with a demure smile, though her cheek against his shoulder seemed to render the words meaningless.

"You keep out of this," Rath yelled, sliding out of bed as if to distance himself from her. He swiftly adjusted the sheet around his waist once again, but as he moved, Marganna had no choice except to go with him, his motions causing her to bob like a puppet.

Rath laid his free hand on Bronwyn's shoulder. "It won't

be like this every night, I assure you. I intend to find some other way of doing things, even if I have to drug the little witch each night. Be patient with me, Bronwyn, and we will soon be together again."

As he spoke, he was gently guiding her toward the door.

"I want to stay with you tonight," she said in a petulant tone. "I want to make sure nothing happens."

"Nothing could possibly happen," Rath assured her.

"I don't trust her."

"Surely you're not afraid I will try to seduce your lover?" Marganna asked with a light laugh. "That's the farthest thing from my mind."

"You're lying!" Bronwyn's hand darted out, her fingers twisting in Marganna's hair and pulling fiercely. "I don't believe you."

"Damnation," breathed Rath, seizing one of Bronwyn's wrists and squeezing until she released her hold on Marganna's hair. "Get out of here—at once! I will speak with you in the morning."

"All right, I'll go. But it will serve you right if she puts a dagger in your black heart."

Bronwyn started to stalk from the room; then, as an afterthought, she stepped close to Rath and slipped her arms around his neck. Before he could move away, she kissed him full on the lips, her restless hands sliding over the muscled shoulders. He lifted his hands to push her away and the sheet around his waist slipped precariously.

"Bronwyn, go away," he all but pleaded.

"Very well . . . but I will be waiting to discuss this with you in the morning."

With a last hateful glare at Marganna, the black-haired beauty slipped through the door and was gone. Rath shot the bolt with a vicious motion.

"Get back into bed and don't dare say another word," he said warningly. Marganna did as she was told, but he still grumbled, "I suppose you think this is all very amusing?"

"No, of course not," she said, clearly suppressing a smile. "What could be amusing about being shackled to a stranger? Especially one with so many pressing . . . obligations."

He dropped onto the bed, not caring that in doing so he gave her wrist another nasty wrench. "God, but you've got a wicked tongue. Give it a rest for a while, will you?"

"Gladly."

They fell into a profound silence, neither moving nor speaking for many minutes. Finally, unable to will himself to sleep lying flat on his back, Rath stirred and turned to his right side. The action brought Marganna up against his back, but now, in the quiet intimacy of the darkened room, their proximity lacked humor.

She opened her mouth to complain, but he said tersely, "Don't say a word—just go to sleep."

She clamped her lips shut but doubted she could ever fall asleep in such a compromising situation. They were back to back, her hip thrust up against his rock-hard thigh, the backs of their legs touching. Even though the sheet and her clothing separated them, she could feel the overpowering heat of his body.

For a long time Marganna lay awake, battling feelings that were entirely new to her. Nothing in her upbringing had prepared her for dealing with men, especially men like Lord Rathburn, who in the space of one short day had reacted to her with a wide variety of emotions, ranging from sensual cajolery to blazing anger to cold implacability. Shifting restlessly, she remembered the way he had kissed her, not asking polite permission as a gentleman would have but taking what he wanted despite her objections. There was no doubt he was an unscrupulous rogue, so why did her mutinous mind keep recalling the feel of his warm chest beneath her fingers, the sight of his naked back in the firelight?

Lying on his side of the bed, Rathburn willed himself to forget the soft, feminine body next to him. She was, he reminded himself, an enemy—someone to be scorned. He must not dwell on the subtle perfume of her hair, the tempting curve of her hip, or the havoc her hands had wreaked on his skin. Cursing himself for a rutting boar, he edged as far away from her as possible and squeezed his eyes shut, determined to sleep.

But slumber did not come easily for either of them. It was well after midnight before the room filled with the even breathing of the two exhausted sleepers, the only sound besides the soft, soothing hiss of the fire.

In the morning, Rath awakened to find that sometime in the night he had turned onto his back again, pulling Marganna across his body, their manacled wrists caught between them. Her head and free arm rested against his chest, and her spicy brown hair spread over his shoulder and onto the pillow. He breathed deeply of its soft fragrance. Their legs had become entangled with the sheet and each other, and he was well aware of the effect the soft weight of her body had on his. His first inclination was to kiss her awake, his imagination fired by curiosity at what he would see in her gaze. Would she be shocked to find herself in his embrace? Or would the sleepy depths of her eyes reveal an awakening of the passion he sensed she was capable of feeling? Thoroughly aroused by the thought of being the one to stir those emotions to life, he lowered his head to hers . . .

With a sudden, frustrated groan, he pushed her away, forcibly reminding himself she was a spy, a threat to his beloved king. With a heavy sigh, he reached for the key on the bedside table that would unlock the metal bracelets.

Marganna was startled into wakefulness but said nothing as she watched him unlock the bracelet on his wrist. He wrapped the sheet around himself once again, then gestured for her to slide to the foot of the bed where he fastened the manacle to the bedpost. At least this time she was in a sitting position on the bed instead of suffering the discomfort of crouching on the floor.

Marganna knew she should keep her eyes averted as her jailor dressed, but she could not resist a quick peek. It seemed the sheltered circumstances of her life were destined to come to an abrupt end! Not only was she staring boldly at a naked man, she found she was frankly fascinated by the stark contrast between the tanned smoothness of some areas of his body and the hairy roughness of others. She felt surprise at her lack of modesty but waited until he had left the room, locking the door behind him, before scolding herself for its absence.

Rath was gone for nearly thirty minutes, and when he returned, he was carrying bread and wine which he thrust at her.

"Eat your breakfast as quickly as you can. We must leave for Yorkshire before first light, and the king has ordered that you be allowed to gather your belongings to take with you."

She could tell from his tone of voice that he considered it another mistake to pamper her thusly, and she wisely started eating, saying nothing. She couldn't help but feel somewhat more cheerful—if she was to be allowed to take her clothing and personal effects, there must be no plans at the moment to execute her.

Before they left Rathburn's room, he removed the manacles and tossed them aside.

"Don't worry, I plan to keep them handy," he said grimly, shoving her down the hall ahead of him. "We've got to make haste now, and you will be able to gather your things more quickly if you are unhampered by the irons. Just don't think I will hesitate to put them back on if it becomes necessary."

An hour later, Lord Rathburn and his female prisoner, along with a small entourage, rode through the dawn-lighted stillness of Nottinghamshire, following the winding road north. Rathburn rode in the lead and Marganna followed, her eyes on his broad, cloaked back. Occasionally a small smile flitted over her face. How angry he would be if he knew that, right under his own watchful gaze, she had managed to leave a message for Lady Margaret.

Making a great show of fumbling through a drawer of the vanity table to find her own belongings, she had left what she hoped would be an unmistakable clue. With the ivory hairpins, a gift to her from Lady Margaret herself, she had formed an arrow, pointing north, and beside it she had left a brooch—not the enameled white boar now worn at court but the elegant sunne-in-splendor brooch presented to Lady Stanley when Edward IV was king . . . Edward, whose sons had been spirited away by his younger brother Richard.

It was Marganna's fervent hope that when Lady Stanley saw the seemingly innocent arrangement left on top of her vanity she would immediately surmise what Marganna had been trying to tell her—that Edward IV's sons were alive and hidden somewhere in the north of England.

Chapter 4

The day went on endlessly. Marganna leaned forward, trying to ease the tired muscles in her shoulders and back. Though she was an adequate horsewoman, she was not accustomed to spending so many long hours in the saddle, and she was aware of her growing exhaustion. She sighed and fought the urge to grimace childishly at the stiffly upright back of the man on the horse ahead of her. It seemed he never tired, never got hungry or thirsty, and never had to make a sojourn into the bushes growing alongside the narrow roadway.

Marganna glanced at the man riding beside Lord Rathburn, and at the same moment Will Metcalfe turned to throw a concerned look back over his shoulder at her. Though his faint smile was apologetic, she knew no matter how sympathetic to her plight he might be, he would never gainsay his friend. His steadfast loyalty to Rath was the main reason King Richard had chosen to send him on this return journey to Yorkshire, and Will was not the sort of man to betray such a trust.

Four silent men at arms accompanied them and, though they never spoke, even to each other, Marganna had noticed the covert looks that signaled their curiosity about her. If ever the iron-willed Lord Rathburn deigned to stop for a meal or to rest, she would attempt to communicate with one or more of them. Of course they probably would not think helping her escape the evil-tempered North Country man worth the risk they would have to take, but she had to chance it. She would offer them money and then pray that Lady Margaret would honor her debt . . .

There was a sudden flurry of hoofbeats as Marganna's own mount was overtaken by a high-stepping white stallion ridden by the ballad singer, Bronwyn. Her black hair streamed out behind her, making a striking contrast with the scarlet cloak she wore and the stallion's black and gold trappings. In her hand was a lithe hazelwood switch that she snaked back and forth against the horse's flanks, urging him forward.

With a disdainful toss of her head as she passed Marganna, Bronwyn drew in rein beside Rathburn and leaned toward him to murmur a few words. With a frown, he turned to stare at his prisoner; then, with a disgusted shrug, held up one hand, causing the small party of riders to come to a halt. As he dismounted, he announced they would pause long enough for a meal of bread and cheese before continuing their journey. Their faces breaking into broad smiles, the men at arms also began dismounting, their silence finally giving way to a confusion of cheerful banter.

As she rode past Marganna a second time, Bronwyn laughed lightly. "I told Rath you were beginning to look like a wilted rose and probably couldn't go on much further without rest."

"Why would you tell him such a thing?"

"It's true, isn't it? Look at yourself."

"I don't want your pity," Marganna snapped, "or his. I am perfectly capable of continuing the journey!"

Giving way to ill temper, Marganna slapped the reins across her palfrey's rump, causing the animal to give a startled whinny and lurch forward. Thrown off balance, Marganna could only clutch at the reins as her horse broke into a full-scale gallop, scattering Rathburn and his men at arms like grouse before its flying hoofs.

As they shot past him, she heard Rath shout, "Stop! Damnation, woman, come back here!"

If only I could, she thought, terror stricken by the speed with which the trees seemed to be flashing past her eyes. Knowing a fall could well kill her, she wound one hand into the animal's mane and leaned close, hugging its neck.

Hoofbeats echoed in her ears, but it was several moments before she realized someone was pursuing her, matching her breakneck pace. Praying whoever it was would be able to overtake her mount, she dragged back on the reins she held gathered in her left hand. Without warning, the horse wheeled and plunged into the forest, following an ancient side road that was little more than a path. Crouching low to avoid the overhanging tree limbs, Marganna glanced desperately over her shoulder to see if her rescuer had followed the same dangerous course.

Behind her came Lord Rathburn, now so close she could easily see his features, which were set in a furious scowl. Certain that the longer her horse ran, the more vengeful he would be, she put her mouth to the mare's ear and urgently pleaded, "Whoa! Whoa!"

As eager as she was to be rescued, she cursed the fact that her savior was not Will Metcalfe or one of the men at arms.

She could hear someone shouting Rathburn's name, and as Marganna darted another swift look backward, he did the same. She cried a warning, but it was too late–a low-hanging branch delivered a resounding blow to the back of his head, sweeping him out of the saddle and into the surrounding brush, where he lay unmoving.

Frantically, she sawed at the reins, now using both hands, and the little brown mare finally broke pace and slowed. Apprehension overcame Marganna's fear and gave her strength; somehow she managed to turn the horse and guide it back toward the prone figure of her captor. With relief, she heard his groan of pain and saw that he was beginning to stir.

Just then, Bronwyn and Will came onto the scene and, seeing Rath lying in the grass, flung themselves off their horses to rush to his aid.

Now that she was certain the man would be cared for, Marganna was filled with an overwhelming desire to resume her flight. If she could take advantage of Will and Bronwyn's preoccupation, perhaps she could put enough distance between herself and the others to effect an escape.

All day long, as they had traveled northward, the landscape had undergone subtle changes, and with a sinking heart she had come to accept the fact that she was being removed from everything familiar, that she might never see her home or the people she knew again. Even then she had not dared to think of escape. It had been the farthest thing from her mind . . . until this moment. Suddenly she experienced such a surge of longing for freedom that she had scarcely entertained the thought before she was acting on it. With one last backward glance, she spurred her horse and was off again—galloping madly, wildly—but this time with a purpose. This time she was riding to regain her freedom.

Traveling steadily, Marganna maintained the grueling pace, but after a time both she and her mare began to tire. She had just noticed an approaching caravan of tinkers when her fatigued palfrey stepped into a pothole in the road, stumbling to its knees and tossing her inelegantly over its head.

"Are ye injured, lass?"

She was looking into the seamed and wrinkled face of a man no taller than herself. His jaw bristled with black whiskers, and eyes like two sloeberries peered out curiously from beneath tangled, overhanging brows.

"Who might ye be?" he asked, making no effort to hide his interest. He glanced at the woman who had come to stand beside them. "We don't often see ladies traveling alone, do we, Mother?"

The woman, stout and sour visaged, shook her head.

Marganna thought feverishly. Her horse, even though it had struggled to its feet, was too tired to go on—indeed, so was she. If she threw herself on their mercy, these good people would almost surely help her. Yet instinctively she knew she could not tell them the entire truth, for if they found out her pursuers were agents of the king, they would be reluctant to interfere.

"I'm . . . I'm running away from my husband," she improvised. "He was forced to marry me—for my dowry—but he hates me and would just as soon see me dead." Marganna dropped her head, as if shamed by the admission. "Not only does he beat me, but last night I think he tried to poison me. When I refused the wine he wanted me to drink, he grew abusive and flew into a rage. I just couldn't stay with him any longer."

"He tried to kill ye?" The man's question was indignant. By his code of ethics, it was perfectly permissible for a husband to beat his wife—most of the time, he was convinced, they needed it—but murder was another matter altogether.

"When I saw my chance to escape, I took it," Marganna went on in a low voice. "If you would give me shelter within one of your wagons, perhaps I can elude him."

The man rubbed his stubbled chin with a grimy hand. " 'Twould be a risk if yer husband should stop us."

"But why would he? He'd never expect me to be traveling south again."

"Have ye money to pay us?" the woman asked bluntly.

Marganna made what she knew was a rash offer. "If you would trust me, I can send you money when I am safe again. I have an aunt who is very rich."

The peddlar and his wife eyed each other for a long moment, unspoken words seeming to pass between them.

"Crawl into that wagon there," the man said suddenly. "Ye'll be well hidden should we pass anyone on the road."

"What about my horse?"

Kneeling beside the animal, the man carefully ran his hands over both its forelegs, his blunt fingers molding and testing bone, sinew, and tendon. "I'm a peddlar and mender by trade," he explained, "but I know about horses too. This one will do. She may have strained the muscle a bit when she fell, but she'll be all right in a day or two. We'll tie her behind the wagon with old Dapple."

"What if my husband should pass us? He'd be certain to recognize her."

The man got to his feet and began unsaddling the mare. "Mother, fetch me some of that horse liniment and a bit of the axle grease. We'll toss this saddle into the wagon. . ."

Marganna watched in astonishment as the tinker set to work to disguise the palfrey she had ridden. While he rubbed its front legs with liniment, his wife obscured the white blaze on its forehead with a few daubs of black grease. Then they smeared handfuls of mud from the roadside along the horse's flanks and rump; with the addition of a filthy and moth-eaten blanket, the mare appeared just as neglected as the horse next to which it was tied.

Marganna climbed into the back of the second wagon, a covered wooden cart in which the tinkers took shelter from the elements. It smelled of stale bodies and moldy bread, and she had no doubt the nest of blankets in which she found herself was flea infested, but she was too tired to care.

The pots and kettles hanging along both sides of the cart began to clang and rattle as the horses pulling the vehicle lurched forward. For a short while the noise was disconcerting, but gradually she grew used to the clamor and, curling up on the makeshift bed, abandoned herself to sleep.

Some time later she was awakened by the sound of voices and realized the cart was no longer moving. She lifted the burlap curtain that covered the back end of the wagon, and though she could see nothing but the road behind, shadowed by a late afternoon sun, the voices were now distinct enough for her to recognize them as male. Quickly she dropped the curtain.

As her ears strained to catch the words being spoken, Marganna idly scratched the flea bites on her arms and wondered how long it might be before the peddlars stopped for a meal. She had eaten nothing since daybreak and hunger gnawed at her stomach. Her eyes roved the darkened interior of the cart. At this moment she wouldn't be above stealing a bite of bread or cheese.

"Psst, lass, where are ye?"

As she leaned forward to speak to the peddlar, his hand closed over her forearm and he pulled her from the wagon. No sooner had her feet touched the ground than he was half dragging her around the side of the shabby vehicle.

"Here she is, gentlemen—the lass I told ye about. She's a beauty, isn't she?"

With dawning horror, Marganna found herself thrust

forward into a semicircle of men. Her eyes went immediately to those of the tallest man present and clung there.

Lord Rathburn! She couldn't believe it . . .

"Here, have a look at her without the cloak," invited the peddlar, a smug smile on his bewhiskered face as he unfastened the cloak and dropped it on the ground at her feet. "I believe ye'll find I am offering ye choice merchandise."

Rathburn stepped forward. "I thought you said the lass you had to sell was docile. This one appears to be contentious."

"Oh, no, sir—'tis only that she . . . well, she has been ill treated by her husband and is frightened of men. Once she sees ye mean her no harm, she'll be as tame as a tabby cat."

Marganna swung on him, not believing her ears. "You are trying to *sell* me to these men? After I appealed to you for help? How could you!"

"Now, girly, ye said ye didn't have the money to pay us," said the tinker's wife. "We helped ye hide from yer husband; now ye do us this little favor. If ye go with these nice men, ye'll have protection from yer husband, and we'll have a bit of extra money in our coffers."

"I'm not at all certain I would be interested," spoke up Rath. "She's not exactly what I had in mind."

"Oh, but sir, think of it! A pretty lass to cook yer meals, wash yer clothes."

"I don't know. She doesn't look strong enough."

"Oh, she's strong all right. Here . . . feel the muscle in that arm."

The peddlar dragged Marganna toward Rath, who simply stood observing her, his hands on his hips. She could not determine what emotion darkened his eyes and drew his mouth into a hard, straight line.

Instead of feeling the proffered arm, he began a leisurely survey of her person, walking slowly around her, his gaze as impersonal as if her were considering a ewe for sale at a country fair.

"No, I'm sorry . . . she's too skinny. I don't think I could get a decent day's work out of her."

"Then what about a decent night's work?" quipped the tinker. "Give the lass a bath, comb her hair, and she'd be a fine bedmate."

"Open your mouth, girl," Rath commanded. "I want to see if your teeth are sound."

Her mouth fell open, but more in astonishment than in obedience. The man grasped her chin between his thumb and forefinger, and he tilted her head this way and that, examining her teeth. Angrily, she twisted her chin away and met his calm gaze with a malevolent glare.

"The teeth are fine, but look at that nose and chin," muttered Rathburn. "They both look as if they spend an uncommon amount of time high in the air. Methinks this one is a haughty piece, my good man, and I can't think her . . . charms would be worth putting up with her temper."

Temper! Marganna opened her mouth, ready to demonstrate how very true that statement was, but Rathburn's deep voice cut smoothly into her intended tirade.

"Lift your skirts. I want to see your legs."

"I most certainly will not! This farce has gone on long enough—oh!"

The tinker grasped her arms and held them firmly behind her while his wife lifted the skirt of Marganna's traveling dress, revealing long, well-shaped legs clad in dark hose.

"Hmm, not too bad," murmured Rathburn, his tone considering. He went down on one knee and wrapped lean fingers around each ankle. "I'll admit, she has nice ankles . . . though the thighs are a little thin for my liking."

"Oh!" Marganna jerked her body in a desperate attempt to kick him, but he only laughed and moved both hands up her legs, fingers playing over the contours of calf and knee, lingering along the smooth thighs before sliding up her hips right to the waist.

"She'd need fattening up," he stated, getting to his feet and stepping back just in time to avoid a well-aimed kick. "A man could be slashed to ribbons against those sharp hip bones."

"You foul-mouthed wretch," Marganna cried.

"You can put her skirt down now, madam. There is only one thing more that interests me."

With a curious half smile on his face, Lord Rathburn again moved closer to Marganna. Before she could sense his intention, he encompassed her ribcage with his hands, slowly easing them upward to cup her breasts as though measuring them, his thumbs smoothing over their tops and down their rounded sides.

Marganna, still restrained by the tinker, was too enraged to do anything but close her eyes tightly and pray Rath would tire of this indecent display.

Abruptly he removed his hands, and she heard his dispassionate voice saying, "She's barely adequate, but just for the sake of curiosity, what price are you asking?"

"She's a fine specimen."

"It seems to me she leaves a lot to be desired," Rath calmly interrupted. "Too weak to work, bad tempered—not even enough bosom to fill a man's hands. No, I think I would be doing you a favor if I took her."

"Remember, she's been married, so she's no inexperienced virgin. She'll know just how to—"

"How much?"

The tinker drew himself up and stated loudly, "Ten pounds."

"Ten pounds?" Rath laughed. "You must be out of your mind."

"Ten pounds ain't nothing to a fine gentleman like yerself. As soon as I saw the king's banner, I knew ye'd be a man of importance, one who can easily afford a plaything such as this pretty one."

Again Rath ran his eyes over Marganna's face and body, his look frankly insulting. "I fail to see the value, peddlar. I'm afraid you'll have to come down on your price or sell to someone else."

"But who's to say the next man we meet won't be her husband? I don't need trouble like that!"

"What property comes with the wench?" Rath asked abruptly. "She surely owns a horse, does she not?"

"Well, the mare she was riding is a bit worse for wear . . . I thought to keep it so I might restore it to good health. Of course, she has the fine clothes on her back . . . for as long as ye wish to keep them there.'' He snickered lewdly, his attempt at bawdy humor making Marganna feel slightly nauseated.

She found herself almost wishing Rathburn would pay the outrageous price so that she might be free of the avaricious peddlar. If he did not sell her this time, he would only try again, and the next customer might be even less gentlemanly than the insufferable Rathburn. She could be passed from hand to hand, utterly powerless to help herself. No, Lord Rathburn was furious and would make her life miserable, without doubt, but even she had to acknowledge that returning to her status as his prisoner would be preferable to the alternatives.

''I'll give you five pounds for the female, and you can keep the horse.''

''I can get more for her from someone else,'' declared the peddlar, a spark of anger lighting his black eyes.

''Then do so,'' replied Rathburn, turning on his heel and signalling to his men.

''Please . . . wait!'' The words were out before Marganna realized it. She could gladly have bitten off her tongue for revealing her fear of being abandoned by her one-time jailor. As he came to a halt and turned to look at her, she saw a triumphant expression pass over his stern face.

''Well, well,'' murmured the peasant. ''It seems the lass has taken a fancy to ye, sir. Surely that makes a difference to ye?''

''Five pounds and not a shilling more.''

''It's robbery, that's all I can say,'' the old man grumbled.

''How can you complain about being robbed?'' cried Marganna. ''What about me? I . . .''

''Silence!'' thundered Rath. ''I don't want to hear another word out of you.''

He tossed a handful of coins at the peddlar's feet and reached out to lift Marganna's cloak from the dust. He thrust it at her. ''Here, take this and come along.''

A look of mutiny settled on her face. "Don't tell me what to do!" she snapped.

He grabbed her arm and shoved her ahead of him. "From now on I will tell you each and every move to make, and by the saints, you'd better obey."

"You don't own me," she gasped.

"Oh, but I do. You've been bought and paid for, and don't ever forget it."

It was dusk when they finally stopped for the night, making camp outside a small village. While two of the men at arms gathered wood and started a fire, the others plucked small game birds they had shot earlier in the day, preparing them for the spit. Bronwyn, watching with a bored expression, turned to Rath.

"I don't see why we couldn't stay at the village inn tonight. I'm tired of sleeping on the ground."

"We aren't going to take any more chances with our prisoner," he said shortly. "She nearly escaped us once today, and I intend to see it doesn't happen again. I'm not going to take her anyplace where she can enlist further aid from strangers."

Marganna, huddled silently by the newly built fire, stifled a bitter laugh at the memory of where her last appeal for aid had gotten her. After a temporary taste of freedom, she was worse off than before. Once she had been given a fresh horse to ride, Rathburn had shackled her hands together and, had it not been for the objection raised by Will Metcalfe, would have placed irons on her feet as well. For the rest of the afternoon, she had ridden between the two men, with the glowering face of Lord Rathburn telling her more plainly than words that she had best behave.

Now she was determined to act meek and well mannered, at least until she had had a decent meal and a good night's rest. After that—tomorrow, perhaps—she would surely find another opportunity to prevent herself from disappearing into the lonely northern moors, a prisoner to be locked away and forgotten.

"I would have a word with you."

Rath's steely voice broke into her thoughts, startling her. Wide eyed, she gazed up at him.

"I want to know exactly what you told the peddlar and his wife."

"I told them nothing except that I was running away from a cruel husband. I thought if I told them the truth they would refuse to help me."

"Did you mention the king?"

Her resolve to be meek quickly forgotten, she gave an unladylike snort. "Of course I did! I made certain they knew immediately that I was an escaped prisoner of the Crown."

He ignored her sarcasm. "I want to know if you said anything about the princes."

"Naturally, I related everything I knew."

"What do you mean?" His voice lowered to a threatening growl.

As always, Marganna was irritated by his manner and lost all sense of propriety. "I informed them that the king has hidden his nephews away so he can dispose of them whenever it pleases him to do so."

"My God, why would you say something like that?"

Her lips twitched. "Why, because I expected the poor itinerant to mount an army to save the princes, of course. Think of it—hundreds of outraged tinkers, armed with teakettles and stew pots, storming every prison and hiding place in Yorkshire. The very thought should give you nightmares."

"Curb your tongue, my lady. You don't know what you are talking about. Though, womanlike, you don't let that stop you from talking loudly and long."

"Good Lord, Rath, are you two at it again?" Will Metcalfe sauntered up to the fire, holding out his lean hands to its warmth. Although it was June, the night air was damp and chilly.

"I've had a gullet full of this impudent trouble-making wench. Right now I'm entertaining pleasant thoughts of taking a carving knife to her traitorous tongue. Then she would certainly be less trouble."

"While you're at it," taunted Marganna, "why don't you just slash my throat and save all of us some misery?"

"Don't tempt me," he shouted.

"Easy, man," cautioned Will, grasping Rath's arm and dragging him away from the campfire. "Use a bit of restraint."

"Restraint? Christ, the woman tried to run me down with her horse, then left me for dead in the forest. It was an unbelievable stroke of luck that we happened to be the first travelers approached by that greedy peddlar. Do you realize how very close we came to never seeing our little traitor again? Her damned foolhardy attempt to escape nearly saw me on my knees before Richard explaining how I managed to lose a prisoner of the Crown. You can preach restraint, Will, but I swear if you were in my position, you'd see no need for it either."

"Rath, be reasonable. Two of the men at arms swear she didn't plan to escape. The mare simply ran away with her. And I've told you she made certain you were all right before she rode on. I don't believe she said anything to the tinker about the princes, so why don't you just consider no harm was done? Shouting at her serves no useful purpose."

"Oh, all right, have it your way. But I won't mollycoddle her, and I won't be so lenient if she tries anything like that again."

Rath leaned against a tree trunk and stared moodily at Marganna's profile, bathed in the light of the fire. Finally he allowed himself a small chuckle.

"You know, Will, I have to admit something—the girl does have spirit. It took a certain recklessness to try what she did."

"I'm not sure I'd have tried it myself," Will confessed. "Especially not if I had to answer to you." He eyed his friend carefully. "But then, you knew from the start she wasn't meek, remember?"

"Why wouldn't I remember?" Rath asked dryly. "She has given me little opportunity to forget it."

Marganna's spirits rose after a hot meal but fell just as quickly when it came time to retire for the night. With a look of determination on his handsome features, Rath clamped the manacle bracelets around her wrist and one of his own, dropping the key into the pocket of his leather jerkin.

"This is as unpleasant for me as for you," he muttered. "But I don't plan to wake up in the morning and find you gone."

He dropped to the pallet he had made before the fire, pulling her down beside him. Angrily, without saying a word, she turned away from him, heaving gusty, impatient sighs as he drank a last cup of wine and discussed travel plans for the next day with Will. Each time he moved his arm, she jerked back on the short chain, receiving perverse satisfaction from annoying him.

Across the campfire, a sulky Bronwyn took up a lute and strummed a sad melody. The last thing Marganna remembered was the woman's low voice, as elusive as smoke in the night air, singing of lost love.

When next she awoke, the moon was high in the sky, and she decided it must be well after midnight. She found herself pressed close to Rathburn, warmed by his body, one hand lying across his wide chest. She breathed deeply of his masculine scent—leather and a faint lemony tang—and moved her fingers upward to lightly brush the bare skin at the base of his throat. Odd that in an unguarded moment like this his nearness could do things to her that had no relation to the usual irritation he provoked. She was filled with a pleasant languor, as well as strong curiosity about what might happen if he were to awaken and kiss her as he had in the privacy of the king's chambers.

Vexed by her indiscreet thoughts, she started to move her hand away when she suddenly remembered seeing him drop the key to the manacles into his pocket. She wondered if she dared . . .

Raising her head a few inches, she gazed into his peacefully sleeping face. A slight snore issued from his lips; his breathing was deep and relaxed.

Slowly, holding her own breath, she eased her hand downward along his ribs and hip, searching for the opening of the pocket. When she found it, she slipped her fingers inside, sliding them deep, reaching for the key.

Suddenly she found herself hauled up to lie atop Rath's body. His low laugh stirred the hair at her ear. "While your method of seeking the key feels exceedingly pleasant, perhaps I should tell you that I took the precaution of removing it to my boot before I went to sleep."

"Oh!" she gasped, filled with a desire to scream in frustration. Then she became aware of his lean frame beneath her, and his obvious state of arousal made her face flame. "Oh," she muttered again, rolling to her side and away from him.

She could not shut out the sound of his rumbling laughter as she flounced about in the blankets, keeping her back turned and refusing to speak further.

Chapter 5

The journey north continued just past dawn the next morning. Breakfast was a cold, hurried meal with a disgruntled Rathburn urging everyone to make haste.

"Why is he in such a hurry if he does not want to return to Yorkshire?" Marganna asked Will Metcalfe later when he reined in his horse to ride beside her. Her hands were again shackled together, her temper flaring higher with each scrape of iron against the tender skin of her wrists.

"It isn't that he doesn't want to return to Yorkshire," Will replied. "It's just that he did not count on returning so soon. Evidently since he must go back, he sees no reason to delay along the way."

Marganna cast him a puzzled look, causing him to explain further.

"You see, winters in the north are long and dreary, and Rath has looked forward to summer. He'd wanted to spend some time at court, both at Nottingham and in London. Even that somewhat jaded society can begin to look inviting after months of nothing but wind and snow. We had business to attend to . . . dispatches for the king, things of that nature, and Rath wanted to make a holiday of it. He's just in a temper because his plans came to naught."

"He's upset because he has to escort me to Yorkshire, you mean, and he blames me for ruining his pleasure jaunt. And because he is angry with me, he makes everyone else pay for it." She shrugged. "Why can't he simply place the blame where it really belongs?"

"And where is that?" Will's sandy eyebrows quirked up in interest as he awaited her answer.

"With his precious King Richard, of course."

"Oh, I forgot . . . you don't know Rath very well. I assure you, he would never blame Richard for anything."

"Then he must be blinded by his loyalty."

"How so?"

"Well, even if I was guilty of spying—though I'm not admitting I was, mind you—the king should have resolved the matter then and there. He had no reason to put me into Rathburn's custody, no reason to send us away from Nottingham. I think he was indulging himself in some kind of . . . prank or something."

"Unfortunately, a king can do just that."

Marganna made no response, knowing that what the man said was true. All of them were subject to the king's whims, pointless as they might seem.

"What do you think Lord Rathburn will do with me, Will?" she asked presently.

"I don't know," he said quietly, "but I can tell you, he is a fair man. The king would never have entrusted you to him otherwise."

Marganna nodded, though she was not all certain the king had spent much time worrying about her security; after all, she had been caught in an act of treason. In reality, she could not expect much effort to be spared on her behalf. She had been placed in Rathburn's hands for good or ill, and it was going to take an exceptional stroke of luck for her to change that.

With a sigh, she turned her attention to the countryside through which they were passing. Peaceful villages nestled in the folds of forested hills, with fields of lush grain and grasses and sleek, well-tended farm animals bespeaking a life of plenty. A heavy dew covered everything, sparkling like diamonds along the hedgerows and bejeweling the trees that arched above the road. Every leaf, every blade of grass, every cobweb was outlined in a shimmer of light as the morning sun began to make its presence known.

Rath did not lessen the pace as the day wore on. The only stops were brief with no loitering. Late in the afternoon a new landmark appeared on the horizon, and she asked Will what it was.

"'Tis the York minster," was his reply. "Its towers dwarf the city and can be seen for miles."

"It looks beautiful. Will we be stopping in York?"

"No, not this time. Rath wants to spend the night at my estate, Moor's End, which is near the city. He has already sent a man ahead to warn them of our arrival."

They passed close enough to York for Marganna to glimpse the white stone wall surrounding it, to smell the aromas and hear the sounds of a large city ceasing its labors for the leisure of eventide. Having been raised in the country, she found the noisy bustle of a city fascinating and regretted that their route would keep them outside one as lovely and interesting as she imagined York would be.

As they left the flaring lights of the town behind, the road began to climb, and a colder wind commenced blowing down from the moorland above. Darkness descended quickly, and an hour or so later, when Will pointed out the lights of his home, a sense of relief washed over Marganna.

Moor's End was a gray stone manor, its grim exterior forbidding in the torchlight despite the swaths of ivy that spilled down its walls. An inviting warmth poured from the open door where Will's housekeeper stood to greet them.

Thoroughly chilled even through the cloak she wore, Marganna moved to the blazing fire in the hall and held out her hands to its heat. When she looked up, she saw the housekeeper eyeing the manacles on her wrists in astonishment and, with a feeling of shame, she swiftly hid them beneath her outer garment.

Noticing her discomfort, Will came to her rescue. "We will be requiring supper immediately, Mrs. Dawson. Will you see to it, please?"

"Certainly." The woman adopted her most regal bearing and swept from the room, giving Marganna one last appraising glance as she went.

Rath strode into the hall, issuing orders to his men at arms and removing his cloak as he did so. "God, I'd like to rid myself of the dust of travel, friend. Have you a bath and a bottle of wine to offer?''

''Follow me,'' Will said laughing, ''and I'll see what can be arranged.''

Rath put out a hand to grip Marganna's arm. ''Come along,'' he said tersely.

''But . . .''

''Rath, I've ordered a private chamber for Marganna . . .''

''A private chamber, Will?''

''Yes. I thought she might appreciate some time to herself. I'd hoped you would approve . . .''

''She's a prisoner, damn it, not a guest in your home!''

''You can lock her in the room. She'll be on the third floor, so I daresay you'll not have to worry about her escaping.''

''I don't trust her . . .''

''I wish you would not discuss me as though I were not standing here,'' protested Marganna.

''Keep out of it,'' Rath said shortly.

''I know Marganna is your prisoner, Rath, and that you feel responsible for her, but there is virtually no way she can escape from Moor's End. Take off the manacles and lock her into the room—let her have a bath and a change of clothing. I would think you owe her that much after the ridiculous humiliation you put her through yesterday.''

Marganna was frankly shocked to hear the note of disapproving anger in Will's voice, and she could tell by the strained expression on Rath's face that he had not often heard his friend speak in such a manner.

''All right, if it will appease you, Will. But if anything happens, I will hold you personally accountable, and the consequences won't be pleasant.''

Together they climbed to the third floor of the manor house, and Will indicated the room that was to be Marganna's.

Impatiently Rath insisted on waiting until the maids had filled an oaken tub with water for Marganna's bath.

''I don't want her talking to them,'' he snapped before Will could voice yet another protest.

When the others had gone, Rath unlocked the manacles

and removed them. His eyes widened as he caught sight of the raw, reddened skin and, with a quiet curse, he seized her chafed wrists in surprisingly gentle hands. "You must have been in pain, Marganna. My God, why didn't you say something?"

"Would it have done any good?" she asked dryly.

"It might have," Rath said. "I'm not completely unfeeling, after all."

She laughed softly. "If there is one thing I did not expect from you, it is mercy."

She glanced up, and for a long moment his eyes held hers, the expression within the green depths unreadable. Finally Marganna lowered her lashes and stepped back, causing his hands to fall away from her wrists.

"Will told me about your plans for a holiday in the south," she said. "I . . . I'm sorry I was the ruination of those plans."

His chuckle surprised her, and she looked up quickly to find him smiling at her. "If there is one thing I did not expect from you, it is an apology!"

"Well," she said, smiling back, "I guess that makes us even."

A few seconds later he seemed to realize he was staring at her. He cleared his throat and said, "I'll go now so you can get on with your bath while the water is hot. Bronwyn will come for you when it's time for the meal." He started from the room, then paused. "After supper I'll ask Will for some salve for those wrists. There's no point in letting the injuries get any worse than they already are."

Marganna watched him go, the conflicting emotions she was feeling plainly visible on her face. Would she ever learn what to expect from the man?

As she and Bronwyn began descending the last flight of stairs, Marganna could hear Rath and Will, their voices raised in what sounded like a heated argument.

"It isn't as if she's a murderer," Will was saying.

"Who's to say she wouldn't be with half a chance? No, you're too soft, Will. I've never seen you so besotted."

"And I've never seen you so pigheaded and stubborn.

I can't think Marganna is nearly as devious as you insist she is."

Bronwyn stopped short to listen, forcing Marganna to do likewise. The two men were so engrossed in their discussion they did not look up.

"She's devious enough to see the advantages of ruining our friendship," Rath pointed out. "Look at us—fighting like schoolboys. She is succeeding in turning you against me, Will. As soon as we get to Middleham, I ought to find a competent jailor who will lock her in the darkest cell in the dungeon and forget her."

"Well said, milord." Bronwyn's laugh trilled as she skipped down the remaining steps, throwing her arms around Rath. Surprised, he looked past her to Marganna, but she averted her face, refusing to meet his eyes.

Sensing her dismay, Will quickly came forward to take her arm. "Come, Marganna, you look in need of a good, hot meal. I think the cook has prepared something special for us."

But there was little Will could do to lighten the mood that had descended upon her. All through the excellent meal, the only thing Marganna heard was Rath's threat echoing in her ears . . . *"lock her in the darkest cell in the dungeon and forget her."*

His carelessly spoken words filled her with such despair that she silently vowed to do anything she had to do to escape. If she did not, her life might as well be over.

Once she had been taken back to her room and locked in, Marganna took inventory of the chamber. The only door in the room besides the one leading to the corridor was one that she discovered opened onto a miniscule balcony.

Cautiously she stepped outside, leaning forward to peer over the waist-high railing into the yard below. Moor's End had been built on a knoll overlooking the Ouse River, and Marganna found herself observing a lighted boat house. She caught her breath. She had not realized it was such a long way down.

Even stripping the bedclothes from the bed and knotting

them together in a rope would not provide enough length for her to lower herself to the ground. Perhaps if she also pulled down the arras? But no, they were sewn from such heavy fabric it would be impossible to fashion the necessary knots.

Disappointed, she turned away from the doorway; as she did so the thick twist of ivy snaking up the stone wall drew her attention. Her stomach lurched with excitement as she began testing the strength of the central branches—yes, she was certain it would hold her weight!

She glanced down, wondering whose chambers were below hers. She didn't care to take a chance on someone seeing her climb past the window.

Just then a knock sounded on the outer door, and she heard Rath's voice calling her name. Rapidly, she stepped back into the room, closing the balcony door behind her.

Marganna moved into the center of the room as she heard the key in the lock and tried to look composed when she saw him standing there, a bowl in his hands.

"I've brought the salve for your wrists, Marganna," he said.

"That is kind of you," she replied stiffly, reaching for the bowl.

"I'll apply it." His brisk tone left no room for objection. "Here, sit in this chair by the window."

She did as she was told, realizing that the sooner she submitted to his ministrations, the sooner he would leave the room.

Rath dipped his long fingers into the pale golden salve and, kneeling on one knee, he took one of her wrists and began applying the medicine with a smooth, stroking motion. Marganna's skin tingled beneath his touch, and it was all she could do to keep from jerking her arm away from him.

"Am I hurting you?" he asked.

She shook her head, still not looking at him. She heard his gusty sigh.

"Look, I know you overheard me talking to Will and that my words worried you. I assure you, I was only making an idle threat."

"I'd like to believe that, because I would rather be dead than spend the rest of my life locked in a cell."

"King Richard wouldn't let that happen to you, so stop thinking about it."

He reached for the other arm.

"How do I know you're telling the truth?" she murmured.

He put one finger beneath her chin and raised her face. "You'll just have to trust me," he said, smiling.

Trust you? was her wry thought. Like a fly should trust a spider!

He rose to his feet, preparing to leave, and Marganna spoke quickly. "Oh, one thing more . . . this is not Will's bedchamber, is it? I would not like to think I was putting anyone out by having the room to myself."

Her guileless question netted the information she had hoped for. "No, of course you're not putting Will or anyone else out. This is a spare room, seldom used. The main bedchambers are on the second floor, along the back of the house. So you see, you're not disturbing anyone at all."

"I'm glad." She smiled faintly. "Good night, then . . . and thank you for the medicine."

"My pleasure. I'll see you in the morning."

When he had gone, relocking the door, she clasped her hands in agitation. So—the bedchambers were located at the back of the house. That meant there was always the chance someone might look out and see her hasty descent. Well, there was only one thing left to do—to be absolutely certain no one saw her leaving Moor's End, she would have to climb up the ivy and onto the roof, scale its sharply peaked height to the other side of the house, and make her way down the ivy she had seen on the front wall.

Her mind made up, she lay down on the bed to try to rest before the ordeal ahead. To give herself the greatest chance of success possible, she planned to wait until the household had retired for the night.

If the other travelers were as tired as she, they would be longing for slumber. And if the events during dinner were any indication, the one from whom she had the most to fear, Lord Rathburn, would not be slow in seeking his bed. Bronwyn had scarcely been able to keep her hands off him, sending him such burning looks that there was little doubt she would welcome his attentions. Even if he did not sleep, he would be far too preoccupied to spare any thought for his prisoner, Marganna mused, a picture of Rathburn and Bronwyn lying together in a tumbled bed flashing into her mind. Suddenly filled with a strange, unidentifiable emotion, she turned on her side and shut her eyes with determination.

Marganna dozed off and on until she thought it must be past midnight; then she rose from the bed and tiptoed across the room to the door leading onto the balcony. Stopping to pick up her cloak, she found herself staring down at it in consternation. If she were to be successful in her attempt to scale the thick growth of ivy, she had to be as unencumbered as possible, and yet she knew she would need the warmth of the cloak once she was safely on the ground.

Resolutely she made a decision and began to undress. Wearing only her white cotton smock and stockings, she wrapped the rest of her clothing and her ankle boots in the cloak and tied it with her girdle, a length of braided leather.

Stepping onto the balcony, she dropped the bundle straight down to the ground below, where she heard it land with a soft thud. Once she was on the ground again, she would reclaim the clothes, even if she had to do so on her hands and knees to avoid being seen. The night wind was so sharp she would not last long without the warmth of her garments.

As soon as she began climbing the ivy, she knew she would never have made it wearing the traveling gown with its long, heavy skirts. Even her undergarment was a hindrance, for a misty rain had fallen during the evening hours drenching the masses of ivy, and by the time Marganna pulled herself up onto the roof, her smock was soaked and sticking to her skin, causing her to shiver violently in the chilling wind.

Perched at the edge of the roof, she looked up at its formidable incline and then started her ascent, carefully groping for hand- and footholds among the rough tiles. The pitch was so steep she found it easiest to proceed on her hands and knees, though the tiles scraped her flesh with every movement.

At one point a tile came loose beneath her foot and slid downwards, rattling noisily all the way until it struck the guttering along the eaves and plummeted into the darkness below. She scarcely breathed, waiting for someone to send up an alarm, but finally, hearing nothing she began inching her way upward once more.

As she neared the peak of the roof, a wild wind flung newborn raindrops into her face, and she crouched, shivering, in the shelter of a stone chimney, hugging herself for warmth and thinking longingly of the woolen clothing lying on the ground below.

There was only a thin slice of moon, and the light it cast was watery at best, but it was enough for Marganna to see her immediate surroundings. She reached the highest point of the roof and started the descent on the other side, finding it easier going down. Once she came to the eaves running along the front of the house, she peered over, trying to see where the ivy growth looked the sturdiest and decided the tower at the end of the house farthest from the front door would be the best place to climb to the ground.

She steadied herself for the short leap onto the tower roof, and though the distance wasn't great, the tiles were so damp that when she flung herself forward, her hands slipped and she felt her body sliding toward the edge of the roof. Desperately she clawed at the tiles, feeling the skin of her hands being painfully shredded. At last, just as one foot skidded off into thin air, the fingers of her right hand found a groove between the tiles and she hung on for dear life, searching all the while for a handhold for her left hand. When she found it, she closed her eyes and lay absolutely still for a long moment, willing her heart to stop pounding. She took several deep breaths before attempting to regain the lost ground. Now she moved only an inch at a time, making certain she had a secure hold before shifting her body into the next position. She circled the tower's round roof until she reached the front edge where the vines were thickest.

Cautiously, she wriggled over the edge, entwining her legs in the ivy and gripping the vines with her stinging hands. Then she slowly eased her way down the side of the tower toward the ground.

She stretched out her legs, toes reaching for solid earth, but just as she prepared to relinquish her hold on the vine, Marganna felt two large hands firmly grasp her hips and lift her backward to imprison her body against a chest heaving in anger.

"Jesus Christ and all the saints!" Rathburn raged as he carried her, kicking and protesting, up two flights of stairs, striding past astonished guests and servants who appeared in the doorways of their bedchambers. "I couldn't believe my eyes when I saw what you were up to. Here's the key," he told a maid. "Unlock that damned door."

Once the door was open, Rath stalked into the room and kicked it shut behind him. With another curse, he dumped Marganna on her bed.

Wearing only black hose and a half-laced black shirt, Rathburn stood over her, glaring, hands knotted into hard fists on his hips.

"I was standing on the balcony looking down at the river when suddenly a bundle of clothing dropped right in front of my eyes. I leaned out to see what was going on and there was your insolent little backside making its way up that ivy. If I could have gotten my hands on you at that moment, I think I would gladly have throttled you! Do you know what a damn-fool dangerous stunt you pulled? You could have been killed, you blasted idiot!"

Marganna stared at him with wide brown eyes, unable to think of a thing to utter in her own defense. Never had she seen anyone as angry as this man.

"Well, don't you have anything to say for yourself?" he roared, coming closer to the bed.

"Of course I do!"

"Never mind! I don't want to hear it!" He shook his head. "I'm too damned angry to listen to any more of your lies right now anyway. Good God, when I think of you up there on that slippery roof—it would have served you right if you had fallen. Of course, it would have been *my* head Richard would have had . . . you know that, don't you? I expect that was incentive enough for you to risk almost anything."

He reached out to close his hands over her upper arms, dragging her from the bed. Green eyes blazing with anger, he began shaking her.

"What . . . the . . . hell . . . did . . . you . . . think . . . you . . . were . . . doing . . . anyway?"

As his harsh words trailed away, Marganna realized his gaze had dropped. Looking down, she saw that the damp cotton of her undergarment was doing nothing to conceal her body from his devouring eyes.

She could almost feel the searing heat of those eyes as they moved over her breasts, barely restrained within the thin smock, darker aureoles and nipples clearly defined against the sheer material. With a gasp of dismay, she crossed her scratched and bleeding arms in front of herself, meeting his look with a semblance of her old defiance.

Rath grasped her wrists, pulling her arms away from her body, and held her immobile before his intimate perusal. His breathing was sharply drawn in and ragged.

"You've tried your best to provoke me, and this time you have gone too far. Damnation, Marganna, you must know every man has a limit to his patience. Why do you keep pushing me?"

She swallowed deeply, then drew a long shuddering breath, her eyes never leaving his. It was clear she did not know what to expect of him.

If she could have known, Rath's next action surprised himself as much as it did her. With a muttered oath, he leaned forward and laid his mouth on hers, drinking in the soft moistness of her lips.

The man's natural arrogance was apparent in the way his mouth claimed hers, as if it was his right, as if she were enjoying it. His tongue teased her lips, gently forcing them to open beneath his assault, to soften under the heated pressure of his mouth.

Marganna felt a small bubble of joy rising within her. If he had thought to punish her disobedience by forcing her to endure his kiss, he had made a mistake. The foolhardiness of her venture was only now dawning on her, making her knees feel weak as she recalled the chill, windswept heights of the roof. It was, she freely admitted, infinitely more pleasurable to be safe and dry, sheltered against the hard warmth of this man whose arms were wrapped around her like bands of iron.

He raised his head and gave her a look filled with some dark emotion she could not identify.

"Why do you persist in being such a reckless little fool?" he muttered. "Just when I think I have you figured out, you do something like this."

"Has no one ever defied you before, my lord?" she dared ask, her brown eyes glowing.

He dragged in a deep breath. "I knew what you were up to the instant you started asking those innocent questions about the locations of the other bedchambers, Marganna. But damn it, I expected you to climb *down* the ivy . . . that's why I was waiting on my balcony. I never thought you'd be stupid enough to climb over the roof!"

He dropped his mouth to hers again, and this time she gave in to a compelling urge to raise her arms and lay her hands softly along either side of his neck, tentatively responding to his kiss.

A frantic pounding sounded at the door. "Rath, for God's sake, what is going on in there?"

Rath lifted his head and then, suddenly groaning, pushed her away, though not roughly.

He shook his head as if to clear his senses. "What am I doing?" he asked, apparently of himself. "Nothing is going on, Will. Everything is all right."

The door opened and an obviously agitated Will Metcalfe peered around it. "The servants woke me because they heard you shouting and thought you would surely kill Marganna. Thank God they were mistaken."

Standing so that he was shielding her near nakedness from Will's view, Rath said quickly, "Let's go belowstairs and I'll explain. I find myself in need of a drink." He turned back to Marganna. "Get under the bedclothes and go to sleep. I don't want you to stir for the rest of the night."

Marganna did as she was told without question, silently watching the two men leave the room and hearing the door lock after them.

She remained huddled beneath the blankets, not even venturing a peek when, fifteen minutes later, one of Rath's men at arms, with a warning tap on the door, unlocked it and entered the room. He dropped the bundle of her clothing at the foot of the bed, then went out onto the balcony and with an axe began to chop away the thick vines that had so prettily graced the old stone wall.

Chapter 6

The next morning Will Metcalfe appeared in the courtyard dressed for traveling. As they waited for the groom to bring their horses, Rath regarded him sardonically.

"What's this, Will? You're going with us? I thought you intended to stay here at Moor's End and take care of some business matters."

Will's face reddened, but taking his reins from the groom, he resolutely stood his ground. "I've changed my mind. I think I'll go to Middleham with you. My business here can wait."

"It's because you don't trust me to look after Marganna properly, isn't it?"

"I think you will treat her as you feel a prisoner should be treated."

"And why not? She *is* a prisoner."

"Just remember your lack of control last night."

"It was a tiring day, and Marganna had no business trying something like that. Hopefully she learned a lesson and won't attempt any more escapes."

"You haven't exactly treated her kindly, Rath. She's not to be blamed for wanting to escape. I intended to travel on with you to act as . . . as an intermediary when necessary."

"You'll only make things worse, Will. If you remember, you were the one who thought she should have a private room—look where that got us!" He shook his head. "I don't need you complicating matters with your well-intentioned but misplaced compassion."

"Whether you need me or not, I'm going." Will's

mouth was set in a straight line, and he busied himself pulling on a pair of gloves.

"You can't deny we have argued more since that girl came on the scene than we ever did in all our years of growing up together." Rath shrugged. "But have it your way. Just stay out of mine."

Beyond Moor's End the road rose steadily through rocky fields of wildflowers, the early morning air frosty even in summer.

Marganna's palfrey labored up a steep incline, then unexpectedly plunged into a dense fog at the top. The horses ahead were swallowed up by the swirling white mass, and every sound was muffled. A dark shape loomed as Rathburn dropped back, reining in his horse beside hers.

"What has happened?" she asked.

"Nothing unusual for this part of the country," he assured her. " 'Tis a sea fret caused by the wind blowing in from the North Sea."

"Will it last long?"

"That's difficult to say," he replied. "If a west wind would spring up, it could be gone in minutes; otherwise it might last for hours or even days. The ancient Celts called the east wind the purple wind—'tis a treacherous bringer of fog and cold, rainy weather."

It was easy to understand why the ancients would have thought such weather the embodiment of evil. As Rath and Marganna rode along, they looked like silent silver ghosts moving through the undefined boundaries of a dream. Marganna was suddenly glad of Rath's comforting presence.

After the occurrences of the night before, she was somewhat surprised by his willingness to speak so amiably with her. Each time she decided to try being docile, fearing she had pushed him too far, he confused her by becoming pleasant. It made him more human somehow . . . almost likable!

"You seem a million miles away, Marganna," she heard Rath saying, his voice oddly distorted by the enveloping fog.

"Mmm, just thinking."

"I probably shouldn't ask, but . . . what are you thinking about?"

"Oh, about how easy it would be to lose oneself in this fog."

"You're not thinking of trying it, are you?" His tone was stern. "It would be most unwise, believe me. While this sea fret makes an excellent screen, it is also quite dangerous. Without warning you could wander over a precipice or find yourself up to your neck in a bog."

There was a hint of laughter in her words. "Why, you sound as if you suspect I might try to elude you."

"I wouldn't put anything past you, Marganna."

"Well, you needn't worry—I'm not planning my escape. Though if last night hadn't been such a disaster, I might be tempted to try it!"

With a toss of her head, she gently spurred her horse forward, leaving him to stare after her hazy figure with a half smile on his face.

The fog persisted for another hour, but as they traveled farther inland, Marganna began to realize the air felt warmer, thinner. Before long, she could discern the vague shapes of those riding ahead and behind her, obscured only by floating mist, tossed this way and that by a new wind lifting out of the west to disintegrate the sea fret and blow it away.

Now the road wound steadily upward and for several miles embraced the crest of a steep, rugged hill. Rath pointed out the River Ure far below them. It looked as if a handful of blue-gray ribbon had been tossed into the air and left to lie as it had fallen, looping across the length of emerald velvet spread beneath it. Rath told her the river ran all the way to Middleham, where it was joined by the Cover River just a short distance from the castle. By the close of day, they would see journey's end.

Middleham Castle had been built on the southern slopes of Wensleydale, with the solemn splendor of the Yorkshire moors surrounding it. On their approach to the huge for-

tress, it seemed to Marganna, that it was a last bastion of civility and security. She felt a growing sense of excitement as they rode through the steeply tilted streets of the little market town huddled against the castle walls and entered the inner ward over the drawbridge at the north gate.

The present keep at Middleham Castle had stood guarding the dale for nearly three hundred years, though, as Rath told her, the first castle on the site was considerably older. The remains of a Norman motte and bailey, which had consisted of a simple wooden structure erected on a mound of earth and surrounded by defensible ditches, could still be seen a short distance southwest of Middleham.

The impressive gray stone fortress that rose above them was aloof and austere. While not entirely forbidding, it seemed to tender a welcome laced with reserve, as well it might. In the lonely north country, where no one ventured without strong purpose, it was always advisable to know a visitor's intention before admitting him inside one's castle walls.

As their horses' hooves clattered over the cobblestones of the courtyard, Marganna was awed by the size of the massive keep. Aware of her interest, Rath continued to talk about the castle's history.

"Middleham fell into the hands of the Nevilles about 1270, but it was when Richard, Earl of Warwick, became the owner that King Richard's association with the castle began. He was trained in the arts of knighthood at Middleham while still a young lad—that is how Will and I first met him. In those days it was a mark of position to be able to board a son at Middleham under the tutelage of Warwick."

Warwick the Kingmaker—who had not heard of him? At one time he had been considered England's god of war, the man who created and commanded kings. Warwick had been responsible for placing Richard III's older brother Edward on the throne, Marganna knew, and she suddenly remembered that Anne, Richard's recently deceased wife, had been a daughter of the Kingmaker.

"When Warwick was killed at Barnet trying to destroy the very king he had once championed, the castle fell forfeit to the Crown, and Edward deeded it to his brother Richard as a reward for his valor in battle. Later, after Richard married Anne Neville, they made this their home. Middleham was always their favorite castle."

While grooms and stableboys took over care of the horses and male servants began unloading the litters, the travelers were ushered into the keep by the castle steward. The approach to the great hall was up a long flight of open stairs along the eastern wall of the castle, past the porter's lodge and through the forebuilding into the main room of Middleham.

Marganna was not prepared for the impressive elegance of the chamber. She had expected a cramped, dark hall lined with crude tables and benches. Instead she found herself in a huge room with a gabled wooden roof, the colorful tapestries covering the gray stone walls lighted by flaming torches and oil lamps. The brightness of the tapestries and the blazing logs in the fireplace added a warmth and comfort that dispelled the chill of the oncoming northern night. Boars' heads with sharply upturned tusks were mounted at each side of the stone fireplace, honoring King Richard, and the coat of arms of the York family was centered directly above the mantel.

The steward was busily fussing about, assigning pages to direct the visitors to their various rooms so they might refresh themselves before the evening meal was served. He smiled broadly at Rathburn.

"Welcome, my lord. 'Tis good to see you again. I was most pleased to receive the message from His Grace informing me that you would be staying here. I expect you will want to occupy your usual chamber?"

His voice was resonant, with a broad accent Marganna found difficult to follow. Traces of that same accent lingered in Rathburn's speech, yet somehow in him it had been tempered and softened, making it almost indiscernible except in moments of anger or emotion.

And there have been many of those, she thought with

silent mirth, though for the first time she experienced a feeling of curiosity about the man and his life.

"Yes, that would be fine, Pickering—and give this young lady the adjoining room, if you would."

"To be sure. King Richard explained the . . . er, circumstances."

"One more thing," Rathburn said briskly, noticing Pickering's welcoming smile to Marganna, "I'd like a supper for two sent up to my chamber—no, better make that three. It would no doubt be wise to ask Will to join us."

"And what about me?" Bronwyn spoke up, a threatening look in her dark eyes.

"Another time, Bronwyn. Dine in the great hall where there will be music and dancing."

Before she could protest, Rathburn turned back to the steward. "By the way, where is Mrs. Biggins? I haven't so much as caught a glimpse of her since we arrived."

"Why, she's down in the village, sir." Pickering leaned closer to speak in a more confidential tone. "One of the merchants sent for her to attend his wife . . . difficult childbirth, I believe." He straightened. "But she knew you'd be arriving, so rest assured she will return as soon as possible to greet you."

"Good, good. Well, I think we should gather our things and go up now."

"Of course. I'll send the lads with your travel bags and . . . oh, here's Amelyn now. She will show you to your chamber."

Marganna saw a slender woman of medium height approaching, a pleased smile on her lovely face.

"Good evening, Lord Rathburn—welcome back to Middleham. It has been some time since we've seen you here."

"Yes, it has," Rath agreed. "But I haven't forgotten how much I enjoy your hospitality."

The woman turned to smile at Marganna. "You must be Marganna," she said as though meeting any ordinary guest. "I'm certain you are tired and would like to rest awhile before dinner, so if you would just follow me, I will show you to your bedchamber."

Rath began to look amused. "You people must understand that this woman is my prisoner. There's no need to treat her as if she were an honored guest, you know."

"But, sir," said Pickering, "the king sent word . . ."

Rath waved an imperious hand. "I know, don't tell me—King Richard wants her treated kindly. For some reason he chooses to ignore the seriousness of her crime. I, on the other hand, intend to keep her under close supervision while here at Middleham."

He started toward a door set into the west wall, and Amelyn, smiling sweetly at Marganna, took a torch from its bracket and inclined her head to indicate that they should follow him.

"This chamber is to be yours for as long as you are a guest at Middleham," Amelyn was saying as she opened the heavy arched door before her. "It is small, but I think you will be comfortable."

Marganna stepped into a quietly beautiful room and couldn't help but exclaim in pleasure, "How lovely!"

"When Pickering received the king's message, he assumed Rath would want you to stay in this room, so he ordered it refurbished. It has been used as a sitting room in the past, but he had the servants bring in the bed and wardrobe. He even chose the tapestries himself."

Though a large oak chest and the four-postered bed with its hangings of hunter's green velvet dominated the room, Marganna's eyes were drawn immediately to the delicate tapestries covering both long walls. Amelyn moved closer with the torch, and the patterns sprang into relief. Woven into the tapestries were dozens of flowers, each with a tiny human face, their leaves forming long green gowns and the subtle purples, blues, crimsons, and golds of their petals glowing softly against the black background. The flowers were dancing in a circle around a different mythological creature on each of the tapestries—a dragon, a sea-goat, a silver unicorn.

Hunter's green draperies were pulled across the windows at the south end of the room; a fire burned in the

carved stone fireplace, and a thick fur rug covered the floor in front of the hearth.

"Everything is wonderful," Marganna said.

"You sound surprised," Amelyn remarked in amusement. "Why is that?"

"Well, for two reasons, I suppose. First, I thought Middleham would be a bleak and barren place—cold, ugly . . ."

"Like a prison?"

"Yes, that's what I was expecting. And I certainly never thought to be treated so well or given such pleasant sleeping quarters. I fully expected to be chained in the cellars."

"The cellars? My heavens, why would you think that?"

Marganna shrugged and, taking off her cloak, dropped it across the bed. "Frankly, the way Lord Rathburn feels about me, there were times I feared the worst once we arrived here."

Amelyn's laugh bubbled. "Oh, Rath! He can be cross. I suppose escorting female prisoners—oh, excuse me . . ."

"Don't apologize, Amelyn. The fact is, I am a prisoner."

"I don't believe the king means you to be—at least, not an ordinary one. His orders were to treat you kindly and make you comfortable."

"I don't understand the situation at all." Marganna sighed. "The king's leniency is another reason Rathburn is so irritated with me. It's almost as if the king is amusing himself at our expense."

"That doesn't sound like him," remarked Amelyn, "but I expect you will soon learn his true purpose. All in good time, as they say."

"No doubt. Meanwhile, I will certainly appreciate this bedchamber."

"Of course, it adjoins the one where Rath will sleep, but as you can see, the key is in the lock if you want to secure the door between the two rooms. Please let me know if there is anything you want or need."

"Yes, I will. Thank you, Amelyn."

"It will be my pleasure to have someone close to my own age in the castle again."

"Do you mind my asking how you came to be at Middleham? I mean, are you a member of the king's family?"

"No," Amelyn answered. "Actually, my father was one of Richard's household knights. That is why we first came to Middleham to live. Then, after my father's death, since I was unmarried and had no other family, I remained under the king's protection. Eventually I fell into my present role, which is something between a housekeeper and a hostess. The truth is, now that Richard resides in London, he doesn't need many retainers at his castles in the north, but he allows me to live here because I have no place else to go."

"However, one should not feel sorry for her," came a deep voice from the doorway. "She has been offered any number of marriage proposals from handsome knights and wealthy squires."

They looked up to see Lord Rathburn leaning on the frame of the open hallway door.

"Why haven't you ever accepted one of those worthy swains, Amelyn?" he asked, approaching with a smile. "Wouldn't you rather be running your own household than staying on in this big, empty place?"

"You know I love it at Middleham, Rath," she exclaimed laughingly, laying a hand on his arm. "Besides, I haven't received the one proposal I am waiting for. None of the others have given me reason to think of leaving here."

"Well, that is fortunate for those of us who have occasion to visit this castle now and then. It is no hardship to enjoy the comfortable bedchambers or the magnificent meals."

"I thank you," Amelyn said, bowing her head, an attractive blush staining her fair skin. "Speaking of meals, however, I suppose I really should see to this evening's. I imagine you are all hungry." She turned back to Marganna. "If you need anything, please let me know."

"Yes, I will. Thank you."

Amelyn slipped past Rathburn and left the room, leaving him and Marganna to face each other.

"The lads will be here shortly with your baggage," he

informed her. "As soon as you have freshened up, present yourself in my chamber for the evening meal."

"Very well."

"I won't lock the door to your room," he continued. "I don't believe it will be necessary, as I think you are sensible enough to realize the merits of a hot supper over those of wandering through the cold, dark corridors of a strange castle looking for some nonexistent means of escape."

Marganna nodded briefly.

He rested the heel of one hand against the wall and leaned casually toward her. When she looked up, his lean face with its elusive dimples was only inches away.

"It seems I have unwittingly discovered the perfect way to keep you obedient."

He chuckled when he saw the question in her eyes. "Kissing," he explained. "Ever since I attempted to punish you last night and ended up kissing you instead, you have been extremely well mannered." He reached out his free hand and took up a strand of hair lying over her shoulder. "You know, Marganna, if I had only known what it took, I would have employed that method much sooner."

She didn't know what to say. His face was so close to hers, she could only stare at his mouth, experiencing a tiny thrill as she imagined it coming down on hers, warm and softly caressing. Her own lips parted in expectation as she lifted her face a fraction of an inch.

He gave an unsteady laugh. "If you don't stop looking at me that way, I'm afraid I will be inclined to explore the merits of punishment yet again."

Afraid he might have sensed her eagerness, she drew back and affected mock horror. "Oh, but for once I have done nothing to deserve it."

"Perhaps not, but I am willing to give you a little time. I don't trust you to behave for long." Grinning, he gave the strand of hair he held a slight tweak. "Get some rest. I'll see you at dinner."

Their truce, shaky as it might be, still held. For the moment she would ask for nothing more.

* * *

Marganna was already present in Rath's chamber when he appeared for the evening meal. Having been informed of Mrs. Biggins' arrival, he had gone belowstairs to greet her; upon returning to his room, he was arrested by the sight of Marganna sitting before the fire, staring into the flames. Unseen, he stood in the doorway and observed her. The flickering light cast a sheen on Marganna's hair, emphasizing the contrast between its darkness and the pale oval of her face. As he watched, she leaned slightly forward, lost in thought.

Rath's lips clamped tight as he experienced a pang at the implied intimacy of the scene. Marganna looked so at home sitting there, as if she were a wife waiting for the husband with whom she would spend a relaxed moment before sharing the supper laid on a nearby table. A meal, he envisioned, that would begin with laughter and frequent touching of hands, proceeding steadily toward a fevered end, with inflamed kisses inevitably leading the partners to the bed in a shadowy corner, to while away the hours of the night in the impassioned expression of their love for each other . . .

Damn, thought Rath, what is there about this castle that makes me start thinking of hearth and home?

Taken from the security of his family at an early age, he had been raised to a harsh and demanding existence, and years of training as a knight, followed by countless forays and skirmishes along the Scottish border, had toughened and hardened him. He'd thought his enjoyment of the rough life on the moors and the company of the men who followed him were enough, but as he grew older, he found himself longing for more. There seemed to be a void within him, and for some reason, each time circumstances brought him back to Middleham, he began to question whether that void could be filled by anything but the possession of home and family—something a man in his position was unlikely ever to have. To be truthful, most of the time the idea of such responsibility seemed unappealing but somehow Middleham had a way of continually presenting domestic scenes such as the one before him, and he couldn't help but wonder what it would be like to have someone special waiting by the fire.

Impatient with his thoughts, he slammed the door behind him; startled, Marganna glanced up. The tentative smile on her face died instantly as she saw the frown on his, making Rath regret having shattered her mood.

"Well, I'm glad you're here already. Shall we eat?"

"What about Will?"

"Oh, he'll be along directly. He sent word he was going down to the stables on an errand and that we were to start without him."

"Very well."

He held the chair as she slipped into her place at the small table near the hearth. Rath sat on the opposite side, facing her.

Marganna stole a quick glance at him, but he seemed intent on uncovering the dishes before them and did not raise his head. She felt uncomfortable without Will's calm presence, at a loss as to how to act or what to say. Taking refuge in silence, she nervously smoothed the linen napkin on her lap, waiting while he served the food.

The meal was delicious—roast Yorkshire mutton with fresh vegetables, followed by cheeses and a gooseberry tart. They were halfway through the first course before Rath spoke.

"What do you think of Middleham?" He leaned forward and Marganna found herself studying his face. The lean, handsome features were devoid of sarcasm or reproach, eliciting an honesty she had not intended.

"I expect it is as comfortable as any prison," she replied. Realizing what she had said, she drew back slightly, expecting an angry eruption from Rathburn. Instead, a half-smile played about his lips.

"And do you know a great deal about prisons?"

"Enough to know they are stifling, unhappy places."

"Do you mind if I ask why you say that with such certainty?"

"I grew up in one, you see." At the look of surprise on his face, she went on. "Oh, not a prison in the usual sense, but a place with walls and locks and restrictions."

Rath sat back in his chair, toying with his wineglass. "You intrigue me, Marganna. Exactly where did you grow up?"

"I was raised in a Welsh convent, where I lived until I was fifteen."

"A convent?" Rath frowned. "Yes, I can understand how that must have seemed like prison to a child."

"I was glad to leave."

"You say you grew up in Wales. Does that mean you are Welsh?"

"Part Welsh, part English." Marganna drew a deep breath. This conversation was beginning to lead in dangerous directions. "I expect I am like most people, a complicated blend of many nationalities."

"Yes, that seems to be the way of it," he said with a return of the half smile. "I, too, have a mixed heritage. My father was born a titled Yorkshireman, but my mother was from a clan of Lowland Scots—a people the English consider little more than heathens." His grin widened. "When he announced he was bringing her back to Wensleydale, all the neighbors expected her to murder him in his bed. They still thought Scotsmen ran naked through the bracken, playing unearthly music on the pipes and killing innocent Englishmen with their claymores."

Marganna laughed softly. "And did your mother live up to their expectations?"

"Not at all. She was a beautiful, highly educated, soft-spoken lady. People had just gotten over the shock of that when her four brothers came for a visit. Now they were more what the locals had expected. They played the pipes and drank every man under the table." Rath leaned forward again, forcing her eyes to meet his sparkling gaze. "And it is rumored that, on occasion, they were even seen running naked through the bracken, usually pursuing some giggling village lass."

Marganna's laughter joined his low rumble.

"My uncles were a wild and merry lot," he continued. "I strongly suspect I have more than a drop or two of their blood in my veins."

She pretended astonishment. "You? Why, I'd never have thought it."

"Don't goad me," he warned, but his eyes were twinkling. "Let's talk about you. Tell me, what does a child do for . . . er, entertainment in a convent?"

She picked up her goblet and took a sip of wine. "I escaped to the garden whenever I could. It was pretty there, quiet and peaceful. And I spent hours playing the harp."

"Did the nuns teach you to play?"

"Yes. There was a harp among my belongings, and one of the sisters decided I should learn to play it."

"Well, I enjoyed your playing at Nottingham, if not the ballad you chose to sing."

For a moment a spark of humor seemed to leap between them. Marganna found herself wishing she was not so opposed to his politics and could admit to the rapport they seemed to share.

"Don't tell me the sister is the one who taught you that risqué melody."

She grinned as she set her goblet back on the table. "There was an old man who earned his keep by working in the garden. He taught me all the ballads and folk songs he knew."

"That one too? I can hardly imagine the nuns permitting it."

"No, they'd never have approved. We sang that particular tune only when no one was around. Actually, he didn't intend to teach the ballad to me, but I overhead it and demanded to learn the words. I used to crouch behind the blackberry hedge, you see, and listen to him talk and sing to himself." Growing uneasy at Rath's undivided attention, she finished lamely, "There wasn't much else to do. I mean, there were no other children."

"You must have been lonely."

"It was a solitary existence," she admitted, searching for a means of turning the conversation away from herself. "But what about you? Where did you receive your musical training?"

"My musical abilities, such as they are, were fostered

here at Middleham when I was a boy. In addition to weaponry, Warwick believed his pupils should have an adequate knowledge of music and languages. I struggled through Latin and the lute."

"You play the lute?" Marganna's brows went up as she digested that fact. She could not imagine such a delicate instrument in his large, masculine hands.

Now it was Rath who sought to turn the discussion in a different direction. "You said you left the convent when you were fifteen. How did that come about?"

"I was taken into Lady Stanley's household as a musician . . . and to learn to be a lady's maid."

Suddenly, to her surprise, he reached across the table and swiftly captured one of her hands in his own. "You puzzle me, Marganna. You say you have worked to earn a living, yet you look like a lady." His fingers closed gently over her forearm, lifting her hand to place it within the grip of his free one. She caught her breath at the intimate rub of her palm against his, but when she would have pulled away, his hold tightened. Her hand looked slender and fragile, paler than the bronzed skin upon which it lay. "At first glance, you even have the hands of a lady." Releasing her wrist, he slid his fingertips slowly across her knuckles, then up the length of her slim fingers, brushing the neatly clipped nails. "But you do not wear jewelry, and no lady I've ever met would keep her nails so short." He turned her hand over, and a large, roughened thumb began an unhurried survey of her palm and the calloused pads of each finger, its circular motion stirring strange feelings to life within her. "This side of your hand reveals that you really have worked for your living . . . and not just at playing the harp. I wonder who and what you truly are, Marganna."

Disturbed by his unprecedented tenderness, she turned her face away and, without warning, found herself staring at their reflections in a mirror that hung on the opposite wall. Something deep inside her twisted painfully. It wasn't fair! The two people in that mirror looked as if they belonged together, locked forever in cozy, firelit contentment. The man, splendid in dark velvet, seemed to hover protectively over the woman, who sat so serene beneath his touch. There was nothing to reveal the truth—no indication the two were bitter enemies, each despising the other's beliefs.

A sigh escaped Marganna's lips as she stole another glance at the reflection. How many times during her austere childhood had she dreamed of just such a scene? How many times had she consoled herself with the promise that one day she would have a home and husband of her own? That she would be loved and cherished by one man—a man who could give her the affection and companionship for which she longed? The dream had sustained her during hours spent kneeling in a chapel filled with icy drafts, through the long nights when her nearly empty stomach grumbled so persistently she could not fall asleep, and even through the dreariness of life in Lady Stanley's household. But now, seeing the charming false image before her, she wondered if the dream would prove to be like the reflection—a lie.

Marganna quickly pulled her hand from Rath's and placed it behind her back while she stared at him with wide, confused eyes.

An expression of impatience passed over Rath's face at that moment, as though he had just recalled their situation and was mentally upbraiding himself for showing such personal interest in her. He cleared his throat.

"What about your family?" he asked. "If you grew up in a nunnery, where were they?"

The abruptness of his tone jolted her back to reality. "My mother died when I was very young," she said stiffly, returning her attention to her food.

"And your father?"

"Is this an interrogation?" she asked, raising troubled eyes to his.

"Why should you consider such casual inquiry an interrogation? I wonder what you have to hide . . .?"

"I . . . I have nothing to hide!" she declared hotly. But she did—he must not learn she was a Tudor.

Candlelight played over Marganna's face, tinting the fine-grained skin with ivory, turning the wide eyes golden brown. Rath studied her for a long moment; then, as if suddenly remembering their discussion, he said, "I don't believe you."

Hands gripping the edge of the table, Marganna leaned forward to ask, "Are you calling me a liar?"

"I am." On the opposite side of the table Rath, too, leaned forward. "You have declined to tell me anything significant about yourself. It's obvious you are hiding something."

"I repeat, I have nothing to conceal."

The door opened to admit Will Metcalfe; he had assessed the situation before he was halfway across the room. He murmured an apology for being late and sat down at the table, studying his dining companions with an odd mixture of amusement and impatience. By the saints, Lord John Rathburn had finally met his match in stubbornness!

The girl, no matter how pretty and womanly she appeared, could set her jaw just as tightly as could the man—could toss her head and flash her eyes and bite off her words with just as much sarcasm as he.

Never in the fifteen years he had known Rath had any woman dared stand up to him as this one was doing. Mostly when Rath was on the scene, women were sweet, biddable, and overanxious to please.

"How did you come to spy against the king?" asked Rath.

She leaped to her feet. "So this little dinner *was* for the purpose of further interrogation!"

"No," he retorted, "but you can't deny my right to curiosity. You claim to have no secrets, yet you are part of a plot against King Richard."

Marganna turned away, crossing the room to stand by the darkened windows. "Why do you believe there was a plot?" she asked. "Perhaps I'm simply a citizen motivated by outrage."

"What outraged you so?" he asked with interest.

Marganna took a deep breath. "It wasn't right for King Richard to depose his nephew simply by trumping up a claim of illegitimacy."

"Ah, but it was not trumped up," Rath stated firmly.

"First of all, the king had nothing to do with the charge. Stillington, the bishop of Bath and Wells, announced that King Edward's marriage to Elizabeth Woodville was invalid and therefore all his children by her illegitimate. The bishop had proof that Edward was legally plight-trothed to another woman when he secretly married Woodville."

Seeing her look of surprise, he went on. "Furthermore, it was the King's Council who declared young Edward a bastard, not fit to rule the country. They are the men who begged Richard to drop his role of Protector and take the crown."

"He could have refused their offer."

"Good God, do you think he wanted to be king? The council was not going to have the boy Edward on the throne, and Richard knew that if he did not allow them to back him, they would choose someone else. Think on it. What might their choice have meant? What if they had chosen someone like Buckingham . . . or, God forbid, the ambitious Henry Tudor, that Welsh jackanapes!"

Marganna bit her tongue and turned away, pretending to look out the window. In truth, the night beyond was so dark all she could see was the reflection of the burning candles in the room behind her.

"Richard agreed to their entreaties out of his love for England and his sense of duty to her. Not, as you would like to think, because he was greedy or power mad."

"Then what reason could he have for secluding the princes in the north?"

"Did you ever stop to think that the king may have taken them out of London to protect them?"

Marganna's laugh was scornful. "Whom could they possibly have to fear as much as the man who usurped the throne?"

"You don't really want to hear the truth. You want to believe the king is guilty."

"I'm not the only one who thinks that way."

"Rath, Marganna! Calm down, both of you." Will advanced, taking Marganna's arm and leading her toward the door to the adjoining room. "Let's end the evening, shall we? There will be ample time to resume this . . . conversation later."

Rath glowered. "I see no point in resuming it. Neither of us is going to be persuaded to listen to the other's point of view. For all I care, we can lock the witch in her room and leave her there."

Marganna paused in the doorway, eyes sparkling with fury. "Fine! I'm certain that would be preferable to enduring your company."

With that she stalked into her bedchamber and would have slammed the door behind her had not Rath moved across the room to prevent it from closing by sticking out a booted foot.

"Since you feel that way, I'll just take this to insure your privacy and mine." His long fingers pulled the key from the lock before he allowed the door to swing shut.

Marganna ground her teeth in anger as she heard the key being turned. She hurried to the door that opened into the hallway outside, but it too, had been locked.

So . . . she was to be a prisoner once more. Very well; at least she would be comfortable and, most important, she would not be bothered by the insufferable Lord Rathburn again.

However, as it turned out, she was very much bothered by the man within the next few hours. Just as she prepared to climb into the high four-poster bed, she heard people talking in the adjoining bedroom. Curious, she stepped close to the door separating the two chambers.

She recognized Rath's deep tones and knew beyond a doubt the voice replying was Bronwyn's. She heard laughter, and then it grew silent. In a few moments, the faint glow of candlelight shining beneath the door was extinguished, and she could only assume they had retired.

The man was utterly crass, to entertain his courtesan in the room next to hers. Had he no decency? Did he give no thought to the possibility of offending Marganna?

Of course not, she admonished herself. He would enjoy knowing that his actions disturbed and disgusted me! That's the crude sort of person he is.

With a sigh she returned to her bed, blowing out the

candles and snuggling deep within the comforting warmth of the feather mattress. Outside the wind howled in the black night, occasionally rattling the glass in the windows or stirring the heavy draperies that covered them.

Unaccustomed to the noise and force of the gale sweeping down from the moorlands, Marganna told herself that was why she could not fall asleep. She lay wide-eyed and restless, staring into the darkness . . . but all the while she was tensed for the sound of laughter from the room beyond.

The dimming fire was the only light in the room, the faint hiss and crackle of burning logs the only sound. Bronwyn lay beside Rath, limbs sprawled carelessly, black hair streaming across the pillow.

Even now he recalled her look of astonishment when he had rebuffed her attempt to seduce him. When she had first come into the room, they had teased and laughed, like so many times before, but when they undressed and got into bed, he had felt not a flicker of desire.

"Don't tell me it is like the night we stayed at Will's house," she raged. "You cannot be exhausted tonight."

No, not exhausted—just suddenly disinterested. Of course, he couldn't tell her that unless he was prepared to handle one of her emotional temper tantrums. He made one feeble attempt at an excuse.

"It seems the mood for dalliance isn't upon me tonight, Bronwyn. Mayhap I have too much on my mind."

"Yes, and don't think I don't know exactly who it is," she snapped, her full lips forming what he might once have thought an inviting pout. "You have not paid a moment's attention to me since you met that woman. Do you find her more attractive than I?"

He looked startled. "Good Lord, no." But even as he spoke the denial, he remembered the shimmer of candlelight against high cheekbones, the insolent tilt of a small, square chin, the soft caress of her fingers as they lay in his. Impatient with himself, he turned on his lover.

"I do not intend to listen to your nagging tonight, Bronwyn. Take your suspicions back to your own chamber and leave me in peace."

She looked stricken. "Please let me stay, Rath. If I go back to my own room, everyone will know you sent me away, and word of it will spread throughout the castle."

"You've never worried about gossip before . . . oh, very well, you may stay. Just be quiet and go to sleep."

Now, arms crossed behind his head, Rath watched her sleeping. To his chagrin, her accusation kept insinuating its way deeper into his mind. In the beginning, Bronwyn had been an exciting challenge, but at this moment he felt nothing for her. It was almost as though she were a stranger. What was worse, no matter how hard he tried to concentrate on the honey skin and ebony hair before him, he could see only the pure, blazing anger in a pair of spice brown eyes.

Chapter 7

Marganna awoke to the sound of a door opening, followed by the thud of booted feet on the stone flooring. She sat up in bed and found herself regarding a disgruntled looking Rathburn, who had crossed the room to stand at the foot of her bed.

Pulling the bedcovers up around her throat, she glared at him and waited for him to speak.

Two things were immediately clear to Rathburn: one, the little baggage was still smarting from their row the night before; and two, she had no idea how appealing she looked sitting in the middle of a rumpled bed, hair loosened and curling around her shoulders, eyes still dreamy from sleep. Silently he warned himself to concentrate on the first fact and ignore the second. She was far from the first woman he had seen in the early-morning intimacy of a bedchamber—most of the others had been unashamedly seductive—so why did he find himself so stirred by her innocent outrage?

"I trust you spent a restful night," he said roughly.

His brusque tone only irritated her further. If the clod expected her to make some comment on his . . . his lack of morals, he would be disappointed.

"Yes, indeed," she answered in a deceptively sweet tone. "I went to sleep right away, and nothing disturbed me all night long."

Little liar, he thought, noticing the faint smudge of shadow beneath her eyes. She slept about as well as I did.

Deciding to let her small deception pass, he went on.

"I've just spoken with Clovelly Biggins and requested that she come up and see you. She promised to bring you some breakfast and take care of any needs you might have."

"Who is Clovelly Biggins?"

"Only the most important resident of this castle," he replied solemnly. "She is a combination of housekeeper, gardener, and doctor. But most significantly she is one of the rarest of creatures . . . a woman who is both honest and dependable." He gave a brisk nod. "Tell her if there is anything you require."

He turned on his heel and strode out of the room before she could respond to his deliberate insult.

Fuming, she tossed back the covers and reached for her bed robe. After donning it and tying the sash, she walked to the windows and drew aside the heavy draperies. Morning sunlight slanted in through the thick glass, warming her as she sat on the cushioned seat and tucked her bare feet beneath her.

Her room was toward the southeast corner of the castle, the side away from the town, and this was her first look at what lay beyond the windows.

The hill behind Middleham rose steeply to a high moor, the breadth of which was visible to Marganna from her lofty vantage point. She was looking at a stark vista she had not known existed in England—acres of windswept grass, and nothing else to mar the landscape. By leaning close to the glass and looking around to the east, she could see a line of wind-scragged trees struggling to the summit of a distant hill, and even farther away, a range of low mountains. Over the entire scene hung a wide, bruised sky, filled with the towering swirls and peaks of wind-whipped clouds.

Marganna leaned her forehead against the glass in a moment of total despair. There was no gentleness in this country, nothing to welcome or comfort her. She had grown up in a land of shady dells and quaint villages. She was accustomed to rural lanes that meandered across fields of wildflowers, quiet brooks where swans glided in majestic silence. Even at the convent there had been gardens and an orchard. How could she bear to be constrained in this harsh, ugly place? Would she ever be allowed to leave here?

She sat staring out the window at the gloomy scene for another ten minutes before a movement close to the castle caught her attention.

Two men on horseback were riding along a path worn in the grass of the slope. Halfway up the path, they came to a halt and seemed to be having a lively discussion. Just as Marganna realized the riders were Rathburn and Will, they suddenly spurred their mounts to a gallop. They were racing; she could see Rath lift his face to the wind, shouting with laughter, as Will shouted back, hair gleaming red-gold in the morning sunlight.

Marganna turned away, a feeling of resentment in the pit of her stomach. Why couldn't she be free to experience the sunshine and fresh air—even that of the desolate moor—instead of being cooped up in this room, without as much as a book to read? Five days of captivity were beginning to seem like a lifetime.

A key scraped in the lock and a tall, spare woman stepped into the room, a covered tray in her hands.

"Gooid mornin' ta ye, miss. Aw be Missus Biggins and Aw've brought sommat fer yer breakfast. An' here's a piggin o' hot water fer washin' oop as well."

Marganna gazed in wonder. Was this Clovelly Biggins? Somehow the name had conjured up the image of a rotund countrywoman with rosy cheeks. Nothing could have been further from reality.

"Thank you." Hesitantly Marganna accepted the pitcher, then disappeared into the garderobe where she made quick work of washing up and slipping out of her nightclothes. Dressed in a day gown of lightweight gray wool, her hair brushed back and tied with a black ribbon, she reentered the bedchamber to find that Mrs. Biggins had arranged the breakfast tray on a small table before the fire.

The woman turned a curious look on Marganna. "Lord Rathburn has told me ye are not pleased ta find yerself a guest at Middleham."

Marganna's chin came up. "Well, it's true I would rather not be here under these circumstances."

After settling herself in a chair close to the fire and pouring two cups of tea, Mrs. Biggins squinted a look at Marganna and indicated the other chair. "Sit ye down, girl."

Somewhat at a loss for words, Marganna did as she was told, accepting the cup the older woman handed her.

Mrs. Biggins continued. "Iver since Aw've known Lord Rathburn—Johnny, as Aw call him—he's been causin' gooid females ta go all flighty. Seems ta me 'tis aboot time a female caused him some trouble of his own!"

Mrs. Biggins chuckled again, then took a long, noisy swig of tea. "Drink oop, lass—'tis a fine red clover tea Aw've brought ye. 'Twill soothe yer nerves."

Clovelly Biggins' good will could not be disguised, even when it took the form of bossiness.

Marganna smiled faintly and took a sip of the fragrant brew. Surprisingly it tasted rather pleasant.

"Eat yer breakfast, that's a gooid lass. Noo, is there anythin' ye be needin'?"

"I would like some freedom to leave this room," Marganna answered crisply.

"Aye, Aw can believe that. Howiver, only Johnny can grant ye that."

"And he'll never do it. I tell you, Mrs. Biggins, I just don't understand the man. First he is furious with me, then he acts as if he is willing to consider a truce. And then, without warning, he becomes hostile again. Are all Yorkshire men that way?"

Mrs. Biggins laughed heartily, her deep-set hazel eyes twinkling. "Ooh, ta be sure. As a matter o' pure fact, lass, men everywhere are like that. But right at this minnit, young John be in a worse state than most because 'tis fair hard fer him ta be stern with a comely lookin' female."

Marganna blushed rosily as she remembered her first meeting with the man. Indeed, he had been all smiles and flattery then, and he had kissed her on the occasion of their second meeting, even in the midst of his anger at finding her in the king's private chambers. No doubt such meaningless and lighthearted lechery was his usual way of dealing with females.

"Well, he seems determined to make life as difficult for me as possible."

Mrs. Biggins wagged a bony forefinger. "Noo, lass, even ye must admit he could treat ye much worse. Aw shudder ta think how he would have dealt with a man in the same situation. The poor buggar'd have seen nowt but the darkness of the dungeons, tha knows."

"Yes, I'm well aware of it. However, I fully believe he would have done likewise with me, had not the king issued his own orders on the subject. Your Rathburn is a harsh man."

"Ye have ta understand summat aboot the lad, Marganna. He has no one but King Richard and Will Metcalfe. His parents and a sister died when the plague struck Yorkshire, and Johnny nowt but ten years old. He and his brother were here at Middleham at the time bein' trained for combat. 'Tis all that saved 'em from the sweatin' sickness themselves."

Despite herself, Marganna felt a pang of sympathy. Until Rath had mentioned his parentage the evening before, she had not thought of Lord Rathburn as a member of a family. He seemed so strong and aloof, and now she knew why. She still had difficulty picturing him as a son or brother, or even as a child, for that matter.

"He did mention his family, but I wasn't aware they were no longer living. Where is his brother now?"

"Daid, like the others. Killed at the Battle of Barnet, fighting against Warwick, the very man who taught him the art of warfare." Mrs. Biggins shook her head, coiled iron-gray braids teetering above each ear. "Poor laddie, he died in King Richard's arms—they were best of friends, tha knows. The king is the one who told Johnny aboot his brother, the one who stayed at his side when he was wild with grief. After that, King Richard became the only family Rath had. Aye, 'tis noo wonder his loyalty is strong."

"I suppose not," Marganna murmured.

"Well, when ye know the lad a bit better, mebbe ye will see what lies behind his actions. The events of his life have taught him ta be hard an' mistrustin'. Aw've prayed someone will come along ta teach him how ta forget all that."

"I'm sorry for his tragedies, of course, but even so, it doesn't make his temper any easier to endure."

"Oh, he'll coom around, soon or late. Just be patient."

"I'll try, but it's not easy. I'm unaccustomed to sitting around with nothing to do," Marganna pointed out. "Perhaps you would ask Lord Rathburn if I might help in some way about the castle?"

Mrs. Biggins studied her with shrewd eyes. "Ye mean work? Noo, why would a laidy like yerself want ta work? Aw've never heard of such."

"I'm not really a lady, Mrs. Biggins," Marganna explained. "I've always worked in some way or another. And truly, I wouldn't mind helping out. I much prefer to stay busy."

"Saints above, what am Aw hearin'? A female of quality like yerself offerin' ta do housework, when that useless Bronwyn refuses ta lift her hands for nowt."

"Will you speak to Rathburn about it?"

"Aye, that Aw will, but Aw'm promisin' nowt, ye know."

"I know." Marganna accepted a second cup of the clover tea and took a careful sip before she asked another question. "Tell me, Mrs. Biggins, how did you come to live at Middleham? Have you always been here?"

"There's those who'd swear Aw have." The other woman chuckled, refilling her own cup. "Aw came here ta work as a maid when Aw was young. Then Aw married one of the castle guards, and somehow we just always stayed on at Middleham. Aw remained even after my husband died. Aw was too old ta go somewhere different, and besides, King Richard and Queen Anne and their poor little tyke were like family ta me, Aw couldn't leave 'em."

"Do you have children of your own?"

"Nay, noo children of my own, though Aw like ta think of Richard, Johnny, and Will as my lads. Aw fair raised 'em, Aw did."

Marganna smiled at the look on the old woman's face. It was doubtful a real parent could look any prouder.

"My husband passed away many years ago," Mrs. Biggins added, "and lookin' after the children at the castle has been my whole life. My mither always said Aw took after my father's folk, for they were Yorkshiremen an' could never leave the moors."

Marganna thought it must be nice to feel such contentment with one's lot in life, to find one's niche and be happy to remain there forever.

"Well, Aw've purely enjoyed chattin' with ye, Marganna, but Aw do need ta get on with my chores. Are ye sure there's nowt Aw can get fer ye?"

"Just Rathburn's permission to leave this room."

Mrs. Biggins winked. "We'll see, lass."

When the woman had gone, Marganna set about tidying the bedchamber. When she had done everything she could think of to pass the time, she returned to the window seat and looked out at the high moor.

Idly she wondered what Margaret Stanley's reaction had been when she found the message left on the vanity table. There could have been little doubt as to its meaning, but would her ladyship respond in any way?

Marganna was almost certain she would. Finding the princes was of the utmost importance to Lady Margaret; even her anger at her niece's clumsiness would not prevent her from making the most of this opportunity.

There must be people in Middleham who knew where the princes had been hidden. It was even a possibility the boys were in this very castle. It was a huge fortress with dozens of chambers. If only she were free to search!

She glanced at the door connecting her room with that of Lord Rathburn and had a sudden thought. The man had seemed hurried and distracted that morning, and she could not remember hearing the turn of the key when he left. Perhaps he had forgotten to lock the door.

It opened easily, and she smiled to herself. In his carelessness, Rath had provided a means for her departure from her chamber.

She stood in the doorway of Rathburn's bedroom, staring about her. It seemed his dominant personality was already stamped on his quarters, even after cnly one night in residence. She could not help but wonder whether he as easily marked the people he chose to make his.

Her glance moved to the bed, but instead of the smooth satin coverlet, she was imagining rumpled sheets and scattered pillows, with Bronwyn's hair spread over them like black silk. And Rathburn, as magnificent in his nudity as he had been that night in his chamber at Nottingham, leaning over her . . .

Marganna closed her eyes, shutting out the scene. When she reopened them, she determinedly turned her gaze to other corners of the room.

Tossed casually over a chair near the fireplace was the brown velvet doublet Rath had worn the night before, and on the floor next to a massive wardrobe was a pair of soft, dark boots. Crossing the room, she opened the doors to the wardrobe and in so doing released a pleasant scent which she immediately associated with Lord Rathburn. It was a heady combination of leather, faint wood smoke, and the fresh, citrus odor of bergamot. She reached out to stroke the sleeve of one of his garments, breathing deeply of the masculine scent.

Quickly closing the wardrobe doors behind her, she strolled around the room, coming to a stop in front of a cushioned seat along the high windows. Lying among the scattered pillows was a lute. So Rathburn had been telling her the unlikely truth! She reached down to pick up the instrument and idly ran her fingers across the strings, noticing as she did so the green and blue streamers adorning its slender neck. A lady's favor no doubt, given in exchange for a pretty song. Marganna smiled to herself. Somehow she thought Rathburn would exact more in the way of payment than a handful of ribbons. Then she thought of Bronwyn, and her smile faded.

She did not hear the door open, only Rath's soft words behind her.

"Old habits are difficult to break, I see. Once a spy . . ."

Marganna whirled to face him. Instead of the intense glower she expected, his face held a teasing smile. He came closer, reaching out to stroke the satiny wood of the lute.

" 'Tis made of rosemary wood. They say it makes a lover's madrigal sweeter. I'll play it for you sometime, shall I?"

"Yes," she said, relieved he was not going to subject her to his usual temper, "perhaps we could sing another duet."

"God forbid." Rath took the instrument from her and placed it back on the cushions. "Now, Marganna, would you care to explain why you are in my chamber?"

"You left the door unlocked. Can you blame me for looking around?"

"Ah, you were trying to learn more about me." His grin was insolent, his eyes laughing.

She sniffed audibly. "More likely, I grew tired of being called a spy and simply decided to act like one."

"And what exactly did you hope to find here?"

"I'm not certain."

He eyed her speculatively. "Well, since you were brave enough to breach the privacy of my bedchamber, I won't hesitate to show you the rest of Middleham."

Before she could speak, he ushered her out of the room and down the hall, stopping to let her look into one chamber after another. When they approached a pair of polished wooden doors, he flung them wide.

Marganna stepped into a pretty room that was simply but elegantly decorated. The walls and bed were hung with blue velvet, and above the fireplace was a portrait of a young woman dressed in a gown of the same color. She moved to study the painting more closely.

Something lying on the mantel caught her eye, and she picked up a brooch. It was fashioned in the shape of a rose—a white Yorkist rose made of pearls and emeralds, a diamond dewdrop flashing fire even in the dimness of the empty chamber.

"This was King Richard's room," she said with certainty.

"Yes, his and Queen Anne's. Everything is just as they left it, their books, jewels, their gifts to each other. Anne had the portrait painted to surprise Richard when he returned from one of his campaigns in Scotland. He brought her the brooch from London. The chess set on the table is carved of wood from the Holy Land, with the chessmen fashioned to represent archangels and prophets. In the old days Richard and Anne used to play chess every evening here in this room."

Marganna did not relish the sudden ghostly images of the king and queen that began to drift into her mind. Seeing their possessions, their gifts to each other, sensing the intimate atmosphere about her—it was not so easy to summon the usual animosity once she began to think of them as ordinary people.

"Go on, look to your heart's content. Perhaps you will learn something of their lives, their enviable marriage."

Marganna glanced up from the chess board. "Enviable? I don't understand. Wasn't Anne forced to marry Richard?"

"Not at all. 'Tis another of the rumors."

"But King Richard was responsible for the death of her father."

"Only because the king was one of the Plantagenet brothers Warwick wanted destroyed. Richard and Edward fought against Warwick in battle, but they neither killed him nor ordered him slain. In fact, both were saddened by his death."

"I see."

"As for Anne, marrying her childhood sweetheart was the one good thing that happened to her in her short lifetime. No, she married Richard because she loved him. And," he added fiercely, "those who claim otherwise are damned liars. I saw them together many times, and it was more than evident they were deeply in love. As a boy I sat at meals and watched them share a trencher, eyes only for each other, creating a world of their own within the crowded, noisy castle. Sometimes Richard whispered endearments in her ear that caused her face to turn rosy, and then they would slip away to this chamber . . . their sanctuary, the only place they could be alone and avoid the rest of the world.''

Lost in thought, Rathburn rested one hip on the window ledge and continued. ''Their marriage seemed so perfect to me that it is probably one of the reasons I myself have never married.''

Marganna gave a small laugh. ''What do you mean?''

''I decided at an early age that if I couldn't have a marriage like theirs, I would prefer to remain a bachelor. The years of seeing them together set the pattern for what I anticipated for myself.''

She was surprised to learn a man like Rathburn would harbor thoughts of marriage. He seemed far too self-sufficient to need anyone.

''So, you will settle for nothing less than a marriage for love?''

One black brow tilted upward. ''It doesn't seem likely I will every marry, does it?''

''No,'' she laughingly agreed. ''Especially considering the imperfections of mere women.''

''Something I would not have expected you to admit,'' he said wryly.

''Oh, I was speaking strictly from your point of view, of course.''

''And what is your viewpoint, may I ask?''

She lowered her lashes to hide the wicked look in her eyes. ''It would be my opinion that, in light of your own imperfections, you'd best prepare yourself for perpetual bachelorhood.''

He put his hands on his hips and tilted his head sideways as if deep in thought. ''Good Lord, do I have imperfections?''

''This may come as something of a shock to you,'' she dared to say, ''but you have an abominable temper and no patience. And there is the matter of your arrogance and lechery and—''

"Stop!" He raised one hand. "I'd appreciate it if you would leave me at least some small measure of self-esteem."

She shrugged, giving him an innocent smile.

Again he took her arm, gently pushing her out of the room and down the hall before him.

"What about you, milady? For what sort of husband do you search?"

"Why would you think I am searching for any sort of husband?"

He looked surprised. "I thought marriage was something all women wanted."

"A typically male assumption," she informed him. "I have survived very well to this point in my life without a man."

The corridor made a turn, and they were facing a door set into the curving wall of a tower. An old hound, lying in front of the door, raised his head and observed them, his tail beginning an eager thumping.

"Hello, Caesar, old lad." Rath knelt beside the animal to scratch its ears. The dog bumped its head upward against Rath's hand, clumsy in its effort to greet the man. "Caesar belonged to Richard and Anne's son, Edward. Since the boy's death a year ago, the dog refuses to sleep anywhere but here, outside the nursery."

He rose and reached out to open the door, pushing it wide. The faintly musty odor of disuse swirled around them. Stepping across the threshold, Marganna peered inside. She could see the dim outline of a small canopy bed and shelves built to fit the arc of the wall. Beneath a long, narrow window was a child's desk, littered with a slate and several papers.

The dog had come to stand beside her, and now he, too, gazed into the empty chamber. Suddenly, the erratic motion of his bony tail ceased; he became perfectly still, and a low, keening whine issued from his throat.

"My God, what is it?" Marganna whispered.

"He expects to find Edward here. I think he misses the boy."

"Oh, how pitiful! The poor thing."

Marganna rested her hand on the hound's broad head and looked back into the darkened room. In her mind's eye she could see a slight figure seated at the desk, a stray beam of sunshine picking out the gold in his flyaway hair as he bent over his writing. She did not know why she thought he would be fair-haired, but somehow she knew he had been—just as she knew his shoulders would have been sharp beneath the scarlet doublet he wore, and that his voice would have been childishly high and merry with mischievous laughter.

She turned away quietly, nearly bumping into Rath. For a moment, their eyes locked and held; after their light-hearted banter of several moments ago, it now seemed they were experiencing a mutual feeling of poignancy. She had not expected such elemental emotion from a man who, until they arrived at Middleham, had seemed harsh and invulnerable.

"Aren't you going inside?" he asked.

"No . . . I don't care to go into that room."

His nod was strangely understanding. "Very well, then. Come along."

In vain Marganna tried to coax the dog to follow them; as soon as Rath closed the door to the nursery, Caesar took up his former post and refused to move.

As they crossed the hallway toward the main part of the castle, Marganna looked up in time to see a self-satisfied smile flit across Rathburn's face.

"You look pleased with yourself," she commented dryly. "I suppose you think this . . . tour is accomplishing just what you had hoped for."

"And what do you think that might be?"

"I think you intended to play upon my sympathies . . ."

"While that thought may have crossed my mind, I was actually smiling because we've passed nearly ten minutes without an argument."

His smile deepened and despite herself, even a haughty toss of her head could not hide Marganna's answering smile.

Rath led the way through the great hall and down the long flight of stairs to the courtyard. His stride lengthened as he crossed the inner bailey, and Marganna hurried to keep up with him.

She was interested to see they were entering a deserted-looking tiltyard. Two quintains were staggering from disuse, and the straw targets for archery were moldy with age and damp weather.

"This is the best place to come if you want to know Middleham," Rath said quietly. "This is where many a lad got his introduction to the rigid expectations of Warwick, his tutor in warfare."

She felt his gaze upon her and met his dark green eyes.

"Richard spent hours here. He was a small boy, weaker than the others his age, but so great was his determination to excel, he did not let that deter him. He practiced with the broadsword and battle-ax much longer than did the rest of the lads, refusing to let his size limit his ability. To this day he is more dangerous with a battle-ax than any man I know."

Rath approached one of the quintains and gave the weighted target an idle push, causing the frayed rope to creak in protest.

"And what about you?" she asked. "Did you enjoy the training?"

"It was what I wanted, or so I thought at the time."

"Would you tell me about it?"

"There's not much to tell. Each day we were expected to rise early and hear Mass before breaking our fast. Then there were lessons with the chaplain and afternoons were spent here in the tiltyard practicing combat. In full armor, we learned to ride and wield weapons at the same time. We took part in mock tournaments, during which most of us received our first battle scars. There were plenty of those, for it was deadly serious play. Our masters tolerated nothing less than intense concentration, bullying us into becoming the strongest, most efficient fighting men it was possible to be.

"When I was first sent to board at Middleham, Richard was still here. Because he and my brother Stephan were close friends, I was allowed in their company. They were five years older than I—fully grown, in my eyes, and everything I thought a man should be. How I envied them their skills at weaponry, the muscles developed by long hours on the practice field—even their book learning! Then, not many months after my arrival, King Edward recalled Richard to London, and I did not meet him again until he returned from exile in the Low Countries.

"As soon as he heard that Edward and Richard had come back to England, Stephan set out to join them." Rath turned to leave the tiltyard, waiting for Marganna to precede him. "He was eighteen years old when he was slain at the Battle of Barnet—the battle Edward fought to regain the throne." He threw her a fierce look. "And please don't bother to tell me you are sorry . . . you didn't know Stephan, and his death can mean nothing to you."

Her lips closed over the trite comment she had been about to make. He was right; it was meaningless to offer perfunctory sympathy on the death of a person she had never known.

She glanced back at the tiltyard, almost able to believe she could hear the shouts of the boys, the clumsy clashing of steel. Rath noticed her hesitation.

"You feel it too, don't you?"

"Feel what?" she countered.

"If ever there were a haunted castle, 'tis this one."

Marganna laughed uncertainly. "Haunted? Surely you—"

"You sense the ghosts—no need to deny it. I can see it in your eyes. But these are not evil, menacing spirits. No, they're gentle ones, lonely ones. Anne . . . her child . . . the boy Richard . . ."

"I don't believe in such things . . ."

"Spend a little more time at Middleham and you will," he assured her. "I think you are already beginning to realize these people are not the monsters you would like to believe them to be."

Carefully she averted her face. "Do you mind if I walk around the courtyard for a few minutes before returning to my room?" she asked.

"Not at all."

Well, she thought, as she gathered her skirts and started across the lawn, at least I have learned something about Rathburn. Beneath that arrogant exterior lurks a small lad still reeling from the shock of losing everyone dear to him. A man who clearly remembers what it was like to endure a lonely youth. He isn't so invulnerable after all.

Perhaps the fact that he had been a child thrust prematurely into a man's world had given him his outward air of insolence and callousness. Perhaps it was an important clue in the solution of the puzzling mystery that was Lord John Rathburn.

Just then a loud shout sounded from the guard tower overlooking the main gateway to the castle.

"Your Lordship, there are riders approaching."

Rath stopped walking to tilt his head and look upward, shielding his eyes from the sun. "Whose standard do they bear?"

"That of the Stanleys," came the reply. "Should we lower the drawbridge?"

Rath turned to throw Marganna a quick look, missing nothing of the sudden flush of color on her face, the elation in her eyes. His jaw tightened and he shouted an angry command.

"Lower the bridge, but keep the portcullis closed. I want to determine their business before granting them entrance to the castle."

The portcullis, a vertical grillwork made of iron-studded wood, protected the main gateway into Middleham. Grimly Rath went forward to grasp one of the crossbars and watch as the outer drawbridge was lowered.

Marganna drew closer and saw a small party of ten or twelve riders halted on the other side of the moat. Two men broke away from the group and rode onto the bridge, their horses' hooves thundering on the wooden planks. A small cry of joy broke from Marganna's lips as she recognized Donal FitzClinton, the handsome courtier from King Richard's court. Lady Stanley had sent the men for her, she realized with mounting excitement. She was to be rescued at last!

FitzClinton dismounted and approached Rath, the thick bars of the portcullis making an effective barrier between them.

"State your business, FitzClinton," said Rath.

"We wish lodging at Middleham for the night. Lord Stanley has sent us to survey some of his estates, and we—"

"I know of no Stanley properties this close to Middleham," Rath interrupted brusquely.

"We are on our way farther north." As he spoke, the young man ran a hand through his thick blond hair, but the gesture did not conceal the searching look he cast over Rathburn's shoulder. As his eyes met Marganna's, he gave a small, almost imperceptible nod.

"I suggest you try to find lodging at Castle Bolton. 'Tis only four miles farther."

"But it grows late."

"Do you have an order from His Grace?" Rath interrupted.

"Nay, but—"

"Then I cannot allow you to enter this fortress. We are guarding a prisoner of the Crown, as you are well aware, and it would not be politically expedient to risk exposure to strangers."

"Rathburn, you can't mean to send them away!" Marganna moved to his side and clutched his arm.

"That is precisely what I mean to do."

"Wait! At least let me speak with them."

"You credit me with little intelligence, my lady. Do you think I don't know these men were sent by Lady Stanley?"

"Just because they bear the Stanley colors does not mean they were sent by her ladyship. Surely the Lord High Constable is more likely to have sent his men on the king's business."

"That's the problem. All too often Lady Stanley has made the king's business her own. She is not to be trusted and, as I have learned to my regret, neither are you. I suggest you return to your room immediately and leave this matter to me."

"No" she cried.

"No?" he said softly. "You are telling me no?"

Marganna flung herself against the bars of the wooden grille, appealing to FitzClinton. "Please, give me some news from the court! Tell me how my . . . her ladyship fares. Is there no message from her?"

A steely arm went around her waist and, with a growl of fury, Rath wrenched her away from the portcullis and swung her around, giving her a shove toward the castle. With a cry, Marganna fell to her knees.

"For God's sake, Rathburn!"

"Stay out of this, FitzClinton! This woman is a traitor, and if you do not wish to be the cause of her death by execution, you will leave at once. I warn you!"

Seeing the courtier's hesitation, Marganna caught back a sob. It was cruel and unfair! Gone was the friendly and relaxed man with whom she had just spent the last hour. Now, as usual, the high-handed North Country lord was in control of the situation; his word was law, and the rest of them were powerless to say him nay. FitzClinton had no choice but to abandon his quest and ride away. He could not gain access to the castle, and Rathburn was not going to relent and let them so much as speak to each other. She clenched her fists in frustration and pounded her heels against the ground.

"Stop acting like a child." Rathburn reached out a hand and yanked her to her feet. With a cry of outrage, she flew at him, butting him in the chest with her head. Her arms flailed as she sought to land a blow against his face.

"Stop it," he thundered, pinioning her arms at her sides and shaking her violently. "Do you wish to find yourself in chains?"

Rage threatening to give way to tears, she forced her body to go limp. It was no use. She dropped her head and stared unseeingly at the grass beneath her feet.

Rath turned and issued yet another terse order. "Guards,

give these men exactly one minute to clear the drawbridge, then raise it."

"And if we refuse to leave?" FitzClinton asked.

"I expect you will find yourself swimming back to your companions."

Rath grasped Marganna's arm and began escorting her toward the keep. Behind them, FitzClinton's deep voice rang out.

"Never fear, my lady! Your mistress sends greetings. You may be certain she will persuade King Richard to release you. Even now she is beseiging him with petitions. We shall return for you."

Marganna cast one last desperate look over her shoulder and was dismayed to see the two men turning to go. A low moan escaped her lips, causing Rathburn's grip to tighten.

"I hate you," she whispered. "I hate you and your king and everything you stand for!"

Following her up the long flight of stone steps, Rathburn told himself he was glad she felt that way. If a feeling such as hatred could be kept alive between them, it would allow room for no other emotions—especially those that might confuse matters.

That night Rath sat at his window staring out into the darkness, listening to the soft sounds of harp music from the next room. The melody was disturbing, melancholy. He stirred uneasily, picturing Marganna bent over the harp, her features etched with sadness. He was caught up in the imagery of a sorrowing woman easing her emotions with the music that drifted and faded into the black Yorkshire night.

In the last two days he had felt a lessening of the tension between them, and it had seemed almost as if their animosity could be put aside. But then, once again, her unreasonable attitude had interfered and their relationship was right back where it had started. Damn the contrary wench!

Just then there was a knock on the door, and he heard Bronwyn's voice. Tonight he was sorely tempted not to turn her away, and as he crossed the room he allowed himself to imagine the woman standing on the other side of the door. She would be dressed in thin silk and lace, her hair swirling about her hips in a seductive tangle. His hand dropped to the door latch, but then the other, more haunting image of Marganna filled his mind.

"Go away, Bronwyn," he said wearily, raising a hand to slide home the heavy bolt.

Chapter 8

The next morning it took Marganna a few seconds to remember why she felt so depressed, why her spirits were so leaden. But then, along with memory of yesterday's incident, came such a white-hot flame of rage against Lord Rathburn that it was all she could do to keep from running across the room to throw open the door between their chambers and burst into a vengeful tirade.

She fell back against the pillows with a sigh. What good would it do? What good would anything do?

Just when she thought there might be a way to dissolve the enmity between them, just when she had begun to admit to a grudging admiration for the man, Rathburn had suddenly and cruelly reverted to being the cold, implacable jailor once more, leaving her more confused than ever.

A tapping at the door was followed by Mrs. Biggins' cheerful voice. "Oop with ye noo, lass. The hour grows late and there's much ta be done this day."

The older woman poked her head around the edge of the door.

Marganna looked at her in surprise. "What is to be done?" she asked, curious despite her bad mood.

" 'Tis sheep-washin' day over ta Rathburn Hall. His lordship thought ye might like ta go and lend a hand."

Anger blazed in Marganna's dark eyes. "Tell his lordship that I would rather—"

"Ah-ah!" warned Mrs. Biggins. "Aren't ye the one who was beggin' me ta find a way ta get ye oot of this castle?"

"Well, yes, but—"

"Get oop and look oot the window. Ye'll see 'tis a rare fine day—a day ta be oot and aboot."

Marganna had to smile at the country woman's odd accent and suddenly she began to feel better. Tossing back the bedcovers, she scurried across the chamber to unlatch the windows and throw them wide to the brisk morning air. Sunlight fairly shimmered along the rocky ridges of the hill behind Middleham, and for once there was no wind, only a balmy breeze.

She drew in a deep breath. "What is a sheep washing, Mrs. Biggins?"

"Ye'll find oot in gooid time. Right noo, ye'd best get dressed and have a bite o' breakfast. We'll be leavin' for the hall shortly. Oh, an' wear sommat old, lass, fer Aw intend ta put ye right ta work."

The prospect of getting away from the confines of Middleham Castle, even for a day, was so appealing to Marganna that as she dressed, she was filled with growing excitement.

When she went down to the courtyard, she was surprised to find Rath waiting for her.

"Where are the others?" she asked, her voice a trifle breathless.

"Mrs. Biggins and Amelyn have already started for Rathburn Hall with the carts of supplies. I thought you might like to take the long way around and see something of the countryside."

Not ready to trust his apparently amicable mood, Marganna merely nodded her agreement.

As they rode away from the castle, down the winding village street to the banks of the Cover River, she felt such a sense of freedom that not even thoughts of the desolate moors could dampen her spirits.

Rath watched as she lifted her face to the warm sunshine, letting her hair spill down her back in a dark russet cloud. An all-too-rare smile hovered about her mouth, and he turned away, trying to control the tightness in his chest.

He was annoyed by the subterfuge he had used in sending the others on ahead. With the pretense of keeping a closer eye on his prisoner, he had chosen to escort Marganna to Rathburn Hall alone, thinking that perhaps, in some small measure, a few moments of liberty would make up for her bitter disappointment in not getting to talk to FitzClinton. But why had he contrived some noble motive when all the time he knew he was only inventing reasons to keep her within his sight? Sternly he reminded himself that an obsession with this woman was something he could not afford.

Just then Marganna turned to look at him, her face still lit by the happy smile, and he heard himself asking, "Have you ever been to a sheep washing before?"

"No. I'm not even certain what a sheep washing is," she replied.

"Well, it's just what it sounds like," Rath answered. "The sheep are herded into the beck—a stream—and washed. The washing takes place about ten days or so before the shearing in order to cleanse the wool."

"What purpose does that serve?"

Rath smiled again. "First of all, a farmer is paid a better price for washed wool, so it makes sense to rid the sheep of the foul-smelling salve they are smeared with in the autumn."

"What sort of salve?"

"It's an ointment made of fats and tar, used to prevent disease and infestation. The second thing the washing accomplishes is to encourage the growth of the 'rise'—the new wool that lifts the fleece up from the sheep's skin to make the clipping easier."

There was an expression of distaste on her face. "I don't understand what my role is to be. As you said, I know nothing about sheep."

"You aren't expected to help with the animals, Marganna. You're to help Clovelly and the others with the cooking."

"Oh!"

"I must say," he commented, chuckling, "you look relieved."

She tried to overcome her self-consciousness by tilting her chin upward in what had become a habitual gesture of defiance since meeting Rathburn, but a guilty flush crept up her neck. "I . . . well, if you must know, I'm glad I don't have to touch those . . . those . . . smelly sheep."

He tried to look stern. "Marganna, I won't lecture you this time, but no Yorkshireman likes to be told his sheep are smelly." He studied her a moment, enjoying the play of vivid color over her high cheekbones. "I assumed Mrs. Biggins explained your duties."

"No. She was in a hurry, I believe."

"Well, you see, the cooking will be almost as important as the sheep washing—true to form, Yorkshiremen turn even a working day into a holiday. All my neighbors and hired men will be helping, and when the work is done, there will be a meal, followed by games and music and maybe a little dancing."

"I had no idea . . ."

Just then the track they had been following topped a ridge, and below them lay a valley, neatly incised by the curving river. Between the river and the rocky hill behind sprawled a manor house and its numerous barns and sheds, the whole surrounded by an intricate network of stone fences.

"That is Rathburn Hall," Rath pointed out.

"It looks very impressive from here," she stated. "I had no idea it would be so large."

They started down the trail that wound its way to the hall, but after a time Marganna was surprised to see it looked no closer than before. This was her first experience with the distorted perspective of the moors.

When she questioned Rath about the strange phenomenon, he replied, "The North Country men think it has something to do with the clearness of the air—it seems to make objects look closer than they really are. 'Tis one of the factors that makes it so easy to become disoriented out here."

The closer they came to Rathburn Hall, the more imposing it appeared. The manor house itself was built of gray stone, its massive proportions softened by the wealth of climbing roses that swept up its walls, swathing every window on the ground floor. A carved stone lintel over the front entrance bore the date 1320, and they stepped into a hall whose flagstone floor was smooth with age.

"It's beautiful," breathed Marganna. To her the polished woods and gently faded upholsteries represented generations of heritage and family tradition. "If all this belongs to you, why don't you live here? I would, if it were mine." She ran a reverent hand along the smooth wood of a curving banister. "It must be wonderful to be a part of this house, to know you belong here."

Rath felt an almost forgotten pride in his ancestral home as he tried to see it through Marganna's eyes. He knew she was thinking of the convent where she had grown up; in comparison, the few short years he had spent in this house had been warm and filled with love.

"Yes, I suppose so." He quirked an inquisitive brow. "Tell me, is there no particular place where you feel you belong?"

"I . . ." Marganna's voice faltered, and she frowned. "Do you know, I don't think I've ever considered that question before. In truth, I can't think of any place I have lived where I really felt as though I belonged."

He was startled. "Surely there has been somewhere?"

"Definitely not the convent," she answered, with a rueful smile. "I hated the regimentation of that place. Then, later, when I went to live with . . . the Stanleys, it was regimentation of a different sort."

"What do you mean?"

"It's difficult to explain. Even though we lived in an elegant house and I loved Lancashire, I never felt as though I was settled there. It was always as if I were biding my time . . . waiting. I guess I felt that way because I was treated like a servant, not like a member of the family." Her gaze flickered to his face and she went on hurriedly. "Of course, I was a servant, so I could expect nothing more, but it seemed an awkward circumstance. I think that to feel you belong someplace, you must have some claim on the property and not be living there through charity. Perhaps it takes being part of a family, and that is why I have the disturbing notion I will never really belong anywhere."

"Nonsense, there's a place for everyone," he stated firmly, though he could not help thinking of his own dilemma. As a lad he'd loved Rathburn Hall, but later, after his family was gone, it had become a desperately lonely place for a man to live. Whenever he came back, he seemed to find himself wandering through the rooms, listening . . . for what? Footsteps, the sound of laughter? No matter—all he ever heard was the sad keening of the wind. Each time he'd stay as long as he could bear the isolation, and then he was away, seeking the clamor and crowds of the cities or the company at Middleham. The only times he truly felt at home were the days like today, when friends and neighbors would overrun the house and gardens, filling the empty, echoing rooms with noise.

"As for this place, I do actually live here part of each year," he went on. "I'm here for the lambing season and again for the shearing. The rest of the time I suspect it is just too quiet for me."

"Still, it seems a waste to leave such a lovely house unoccupied."

"Rathburn Hall is never entirely empty. My household staff remains here at all times, so the place is kept in good repair."

He ushered Marganna into the kitchen, where they found Clovelly Biggins busy issuing orders to a small staff of workers. The room was steamy despite the opened windows, and delicious aromas of baking bread and sizzling meat assailed the senses. Two men were standing watch over a side of beef roasting on a spit in the fireplace, and two young girls were placing freshly baked custard tarts on the wide window ledges to cool.

Pleased to find she was to be a part of the bustling scene, Marganna donned the huge white apron Mrs. Biggins handed her and began paring vegetables. With a grin, Rath seized a custard tart and dashed out of the room, promising to see them later.

Upon his arrival at Rathburn Hall a few hours later, Will Metcalfe found Marganna packing pewter plates into a basket, chattering gaily with one of the kitchen girls. When she saw Will, she favored him with a brilliant smile.

"Will, did you know the meal is to be served outdoors?"

"It's a tradition," he explained. "We northerners don't have much chance to enjoy summer weather, so we take advantage of every opportunity."

"Have ye been up ta the beck?" asked Mrs. Biggins, lifting the lid on a blackened stew pot and releasing a cloud of steam into the room.

"I'm on my way up there now," Will assured her. "I stopped by the kitchen to see if Marganna might like to ride with me. I doubt she has ever seen a sheep washing."

"By all means, lass, go with him. And ye can tell the men we will be ready with their dinner by midafternoon."

Marganna paused in the act of removing her apron. "Shouldn't I stay here to help?"

"Noo, away with ye. Ye've earned a rest."

Will and Marganna crossed the field of gorse and bracken that lay behind the house, their horses carefully picking their way through the underbrush. As they neared the beck, they could hear shouts and laughter, as well as the disgruntled bleating of sheep.

Halting on the rocky bank, they watched as two men standing on the opposite side grasped a pair of sheep and tossed them into the beck hindquarters first.

"They throw them in backwards so they don't splash so badly," Will told her.

Marganna scarcely heard him, for just then she noticed that one of the two men standing in the water was Rathburn, looking quite unlike his usual aloof self. As he leaned forward to collar the animal by grasping a handful of wool on its neck, he glanced up and saw her watching him. He gave a nod that caused his dark hair to tumble carelessly across his forehead, and a broad smile broke over his face, making dimples deepen in each lean cheek. There was a smear of mud along one side of his jaw.

Despite his mild mood earlier, Marganna was startled that he looked so pleased to see her and she couldn't resist smiling back.

Unlike the other men, Rath wore no shirt—indeed, from her vantage point, there was no way to be certain he was wearing anything at all. The dark hair that started at the hollow of his throat and covered his broad chest glistened with droplets of water, drawing her eye. As he vigorously scrubbed first one side of the sheep and then the other, his powerful muscles tensed and stretched beneath his tanned skin.

Watching Rath, Marganna was instantly transported back to the night they had spent together at Nottingham. Her mind filled with the image of his unclothed body outlined by the fire, and she recalled the breadth of his shoulders, his lean hips and softly furred legs. She had spent the night lying next to his splendid masculinity, had awakened to find her head on his chest and her fingers curled against his warm skin. At that time, thank God, she'd had her anger and outrage to insulate her from the reality of the situation. Now there was less to protect her from the effect he was having on her senses. An appealing rosiness suffused her face, and she forced her gaze upward, fixing on the smear of mud along his jaw.

With another quick glance at Marganna, Rath turned the animal in the water, managing to do so by putting one arm under its neck and the other on its loin section while being careful to keep its head above the water.

One of the men standing on the bank observed Marganna's interest and called out, "Give 'er a good dolly, Johnny! Show the lady how it's done!"

The others whooped in glee and Marganna turned to Will, a questioning look on her face.

"Dolly? That's just the term they use for washing," he explained.

"Oh." She blushed faintly. "I wasn't certain what it might mean."

Will threw back his head and laughed loudly, causing all eyes to turn to them. "With these fellows, you can never predict what they might say. Thank the saints they are on their best behavior because they don't know who you are!"

Marganna laughed too, unaware that Rath cast a dark

look in their direction, as if envious of their easy rapport.

When the two sheep in the beck were thoroughly washed, the man working alongside Rath released his, letting it swim to the opposite bank, where other workers waited to lift it from the water and send it on its way. Rath, on the other hand, made a show of raising the animal he held high above his head and striding through the water to set it directly on the dry ground, where it gave an angry bleat and scrambled away. As Rath rose from the water, amid catcalls and encouraging cheers, Marganna was glad to see he was wearing leather chausses, wet and clinging though they were. She meant to look away, but his single garment left little to the imagination, and her disobedient eyes kept surveying the intriguing contours of his body. The sheer beauty of his maleness made her breath catch in her throat and brought to tingling life feelings deep within her. Realizing she was imagining how it would feel to caress the hard, warm planes of his chest and ribs, her fingers tightened on the reins and she glanced around guiltily.

Will gave a low laugh. "If I didn't know better, Marganna, I would think Rath was trying to impress you."

Her face burned as she haughtily tossed her head. "Don't be silly, Will. The man despises me!"

"Hmm—sometimes I wonder."

One of the men lounging near the pen where the last of the unwashed sheep were being kept came forward with a stone jar in his hand. One by one, the workmen passed the jar among themselves, tipping it up and taking long draughts of its contents.

"What's that?" she asked.

"Barley ale," answered Will. "The men need it to sustain them until the washing is done. They start work early in the day and eat nothing until they are finished. All they have to keep them going is an occasional sip of ale."

When it was Rath's turn, he threw back his head, exposing the strong line of throat and jaw as he drank.

With a shout of laughter, his companion jostled his arm, saying, 'Doon't drink it all, Johnny—save soom fer me!"

Obligingly, Rathburn passed the ale to the next man, wiping several drops of amber liquid from his chin with the back of one hand. Just then he looked up to see Marganna watching him, and his gaze locked with hers. With an effort, she tore her eyes away, but not before she saw the gleam of white teeth.

Curse the man! He was fully aware of the virile picture he made. Why was she allowing him the satisfaction of seeing her staring at him? Instinctively she knew he had more than enough power over her as it was, without making him think she found him attractive. That knowledge would be more dangerous in his hands than manacles or chains could ever be.

"Will, I think I should go back to the house and see if Mrs. Biggins needs help."

"Very well. I'll accompany you."

"No need. I can find my way."

Will grinned. "You're still officially a prisoner, my dear, and I would place myself in jeopardy if I permitted you to simply ride away by yourself. Since I care neither to find myself being given a good dolly in the beck nor to explain my lunacy to Rath, I think I should ride with you."

"Oh, very well."

As they rode away, Rathburn stared after them, a self-satisfied smile played about his mouth. He had seen Marganna's covert glances give way to a rapt expression that had lingered as she watched him. It seemed the lass was not as prim and proper as she would have him believe. Interesting thought . . .

"Look oot, yer lordship!" The warning came from the man on the bank, who had just released another sheep into the water, but it came too late. The frightened animal kicked out in agitation, its sharp hooves catching Rathburn in the chest, sending him reeling backwards. Losing his balance, he sat down abruptly in the muddy water, amid raucous shouts of laughter from his comrades.

Marganna heard the laughter and turned back toward the stream. Seeing Rath sprawled in the beck, a look of consternation on his face, she quickly summed up the situation. Knowing Will was looking at her with an amused glint in his eye, she stifled her smug grin, but there was no way she could damp down the bubble of happiness that burst inside her, flooding her with warm pleasure.

A few hours later Lord John Rathburn, now dressed in a woolen doublet and dark hose, leaned casually against the garden wall and watched as the women hurried hither and yon, bringing the food they had prepared from the kitchens to makeshift tables in the yard.

Again and again his eyes strayed to Marganna. She stood at one end of a long table, pouring mugs of ale from a pitcher. Her pretty face seemed to have drawn every eligible man in the crowd, and Rath frowned at their efforts to coax a smile from her lips.

He started to rise, but a large hand fell on his shoulder. "Leave the lass alone, Johnny," said Mrs. Biggins. "Let her have a little fun."

"You're as bad as Will, Clovelly. You seem to forget the girl is in my custody because she is a spy. How do I know she isn't busy gathering information right here before my very eyes?"

"Gooid lord, man, are ye daft? Ye can see fer yerself she is barely speakin' ta any of those young blades. She nods and smiles but rarely does she say onnything. Aw don't think ye need ta worry that state secrets are bein' passed aboot!"

"Mayhap you are right, Clovelly, my love. I've had nothing but a custard tart and an abundance of ale all day—perhaps my brain is addled. What I need is some food!"

The woman laughed heartily. "Then call yer men an' let's eat."

By midafternoon, when the meal was served, the families of the workers who had been assisting with the sheep washing had arrived. The women came carrying dishes of food, calling out greetings to each other and cheerfully admonishing the children, who were darting here and there through the crowd of people, as if giddy with the warm sunshine and fresh air.

Hungry folk piled their platters high with sliced beef and roasted vegetables; with various kinds of fowl basted in wine; with spiced eggs, hot breads, and creamy butter; as well as with fruit, cheese, and tarts reserved for dessert. They washed down the food with more ale or mugs of tart cider; the women drank wine, and the children dipped into pails of cold milk.

Marganna sat on a low stone wall close to the rose-covered house, balancing her dinner plate on her knees, too excited by the hubbub around her to have much interest in eating.

Rarely had she been at such a large gathering, and the few times she had were either at court or at one of the Stanley's country homes. In no other place had she experienced such open friendliness, such camaraderie. Here it seemed everyone knew everyone else; each man was genuinely glad to see his neighbor and pleased to spend time in his company.

"You'd never believe these people were together at another sheep washing just three days ago, would you?" asked Amelyn, settling herself on the wall beside Marganna.

"Why, no. I thought they probably hadn't seen each other for weeks."

"What's more, they will all be together day after tomorrow and several more times before the sheep washings and clippings have ended. Most of our social activities take place in the summer," Amelyn explained. "We have only a short time to store up memories to last us through the long, dark winter months."

Marganna shivered. "It sounds so dull and dreary."

"One gets accustomed to it." Amelyn sighed. "Besides, I'm told winter can be the most tolerable . . . with the right companion."

Marganna regarded the other woman. "I know Rathburn said you scorned your suitors, but isn't there someone a bit more . . . special than the others?"

Amelyn colored slightly. "Yes, there is someone special." She gave a bitter laugh. "But thus far I have failed to win his attention.'' At Marganna's questioning look, Amelyn made a self-deprecating face. ''We are supposed to be in a festive mood today. I will tell you all about my sad affair some other time.''

The promised sharing of secrets between them pleased Marganna. She had never had a friend her own age, and the prospect of getting to know Amelyn better in the long months ahead was delightful.

''Oh, look over there—what are those men doing?''

''They are preparing an obstacle course for a race. Would you like to watch?''

The race proved to be a hilarious diversion. Marganna had never seen grown men leaping hedges, crawling through hollow logs, or swinging across garden pools on ropes strung carelessly over the largest branches of oak trees. She laughed helplessly at their antics, joining the rest of the crowd in noisily cheering them on.

She caught sight of Rath sprinting toward the fluttering ribbon that marked the finish line, his long strides carrying him to certain victory. Suddenly a tiny girl in a scarlet gown broke away from the rest of the onlookers, and in pursuit of her puppy, she dashed right into Rathburn's path. With a comical grimace, Rath leaped high in an attempt to avoid the dog and the little girl, but his feet became entangled in the long streamer that had served as the animal's leash. Losing his balance, he gave a warning shout and somersaulted head over heels, coming to rest right at Marganna's feet. She clapped a hand over her mouth to stifle her giggles.

''You appear to be enjoying yourself,'' Rath commented dryly, getting to his feet and brushing the dust from his clothes.

''I must admit I did not expect the games to be so . . . entertaining,'' she said with a saucy grin. ''Though of course I suppose it is a breach of manners to laugh at *the* Lord Rathburn, even when he's curled in the grass like a hedgehog!''

Rath quickly assured himself the child and her pet were not injured, then turned back to Marganna. ''On the contrary, Clovelly informs me you have worked hard enough to earn a bit of fun. I don't begrudge you your reward, even if it is making sport of a poor, hapless wretch."

Just then one of the men slipped from the rope and landed in the garden pool with a resounding splash. Shouts of merriment echoed all around them, and Rath murmured, "If you will excuse me, I think I should make an attempt to instigate some new, less hazardous game."

Marganna watched as he efficiently organized games and races for the children, getting the youngsters into place with a combination of teasing banter and cheerful pats on rumpled heads. To her amazement, not one of the children seemed afraid of the man she had ofttimes thought an ogre; the boys looked up at him with something akin to awe, carefully aping his every move, and the girls reacted to his attentions with blushes and giggles, a startlingly adult response. The little black-eyed lass whose dog had created havoc tugged at the hem of his doublet until she caught his notice, then thrust a handful of bedraggled bluebells at him. Marganna held her breath, fearing for the child's fragile vanity. What if Rathburn, impatient as always, brushed her aside and hurt her feelings?

But Rathburn, a delighted smile on his face, knelt beside her and humbly accepted the flowers. Tucking them into the loosely laced neck of his shirt, he announced, "In Yorkshire, when your sweetheart gives you flowers, you wear them next to your heart."

The little girl beamed, then planted a loud kiss on his cheek, to the amusement of the onlookers. With a deep chuckle and a whispered comment to her, Rath swung the child onto his shoulder and rose to his feet, wringing a chorus of cries from the other children as they witnessed their companion's enviable position high above the crowd.

Prankishly, Rath extracted a single blossom from his shirt and draped it over one ear. Then, with unerring accuracy he looked directly into Marganna's eyes. A strange sensation rose in her throat as she gazed at the deep-blue flower lying against his bronzed skin and curling black hair. With a devilish grin, he closed one eye in a broad, insolent wink and then, before she could make any response, walked away with a bouncing step that caused the child to squeal in mock terror.

As Marganna stared after him, she realized the whole incident with the children had shown her a side of Rathburn she had not known existed, and that this new image would make it difficult for her to remember the high-handed, overbearing brute she had once thought him to be.

Several glasses of wine had made Marganna giddy, though she had little doubt she was among the most sober at the celebration. The music seemed to grow louder and faster until the dancers were merely colorful blurs as they spun around the lantern-lighted yard. From where she sat in relative darkness Marganna watched with envy, wanting to share the fun but unwilling to risk Rath's disapproval. It had been a most interesting day, and she wanted to enjoy it as long as possible before returning to her confinement.

"Here you are, lurking in dark corners again."

Rathburn loomed before her, large and substantial looking in his dark blue doublet. She could not control a small shiver of alarm at his unexpected appearance.

"I am not lurking," she replied.

"Then why are you sitting in the dark? Why not join the dancing?"

"I am quite content to watch."

"But I would think you would be ill at ease sitting in this particular spot."

"And why is that?"

"Did you not realize you are surrounded by white roses? It seems to me that such a well-known Yorkist symbol would make a rebel like you uneasy, to say the least."

"I hadn't noticed," she declared, tossing her head.

He grinned. "This house is fairly smothered in white roses—do you mean to tell me you didn't even notice them? I thought a spy needed a good eye for detail."

"You know," she drawled, "it seems a pity someone has obviously expended so much time and effort cultivating white roses when surely the day will come that they must be torn away and destroyed by conquering Lancastrians."

"I assure you, the vines will die of old age before that happens."

"Perhaps." Marganna smiled with deceptive sweetness.

"I came to ask you to dance with me," he said abruptly.

"No, thank you—I recall the disastrous occasion of our last dance!"

"Ah, but there's a difference. You cannot have been up to mischief this time. Or perhaps I should examine your bosom just to make certain . . . ?"

"What a horrid . . . !"

Marganna's voice died in a faint squeak as she looked up to see him leaning toward her, his face coming close to hers. A sigh of relief escaped her lips as she realized he was merely leaning forward to pluck a rose from the vine behind her.

"Ouch! Damned thorn!" He sucked at his finger, eyes full of amusement as they met hers. "Sorry if I frightened you, Marganna. Did you think I meant to carry out my threat? Or perhaps you thought I wanted to kiss you."

"Oh! You are the most insulting, the most irritating . . ."

"Shut up or I *will* kiss you," he warned, laughter lingering on the edge of his words. Marganna's mouth snapped shut.

Rath busied himself stripping the thorns from the rose he held; then he thrust it into the low neck of her gown and murmured, "In Yorkshire, when your sweetheart gives you flowers . . ."

He laughed at her expression as he grabbed her hand and pulled her out of the dark and into the kaleidoscope of the dance, despite her mutters of protest.

"Hush," he said close to her ear, his arm going around her waist. "Since I saw no stolen letters tucked into your bosom, this dance should be relatively uneventful. Besides, it is the payment you owe me for a day of freedom."

As her feet began to move in time to the music, Marganna reconsidered the insult she had been about to fling at him. Even she had to admit the day had been worth a great deal; perhaps a lively dance or two with a handsome man was not too harsh a price to pay.

She shook her head—what was the matter with her? She couldn't be falling under his spell too, could she? Was she destined to become like every other simpering female within the radius of his charm? No . . . no! It must be the wine, she told herself . . . it had to be the wine!

Rath whirled her away, then back toward him, his dark head bent close, his smile dazzling in the dim light. Across the yard, Marganna caught sight of Bronwyn watching them, her rage evident in every line of face and body. Since there had been no way to avoid Rath's forced intimacy, she decided an effective means of revenge might be had by stoking Bronwyn's jealousy. With inward glee, she recalled the night in his bedchamber at Nottingham, when her seemingly innocent movements had increased Bronwyn's fury at Rath, and decided he deserved another such setdown.

Marganna favored her partner with a seductive smile, smug in her assumption of Bronwyn's eventual retaliation, and slid one hand up along his sleeve to rest affectionately on his shoulder. In response, Rath's own hands tightened their hold, and he pulled her closer. Her smile never faltered, but Marganna was distinctly relieved when the dance finally drew to a close. She sank low in a curtsey, then looked up to see Rathburn execute a rather unsteady bow.

Why, he's as tipsy as I am! she thought. No wonder he acts so pleased with himself and the world in general . . .

She rose and turned away, so as to discourage any further dancing, and came face to face with Bronwyn, whose eyes were glittering icily.

"You slut!" Bronwyn spat, and in that instant threw the contents of a pitcher of wine into Marganna's face.

A murmur went up from the rest of the dancers, and Rath uttered a quiet but explicit curse.

Despite her shock, Marganna nearly laughed, thinking how her plan had gone awry.

Bronwyn and Rath faced each other, almost comical in their rage.

"What in the blazing hell is wrong with you?" Rath

demanded. Before Bronwyn could reply, he picked up a second pitcher of wine and emptied it over her head.

Bronwyn screamed and stamped her feet, causing several people in the crowd to laugh. Frustrated, she flew at Rath, cursing like the coarsest sailor, and he caught her hands tightly.

"Don't hurt her!" Marganna's guilty knowledge that her ill-considered action had been the cause of the other woman's attack compelled her to speak out against a possible reprisal. "I mean, I'm all right . . . she meant no harm."

"It sure as hell wasn't an accident," Rath pointed out, perplexed by her willingness to see Bronwyn go unpunished.

"Nevertheless there is no need to bully her," Marganna insisted.

At that moment Bronwyn broke free, and her flailing hand struck him in the jaw.

"Bully *her?*" he groaned. Turning to the crowd, he ordered, "Someone take this screaming she-cat away. I'll reward the man who can return her to Middleham without risk to his own or anyone else's life."

"I can handle her, your lordship." The crowd eagerly parted for the huge man who spoke. He stood a full head taller than Rathburn himself, with a wildly curling red-blond beard and hair to match. To Marganna he looked like an ancient Norse deity come to life, even though he was clad in wool and worn leather and had the odor of sheep clinging to him.

Rath shoved Bronwyn toward the man, nodding briskly. "Good luck to you then, Erik Vogelman. No doubt you'll need it."

Before Bronwyn could toss the wet hair out of her eyes, the man had scooped her up and thrown her across his massive shoulder. She kicked and struggled, shrieking all the while, but he merely grinned and started off into the darkness. "I'll wait for you at Middleham," he said with perfect assurance.

Rath watched them go, then turned to Marganna. The

bodice of her gown was soaked with wine, and she was shivering in the night air.

"Come," he said, taking her hand.

"Where are we going?"

"You must get out of those wet clothes," he stated firmly, pulling her toward the house. "There are some things that belonged to my mother."

"No, I don't need to change," she cried. "Just send me back to Middleham—I will be fine."

"Riding three miles in soaking wet clothing would be enough to give you a fever, Marganna. Now come along like a good lass and don't be stubborn."

"You are sending Bronwyn home in wet clothes," she argued as he pushed her through the doorway.

"Yes, but her hot temper will be enough to dry her clothing in no time at all."

Marganna was aware of his guiding hand against the small of her back as they started up a flight of stairs. She moved faster, hoping to avoid his touch, but her effort only caused his hand to trail lower, dangerously close to the curves not entirely concealed by the agitated sway of her long skirts.

"Why do you think Bronwyn did such a thing?" he asked, obviously distracted by the enticing motion of her hips so near his hand.

"I'm certain I have no idea." She brushed a damp strand of hair from her eyes. "Have you ever noticed that you are always pulling me along hallways or up and down flights of stairs?"

"Yes, I've noticed. You must learn not to be so reluctant to follow my lead," he said smoothly, throwing wide a door and ushering her inside the chamber.

He left her standing in the dim light by the open door while he fumbled about lighting several candles.

"Choose something from that wardrobe over there to put on," he suggested, closing the door to the hall.

"Surely you don't intend to . . . to stay here while I undress?" she asked indignantly.

"I will turn my back," he assured her. "Here—I'll

stand by the window and watch the dancing below. At least Brownyn's hysterical outburst did not spoil the fun."

Rath positioned himself by the window, but to his surprise, instead of the dancers below he saw Marganna's reflection, clearly etched on the dark glass. At another time his gentlemanly instincts might have come to the fore, but tonight he was made reckless by the wine and the mood of festivity, so he settled himself to watch with little compunction.

He saw her open the doors to the cupboard and peer inside, sorting twice through the dresses before selecting one. It appeared to be exactly what he would have expected her to choose—one that was plain and unadorned.

She is still stiff-necked about accepting charity, he thought with an inward chuckle.

His lips twitched again as he noticed her taking a swift survey of the room, no doubt searching for a dressing screen. Determining there was none, she darted another look at him before raising her arms to start unhooking the back of her gown. She seemed to manage the top hooks easily, but as she reached the lower fastenings, she began to struggle. She leaned forward at the waist, arms straining backward, and he had a sudden and disturbing view of her rounded breasts, half bared by the gaping bodice. He shifted uncomfortably, his avid eyes feasting on the lovely sight. In his current frame of mind, the view was having a profoundly devastating affect on him, and he suddenly found himself spinning around to look at her.

"Are you having difficulties?" he asked, striding across the floor. "Here, let me help you."

"How did you—?" She gave a small scream and backed away. "You could see me! You were watching me in the window!"

He grinned. "I fully intended to watch the dancers. How was I to know the light in the room behind me would create a perfect mirror?"

"Yet you said nothing! You were just going to stand there and watch me undress! You are despicable . . ."

He could not control a shout of hearty laughter. "Turn

around, Marganna,'' he said, his eyes dancing with devilish light. ''I will assist you.''

''I do not want your assistance,'' she stormed, backing away from him. He followed menacingly.

''You are not exactly in a position to refuse me . . .''

''Of course not!'' she snapped. ''You have made certain my position is untenable, as always. I am constantly being put in situations where I can do nothing!''

With a throaty laugh, Rathburn leaned forward, putting his hand against the wall on either side of her head. ''Without wishing to appear argumentative, I would say that at this moment you are in a very good position for certain things . . . this, for instance.''

The heat of his mouth sent a shock down her spine and into her icy limbs; his lips smothered her cry of alarm.

''Lord,'' he breathed heavily, ''I've wanted to do this all day . . .''

Marganna quickly found there was to be no retreat—behind her was the immovable solidity of the wall and in front the unrelenting press of Rath's body. He seemed to be leaning all his weight against her, subduing her with force while his mouth coaxed a response from her. An almost liquid warmth started at the fusion of her lips with his and insinuated its way throughout her body, leaving her weak and boneless, melting against him.

After a few moments, she twisted her head aside, gasping for air. When she managed to tear her mouth from his, his lips simply continued their assault in another area, sliding along her jaw and across the hollows of her throat.

''Mmm—you taste like wine, Marganna,'' he whispered huskily, greedily kissing the sweet stickiness from her skin. She moaned and stirred, pressing her hands against his chest.

The events of the day had taken their toll, leaving her confused and vulnerable. Every way she turned she had caught glimpses of the man behind Rathburn's usual cold, harsh exterior, and now that undeniably exciting and sensual man was doing bold things to her that—heaven help her!—she welcomed.

His hands dropped from the wall beside her head onto

her shoulders, moving in a slow caress up the column of her neck to cup her face and turn it back toward his. This time his lips had gentled, and their searing heat turned to an enticing warmth, eliciting a response from her despite herself. Suddenly she was no longer aware of the painful crush of his body; she felt as if she were falling, as if her knees could no longer support her weight. Of their own accord, her hands slid around his waist.

His hands moved downward again, massaging her shoulders briefly before pressing lower to the small of her back. As his kiss deepened, Marganna realized that his hands had crept inside the gaping opening at the back of the gown and were exploring her naked skin. She was warmed by the delightful heat of his broad palms and splayed fingers, but she caught her breath as he drew her closer, his fingers inching beneath her arms to stroke the swell of her breasts. Her start of protest caught him by surprise, and she managed to pull away from him.

Passion had made his eyes heavy lidded and languorous; it drew his black brows down in a slashing line and gave his jaw the look of being tightly clenched. His chest rose and fell rapidly with each breath he took, and Marganna could feel the hammer of his heart beneath her restraining hands.

Rath stared down into her face, thinking he could nearly drown in the black pools that were the irises of her eyes. Scarcely any of their usual brown coloring was visible, giving her a frightened and defenseless appearance. Her lips were parted, looking swollen and intensely inviting. He felt inexorably drawn . . .

His lips touched hers, not really kissing but rubbing intimately against them, as if memorizing their shape and taste.

"Why are you doing this?" she moaned.

"Marganna, would you mind terribly if I asked you to shut up and kiss me properly?"

"Yes . . ."

His mouth was gentle no longer, but neither was it savage. It simply took command of hers, forcing her lips to part in submission, to soften beneath his conquest, to traitorously return the kiss he gave. At some point her arms crept upward, and she laced her fingers through his thick black hair. Not wishing to do so but unable to prevent herself, Marganna molded her body to his, fitting perfectly against his muscular form.

A sudden knocking at the door was followed by Mrs. Biggins' strident voice. "Johnny lad, there's a message fer ye."

Rath found his voice. "Just a minute, Clovelly."

He released Marganna and, stepping away with a wry expression, straightened her gown, which had fallen over one shoulder. He strode to the door, opening it only slightly so the curious Mrs. Biggins would not see Marganna's disheveled appearance.

Slowly regaining her sanity, Marganna caught sight of herself in the mirror and was shocked. She looked a sight, with her gown twisted and her hair straggling down around her face. What had she been thinking of? How could she have allowed such a thing to happen?

She was only vaguely aware of the low hum of voices, catching just a word here and there. When Rath had closed the door and returned to her side, he, too, seemed perturbed.

For a moment he simply stared down at her without speaking, looking nothing like his usual composed self. Finally, running a careless hand through his hair that left it untidy, he ground out a brief explanation about having to ride to a neighboring estate on business.

"Damn! I don't want to leave you like this, Marganna. It's important or I wouldn't go." He heaved an uneven sigh. "As it is, I suppose I shall have to trust Will to see you safely back to Middleham."

She nodded in agreement. Rath took her hands and pressed them briefly. "Change your clothes, and I'll go find Will. I'll see you in the morning." He brushed a whisper of a kiss on her lips. "Good night."

"Good night," she answered faintly, watching as he left the chamber.

She stooped to retrieve the blue gown she had dropped earlier, and something lying on the carpet caught her eye. With a pang of emotion, she saw that it was the white rose Rath had tucked into her bodice in the garden.

Chapter 9

Hands gripping the edge of the wall along the parapet walk, Marganna lifted her face to the wind, letting it swirl her hair around her head.

Amelyn, her fair tresses bound up in a silken scarf, stood close by, pointing out landmarks. She had spent the morning showing Marganna the kitchens and laundry, where she was to be allowed to lend a hand whenever she wished, and had ended their time together by taking her up to the walkway at the height of the keep, so she might see the magnificent view of Wensleydale spread out below them.

"I never grow tired of looking at this sight," Amelyn said, gesturing toward the countryside beyond Middleham. "The moors are ever changing. Each season has its own beauty."

"It's different from the parts of England where I have lived," observed Marganna, letting her gaze drift slowly along the contours of the barren hill behind the castle. "Do you think I will ever grow used to it?"

"Of course! You just have to give it a little time. It was strange to me, too, when I first came here. Now I cannot imagine living anywhere else."

"Then you are fortunate, Amelyn. It must be nice to have that kind of contentment."

Amelyn's small laugh was tinged with bitterness. "Do I seem content to you?"

"Well . . . yes." Marganna looked at her in surprise. "I mean, you are needed here—everyone likes and respects you . . ."

"But I'm only a female, remember. That means I'm expected to marry, and if I do, chances are I will have to leave Middleham."

"And you don't think you would be happy anywhere else?"

"This is my home. This is where I want to stay. Of course I couldn't be happy elsewhere."

"Why don't you marry someone from Middleham then?"

Amelyn chipped at the lichen on the stone wall with a shapely fingernail. "A clever solution, Marganna, but one not easily accomplished. Most of the suitable unmarried men here are either too young or too old for me."

"What about Lord Rathburn?" Marganna asked casually.

Amelyn sighed. "You must think me daring! How could I set my cap for one in such a lofty position?" She raised her eyes. "Could you be so bold?"

"What do you mean?"

"Have you any interest in the handsome lord, Marganna?"

"None whatsoever! The man is a beast and has certainly made no secret of his dislike for me. He has only contempt for what he thinks I am."

"A spy?"

"Yes, a spy. And a traitor."

Amelyn gave a short laugh. "You sound so indignant, but I saw him tucking that rose into your bodice last night. That looked anything but innocent." A sly smile lifted the corners of her mouth. "And tell me, when the two of you disappeared upstairs, why were you gone so long?"

"Oh, Amelyn, must you believe the worst?" Marganna turned away to study the landscape in the opposite direction.

How could she convince anyone of her innocence when she could feel the heat of a guilty blush staining her cheeks? She lifted her face to the cooling wind, but the burning sensation beneath her skin reminded her of the warmth of Rath's caressing hands.

The worst part, she reminded herself, was the distorted

way she had begun to view Lord John Rathburn. Well, that, at least, was over. Any misconceptions she might have had that they could attempt a harmonious relationship had ended abruptly at breakfast that morning. Coming face to face with him, she had been unable to conceal her confusion, but when she greeted him with a tentative smile, he had frowned and turned away, rudely ignoring her and starting a conversation with the huge man who had volunteered to escort Bronwyn home from Rathburn Hall.

Even now a wave of shame threatened to engulf her. She could not recall ever having been so humiliated—not even at Nottingham when he had wildly accused her of being a spy. She would never know how many people in the great hall had witnessed the curt dismissal. She did not want to know! But she had already promised herself it would never happen again. It would be a winter's day in Hades before she so much as looked at the man again.

"Good heavens, Marganna," Amelyn was saying. "Where is your mind? I have asked you the same question twice and I don't believe you even heard me."

"Oh! I'm sorry . . . what were you saying?"

"I asked if you did not agree that Rath is a handsome figure of a man. I mean, see how he sits his horse."

Marganna's eyes followed Amelyn's gesture, and she was shocked to find the subject of her ire in the courtyard below, just swinging onto the back of his spirited steed. As he did so, he raised his face toward them, and across the distance, his gaze seemed to lock with Marganna's. This time it was she who deliberately turned away.

A disgruntled Lord Rathburn stirred uneasily in the saddle as he thought of his meeting with Marganna that morning. He hoped she would never know the effort it had cost him to turn away from the welcome in her brown eyes, from the smile trembling on lips he so vividly recalled kissing. His rebuff had brought such a stricken look to her face that it had been almost more than he could stand, and it had required a supreme physical effort to keep himself from taking her into his arms then and there. But Jesus Christ and all the saints, he must not ignore the reality of what she was—a spy. He could not permit such a thing ever to happen again!

Now, seeing Marganna standing high above him on the parapet, her hair streaming in the wind, he felt the same heady effect he'd attributed to the barley ale he'd drunk at the sheep washing. And when she so pointedly turned her back on him, something in his chest tightened painfully, and he fought the urge to leap off his horse, storm up the stairs to the walkway, and make her listen to reason.

Instead Rath resolutely guided his horse onto the narrow roadway leading across the moors to Aysgarth Falls and the isolated manor house of Nappa Hall, determined to confine his thoughts to the business he had to attend to this morning.

Coor-lee!

The eerie cry echoed across the loneliness of the wild moor as a pair of curlews wheeled overhead.

"What a melancholy cry those birds have," Marganna said. "They sound so sad."

Will, riding beside her, nodded as the double-noted cry trilled upward again. "I've always thought that sound added to the mystery of the moorland. It's such a beautiful, haunting cry."

"Like some poor lost soul, alone and afraid." She shivered. "How much farther to Aysgarth Falls?"

"Don't worry, they're not far." Will grinned. "I don't believe you like the moors much, do you?"

"They're so empty. There's nothing here—no people, no animals, no trees—nothing."

"Now, that's where a true Yorkshireman would say you are wrong, my dear. Completely wrong. Why, the moors are anything but empty."

"But I see nothing except gorse and bracken and the occasional wind-warped bush."

"That's because you haven't learned the proper way to observe," he informed her. "You must look at them differently than you would look at, say, a Staffordshire meadow. The birds and animals that live here are designed to blend with the land for their own protection. Just because you can't see them doesn't mean they don't exist. And if you would carefully examine an acre of this ground, you'd find as many wildflowers as—'' He broke off in mid-sentence to glance behind him. Marganna heard the thudding echo of hooves against the boggy grass and turned to look also.

Head held high, Bronwyn was rapidly approaching. When she drew closer, Marganna could clearly see the challenging light in the woman's dark eyes.

"What a surprise to meet up with you, Bronwyn,'' Will said dryly.

"I saw you two leave the castle. I thought it might be interesting to learn where you are going and why you sought the privacy of the moors.''

"I'm taking Marganna to Aysgarth Falls, if you must know. It's a beautiful place, and I thought she might enjoy seeing it.''

"Then this is only an innocent sightseeing jaunt?'' Bronwyn jeered.

"That's correct, '' Will answered quietly.

"In that event, you won't mind if I accompany you, surely. Indeed, it has been an age since I have seen the falls.''

Eventually they left the plain to enter the shade of an unexpected forest. The Ure, heretofore a quiet, unspectacular river, now gathered force for its suicidal leap into a deep, rocky gorge where it would froth and foam over a series of falls. As they passed an ancient church with a graveyard of crooked, moss-covered headstones, they began to hear the roar of water.

Will led the way onto a packhorse bridge that spanned the river, pausing to let Marganna have her first view of the falls.

"To the left are the upper falls,'' he shouted above the noise of the water. "Down below are the middle and lower.''

It seemed to Marganna the river had gone mad, twisting and turning, flinging itself over the shelves of rock to spume up through jagged crevices, the glistening water drops looking like handfuls of diamonds tossed into the air. Below them the river was churned into milky whiteness, contrasting with the deep green of the trees that lined the banks.

She and Bronwyn followed Will as he crossed the bridge and turned onto a path that led upward toward the top terrace of the falls. As the path leveled out, they could see a horse standing in the shallow water along the edge of the river, its rider sitting motionless as if lost in thought.

Rathburn heard their approach and looked up, startled not only to be disturbed in such a lonely place but equally surprised to find himself looking into the eyes of the very woman about whom he'd been thinking. His mouth firmed in anger, and he wrenched his gaze away from Marganna to turn on Will.

"What in God's name are you doing *here?*" he asked through clenched teeth.

"It was my intention to show Marganna the falls," Will answered evenly. "I had no plans to go farther."

"Use your head, Will! You never used to be such a dunce."

"I'm growing weary of your everlasting temper, Rath," Will snapped, his freckles standing out against his pale skin.

"And I'm growing weary of your everlasting carelessness," Rath countered.

"*My* carelessness? Oh, hellfire and damnation!" Will swore. "What about you? How was I to know you would be here instead of at—"

The two men stared at each other for a long moment; then Rathburn spurred his horse forward onto the bank. He and Will engaged in a low conversation, at the close of which, without explanation or farewell, Rath crossed the bridge and rode out of sight.

"I hope you will excuse Rath," Will said a little too heartily. "He had . . . er, business to take care of and had to be on his way. He'll probably join us for the return to Middleham."

Marganna's curiosity was piqued, but because she was

aware of the black mood that had fallen on Bronwyn, she said nothing. Rath, in his displeasure at seeing them, had neglected to spare her even a word. It was almost certainly not the way a man would treat his paramour if all was well between them.

When Will suggested a walk around the falls, Marganna was glad to accept and even more glad when Bronwyn gloomily announced she would wait for them there. They tethered the horses at the water's edge and left her reclining against a small, sun-splashed boulder.

When they returned more than an hour later, Bronwyn was not in sight, though her horse was still with the others.

"She must have decided to go for a walk after all," Will said, dropping onto the grass.

Feeling too restless to join him, Marganna stood tossing a handful of pebbles into the water, then wandered aimlessly along the bank.

She thought the falls were beautiful, by far the prettiest place she had seen since coming to Yorkshire. She loved the sight of shadowy green woods and the roar of turbulent waters.

Standing on the edge of the riverbank, she watched the clear, peat-colored water swirl past, rippling shallowly over rounded stones. After the long walk she had taken with Will, she was uncomfortably warm in the riding dress she wore, and the water suddenly looked coolly inviting.

Marganna sat down on the grassy bank and slipped off the hose and boots she was wearing. Rising, she cast a glance in Will's direction. He was barely visible through the curtain of leaves as he leaned against a tree trunk, eyes shut as if taking a nap, so she hitched up her skirts and stepped carefully into the water.

She could not control a shocked gasp as the icy water closed around her ankles, but after a moment she grew used to the chill and took a few tentative steps. The stones felt cold and smooth beneath her feet, but they were slippery with moss, so she moved cautiously.

Finding such simple pleasure in her surroundings was cheering, and it freed her mind from the desolation that had gripped it all morning. Thinking about it now, she realized Rath's actions the night before had undoubtedly been the result of too much wine and not an indication of his true feelings for her as she had first thought.

It is no wonder he acted the way he had in the great hall this morning, she mused—he must have been worried that I had taken his drunken wooing seriously!

Idly she kicked at the water, making small, angry splashes.

He needn't have worried, she fumed silently.

As she turned and started back toward the bank, she was surprised to see Bronwyn standing nearby watching her.

"What are you doing?" the woman called out.

Marganna moved closer to the river's edge. The very fact that Bronwyn had deigned to speak after the night before seemed a good sign. "I'm cooling off after my long walk with Will."

"You'd better not go out that far again," Bronwyn said warningly.

"Why not? Surely there can be no harm in it."

"Rath wouldn't like it."

"What objection could he possibly have?"

"Perhaps he would fear for your safety," Bronwyn replied with a slight sneer. "He does seem to regard you highly."

"You're mistaken about that," Marganna said quietly.

"Am I?"

"Yes, you are. There is nothing between Lord Rathburn and myself. And I would like to explain to you about last night—about what you thought you saw."

Bronwyn laughed nastily. "There is nothing to explain. And don't, for one minute, think I regretted pouring that wine over your head."

"I saw you watching us dance," Marganna confessed, "and I thought it might be interesting to try to make you angry at Rath." She shrugged, half smiling. "I realize it sounds ridiculous now, but at the time I deemed it a worthy idea. How was I to know you would see fit to punish me instead of your—instead of Rathburn?"

"This morning Rath spoke to me in a way he never has before," Bronwyn informed her, her lovely face taking on a morose expression. "He told me he has no further interest in me. I didn't believe him at first, but now I know he meant it. You saw how he treated me when we came upon him at the falls. He wouldn't even look at me! I should have known last night when he sent me away with that strutting, ill-bred Norseman."

"Whatever Rath told you can have nothing to do with me," Marganna insisted.

"Oh, but it does. Ever since Nottingham, he has acted like a besotted fool. I wish he had never seen you."

"I'm sorry that—"

"No, don't feel sorry for me!" Bronwyn suddenly raged. "I don't need your pity. Save it for yourself. He may want you now, but you will never make him love you."

"That is not my intention," cried Marganna. "I could explain, if only you would listen to me."

"I pity you if you think he will treat you differently than any of his other women. Once you have given in to him, he will soon grow bored and seek another. It is always that way."

Marganna's arguments died quickly. Stunned by Bronwyn's revelation of Rath as a womanizer, and smarting under the dismal prediction of his faithlessness, she turned her back and began wading into the river again. She couldn't bear to have the woman see how much those words had hurt her.

Now her arguments were turned inward as she tried to tell herself Bronwyn's taunt meant nothing. She had already analyzed Rathburn's affections and her response to them, hadn't she? Why should she care if he had bedded every woman in the north of England?

She scrambled over the rocks, skirts sodden and dragging, and behind her she could hear Bronwyn's voice.

"Don't be stupid—come back here!"

She held her head a little higher, fastening her gaze on the line of trees on the opposite bank. She would rather cross the entire river than have to turn back and face Bronwyn.

A movement downriver caught her eye, and she glanced up to see Rath ride onto the stone bridge. As soon as he saw her, he reined in his stallion and stood in the stirrups, shouting. His words lost in the noise of the falls, he began pointing emphatically. Marganna looked over her shoulder to see Bronwyn, knee-deep in the river and coming after her.

A frisson of fear traced its way down Marganna's spine. Was Rath warning her she was in danger? Did he think Bronwyn meant to harm her?

Another look at the determination on Bronwyn's face convinced her, and she began to splash through the water as fast as she could.

"Stop, Marganna!" Bronwyn cried. "Wait for me!"

"No!" In her haste, Marganna slipped on a mossy rock and with a cry fell full length into the water. The river closed over her, wrapping her in its chilly depths. She knew she was being dragged farther from shore by the swift current.

She must have stepped into a deep pool, because she could no longer touch bottom; the current seized her and whirled her along, plunging her beneath the surface again and again.

A loud roaring drummed in her head, and her chest began to ache. In desperation she struck out with hands and feet, attempting to swim. The force of the current catapulted her body backward, and her last moment of conscious thought was of blinding pain as her head struck a rock. With a sigh, she slipped beneath the surface and was carried downstream like a bundle of rags.

Bronwyn suffered a long moment of indecision. She could not deny feeling a primal impulse to see her enemy destroyed, yet she knew Marganna had never deliberately harmed her.

Surprised at herself for choosing to react in a purely emotional way, Bronwyn lunged through the water and reached for Marganna. Her fingers tangled in the streaming russet hair, gripping it fiercely.

Rath had leaped from his horse to dive into the churning river, and now, as he swam toward them, Bronwyn allowed herself to float with the current, keeping Marganna's head above water until he could reach them.

"Hold on," shouted Rath as he began towing both women out of the deeper water. As soon as his feet struck bottom, he lifted Marganna into his arms and began striding to shore. Will, having been roused by Rath's shouts, waded out to assist Bronwyn.

When they reached the grassy bank, Rath knelt with Marganna in his arms. Her head lolled back, a bruise darkening one side of her temple. He leaned forward and caught the faint sound of her ragged breathing; his relief was evident in his bowed head and slumped shoulders. When he looked up again, his face was gray, with lines etched into his forehead.

"Thank God you got to her, Bronwyn! She would have drowned before I could reach her."

Uneasy at his fervent praise, Bronwyn shrugged. "I tried to stop her. I told her not to go out any farther."

"I, too, motioned for her to go back. That was our mistake. This independent wench doesn't like to be told what to do." His gaze softened as he looked down at Marganna's still face. "The little fool . . ."

Will and Bronwyn exchanged glances of half-amused chagrin, but in that instant Rath's mood changed abruptly.

"She may be badly hurt," he said briskly. "I'm going to take her to Nappa Hall where there's a physician."

"Do you want me to go with you?" asked Will.

"No, just take Bronwyn back to Middleham."

Will held the unmoving Marganna until Rath was seated on his stallion, then gently lifted her up to him. Rath cradled her against his chest, one arm around her protectively.

"She'll be fine," Will assured him.

"I hope you're right."

Rath took one more look at Marganna's unnaturally pale face, then spurred his horse, taking the track to Nappa Hall from which he had so recently come.

* * *

Lord Rathburn stirred restlessly, looking at the two other men in the room. James Metcalfe, master of Nappa Hall, jumped to his feet to refill his guests' brandy glasses.

"I don't need any more to drink," Rath protested, but Metcalfe splashed a good measure into the glass anyway.

"Doctor's orders," he said, smiling.

The doctor himself, a thin, dapper man in a purple velvet doublet, stood warming his backside at the fire. "That's right, my lord. A good tot will ward off the chill of the night."

Rathburn rose and strode across the room to look out the long windows. Evening had fallen. "How long do you think Marganna will sleep, Doctor? It will soon be too late to travel back to Middleham tonight."

"Why not stay here, Rath?" Metcalfe suggested. "We've plenty of room, and I doubt the girl will be in any condition to be moved for a while."

"Yes, why not stay here? It would be for the best," the doctor agreed. "She suffered a nasty blow, but it's nothing that can't be set right with proper rest. Why not spend the night and go back in the morning? I assure you, she will feel more up to the journey after a good night's sleep."

"I don't know . . ."

"Perhaps the prospect of a good meal will decide you," said Metcalfe. "I happen to employ one of the best cooks in the north country."

"Damnation, James, you know who this woman is. Surely it would not be wise to keep her here."

"She is unconscious, Rath. What harm could she possibly do?"

"That's just it—who knows?" He looked from one man to the other and finally shrugged. "Oh, very well, if you think it will be all right. But I intend to look in on her before dinner all the same."

Marganna lay in a wide bed, her face nearly as colorless as the white silk pillows beneath her head. Alarmed at her pallor, Rath crossed the room quickly and sat on the edge of the bed. With relief, he could hear her even breathing and see the faint flutter of her eyelids.

Moaning softly, Marganna stirred and opened her eyes, seeing him through a haze. "Bronwyn?" she whispered sleepily.

"She saved your life."

Her eyes widened. "She wasn't . . . trying to kill me?"

"Good Lord, no," Rath exclaimed softly. "Is that what you thought?"

He reached out to take her hand. Finding it cold, he began pressing her fingers to warm them. "You're safe now—I'll be with you."

A smile lifted the corners of her mouth before she surrendered once again to oblivion.

Tenderly he brushed a stray curl from her cheek, letting his hand move downward to stroke her jaw with his thumb. He felt a heaviness in the vicinity of his chest, a heaviness that had begun the instant he saw Marganna lying injured in the shallow water of the falls. He had never known such helplessness or fear. He never wanted to experience it again.

He heaved a weary sigh. It was no good telling himself he'd felt that way because she looked so young and defenseless, or because she had been put into his care, making him responsible for her. No, he knew it went far beyond that . . . but just how far, he was not yet prepared to estimate.

Twenty minutes later, when the doctor came to tell him they were waiting dinner, Rath was still sitting by her side, her hand clasped tightly in his.

Early morning sunshine streamed into the room, touching Marganna with its warmth. She yawned and stretched her arms and legs.

Good heavens, why was she so stiff and sore?

Slowly she opened her eyes and found herself looking at cream-colored bed hangings instead of her own hunter's green ones.

Where am I? she thought, sitting up in bed. The rapid movement made her head throb, and she winced in pain. What has happened to me?

As she held her aching head, memories of the previous

afternoon began to return—Bronwyn, the river, Rath's anger.

Unexpectedly she heard the shuffling of feet and a faint whisper, followed by a barely stifled giggle.

"Who's there?" she said, finding it agonizing to turn her head.

The room grew silent, but she sensed the presence of someone other than herself.

"If you don't show yourself right now, I will start screaming," she warned.

"Oh, please, miss, don't do that!" A blond head appeared over the back of a striped couch set in front of the windows.

It was followed immediately by another head, this one topped with a tousled mop of dark brown hair. Two round, dark eyes pleaded with her. "If you tell on us, we will be in sixty sorts of trouble!"

"Honestly, we didn't mean any harm."

Marganna quelled a smile. "Who are you?" she asked sternly. "Come out from behind that couch."

She found herself confronting two boys, one about thirteen years old, the other—the dark-haired one—about ten. Suddenly she could not hold back her smile, and the boys, taking it as a hopeful sign, beamed back at her.

Marganna patted the edge of the bed. "Come, sit down and tell me who you are."

The boys advanced readily, though the older one said, "I am sorry, but we are not allowed to tell our names to strangers."

As she studied the lads' patrician features, she found herself doubting that two such self-assured children could have grown up in this isolated part of the country. There was a certain worldliness about them, a hint of sophistication—and not a trace of broad Yorkshire accent.

"Well, that's all right. I understand."

And indeed it was all right, for Marganna had begun to suspect she had just met Edward and Dickon—the missing Plantagenet princes.

Chapter 10

"You won't tell anyone we came into your room, will you?" the dark-haired younger boy asked, sitting on the edge of the bed and gazing up at Marganna with earnest hazel eyes.

"No, not if you don't want me to," she answered.

The older boy breathed a sigh of relief. "We're supposed to remain out of sight when strangers visit Nappa Hall, but we looked out the window yesterday afternoon and saw Lord Rathburn carrying you into the house, and I'm afraid we let our curiosity get the better of us."

"We thought you were drowned," exclaimed his brother.

Marganna had to laugh. "I very nearly was."

"What happened?" they asked in unison.

"It's a long and involved story," she replied. "Let's just say I fell into the river."

"But I distinctly heard Rathburn telling Master Metcalfe that the ballad singer, Bronwyn, had to save you," said the older boy, a puzzled look on his face. "Isn't she his courtesan?"

"Oh!" Marganna was astonished. The lad was such a mixture of childishness and maturity that he was disconcerting.

"I should think she would rather drown you. Isn't she jealous because you are so pretty?" The younger child grinned widely enough to display gaps between his front teeth.

"Dickon! One doesn't speak to a lady in that manner," scolded his brother.

"You forgot and called me by my name. Now she knows who I am."

Marganna laid a hand on his shoulder and smiled gently. "Please, I have a confession to make. I think I know who you are without being told. You are Richard, and your older brother is Edward. Am I correct?"

"Did our uncle send you?" demanded Edward warily.

"No, not really. I . . . well, I'm a guest at Middleham for a while . . . and of course I have heard about the two of you. As soon as I saw you, I knew who you must be."

"Then you may call us Ned and Dickon, if you like," spoke up Richard. "My brother used to be King Edward V. Now he's just plain Edward, but I don't think he minds, do you, Ned?"

"Of course not. And anyway, I still retain a number of titles—not that I plan to use any of them."

"Well, I'm the Duke of York," his brother said proudly, "and I plan to use that. I like the sound of it!"

Again Marganna's laugh rang out, her headache forgotten. They were delightful!

"Won't you tell us your name?" queried Edward.

"Certainly; it's Marganna."

"You know, Marganna, you don't sound much like the people here in Yorkshire," Dickon commented. "Where do you come from?"

"I'm from the south," she said, wondering just how much information she should divulge. "Like the two of you."

"Oh, we consider ourselves Yorkshiremen now," Edward told her. "Like our uncle Richard and Lord Rathburn."

"Then you don't miss your old home?"

"Not so much anymore. Oh, sometimes it would be nice to see our mother, but as long as she is surrounded by the Woodvilles, we know our uncle will not allow it."

"We miss our sisters sometimes," Ned said, "though they are mostly babies, except for Bess and Cecily. And anyway, we may get to see them soon. Uncle is having them brought north to the castle at Sheriff Hutton, and as soon as the danger is past, we will get to live with them again."

"The danger?"

"Have you not heard of Henry Tudor?" Edward asked.

"He is a very bad man," Dickon informed her, "who wants to take the throne away from our uncle. He's going to sail to England from France and start a war."

"I see." Marganna was completely at a loss for words. It would seem the Yorkists had done a thorough job with the two young princes.

"Would you care to play a game?" Dickon was asking. "We know several good ones."

A few minutes later, engrossed in their merriment, none of the three heard the door opening. Marganna had just thrown herself back against the bed cushions, laughing heartily, when she looked up and saw Rathburn scowling at her, his face suffused with rage.

"Oh! Lord Rathburn!" Edward choked and sat down abruptly in a nearby chair.

Dickon rolled his eyes at his brother and half whispered, "Uh-oh. Now we're in for it."

"What is the meaning of this, Marganna?" Rathburn demanded in clipped, icy tones.

"Well, I . . . we . . ."

"It's not her fault, sir," Edward said quickly. "We're the ones who came in here."

"We wanted to see if she was really drowned," Dickon added.

Rath clapped a hand to his forehead and turned away. "Damnation!" He began pacing up and down the length of the room. "Damnation!"

"If you would only listen to us," Marganna began. Her low voice caused Rathburn to spin around to face her. He was obviously waiting to hear what she had to say, so she nervously cleared her throat and went on. "Really, no harm has been done . . ."

"No harm!" he ranted. "No harm! Hell, no—I just neatly arranged for you to meet the objects of your search. Now all I have to do is furnish you with a horse and send you on your way back to London."

"Sarcasm won't help."

"We don't understand, Lord Rathburn—what has happened?" Edward looked from one to the other with a perplexed expression.

"We like Marganna," Dickon said stoutly. "You aren't angry with us for talking to her, are you?"

Rathburn's struggle to gain control of his temper was plainly visible on his face. Finally he went down on one knee beside the boy and, putting an arm around his shoulders, drew him close. "You remember our long talks about danger, don't you, Dickon? Well, this is the sort of thing I meant. Talking to a stranger isn't wise, even if he or she is someone you judge to be harmless. Marganna, for instance—" He cast a scorching glance her way. "For all you know, she might be a spy, one of Tudor's agents."

"Marganna?" Laughter trembled on the boy's lips.

"Yes, Marganna. You have no way of knowing, Dickon, and that is why we have asked you to be extremely cautious. You should never have come into this room."

"Then you are angry with us?" Edward leaned forward in the chair, hands loosely clasped.

"Yes, I'm afraid I am," Rath answered slowly. "But I am also angry with myself for letting my worry over this woman make me neglect my duty to you. And I'm angry with Will for ever bringing her so close to Nappa Hall."

"You're angry at everybody, aren't you?" Young Richard tried unsuccessfully to hide a grin, and when his wide eyes met Marganna's, she could not stifle a small chuckle.

"I'm glad you think this is so humorous, Marganna." Rathburn got to his feet. "Perhaps you haven't realized what this morning's events mean to your own situation."

"I suppose now you must chain me in—"

"We'll discuss it later," he ground out through clenched teeth. "Right now, you had best get dressed while I take the boys belowstairs and have a talk with James. He is not going to be pleased."

"We truly meant no harm," Edward repeated. "Good-bye, Marganna. I hope we will meet again soon."

"So do I, Ned. Good-bye, Dickon."

Rath was leading the way from the room, shoulders slumped as if he regretted the task before him.

Dickon turned to flash her one last smile. "I'll wager Master Metcalfe is going to be furious with us!" he said, as if anticipating the excitement.

Marganna was uncomfortably aware of the man seated behind her on the horse. He maintained such a stony silence that at first she wondered if the reason he had refused James Metcalfe's offer of a second horse was because he had devised a plan for disposing of her on the journey back to Middleham. Perhaps he would drop her over the edge of some steep ravine or toss her into one of the bottomless bogs on the moor. Uneasily she realized that most of his immediate problems could effectively be solved in such a way.

And yet the strong arm he had around her waist would tighten when the track grew rough in what she might have thought was a protective way had she not known how angry he was. She elected to sit as quietly as possible, doing or saying nothing to antagonize him further.

As they caught their first glimpse of Middleham's towers, Rathburn broke the silence between them.

"I'd like to walk for awhile, Marganna. We must talk about what has happened."

She nodded, breathing a little more freely. The very incongruity of her earlier thoughts and the certainty that he would not attempt to murder her this close to the castle brought a smile to her lips.

"It would be wiser if you did not openly display amusement over this latest turn of events," Rath warned, lifting her from the horse.

"If you must know," she said, unable to resist teasing him, "since we left Nappa Hall, I've been thinking you intended to do away with me as we crossed the moor. Now, within sight of Middleham, I feel relieved." She began walking slowly, leaving him to gather the reins and follow.

"And yet you might be wiser to continue to mistrust me," he said softly. "Since you came into my life, I must confess, I have entertained several satisfactory plans for ridding myself of you and the problems you represent."

She looked sideways at him, her eyes amused. His words seemed to be inspired more by frustration than by anger.

"What kind of plans? Did you consider tying a weight around my neck and throwing me in the moat?"

"I considered it."

"And what about leaving me to starve in the dungeons?"

"All that and more," he growled, though his tone was lighter. "Of course, I abandoned that plan out of pity for the rats . . ."

"Don't tell me," she said. "You thought I would talk them to death, didn't you?"

"Something like that." He heaved a sigh. "Believe me, there were times when it would have been a pleasure to drop you from the highest tower at Middleham." He stopped short, causing her to check her own step.

"On the other hand, you will never know how many times I have given thanks that Richard chose to save your troublesome neck from the executioner."

Gently he encircled the base of her throat with hands that in no way resembled the soft, pampered ones of an aristocrat. Hard and work roughened, they slid slowly along the smooth contours of her skin, the thumbs pressing upward in a caressing motion. The ends of the leather reins he still held in one hand trailed over her shoulder and neck, tickling lightly, playfully.

"And now I must be eternally grateful to Bronwyn for preventing your death yesterday. I lived through a nightmare, knowing I couldn't get to you in time."

Marganna could not control the spark that leaped within her, and she quickly lowered her lashes, not wishing to let him see her reaction to his words, his touch. She heard a deep sigh of exasperation and felt his thumbs beneath her jaw, lifting her face.

"Damn you, Marganna," he muttered, "you will drive me insane." In the next instant, he was kissing her, his mouth sweetly gentle as it explored hers. His hands slipped to her shoulders, cupping them and holding her tightly against him. He kissed her forehead and eyelids, then dropped a second soft kiss on her mouth.

After a moment, he gripped her upper arms and held her away from him. "We seem to have had very little discussion of the problem after all," he said with a groan and a laugh. "You've managed to distract me again. Oh, Marganna, if your heart is black, damn me for a weak-willed schoolboy who can't see past the cinnamon spice of your eyes." He paused for another kiss. "And if your words are evil lies, damn me for a fool who believes them because they are spoken by the most tempting mouth I've ever seen." He allowed himself to be tempted once again, then hugged her fiercely. "Why was it my fate ever to lay eyes on you? If you had been a man, if I'd crossed swords with you in battle, I'd have had no trouble knowing exactly how to deal with you. As it is, I don't know what I am going to do."

Marganna's eyes widened, and her heart began to flutter alarmingly. Never had she expected such an admission from him.

Rath took a few steps away from her, then turned back. "The worst of it is, I can't understand what there is about you that makes you different from other women. I've known many who were more beautiful . . . certainly more agreeable. Why should my life be thrown into turmoil by a skinny spinster with doubtful political associations? It makes no sense whatsoever!"

She knew she should be feeling insulted, but for some reason his words warmed her like the sweetest flattery.

"I am not a skinny spinster," she protested halfheartedly.

He pretended to study her. "Well, perhaps not skinny, but you can't deny your political associations."

"Please, may I say something?" she ventured in a more serious voice.

"Have I ever yet been able to prevent you from speaking your mind?"

She ignored the barb. "If you are worried that I might

betray the princes, I can assure you I have no intention of doing so."

"Oh, naturally not!"

"No, I mean it," she insisted. "After all, it would gain me nothing to reveal their whereabouts to anyone at Middleham."

"But what if your noble swain FitzClinton were to appear at the castle gates again? Surely you could not resist telling him."

"You know very well I will not be allowed to speak to FitzClinton or anyone else outside the castle walls. It shouldn't be necessary for you to worry about that. What I am saying is that if it will ease your mind, I give you my word I will say nothing to anyone inside the castle. Am I right in assuming there are very few who know where Edward and Dickon are being kept?"

"Yes—Will, Clovelly, myself . . . and a few of the men at arms. The Metcalfe family and their half-dozen retainers are the only others who are privy to the king's plan to protect his nephews . . ."

"Do you really believe he is trying to protect them by shutting them up in some isolated manor house?"

"They aren't shut up. They go about freely unless there are strangers in the area—and with the several Metcalfe children for companionship, you needn't think they are lonely."

"If they are not lonely, why did they risk so much to talk to me?"

"Probably because you were someone different and intriguing. After all, Dickon himself said they thought you were drowned." Rath permitted himself a smile. "No doubt they had never seen such a wet, bedraggled female."

"While that may be true, it has nothing to do with my proposal. Are you going to accept my word that I will not reveal your secret?"

"I don't know whether or not you can be trusted."

"You northerners are not the only ones with honor. I can keep my word as well as any man."

He eyed her appraisingly. "All right, I'll give you the

chance to prove it. If you say nothing, not even to Will—I will have more than enough to say to him myself—I won't take any action against you. But the moment I think you have broken your word, I will request permission from Richard to treat you as a real prisoner. Is that understood?''

''Yes.''

''I trust you even less when you are meek, Marganna.''

''Would you prefer that I—?''

He held up a hand. ''No! I'll accept meek for awhile, if you don't mind. I am weary to death of defiance.''

For the next few days, Marganna had no more than an occasional glimpse of Rathburn at meals or as he moved through the castle. At those times her eyes followed his tall figure with longing, and she came to realize she missed their verbal exchanges.

To pass the hours, she began helping Clovelly in the kitchen and Amelyn with the housework; at other times she stitched on tapestries or played her harp. It was nearly a week later when, glancing up from the needlework she held, she saw Rath approaching, a mutinous look on his lean face.

''Is something wrong?'' she asked, dreading the trouble she foresaw in his eyes.

''The princes want to see you,'' he stated flatly.

''Is that all? I thought something terrible had happened.''

''It hasn't happened yet, but I am half afraid that it will if I allow you to meet them again.''

''Then I am frankly surprised you are even considering it.''

''I wouldn't, except . . . well, Edward has been ill all week, and he claims a visit from you is the only thing that will make him feel better.''

''He said that?''

''Don't think I'm unaware I am being manipulated,'' he said grimly. ''That seems to be my lot in life these days. Manipulated by children and women . . . Lord, to think I was tired of being a knight! That I deemed tournaments and playing at war a waste of time."

Instead of listening to his words, Marganna was lost in thought. She was recalling the elder of the two princes, realizing his pale complexion and a thinness that bordered on frailty had to be attributed to something other than his youth.

"Edward is ill a great deal, isn't he?" she asked.

"I'm afraid so. Sometimes he goes for months in relatively good health, and then, as happened last week, he experiences bouts of nausea or fever that leave him feeling very unwell."

"Do you believe this illness to be serious?"

"Yes, I do."

"What . . . what is it?"

"The physicians are undecided, but they concur it is some kind of wasting disease."

"Oh, no!" Marganna was horrified. "It can't be. Why should a child who has already had so much tragedy in his life have to contend with something like that?"

" 'Tis a question I have often asked myself," Rath said. "I've never arrived at any satisfactory answer."

"What will happen to Edward?"

"The physicians cannot predict what course the disease will take. A few of them insist he will outgrow it, but Dr. Coombs, the physician you met at Nappa Hall, doesn't agree. Ned has reached his present age with no real indication he is improving. Coombs now feels it is doubtful he will ever overcome the illness."

"Do you mean that he thinks . . . he thinks the boy will never . . ."

"He is of the opinion the disease will eventually prove fatal. There already seems to be a weakening of the bone structure, and apparently there is nothing to be done about it."

"Does the king know?"

"Of course. It was one of the reasons he removed Ned from London. He knew the boy would never have the stamina to rule England. He hoped to provide some sort of normal childhood while it was yet possible."

"It's just so unfair," Marganna murmured. "Rath, please, if you will allow it, I should like very much to visit Ned and Dickon."

He inclined his dark head. "Surely it can do no harm."

"Those boys will never come to any harm through me," vowed Marganna. "I swear it!"

On the second visit they made to Nappa Hall together, Rath and Marganna found themselves being led by Ned and Dickon up the narrow staircase to the top floor of the house. Because the Metcalfe children were spending the day with their grandmother, the princes had been allowed to invite their friends to visit, but both boys insisted on playing games instead of mildly settling down to chat. They had spent an hour in Edward's bedchamber playing with the deck of cards recently sent by his uncle. Playing cards, it seemed, had become all the rage in London, so Richard thought the boys might enjoy having their own. But an hour of sitting still left Dickon restless and fidgety, and when Rath suggested he pick the next game, the boy immediately declared he wanted to play hide-and-seek in the attics.

Marganna was so astonished when Rathburn readily agreed and started for the stairs, leaving them to follow, that her expression was comical. Ned laughed.

"You look surprised, Marganna," he said. "Perhaps you did not know Lord Rathburn likes to play games."

"No . . ."

"You should see him when he pretends to be the Mad Monk." Dickon giggled. "He stretches his arms straight out in front of him and stalks across the floor, moaning and groaning. Last year, when I was younger, I thought he was awfully scary."

"Yes, I can imagine." Marganna's eyes sparkled as she tried to picture the stern northerner in his role as the Mad Monk.

Edward heaved a small sigh. "Now my physician, Coombs, doesn't approve of us playing noisy games. He thinks they are too tiring."

"And I expect he is right," Marganna said quietly.

"I only played them so Dickon would not have to play alone," he explained, the hint of a guilty flush staining his cheeks. "I don't play hide-and-seek anymore, and that is why my brother wants you to play. I will sit in the middle of the room and tell the seeker whether he is warm or cold."

"Warm or cold?"

"Yes, you know . . . warm, warmer when he is getting close—cold if he is going farther away from the one in hiding. Surely you have heard of that?"

"Well, there were no other children where I grew up," Marganna explained, "so I am afraid I know very little about games."

"Don't worry, we'll teach you." Dickon took her hand and pulled her into the middle of the attic room where Rath was waiting for them.

After a chair was positioned in the center of the room for Edward to sit in, it was determined that Rath and Marganna should hide first, making Dickon seek them out.

Dickon went into the next room and covered his eyes to count to ten, giving them the chance to find hiding places.

"One, two, three . . ." he called loudly.

Caught up in the excitement, Marganna flew across the room to some pieces of heavy furniture, thinking to hide behind them.

"Four, five, six . . ."

No . . . it would be the first place the boy would look. She whirled around to survey the room and saw that Rath was already out of sight, no doubt hidden someplace watching her. Quickly she looked around again, and Ned urged her to hurry.

"Seven, eight, nine . . ."

In desperation, she caught sight of a huge wooden cupboard in one corner, and just as Dickon shouted, "Ten! Here I come, ready or not!" she opened the door and backed inside, tucking her long skirt around her legs. Quietly she pulled the door shut and pressed back into the dark corner.

Her shoulder encountered an unyielding object as a low

voice whispered in her ear, "You didn't choose a very original hiding place, Marganna."

"Rath? What are you doing in here?"

"Shh!" His warm breath stirred the hair around her ear and she shivered.

"I'll find another place to hide," she muttered, but a brawny arm came around in front of her, pulling her against him.

"No, it's too late now. We'll just have to take our chances together."

They could hear running footsteps in the room beyond and then Ned's voice: "You're cold, Dickon. Very, very cold."

"Then I shall look behind this stack of old paintings."

"Cool . . . barely warm."

"Aha, I must be going in the right direction. I wonder if Marganna would fit inside this trunk?"

Shut in the dark cupboard, Rath's body warm against her back, Marganna drew a deep breath. His arm, loosely draped in front of her, brushed her breasts, making her uncomfortably aware of the intimacy of their positions. She shifted her feet and froze in embarrassment as her buttocks brushed against Rath, eliciting a sharp gasp and a tightening of his arm.

"For God's sake, stand still, Marganna," he said close beside her ear. "This is supposed to be a child's game, but if you persist in reminding me I am a man . . ."

"Oh! I did not mean—"

"Shh," he repeated, this time his lips grazing her ear.

"You're getting warmer, Dickon!"

"So am I," whispered Rath.

Marganna jabbed an elbow backward, catching him in the ribs. She heard his smothered laughter, but it did nothing to quell the tremors that shook her body. She could not remain in such a compromising situation a moment longer.

"How am I now?" she heard Dickon asking.

"Warm . . . very warm!"

"Ah, someone must be inside this cupboard."

They could hear the boy fumbling with the latch, and

then the door was thrown wide. Rath gave Marganna a tiny push from behind, and she stumbled out into the room.

"Ha! I knew I could find you!" Dickon's round eyes were triumphant. "Now that only leaves Rath . . . and I'll wager he is behind that couch in the far corner."

Just as the lad started off, a horrifying roar sounded from the darkened depths of the cupboard and a pair of twitching, grasping hands came into sight.

As Rath lurched from the cupboard, arms extended in front of him, Dickon gave a scream of delight. "It's the Mad Monk! Run, Marganna, run!"

Both he and Ned scampered across the room, leaving her to face the oncoming specter, whose green eyes were glowing devilishly and whose outstretched fingers were even now fumbling in her hair.

Marganna could not suppress a cry of fright and, ducking away, gathered her skirts in her hands and began to run. Rathburn relentlessly stalked after her, uttering bloodcurdling moans.

"Stop it!" she shrieked. "I'm warning you, stop it!"

"I say," sounded a new and disapproving voice. "What is going on up here?" Dr. Coombs stood at the top of the stairs, shaking his head in disbelief. "Lord Rathburn, surely you don't consider this an appropriate game for the princes?"

"But we like it," insisted Dickon.

"I'm well aware of that, Master Dickon," the physician said, his lips twitching in an effort not to smile, "but it is far too boisterous for Edward. Now . . ." he bent a reproving glance at Rath. "I suggest we go downstairs for a nice, restful glass of wine, shall we? Marganna, after you."

Feeling very undignified, Marganna smoothed her skirts and tilted her chin upward before slipping past the physician and down the stairs. At the first landing, she paused and looked back. Behind her came Dr. Coombs, unaware that Rath, to the delight of the two boys, had once again been transformed into the Mad Monk, eyes rolled back and arms quivering spasmodically. Lowering her head, she bit her lip and hurried a little faster down the remaining steps.

Following Marganna down the narrow track leading toward Middleham, Rath let his eyes roam freely over her back, slim and straight beneath the green riding gown she wore. She sat astride her horse unaware that her skirts had bunched up to reveal shapely calves garbed in dark green hose.

Now a strong wind lifted and tangled her hair, tossing it this way and that; he appreciated the fact that she did not fuss with it, trying to control it with scarves or her hands.

He remembered the spicy smell of her hair as she had stood so close beside him in that dark cupboard, her head resting just below his shoulder. He had certainly been hard pressed to keep his hands off her at that moment.

The silly game in the attic had engendered a score of deliciously lecherous thoughts, and for a few moments Rath let himself imagine Marganna returning a passion as strong as that he felt for her. He envisioned them lying together in the tall, sweet grass of a secluded glen. He pictured the deliberate slowness with which he would unhook the velvet gown she wore, freeing her enticing body for his lips and eyes to enjoy. In his mind, he unpinned her coppery brown hair, loosening it from its neatly coiled braids with irreverent fingers, spreading it across his own naked chest as he pulled her down to his kiss. Somehow he knew their lovemaking would be fierce and sweet.

Rath broke into a sweat. Damnation, he thought, I can't keep thinking this way! I've got to gain control of myself.

He forced himself to recall the more mundane aspects of their visit at Nappa Hall. The afternoon just past had been one of the most entertaining he had spent in a long while, he mused. Even the medicinal glass of wine under the prudently watchful eye of the physician had been enjoyable. Marganna had a natural way of talking to the boys, as though they had always been friends, and Rath heard them recounting stories from their childhood that he suspected even Richard had never heard. He had studied her closely but admittedly had seen nothing insincere in her manner. Could it be that she genuinely liked the princes and found being with them pleasant?

He grimaced, wondering what the king would say if he knew his nephews had just spent an afternoon in the company of the accused Tudor spy. There was no possibility he would be pleased by the revelation.

And yet for the first time Rath found himself considering Richard's initial theory that Marganna had been sent to spy by someone else and was really no threat herself. If only he could be certain of that.

A jagged streak of lightning burned along the horizon, startling him with its intensity.

Damn! He had done it again! Not for the first time, he had let his mind dwell on Marganna to the exclusion of all else. He should have noticed the steady darkening of the sky, the building storm clouds, the ominous stillness of the moor.

He spurred his horse into a gallop, closing the distance between Marganna and himself. As he drew alongside her, the first low rumbling of thunder could be heard, and she turned an agitated face toward him.

"It's going to storm, isn't it?"

"Yes," he shouted above the rising wind. "If we pick up our pace, mayhap we can reach Middleham before it breaks."

She looked doubtful, he noticed, but did not argue. They rode steadily for the next twenty minutes, and occasionally he saw her survey the sky with a sweeping glance. After each look, she urged her mount to greater speed.

They were crossing the highest part of the moor when the storm closed down around them. The clouds began to churn, slowly at first, then faster, obliterating the sun. The day, already old, began to slip rapidly away, leaving premature night in its stead. Another blinding flash of lightning scored the sky, causing Marganna to flinch. The very ground beneath the horses' hooves quivered with the vibrations of the thunder that crashed mightily on every side.

"Look!" Rath shouted, pointing westward. "Here comes the rain."

Marganna followed his gesture and saw what appeared to be a windblown curtain of gray advancing across the breadth of the moor. As she watched, it drew unavoidably closer.

"Hurry! There's an old hut up there in the cleft of that hill. We'll have to take shelter there."

The first raindrops whirled through the air as Rath led the way, guiding his horse off the trail and up the steep incline. Halfway along the rough path, he halted, his head bent against the wind, listening.

"Do you hear anything?" he called back to her.

"No, I don't think so. Wait, there was something."

Below the keening whine of the wind the faint noise came a second time.

"Baa-aah!"

"What is it?" Marganna cried, trying to control the nervous prancing of the animal she rode. "There, I heard it again."

"It must be a lost or injured sheep."

Despite the drops of water now pelting his face, Rath stood up in his stirrups and, shielding his eyes, let his gaze scan the terrain.

Again he pointed. "Up there! There's a sheep wedged in between those boulders. It must have fallen from the rocks above."

"Will it be all right?"

He shook his head. "I'll have to go after it. You go on to the hut and I'll be there as soon as I can."

"I don't know where the hut is!"

Rath settled back into his saddle and started off up the hillside, shouting back at her over his shoulder. "It's straight ahead—you can't miss it! Now go on before you get any wetter!"

"I . . . I don't want to go on alone," she protested, glancing at the darkness overlaying the path. "Let me come with you."

"Good God, woman! Can't you ever just do as you're told? I've got a hurt animal to see to. I've got to get it in out of the storm, and you'd only be in the way. Surely you can see I don't have time to waste arguing!"

"I'm sorry. I didn't mean to waste your precious time," she spat, but he didn't hear her scathing words; he had already ridden out of earshot, his attention on the sheep that continued to bleat in terror.

With a resigned sigh, Marganna rode on in the direction in which Rath had indicated the hut was to be found. As she reached a plateau where the path leveled off somewhat, an enraged wind caught her in a blast of fury. It ripped at her hair and clothing, striking her face with a thousand tiny stinging blows, threatening to topple her from her horse. She bent her head against the gale, shivering as cold raindrops rolled off her hair and down her neck.

Another brilliant streak of lightning flared, and she jerked at the reins, causing her mare to skitter sideways, eyes rolling and hooves clashing on the rock underfoot.

Silently she cursed Rathburn for abandoning her to the storm, for caring more about the welfare of that animal than he had for hers.

She had just about given up finding the hut when, at last, a pile of stones loomed up before her, and she realized she had finally reached shelter. The hut, used in the past by shepherds, was huddled against the hillside looking lonely and haunted.

She tied her horse behind the hut, where it would be protected from the worst of the storm by the overhang of the slate roof, then she went around to the front and tentatively stepped into the only room of the small building.

A cobweb clutched at her face; disgusted, she pulled it away with shaky fingers. She had never felt so alone and miserable in all her life.

God, how she hated Yorkshire and its uncivilized moors and even more uncivilized weather! How could a storm of such dimensions have blown up with so little warning? At this moment she wished herself anywhere else on earth except the north of England—this cold, desolate place!

She was nearly blinded as fiery lightning burst across the sky, momentarily lighting the interior of the room in which she stood. It was followed immediately by an enormous explosion of thunder and the increased drum of rain on the roof overhead.

Wrapping her arms around herself for warmth, Marganna huddled in a corner of the hut, alternately wishing that Rath would be stricken by a well-deserved bolt of lightning or that he would come striding into the tumbledown cottage to calm her ridiculous apprehensions.

Outside the wind howled maniacally, plucking at the slates on the roof and threatening to rip the fragile door from its hinges.

Curse you, Rathburn, she thought angrily. Where are you? What has happened to you?

A loose shutter banged, making her heart lurch. Just as her breathing calmed it banged again, and she jumped, her nerves shattered.

Fear and fury waged battle within her, leaving her shaken and uncertain. She didn't know whether she never wanted to see Rath again or whether she would give everything she owned for a moment's comfort in his arms.

Chapter 11

The door to the shepherds' hut flew open, startling Marganna.

Rath, his wind-whipped cloak swirling around his knees, slammed the door behind him and crossed the room to the stone fireplace, where he dropped the leather saddlebags he was carrying.

Rummaging through one of the bags, he announced, "The animal was a young ram. He was uninjured, although I don't know how he kept from breaking his neck. At any rate, I found the rest of the flock sheltering under a *brot*—an overhang of peat hag, if you don't know what that is—and left him with them."

Finding what he required, Rath began examining the dusty pile of kindling left in the fireplace, nudging it with his boot. Presently two or three mice ran out, scuttling away to safety in the darkness, and he chuckled.

"I thought it more than likely vermin had taken up residence in this old fireplace." He squatted on the hearth, striking the flint he had taken from the saddlebag. "I just hope no bird has seen fit to block the chimney with its nest."

He nurtured the sparks into flame, then added several sticks of wood from a crumbling woodbox beside the fireplace. "Lucky that someone else sheltered here recently. I'd never have gotten a fire going with wet wood."

Just as he rose, dusting his hands, a jagged flare of lightning illuminated Rath's tall figure, followed by a tremendous volley of thunder that jarred the cottage. From the corner where she crouched, Marganna saw him throw back his head to shake the raindrops from his curling black hair, his white teeth glimmering in a broad smile. In that instant he looked like a pagan worshipping the elements. He was obviously exhilarated by the thunderstorm. She could hear the excitement in his voice.

"Now you understand why no seasoned North Country man ever goes onto the moor without being prepared for the worst." Again he was kneeling over the saddlebags. "I've got another cloak and a blanket and bread and cheese as well, not to mention a flask of heather ale." His laugh was triumphant. "Even a candle or two. Of course, this is nothing compared to what we carry in the wintertime."

He lighted one of the candles and wedged it into a wide crack in the wall opposite, from which its glow was drawn back toward the small fire, feebly lighting the main portion of the hut.

"Why don't you come closer to the fire and warm yourself, Marganna? I'll wager you are chilled to the bone . . . Marganna?" For the first time he turned to look at her. "What the devil . . . ?"

He strode rapidly to her side, reached out with strong hands to grip her shoulders, and drew her up beside him. She twisted away, but he captured her chin, ruthlessly exposing her face to the light. Her eyes were huge and dark, her cheeks streaked with the telltale signs of tears.

"What's wrong?" he questioned sternly. "Why have you been crying?"

"I haven't—"

"Don't lie to me." He gave her a gentle shake. "Did something happen after you left me?"

"No." She tried to pull away, but he wouldn't release her.

"Marganna, I want to know what made you cry," he insisted.

He searched her face with a puzzled expression, taking in the vivid hair now hanging damply around her shoulders, the shadows beneath her eyes, the soft trembling of her mouth.

"You were afraid, weren't you? Tell me . . ."

"No, I wasn't afraid."

His hands moved to the sides of her face to gather the mass of loosened hair and hold it back gently. One by one, he kissed the tears from her cheeks, and when his mouth finally touched hers, she could taste the salt on his lips. She leaned away from him to look into his eyes and found they were filled with such an odd tenderness that her breathing was constricted.

Marganna was suddenly overcome by a new sort of panic. She struggled out of his grasp, willing herself to remember the indignant anger she had directed toward the man only a short time ago.

She widened the distance between them. "How can you pretend such concern for me when you left me alone in the storm? You didn't care then whether or not I got lost or . . . or killed! You cared more about what happened to that animal. Why should I believe you are sincere now?"

"What are you talking about?" He took a step toward her, but she warded him off with an imperious hand.

"Don't touch me! I see exactly what you have in mind—how convenient for you that the weather turned so nasty. Here we are . . . a cozy fire, food and ale, blankets. What could be more perfect? Next I suppose you'll suggest I get out of my wet clothing so I won't catch a chill."

"It wouldn't be a bad idea, you know."

"You must think I am the most naive woman on the face of the earth," she snapped. "Well, I think your methods of . . . of seduction are stale and overused and . . . and lacking in imagination."

He could not hold back his laughter. "God, and to think I actually felt remorse when I saw you cowering in that corner. Well, my lady, for all I care you can stay there, chattering teeth and all, until . . . until you come to your senses and realize there is no way in Hades I would be interested in seducing you."

"Oh!" The single word escaped her lips in a gasp of outrage. She backed even further away. "You are the most insulting man I have ever met," she muttered furiously.

"Insulting?" One black eyebrow shot up. "Marganna, what is it you want me to say? You accuse me of seduction, but when I tell you I have no interest, you take offense. Am I to understand you want me to—?''

''No!'' She whirled away. ''Never—do you hear me? Never!''

''Then, pray tell, what is it you want me to do?''

''Go away! Just leave me alone,'' she cried.

''Now see here, I thought you were afraid of the storm. Are you so certain you want to be left alone?''

''If you must know, I find more to fear from you than from the weather.''

''Oh, hell!''

He turned abruptly and stalked to the fireplace, where he bent and scooped up one of the saddlebags. Tossing it over his shoulder, he favored her with an irate glare.

''If it suits you to be alone, that's fine with me.''

''Where are you going?'' Her throat was suddenly dry.

''I'm starting back to Middleham.''

''Now? In this rain?''

''I've been out in worse weather,'' he replied. ''And at least this way your virtue will be in no danger.''

''But . . .''

''You did say you wanted me to leave you alone, did you not?''

''Well, yes . . . but . . .''

''Scared?'' he taunted.

Her chin rose haughtily. ''Of course not! I refuse to beg you to stay, if that is what you are thinking I will do.''

When he yanked open the door, a savage gust of wind doused the candle and filled the room with a whirl of raindrops that sizzled in the fire.

''Good-bye.'' He smiled nastily. ''Have a pleasant evening.''

''Good-bye!'' she spat back.

He slammed the door behind him.

''I hope you break your arrogant neck,'' she muttered, half under her breath.

Just then a loose shutter banged against the window and, startled, she cried out. Embarrassed and glad Rath was not there to hear her, she moved closer to the fire, holding out her arms to its warmth.

How could Rath abandon her again, knowing how frightened she was? And yet, she reminded herself, she was the one who had denied being afraid, the one who had told him to go.

And why? she thought. Because I don't trust myself to be able to resist his advances. Because he makes me feel the way no other man ever has . . . and I don't want that. I am his prisoner in too many ways already.

Unexpectedly the door burst open again. Marganna spun around to see Rath standing on the threshold, water streaming from his hair and clothing.

"Marganna," he said, tossing down the leather bag he was carrying, "I'm going to stay here with you whether you like it or not."

All logical thought fled her mind as she flung herself at him. His arm went around her waist as he lifted her from the floor and held her against him, while with his free hand he closed the door. Still holding her, he crossed to the fire before lowering her feet to the earthen floor.

"Well, my brave lass," he murmured, "it seems you are a bit unnerved after all."

"Y-yes. I lied when I said I wasn't afraid," she admitted in a small voice.

" 'Tis all right—I lied when I said I didn't want to seduce you."

Her head snapped up, but instead of the teasing laughter she expected to see in his eyes, they were filled with an intensity that weakened her knees and caused her heart to hammer hard against her ribs.

"Rath?" she whispered faintly.

"Hmm?" He dropped his rain-streaked cloak, and his hands came up to grip the lapels of the sleeveless surcoat she wore, pushing it backward off her shoulders and letting it fall to the floor. Beneath it her gown was soaked and clinging, but despite its clamminess, she could feel the heat of his hands as they slid down her arms to her wrists.

She cleared her throat. "Let me go," she said more loudly.

"I only want to warm you, Marganna." There was a

husky catch in his voice. His fingers moved to the lacings at the back of the gown. "That is all, I promise—unless, of course, you desire more . . . ?"

"No!"

She pushed hard against his chest. "Rath, have you lost your senses? Do you forget that we . . . dislike each other?"

"Nay, how could I forget that? But, my dear, you know as well as I there is something between us other than dislike, and we've denied it far too long."

"I have no intention of—"

"Marganna, be quiet." He said the words quietly and deliberately, and just as deliberately moved her hands away and drew her back into his embrace.

His mouth took possession of hers, forcing everything from her mind but the sensation his touch was provoking. His face and lips were cold, damp with rain, but the inside of his mouth was warm, the contrast wreaking havoc with her senses. The tension seemed to drain from her body and she slumped wearily.

Deftly he loosened the fastenings at the back of her dress and pulled it forward over her shoulders.

"Please, may I have the cloak to wear?" she asked in a low voice. As he knelt to pull it from the leather pouch lying on the floor, she stepped out of her wet gown and carefully spread it over the woodbox to dry. Wearing only a smock, her hose, and her boots, she blushed to find him watching her; quickly she threw the garment he handed her around her shoulders.

Rath had unfolded a blanket before the fire and now he took her hand, pulling her down into a sitting position facing him.

"I think you will be more comfortable without those wet shoes," he said, taking one of her feet into his hands and proceeding to strip off the ankle-high boot. Then, his eyes never leaving hers, he cupped her heel in one hand and moved the other upward, sliding it along the outside of her leg until his fingers encountered the lace garter she wore. Slipping beneath it, he dragged the garter down to her ankle; even though she was startled by his intimate touch, she made no protest as he peeled away the sodden hose. He then turned his attention to the other leg, and she shivered as the dry heat of the fire touched her chilled skin.

"Better?" he asked.

She could only nod, wondering what he would do next. She did not have long to wonder, for he immediately drew a silver flask from the saddlebag and handed it to her.

"Take a sip," he gently commanded. She did as she was told, grateful for the inner warming the ale offered. Then Rath took a long swallow and passed the flask to her again. She shook her head, recalling the night at Rathburn Hall with a faint smile.

"You are very beautiful when you smile, did you know that?"

"No . . . I . . ."

"Why do you look so shocked?" Rath set the flask aside and studied her with amusement.

"Well, you have called me many things but never before beautiful. You've only referred to me as a skinny spinster . . . or . . . oh! remember all the horrid things you said the day that peddlar attempted to persuade you to buy me?" Her face was rosy, not, he suspected, entirely from the blazing fire.

"I seem to recall I paid a goodly sum for you."

"A goodly sum?" She choked. "Five pounds! Another of your insults."

"Be that as it may, I have not realized any return on that investment," he said teasingly. "At least not yet." He removed his jerkin and started unlacing his shirt.

She cast a sideways glance at him, but he seemed engrossed in getting out of his wet clothing, so she thought perhaps she had mistaken his meaning.

Outside the hut the storm raged on. Inside, a new storm was building. Marganna knew it beyond doubt when Rath, now clad only in dark brown hose, rose to add more wood to the fire and, instead of returning to his position beside her, sat down close behind, putting his arms around her waist and pulling her backward to settle her firmly against him. He stretched his long legs out beside each of hers and whispered, "Now, isn't this better?"

Marganna didn't trust herself to reply; her mouth felt too dry to form words. She knew she should stop Rath right then. If she did not, he would think she welcomed his advances. There was no way she could possibly have misconstrued his motive this time, and if she did not move away from him immediately, events could not help but progress toward their natural conclusion.

She felt the press of his body against her back, then the stirring of his breath close to her ear. "I find I am enjoying this immensely, sweetheart, but I must ask you to remove the cloak. The wool irritates my bare skin."

She was assailed by a series of tiny chills, and in her confusion could not decide whether they were caused by what he said or the fact that, without waiting for her approval, he had already reached over her shoulders and set his fingers to work at unknotting the cords of the cloak to remove it. He knew she was going to give in to him even before she was willing to admit it to herself! It shamed her to be so transparent, so obviously pliable. She half twisted in his arms to demand he let her go, and found instead that his hold tightened considerably and his dark head was bending toward hers, his mouth urgent as it claimed her own.

Rath had nearly come to his senses as Marganna sat quietly within his embrace; he realized she must be trying to sort out her feelings and emotions, and for the space of a few seconds he knew they should stop this madness and go no further. Just as he opened his mouth to tell her so, she had turned toward him, and the delightful brush of her body against his, as well as the sudden, shadowy view of her lovely breasts inside the gaping neck of the smock, cost him dearly. Gone was rational thought, gone was concern for anything more than the feel of her body beneath his, their passions rivaling the dramatic thunderstorm that now seemed out of mind and hearing.

"Oh, Marganna . . . love," he mumbled, "I only meant to warm you . . . believe me. But now . . . I can't seem to stop myself . . ."

His hand dropped to her hip, pulling her closer, then glided up the slender line of waist and ribs to cup and fondle a rounded breast. Marganna gasped in delighted shock, finding herself welcoming the pleasure of his caresses. Finally acknowledging that she did not want him to stop his sensual assault, she allowed herself to relax, to banish uneasy thoughts of what the consequences of their actions might be. Tomorrow would be time enough to worry about that.

"Rath," she murmured against his mouth, "I am so tired of fighting you. I can't do it anymore."

He lifted his face from hers. "There is no need to fight me, love. This is what we both want."

She sighed, knowing he was right.

The sweetness of her surrender served to inflame him beyond all reason. Placing an arm beneath her legs, he lifted her, supporting her body as he shifted his until they were reclining with Marganna half lying atop his long, muscular frame. Her head rested against his broad chest, and she marveled at the rapid beating of his heart. Knowing he was as stirred as she only excited her more.

"Marganna?" He drew an unsteady breath. "Are you certain?"

"Yes," she whispered.

Without knowing where she found the audacity, she pressed her mouth to the taut flesh of his shoulder, moving it along the sinewy surface to his strong neck. She felt him swallow deeply as she placed a light kiss in the hollow of his throat, and when she raised herself slightly to cover his mouth in a gently exploratory kiss, she could feel rather than hear the moan that escaped him.

His hand at the back of her head imprisoned her and brought her lips down on his again. This time the kiss was anything but gentle; he had grown impatient in his ardor. He was finished with persuasive wooing. It seemed he had assumed the role of aggressive, demanding male, sensing instinctively she would play the submissive female. Each time he heard her gasp in delight or felt her body move, straining closer to his, he was elevated to a new level of

passion, knowing that what was happening between them was a rare and extraordinary thing.

He grasped the hem of her undergarment and began easing it toward her shoulders. She obligingly raised her head so that he might slip the smock off and toss it aside, knowing beyond doubt that was the final surrender.

Wrapping her in his arms, he rolled Marganna onto her back, then knelt above her. As his hands moved to the fastening of the single garment he still wore, she could not make herself look away. Then, at last, his virility was completely revealed, and she no longer had to be content with tantalizing glimpses. With something of a shock, she realized he was even more beautiful than the classic statues to which she had mentally compared him, and when she lifted a hand to touch him, her fingers encountered not chilly marble, but the vibrant warmth of pliant, softly furred flesh.

Rath, with equal reverence, let his gaze roam freely over her. The light from the fire slanted across her slender figure, causing flickering shadows to dance erotically along the delicate collarbone, the tautly crested mounds of her breasts, and the shaded hollows beside the soft sweep of her hipbones. Each line and curve of hand and wrist, leg and ankle, was accentuated by the firelight, giving her a fragile look.

She stirred restlessly. "Rath, please . . . !"

Peering up at him through her lashes, she saw the look of triumph that appeared within the dark green eyes, the complacent smile on his firm lips. Much to her own amazement, she did not begrudge him this moment of victory, nor did she regret her own capitulation. After waiting twenty years to relinquish her innocence, she felt she could not wait a moment longer. She reached up and drew him down to her, feeling the finely corded strength of his body as he lowered it over hers.

"Marganna," he murmured, nuzzling his face into the fragrant hair alongside her neck. She turned toward him, and his mouth slanted over hers, absorbing the low moan issuing from her throat. Holding her in the curve of his arm, he permitted his free hand to explore the contours

he had dreamed of for so long. He delighted in touching the smooth skin, stroking and caressing her to an intense arousal, kindling a fire that swept through her body, leaving her nearly frantic with feverish longing.

Her hands slipped over his shoulders, massaging the broad muscles, and he moved to cover her. Her back arched, thrusting her hips upward to meet his downward motion. A small cry escaped her lips and pain clouded the brown eyes looking into his; his own eyes softened in sympathy, then glowed with pleasure and slowly but surely began to smolder with unchecked sensuality.

Overcome by concern for her, he struggled to curb his raging lust. He lay still until the slight frown left her face and she gazed up at him questioningly. Then he started to move, slowly easing into the age-old rhythm, watching the guarded look fade from her eyes. Once she realized there would be no more pain, she hesitantly began to match the motions of his body. Her unstudied reactions to his lovemaking caused his breathing to become harsh and ragged; his features grew rigid with desire and his hands commenced a feverish survey of her flesh.

Marganna knew she would remember this moment for the rest of her life—the drum of rain on the oilskin window, the soft, simmering murmur of the fire, the dusty smell of the cottage floor and the scratchiness of the wool blanket beneath her bare back. But most of all she was aware of the man who hovered over her, his green eyes glowing with an almost frightening intensity. The golden light from the fire sculpted the muscles of his chest, gilding the fine covering of black hair. Again and again her hands stroked him, finding pleasure in the warmth of his skin, the coarseness of his hair. Each time her hands moved, she could feel the muscles beneath them bunching, as though pulled tight by threads of tension.

The pleasurable intimacy they shared was more than Marganna had ever dared hope for; nothing she had heard or imagined could have prepared her for the reality. She felt herself spiraling upward, tensing almost unbearably, and then she seemed to explode in the grip of a powerful release that radiated satisfying tremors throughout her

body. She heard a harsh cry wrench from Rath's throat as his frame was wracked with violent shudders, and then his mouth closed over hers, fiercely possessive, his kiss tasting of heather ale.

Marganna lay cradled in his arms for long moments, her head resting against his chest. Eventually Rath stirred and, placing a finger beneath her chin, turned her face up so he could study it.

"That was wonderful, love," he said softly.

Too weary from the emotional scene just past even to begin an assessment of what it was going to mean in her life, Marganna merely smiled and shook her head.

"Yes, it was," she whispered.

As always, her candor amused him, and he uttered a low, resonant laugh, brushing her lips with a kiss and hugging her closer to him. With his free hand, he reached for the discarded cloak, which he spread over them.

Marganna sighed tiredly and nestled in his embrace. Outside the winds still raged, but inside, at least for the moment, the storm had calmed.

The broken shutter banged in the night wind, waking Marganna from a sound sleep. She glanced at Rath, still sleeping beside her, thinking how much younger and more carefree he looked than when he was awake. He lay with his head resting on one arm, black hair disheveled and falling forward over an unfurrowed brow. A feeling of tenderness surged through her, making her want to smooth back his hair and trail her fingers along the faintly shadowed jaw. She recalled the strength and heat of his body, the thrill of his fevered kisses, the sound of his voice as he'd murmured her name in impassioned urgency.

It had happened so easily! Had anyone warned her she was in danger of submitting to the arrogant northern lord, she would have denied it emphatically. Such a thing would have seemed impossible. But somehow in these past weeks he had managed to disarm her, intriguing her with a gentle boyishness and humor he had kept hidden until recently. She suspected this Rath was someone she could care for deeply, but because an involvement of that sort would only

complicate her life further, she knew he was someone she should avoid.

Carefully she eased out of Rath's encircling arm and sat up, slipping her legs from beneath the cloak, away from his warmth. She reached for the crumpled smock and pulled it on, glad to find it was nearly dry. Her dress was still damp, but she put in on anyway, knowing she would rather suffer that discomfort than the response she could expect if she was not decently clothed when she faced Rath again.

"Here, I'll lace it for you," he said, his deep voice startling in the stillness of the hut.

She whirled to face him, but with firm hands on her shoulders, he turned her and neatly did up the back of the gown.

He rose and reached for his own clothing. She could think of nothing to say, so she sat gazing into the fire, lost in thought, and in a few minutes, fully dressed, he dropped down beside her.

"Are you hungry?" he asked, unwrapping a linen napkin to reveal bread and cheese. "It has been some time since we have eaten."

Unable to face him, Marganna accepted a small piece of cheese and bit into it, keeping her face averted.

"It's still storming," Rath commented unnecessarily.

She drew a deep breath. "When . . . when do you think we will start for Middleham?"

"Not until morning, I'm afraid. I don't think the rain is going to stop any time soon."

Despite herself, she had to venture a look at him. "But won't they be worried about us back at the castle?"

"They will realize we either had to spend the night at Nappa Hall or find shelter along the way. They won't worry about us as long as we are back by midmorning."

Now it was Rath's turn to take a deep and unsteady breath. Looking into her clear eyes, reading the uncertainty of her emotions there, he himself felt shaky.

He could barely believe what had taken place within this grim and deserted hut. Against his better judgment, he knew he was about to broach the subject to Marganna.

Stalling for time, he handed her the silver flask and watched as she took a ladylike sip before passing it back. He took one long swallow, then another. At last he cleared his throat and twisted to face her.

"Marganna, there is something I want you to know."

She started to protest, but he laid a finger across her lips, and she fell silent.

"I want you to know that I did not mean anything like this to happen," he said quietly. "When it started, I meant only to warm you." He reached out and picked up a long strand of red-brown hair lying over her shoulder. Suddenly he grinned, tilting his dark head to one side. "But I can't say I'm sorry."

"Rath, for heaven's sake," she murmured, coloring. "Do we have to discuss it?"

"We must talk about it sooner or later, Marganna. Why won't you look at me? You're not sorry, are you?"

"I cannot believe a gentleman would take advantage of a lady and then . . . question her in this manner."

He chuckled. "I think we have already established my lack of gentlemanly qualities." He gave her hair a gentle tug. "Besides, I'm not so certain *I* took advantage of *you*. It seems to me that you had rather definite ideas about the direction in which matters should proceed."

"I . . . !" What was meant to be a spirited protest died as her lips curved upward. "Yes, I suppose I did."

Rath dipped his head and laid his mouth on hers, kissing her softly. It took nothing more than that to start her heart pounding against her ribs once more. He gently worried her lower lip with his teeth, then pulled away to look at her.

"It was a wonderful experience." He placed a light kiss at each corner of her mouth. "And one I enjoyed sharing with you."

"I did not think it would be . . . so . . . pleasant," she said shyly, her errant fingers reaching out to touch his shoulder.

He laughed exultantly. "Believe me, love, when I say even I was taken by surprise."

"You?" Her eyes were wide with disbelief.

"I shouldn't admit it, should I? As a man of experience, I shouldn't confess that I found more pleasure here in this dirt-floored hut with you than I have ever known before."

"Oh, Rath," she whispered in dismay.

His lips moved over hers again and, as he deepened his kiss, his strong hands clasped her shoulders, bearing her down onto the rumpled blanket.

"You were so sweet . . . despite your fear—so willing to please."

She lay quietly beneath him, offering no resistance. He slid his hands down, caressing her breasts through the fabric of her gown, his fingertips brushing the fullness above the neckline.

"Mayhap we should not have wasted the effort to dress," he said, raising his head to smile down at her.

Despite the smile, Marganna felt the intensity expressed by his touch and, miserably, knew she had already started to respond. She must not let that happen a second time.

"No," she suddenly said, turning her face away. "No . . ."

He looked startled. "Why not? We have the entire night."

She struggled into a sitting position, pushing his hands away. "I . . . can't," she cried.

"Surely you can't mean you don't want me to make love to you. I won't believe that."

"No, it's not that."

"Then what?"

"We can never be lovers again because I do not . . . I will not be responsible for bringing another bastard into the world, yours or anyone else's."

His eyes narrowed. "What are you saying, Marganna?"

Hastily she scrambled to her feet and began to pace beyond the firelight, just at the edge of the darkness. She twisted her hands together, betraying her agitation. Rath swiveled to watch her.

"Marganna?"

"My mother once made just such a mistake, Rath. I do not intend to follow her example."

"You have no father?"

"Everyone has a father," she said bitterly. "I just don't know who mine is."

"Is it so important?"

"I might have expected that callous attitude from someone who had a father. Of course it is important. Or at least it was to me . . . to the child I used to be. The child who stood at the iron gates of the convent and watched people pass by, wondering whether this man or that might be her father."

"And your mother? Why did she never tell you about him?"

"She did not have the chance—she died when I was very young. But I have no reason to think she would have in any case. She never told anyone else."

"She must have had some reason."

"Her family." Marganna stopped pacing and stood in front of him. "They would never have understood the circumstances or condoned her actions. No doubt she feared the measures they would have taken against him."

"So no one will ever know the identity of the man who sired you?"

"No."

"Poor Marganna." Rath unfolded his long legs and stood up. "Then that is the reason you won't let me make love to you?"

"Can't you see I don't dare? I have already taken one chance. It would be tempting fate to take another."

His fingers closed around her upper arms, pulling her into his embrace.

"I know you do not credit me with much sensitivity, Marganna, but I want you to know that I will try to understand your position."

"Thank you."

"You know, it's strange, but I have always thought I grew up without a father, simply because mine died when I was so young. Now I see my situation differently. I mean, he was there to give me a name, a heritage. He was there long enough to assure me he cared about me and about my future. I see now that my situation was infinitely preferable to yours."

"Then you will not insist?"

"Your argument is valid, as much as I wish it were not."

Her eyes were wide and dark, appealing to something deep within him. He rested his chin on the top of her head, speaking quickly before he had time to reconsider.

"I will not press you, I promise. Besides, we both know there can never be anything real between us, so perhaps it is better to stop now before we become even more deeply ensnared."

"Yes, I agree."

"One last kiss and I will leave you alone," he bargained.

He cupped her face in his hands and kissed her, a slow and searching kiss that asked nothing. Feeling comforted, she let him hold her for a long moment, then stepped away.

"Thank you for listening to me . . . and for trying to understand how I feel."

The room was full of shadows as Rath sat in the midnight gloom, staring down at the woman who slept near the hearth. Her head was pillowed on her arm, her hair spread out around her.

God only knew how he would manage to keep the promise he had made her. After making love to her once, he wasn't certain he could resist the urge to do so again. His desire for her had awakened a tender possessiveness that surprised as well as unnerved him, and instinctively he knew it would not be easy being haunted by the memory of this night they had shared.

He no longer saw Marganna as the irritating spitfire he once thought her to be but as a lonely child—a child, it struck him, such as he had been, growing to maturity with no one to call his own. It saddened him to think the beautiful, loving woman beside him had suffered that same loneliness.

If they had not been enemies, they might have taken some measure of comfort from each other, as they had done this night. But it was not meant to be. She had asked for his restraint and he had promised. Tonight had been a mistake she did not want to repeat, and he must honor that. Already he had the feeling it was the worst bargain he had ever made.

He ran a careless hand through his hair and smiled ruefully. Jesus Christ and all the saints, but life had become complicated!

Chapter 12

By morning the storm was gone but not the new constraint between Rath and Marganna. The very air in the hut seemed to be heavy with unspoken thoughts and emotions as they both went silently about the task of gathering their belongings to continue the trip back to Middleham.

Once or twice Marganna glanced up to find Rath staring at her, a speculative expression on his face; each time she struggled to think of something to say, but the words stuck in her throat and she would hastily turn away. When he looked at her that way, she knew he was remembering the events of the night before— the firelit privacy of the shepherds' cottage, his suddenly flaring passion, and her own abandoned response.

Riding along the narrow track, eyes occasionally straying ahead to his straight back, she allowed herself a moment of self-pity. What had happened last night had been unexpectedly wonderful, but why couldn't it have occurred under different circumstances? If only she had given herself to someone who cared for her, someone in a position to marry her . . .

Because the years of her childhood had been spent in the awareness that she was a nuisance, a bothersome creature to be shifted here and there and kept out of the way, she had nurtured her dream of a home shared with a decent husband and noisy children—a place where at last she would belong. The nuns had been kind but distant, too involved with the rituals and petty politics of convent life to realize she was a lonely child in need of affection. So long ago she had vowed to seek the protection of a man who loved her and to raise her own children the way she wished she had been raised—with love, merriment, and caring discipline.

Now one night with Rath had put that dream in peril; if she surrendered to the desires a few stolen hours in a deserted hut had ignited within her, she might be bound heart and soul to a lusty, laughing, black-haired man who would take what she offered and promise her nothing. For the sake of her future, from this day forward she must be careful to do nothing to further her infatuation with him.

She breathed a shaky sigh of relief as they rode through the main gate at Middleham, thinking that once she was out of Rathburn's sight, she would feel more comfortable.

She had not anticipated the reaction they would receive as they entered the great hall. Many of the residents of the castle were still at the table breaking their fast, and when Rath ushered her through the doorway, it seemed to Marganna that all eyes were on them. There was a brief silence before the general hubbub reclaimed the room. Rising above the other voices was that of Clovelly Biggins.

"Praise be, ye are back—we were worried. Come, sit and have a bite of sommat ta eat."

Will came forward to greet them, the frown on his face fading as he determined they were unharmed.

Marganna avoided Will's probing gaze; as she averted her eyes, she happened to see Bronwyn seated at the dining table across the room. For once the woman looked neither angry nor accusing. She gave Marganna a brief, solemn nod, as though acknowledging the changed circumstances between them, then turned back to Erik Vogelman, the blond giant, who sat at her side, a firm arm around her shoulders.

"Did you enjoy your stay at Nappa Hall with my illustrious cousin James?" Will was asking as he escorted Marganna toward the tables.

She couldn't control a quick glance at Rath. "Well, we—"

"Actually, we were halfway to Middleham when the storm broke," Rath cut in smoothly. "We sheltered at the shepherds' hut."

Will looked from one to the other. "The shepherds' hut?"

Mrs. Biggins coughed noisily. " 'Tis a gooid thing you know the moors, Johnny. Noo man nor beast would be likely ta survive long, caught oot in such a storm, tha knows."

Will looked doubtful. "Tell me this, Rath . . . just how is it a knowledgeable fellow such as yourself would not know a storm of that magnitude was coming? I find it difficult to believe you had no forewarning of it when you left Nappa Hall."

Rath's face darkened. "What is it you are trying to say, friend?" He kept his voice low, but several people at the nearby table turned to look, as if sensing the sudden tension in the room.

Will's jaw jutted forward. "I think you fully intended to—"

"Will, please," Marganna interrupted, laying a hand on his sleeve. "I . . . I don't think I care for breakfast right now. Would you mind walking me to my chamber?"

Rath's eyes narrowed. "I will walk with you," he said in a steel-edged voice.

"Johnny, ye'd best eat a bite," Mrs. Biggins spoke up. "Why not let Will take Marganna oop?"

"I'd be delighted," Will said, placing Marganna's hand in the crook of his arm and patting it firmly.

Marganna's eyes pleaded with Rath not to create a scene; finally, he waved them away and settled himself at the table, without another glance in their direction.

Will was waiting in the wooden walkway to the castle's outer chambers when Rath left the dining hall.

"I want to know what you think you're doing," he demanded angrily.

Rath's voice was calm. "What do you mean?"

"Something happened last night between you and Marganna, didn't it? I sensed it the moment I saw you walk through that doorway. And knowing you as I do,'' he said grimly, ''I have little doubt about just what went on.''

''Will, for heaven's sake, don't make this any worse than it already is.''

''So I'm right? You seduced her?''

Rath moved away, riveting his attention on the sight of green hills through the narrow windows of the hallway. ''If it makes you feel any kinder toward me, it wasn't a deliberate seduction.''

Will smashed one fist into the palm of his other hand. ''Damn you for a rogue! I knew you didn't know how to treat a decent woman.''

Slowly Rath turned back to face him. ''It would seem your summation of my character is not far from correct.''

Will could not miss the self-mockery in his friend's voice and his expression softened.

''Are you actually telling me you agree with me for once?''

''I am.''

''Rath, what in God's name happened?''

''We were caught in that damned storm, and somehow, there in the shepherds' hut, we started arguing and . . . matters got out of control.''

''An argument led to . . . ?''

Rathburn nodded, a wry expression on his face. ''You know the woman has driven me to distraction since the first time we met. And lately, I confess, I haven't been able to think of anything but her. I suppose being alone in such intimate circumstances was too tempting. Of course, I take full responsibility, but that doesn't change what happened.''

''It doesn't sound as if Marganna exactly scorned you.''

Will heaved a weary sigh. ''Richard predicted there was something of great importance between you two; I guess I knew he was right, no matter how I wished to deny it.''

''Will, believe me, there is nothing between Marganna and myself, nor can there ever be. Last night was a mistake that won't happen again. I made a vow to leave her alone, and I will honor it."

"Nevertheless I, for one, will be surprised if it ends here. There is a significance about your relationship, and God only knows where it will lead next."

"It's my duty to see that it leads nowhere."

"I think that will be a monumental task, my friend." Will shook his head. "I had intended to tell you I was leaving for Moor's End for a few days, but perhaps I should delay the trip."

"There's no sense to that. After all, you have been away from home for some time, and there's really nothing you can do here. Don't worry that I will force my attentions on Marganna. She has made her feelings very clear, and I will respect them." A corner of his mouth lifted. "Even if it means I can never dare to be alone with her."

"Honor is a hellish thing," stated Will only half jokingly. He clapped his friend on the shoulder. "Good luck avoiding Marganna. I daresay you're going to need it."

Amelyn eyed Marganna over the pile of linens they were folding.

"Surely you have heard the rumors? They are flying over this castle like a barrage of arrows."

"I'm afraid I don't know what you're talking about."

Marganna carefully avoided Amelyn's speculative gaze as she scattered crushed rosemary between the folds of the bed sheets stacked before her.

"They concern you, you know. You and Rath."

"Oh?" Marganna made her voice as disinterested as she could.

'People are speculating about what took place in the deserted hut the night you spent together there."

"Why must they assume anything happened?"

Amelyn smoothed a hand over the linens. "There are those in this castle who have said all along that you and Rath would become lovers. They just didn't know when or how. They like to think the storm gave you a perfect opportunity."

"Oh, for heaven's sake, Amelyn, what senseless drivel!"

Amelyn looked affronted. "Is it? I must tell you I've heard more than one of the men wagering how long it would be before Rath got you into his bed."

"I'm not even going to dignify that ridiculous statement with a response."

"Ridiculous?" Amelyn's eyes narrowed. "I see nothing ridiculous about it. What woman wouldn't want to be loved by Lord Rathburn? At least you could be honest about it."

Marganna was startled by the vehemence of her words. "Amelyn, are you angry with me?"

"No, of course not." Amelyn scooped up an armload of linens. "I'll take these up to Mrs. Biggins now."

"I'll help," Marganna said, gathering up the last of the folded sheets. As they started from the room, she glanced at the woman beside her. "I'm sorry if I seemed short-tempered."

In the doorway Marganna unexpectedly collided with a broad masculine chest, and as she stumbled and fell, the linens flew out of her arms and scattered over the flagstone flooring.

She heard a deep laugh. "Well, good afternoon ladies."

Marganna froze at the sound of Rath's voice above her. Its very timbre sent a thrill piercing through her, and her fingers gripped the one remaining sheet she held so tightly that she knew it would be full of creases.

Just hearing his low, intimate tone immediately transported her back in time; she was helpless against the onslaught of memories—the tenderness of his jade eyes, the scorching heat of his body as he held her close . . .

Marganna made a determined effort to wrench her thoughts back to the moment at hand. Having done so, she was surprised to see Rath bending over her, offering his hand.

"Well, well—who might this rosy little kitchen maid be?" he said teasingly, pulling her to her feet. "I hope I didn't hurt you." He retained his hold on her hand, a half smile on his lips, but his eyes as they searched her face were somber.

"I'm fine," she assured him.

At last he released her, turning his gaze on Amelyn. "And I hope I haven't caused you even more work."

Amelyn blushed prettily as she raised wide blue eyes to gaze adoringly at him. "There's no harm done, Rath."

"Good. At least let me help gather these up."

He knelt, leaving Marganna no choice but to kneel beside him in order to retrieve the linens strewn over the floor. They both reached for the same sheet, and as his warm fingers closed over hers, Marganna nearly gave in to the longing she felt. She struggled against the urge to wrap her arms around him then and there and tell him she didn't want him to honor their bargain. Knowing he was staring at her, she drew an unsteady breath and began to stack the rumpled linens, desperately summoning every ounce of pride and courage she possessed.

"Now," Rath was saying, "perhaps you will permit me to carry these heavy loads of linens for you? By the saints, it looks to be too much for such slender creatures as you."

Amelyn's acceptance almost bubbled forth, she was so pleased. Rath gathered up the laundry, then held out an arm to her, ascending the stairs and leaving Marganna to follow more slowly.

Feeling irritated despite herself, she had to admit he was only attempting to make the best of the situation. After all, even though she had rejected his attentions, they still had to live in the same castle and maintain some sort of civility.

She followed Rath and Amelyn's retreating backs with grave eyes. In reality she supposed it would be a wonderful solution to the problem if he were to find someone else. Amelyn's hints had led Marganna to believe she harbored a secret affection for Rathburn, and there could be no doubt she was pleased by his notice. Perhaps it would be for the best.

Marganna crouched beside the hound, placing a bowl of meat scraps by the nursery door.

"There you are, Caesar, old fellow. I've brought you some dinner."

The hound raised sad eyes, and his tail thumped in pleasure at seeing her. She patted his large, bony head and fondled his ears.

"I'll wager you are lonely, aren't you?"

The dog lapped at her hand, and she laughed softly.

"Well, then, I will just have to come and see you more often. I can't stay now, because I promised Mrs. Biggins I would help in the kitchen, but I'll bring you more food tomorrow."

She rose to her feet and, with a last pat on the animal's head, turned to go. She uttered a small cry as she found herself face to face with Rathburn.

"What is the meaning of this, Marganna?" he asked with mock sternness, hands behind his back, shoulders squared.

"I . . . I only brought the dog something to eat," she replied. "Surely there can be no harm in that?"

"Caesar is capable of going down to eat with the other dogs," he said, his eyes twinkling. "I believe he does, upon occasion."

"That may be true, but he spends so much time up here I thought he might be neglecting his own needs."

"Surely he is the best judge of his needs."

"Am I to understand I'm being forbidden to bring him food?" Marganna drew herself up to her full height, ready to do battle if necessary.

Rath grinned, dimples scoring his cheeks. "No one is forbidding you to do anything, Marganna. You are the prickliest female I have ever known. Bring the dog food anytime you wish."

With those words, he withdrew his right hand from behind his back and, with a wink, tossed the meaty bone it held to the watchful hound. "I try to bring him something every day myself."

Feeling unreasonably upset, Marganna brushed past the man and started down the hall. His first reaction was to put his foot down hard on the trailing hem of her gown. She was stopped short and jerked back against him. His hands came up to catch her shoulders.

"Will you please release me?" she requested through gritted teeth.

"I can't go on this way, sweetheart," he said into her ear.

"What way?"

"Trying to ignore you. I thought it would be easier to keep my part of our bargain if I simply avoided you. It was a commendable plan I'll admit, but it is simply not possible."

"I thought we had done very well," she murmured.

"You're a liar," he accused softly, smiling. "Don't think I haven't seen the way you watch me . . ."

"I do not!"

"I beg to differ."

"Differ all you like—it signifies nothing!"

"I'll tell you how I know you watch me—I spend all my time watching *you!* I try not to, but everywhere I turn I see you. I'm haunted by the sight of you at the evening meal with candlelight on your face, or the way you look with the morning sunlight in your hair as you bend over your needlework. And what a vision you made the day you threw yourself—and the laundry—at my feet, smelling of rosemary and sunshine."

With a groan of anguish, Rath released her shoulders and slid one arm around her waist and the other across her chest, pulling her tightly against him.

"God, Marganna, I want you so much!"

She felt his lips at the nape of her neck, and every muscle in her body turned to liquid, leaving his arms as her only means of support. She sagged against him, fighting to control the wild leap of passion his words had inspired. She must stop this—she had to be strong!

"You don't know how often I think about making love to you, sweetheart. The frustration of seeing you but not touching you is killing me!"

She shook her head fiercely. "You promised!"

"Damn that promise! Tell me you want me, too."

"Yes," she whispered miserably. "Oh, yes . . . I do! I think about . . . loving you all the time, Rath, but I can't!"

She did not realize she was crying until she felt his grip

loosen and looked down to see the tears splashing on his sleeve.

He turned her in his arms, one large hand cupping her head to hold it against his chest. "You women choose the damndest times to cry," he whispered shakily.

She gazed up at him through tear-drowned eyes. "I'm sorry . . ."

He sighed, his mouth curving upward. "I begin to realize what a selfish, unfeeling lecher I really am. I won't bother you again, I swear it."

He dropped a kiss on her hair.

"Thank you," Marganna breathed, reluctantly leaving his embrace.

Rath watched her go, unable to ascertain his own mood, let alone hers.

Rath was scrupulously true to his word and avoided Marganna for the next few days. But instead of easing her mind, his absence only made her feel worse.

Tonight, wearing one of her prettiest gowns in an effort to lighten her mood, she came down to the great hall for supper, determined to let nothing disturb her enjoyment of the evening.

She found herself seated next to Mrs. Biggins and across from Amelyn, who, though she seemed solemn and withdrawn, finally joined the lively conversation. Rath was placed at the end of the table, so although their eyes met occasionally, they were too far apart to speak.

When the meal was finished, Marganna was surprised to be approached by Rath, who asked her to entertain with a song or two on the harp.

"Ah, would ye?" pleaded Mrs. Biggins. "Aw'd purely love ta hear ye."

"Very well. I'll play some of the old folk songs, shall I?"

Seated on a low stool near the fire, Marganna placed the harp against her knees and drew her fingers across the strings. Rath felt spellbound from the very first note of the melody.

The wavering light from a torch on the wall was reflected in her sparkling eyes; it held his attention, as did the hypnotic movements of her graceful hands on the instrument. He was too captivated to notice the arrival of a king's messenger until Pickering, the castle steward, tapped him on the shoulder and summoned him to the outer room.

Marganna had just finished the song when he returned, and the moment she looked into his blazing green eyes, she knew something disastrous had happened. She put the harp aside and stood up quickly.

"What is it?"

"I want to speak with you privately," he rasped out. "Go upstairs." He turned to the portly man standing near by. "Pickering, will you see the messenger and his companions are given a good meal? If you wish, you may convey the news to the rest of the castle."

"But . . . are you sure, my lord?"

"They have to know sooner or later," Rath replied. He whirled to glare at Marganna. "I told you to go upstairs and, by God, I mean *now!*"

Marganna had only a glimpse of shocked faces as she gathered her skirts and ran from the room, filled with the worst dread she had ever experienced. What could have happened to make him so angry?

Rath threw open the door to his bedchamber and Marganna darted inside, not waiting for him to issue the order. She stood close to the fire, in need of its warmth, for an awful chill was creeping over her. Nervously she twisted her hands together, all the while keeping her eyes on Rathburn's livid face.

He paced madly up and down the room for two or three minutes, obviously attempting to gain a hold on his temper. When he came to stand in front of her, she wasn't certain he had been successful in his efforts, for angry sparks seemed to glint from beneath his thick black brows.

"I've had a message from Richard," he said unnecessarily.

She nodded warily.

"It seems a veritable scandal has been created at court

by dear Lady Stanley. She has made a nuisance of herself by proclaiming to all and sundry that the king himself has been an accomplice in a sordid kidnapping scheme."

"What?" Marganna's voice was faint.

"Yes. She dares to accuse the king of conspiring to spirit away her young and innocent niece—one Mistress Marganna *Tudor.*"

"Oh." Suddenly Marganna did not think her legs would support her. She moved to the side of the four-poster bed and sat down, hands clutching a slender wooden post.

" 'Oh'? Is that all you have to say?" he shouted.

She swallowed hard. "What . . . what would you like me to say?"

"I'd like you to say it's all a mistake. Tell me you are not a Tudor, not that old bitch's niece!"

She dropped her head. "I can't."

"How in the name of God could I have been so blind and stupid?" he raged. "I should have known from the beginning."

He resumed his pacing, flinging himself from one side of the room to the other. "How you must have laughed at me, at all of us! A Tudor right in our midst, and we didn't even know it. That must have amused you."

"Rath, I—"

"We should have realized Tudor's mother wouldn't send a mere lady's-maid to do her spying. It was too important to risk sending just anyone—it had to be a family member, someone with a stake in the final outcome. Damn your eyes, Marganna, what did your loving cousin promise to do for you when he became king?"

Her head came up abruptly. "I have asked for nothing," she declared.

"Surely you were to have been rewarded for your loyal services," he said with a sneer.

"I was not."

"Don't keep lying to me, woman! You cannot expect me to believe you were an innocent pawn . . . as Richard so obviously still thinks. What did you stand to gain when Tudor became king? Money? Property? Tell me, what was it?"

"It will do me no good to try and defend myself," she cried. "You won't listen to anything I have to say."

He laughed harshly. "You are right, of course. I've learned time and again you cannot be trusted. Mayhap this time I have learned it for good."

"What is going to happen to me now?" she asked quietly. "Am I to be punished?"

His hateful laugh rang out a second time. "Oh, yes, my dear, most certainly. You are being given a sentence worse than death."

One hand went to her throat. "What do you mean, worse than death?"

Rath pulled a folded parchment from his doublet and tossed it at her. "Would you care to read the king's orders yourself?"

With shaking fingers, she smoothed out the letter and scanned it rapidly. All color drained from her face, making her eyes appear twice as dark as usual.

"Marry?" she exclaimed. "You and I?"

"Exactly. It would seem I am to be penalized for my part in this also."

"Why would the king wish us to marry?"

"To squelch the rumors, of course. Your extremely vocal aunt is telling everyone that Richard used a false charge of treason against you in order to obtain your . . . charms for a certain lusty North Country man he wished to reward. She says I have kidnapped you and am holding you against your will here at Middleham, and that I am turning away all her envoys."

"That much is true."

"It is true you are being held a prisoner and that I have refused entrance to her messengers, but do not permit yourself to overlook the fact there was a very real charge of treason against you."

"I still don't understand why a marriage is required."

"Richard is of the opinion that if we marry, people will think you came with me of your own accord, and that Lady Margaret has just made up her wild tale of intrigue and kidnapping to save the family dignity. If he can provide witnesses who swear you have married me willingly, it will appear to one and all your aunt was simply trying to shore up your crumbling reputation."

"Well, I won't do it."

He stopped at the foot of the bed. "Won't do what?"

"I won't marry you."

"The king orders it. You have no choice."

"Fie on the king," she stormed. "I'd just as soon be executed."

"That should have been arranged long ago, God knows."

"It's not too late."

"I'm afraid it is. Richard has called for a wedding and, my fine, indignant beauty, a wedding there will be."

"I won't do it, I tell you."

"And I tell you you will!"

"You will never be able to make it appear that I am willing," she said scornfully.

"I'll drug you if necessary, Marganna. This is one time you are going to keep quiet and do as you are told."

"You are hateful!"

He shrugged. "You are welcome to think so. Now I am going belowstairs to speak with Clovelly about plans for our wedding so that it will take place as soon as possible."

"I refuse to go through with this marriage."

He started toward the door, then stopped short and turned to cast a challenging look at her. "Believe me, I'm no more thrilled about the prospect of being your husband than you are my wife. But the king commands us, and we have no option but to obey. However, let me assure you of one thing, my lady."

He strode back to the foot of the bed and stood observing her, hands on his hips. "The privileges of married life are few at best, and I intend to make the most of what benefits there are—starting with the wedding night."

"Meaning?"

"Meaning I plan to exercise my husbandly rights, and you'd best not consider refusing me. Is that understood?"

She raised her chin, clamping her lips together.

"Answer me, Marganna."

"You are lewd and disgusting! A lascivious—"

He leaned down and, clutching her arms, jerked her forward until they were face to face.

"Do you understand what I am saying?"

"Yes, but—"

"Good! You may make an obedient little wife after all."

With that, he shoved her backward onto the bed and stalked out of the room, slamming the door behind him.

Chapter 13

Marganna banged the freshly polished pewter mug down on the table with a resounding crash and reached for another; Clovelly Biggins' strong hand darted out to detain her.

"Nay, lass, there's no need for ye ta help here any longer. Why don't ye go oopstairs and rest a bit?"

"But I'm not tired," Marganna insisted. "Besides, I must keep busy today of all days."

"Mayhap ye should find sommat else ta do, then." Mrs. Biggins chuckled. "Aw don't want these mugs dented oot of shape, and the way ye've been bangin' them aboot . . ."

"I'm sorry, Mrs. Biggins. I guess I was thinking of other things and just got careless. I'll be more careful, I promise."

"Why won't ye rest, lass? 'Tis yer wedding day."

Marganna grimaced. That was exactly the reason she couldn't rest. If she didn't keep her mind busy with other things, the significance of this day might overwhelm her, shattering what was left of her composure.

Since the night the messenger had arrived with King Richard's fateful edict, she had nursed a seething anger against the cold-eyed stranger Rathburn had become. He had barely spoken to her except to issue orders in clipped and icy tones. In that same aloof voice he had informed her their wedding would take place on this day, after the sheep shearing.

"We might as well combine the two events," he'd said bluntly, "since our neighbors will be together anyway."

Marganna had merely lifted a disdainful shoulder. If he

expected her to be insulted because she would have to share her wedding day with the smelly chore of sheep shearing, he was going to be disappointed. He was wasting his time trying to ruin a day that was already in ruins for her because she was being forced to marry him instead of the genial, smiling man she had always envisioned.

Had he but known, his next words, tossed over his shoulder as he'd left the room, upset her far more.

"The wedding will take place at Rathburn Hall as soon as the shearing is finished. Be certain you pack extra clothing, as we will spend our honeymoon there . . . alone."

The barely veiled threat behind his words affected her more surely than any of his barbed insults. There was little doubt of his intentions, and each day she grew more and more aware of the fact that she could do nothing to stop the chain of events set into motion by her aunt's political scheming.

Along with her apprehension, a frustrated wrath developed, causing her to suffer moments of sheer panic, severe headaches, and sleepless nights. With Will gone, there was no one to whom she could turn for advice. Each time she approached Amelyn, it seemed the other woman had to rush away to attend to some errand or another. Marganna realized Amelyn was avoiding her and felt guilty as she recalled the other's desperate wish to stay at Middleham. It should have been Amelyn who was preparing to be wed, and they both knew it.

At one point Marganna tried to speak to Mrs. Biggins about the situation, but to no avail. Mrs. Biggins was nothing if not a staunch and stalwart supporter of her menfolk. If King Richard wished the marriage to take place and if Rath agreed, then indeed there would be a wedding at Rathburn Hall, despite Hades or high tide.

"He'll make ye a fine hoosband, lass," she'd said, smiling at Marganna's frowning face. "Just give him a chance."

"But we despise each other."

"Do ye think so?" Mrs. Biggins actually sounded dubious. "Aw myself have often thought there was a grand attraction betwixt the two of ye."

"I'm afraid you are mistaken," Marganna replied stiffly.

"Ah well," Mrs. Biggins uttered mildly, " 'twould not be the first time."

When her wedding day dawned, Marganna saw the end to her hopes of forestalling the ceremony. How could she plead her case or dissuade the others from this course of action if no one would talk to her?

On the trip to Rathburn Hall earlier that morning, she had desperately gone over her alternatives, coming to the bitter conclusion there were only two left open to her. She could give in and comply with the king's wishes, marry Rathburn, and attempt to convince herself it was preferable to being executed. Or she could refuse to obey the order and defy them. Of course, in his present mood, she could well imagine Rathburn beating her into submission and enjoying it immensely.

She looked around her at the gleaming white walls and polished stone floors of the kitchen at Rathburn Hall. Mrs. Biggins had agreed to let her work there that morning only because it would be the last time she could set foot in the room as an ordinary person. By this time tomorrow, Marganna would be mistress of the house, and it would be her duty to give orders and assign tasks to others, not labor at them herself.

There had been some changes in her status already. Once the castle residents had recovered from the initial shock of learning Lord Rathburn was being ordered to marry his prisoner, they began treating her with deference, making certain she had the best chair or the first glass of wine poured. She had even been given a lady's-maid—a shy girl of sixteen who was so in awe of Marganna that she was excessively clumsy. It seemed to Marganna the poor creature was forever stammering apologies or bursting into tears; such nervousness caused her to deal even more gently with the girl, for she was positive Lilibeth, as the maid was named, was the one person at Middleham more miserable than herself.

"Marganna!"

She glanced up to see Will Metcalfe hurrying through

the kitchen doors. He seized her by the waist and swung her around.

"Oh, Will, it is so good to see you," she cried, laughing for the first time in days. "What brings you back so soon?"

"Rath's messenger." He grinned. "I did not want to miss the festivities."

Marganna's smiled died. "Ah, yes, the festivities. Need I tell you they are hardly festive?"

Will cast a look at Mrs. Biggins, who gave a knowing nod. "Marganna's got the bride jitters, tha knows."

Seeing Marganna gather herself for a spirited rejoinder, Will spoke hastily. "Do you mind if I take Marganna for a walk, Clovelly?"

"Lord no, lad. Ta tell ye the truth, Aw think some fresh air will do her gooid. She's pale as milk."

"Come along then, Marganna. Let's walk down by the barn and see how the shearing is progressing."

Without waiting for her reply, he took her arm and steered her through the door into the bright summer sunshine.

As they strolled through the back garden, following the path to the outbuildings, Will studied her carefully. "Clovelly's right, you know—you are pale. I came back expecting to find you radiant, and instead you look like a wraith, all shadow-eyed and hollow-cheeked. Aren't you happy, Marganna?"

She heaved a disgusted sigh. "Will, I wasn't particularly happy when you left. What could possibly have happened since then to change my attitude?"

"Why, being married to Rath," he exclaimed, surprised. "I . . . well, I thought it was the answer to all your problems."

"Hardly that."

"What do you mean?"

"How can you believe something we are *forced* into doing will solve anything? Rath was very angry to find out I am a Tudor; he feels marrying me is a punishment. Therefore, I fully expect to suffer abuse at his hands, as well as every humiliation he cares to inflict upon me."

"Nonsense. Rath isn't like that." Will had to smile. "Marganna, you have nothing to fear from him, I assure you. He may swear and shout, but he would not harm a woman, especially not one he cares about as he does you."

"Cares about? Now who is talking nonsense?"

"There is something between you and Rath, whether you admit it or not. Up to now, I think you have both let your pasts interfere. If you could manage to forget you are a Tudor and he King Richard's man, I think you might deal very nicely with each other."

"And all this time I kept thinking that if only you were here, you would help me find a way out of this mess. Now I see you are just as bad as Mrs. Biggins."

"Surely you did not think I would have any influence over King Richard? Or Rath, for that matter."

"I had hoped you might. Can't you see he'll be so angry at losing his freedom, he'll still want to punish me?"

As they neared the farmyard, they could hear the bleating of sheep overlaid with the shouts and curses of the workers. A fine cloud of dust thrown up by the churning hooves hung over the scene and begrimed the men's faces.

Will, thankful for the opportunity to change the subject, said, "Look at this! It seems like complete chaos, doesn't it? However, in reality, there is a great deal of organization to a shearing."

They stepped inside the stone barn and Marganna, though feeling put out at Will, turned her attention to the strange scene before them.

The clippers were seated on stools along either side of the building, with the sheep herded down the middle. As soon as an animal had been shorn, it was let go and waved toward one end of the barn, where two men posted at the door marked it with daubs of tar before turning it out.

"These workers will shear hundreds of sheep today," Will hurried on. "So you see why they need a reliable method of handling the animals."

The clipper they were watching flashed Marganna a brief smile before beginning the task of shearing the shaggy ewe before him. Wielding the clippers with ease, he began at the animal's right front shoulder and worked down the side to the rump, repeated the process on the left side, then deftly turned the ewe to clip its underside. Nearly finished, he righted the sheep and moved the clippers straight down its spine, leaving the fleece to drop off.

"That requires skill, believe me," Will said as he escorted her past the wrappers, men who received the freshly clipped fleeces and made short work of rolling them into tight bundles, keeping pace with the shearing.

"The wrapper must—"

"Will, please!" Marganna pleaded. "There isn't much time, and I must talk with you."

"Oh, all right." He sighed.

When they left the barn through the door at the opposite end, they found themselves in a small fenced yard. Before Marganna could speak, she was startled to catch sight of Rath. Again dressed in his leather chausses and little else, he was standing at a stone trough, splashing water on his chest and arms.

He saw them and grinned. "So, Will, you got my message?" He scooped up a handful of water to splash on his face; then, shaking the drops from his eyes, he reached for a linen towel draped over the fence.

"Aye, and I had to come see for myself. I couldn't believe the news."

Looking at Marganna, Rath quirked an eyebrow. "It seems you aren't the only one having difficulty believing it. However, I did see the priest arriving a short while ago, so I assure you, the wedding ceremony will go ahead as planned."

Marganna refused to look at him and studied the rough edge of the trough instead. Surprisingly there were tiny flowers floating in the water. She reached out a hand to pick one up, and Will spoke.

"That's flowering mint, Marganna. The workers put it in the wash water to cut the grease and odor of sheep shearing. They say nothing works better."

"So you see, sweetheart," Rath drawled, "you needn't worry that your bridegroom will come to you smelling like sheep."

"Oh! Do you never tire of shaming me?" she cried.

She turned to Will, hands outspread in a supplicating gesture. "Do you see why this marriage is impossible? The man is a crude boor."

"And no doubt you would prefer a gentlemanly husband—someone like Will, for instance? Is that it, Marganna? Have you appealed to him to save you from my clutches?"

"Even if I had entertained such an idea, Will himself would have put an end to it. He has already spent considerable time trying to convince me you are the proper mate for me."

"Is that so? Well, well, I must say, I am astonished."

"So am I," she retorted. "I thought Will was more perceptive than that. Now, if you will excuse me, I have several things I must do."

She put her nose into the air and swept through the open gate. Rath and Will stared after her, bemused expressions on their faces. When she had gone, Will permitted himself a small chuckle.

"You're going to have a devil of a time with her, Rath. Something tells me she isn't going to be as compliant as most of your females."

Rath's white teeth gleamed in a broad smile. "Perhaps that's what makes her so damned interesting. You know, Will, when I first got Richard's orders, I was furious. I thought his plan of marriage between Marganna and me was nothing short of idiotic."

"And?"

"Now I've reconsidered. I'm beginning to find the prospect rather intriguing."

Will grinned. "You always did relish a challenge."

"Aye. Marganna may be stubborn enough that it will take longer to win her over, but do not doubt the outcome of this match. Have you never heard, old friend, that all women are like marionettes . . . just waiting for their master's command?" He grinned roguishly. "And I shall soon learn all the right strings to pull."

Will shook his head. "Lord, I'd worry about you if I thought you were serious! Best beware you don't get so tangled in those strings that you hang yourself!"

* * *

The wedding took place in the garden, just at sundown.

Tired but satisfied after a day of hard labor, freshly washed men joined their wives and children on the lawn. The celebrations that followed sheep shearings were traditionally the most pleasant holidays of the summer months, but there was an added air of anticipation about this one, for there had been much speculation over the marriage between Lord Rathburn and the stranger from the south.

A murmur of admiration met Marganna's appearance as Will escorted her to the ivy-covered arbor where the parish priest waited to conduct the ceremony.

Though the gown she wore was old-fashioned, having belonged to Rath's mother, its simplicity suited her. It was a cream-colored wool, the softest, lightest wool Marganna had ever seen. The low neckline left her throat and shoulders bared, and the flowing lines of the skirt emphasized the slenderness of her waist. The color was flattering, turning her complexion a deep ivory and enhancing the dark sherry color of her eyes. Her cinnamony hair was piled on top of her head and dressed with tiny yellow rosebuds and the newest leaves of ivy, which Mrs. Biggins told her symbolized marriage. In her shaking hands Marganna carried a bouquet fashioned by the young girls who had attended the shearing. They told her shyly that it was a "clipping posy," usually given by country lasses to their sweethearts. Scented with the delicious fragrances of a sun-warmed meadow, the bouquet contained pansies, cabbage roses, columbines, gillyflowers, gorse, and lavender, all bound together with sweetbrier, marjoram, and ribbon grass.

A capricious breeze blew off the high moor, whipping color into Marganna's cheeks and loosening tendrils of hair to curl about her ears. Rath, coming to stand beside her, gazed down at her averted face and felt a constriction within his chest. Inexplicably, a sudden feeling of tenderness threatened to overcome him, and without stopping to analyze the gesture, he reached out a strong, warm hand to capture one of her cold, trembling ones.

"You're not afraid, are you?"

At his whispered words, she raised wide eyes to his face; he smiled, a dimple marking his tanned cheek. In the fiery sunset, his hair was mahogany.

"I'll never be afraid of you," she lied, chin high.

Secretly she was puzzled by his apparent change of heart concerning their marriage. He had gone from blazing anger to something that seemed like anticipation, leaving her distrustful. She feared he had only hidden his rage for the sake of appearances and would bring it forth once more when they were alone.

He tightened his grip on her hand, and she was caught up in the dark liquid fire of his gaze as it moved over her face and shoulders. The colorful garden surrounding them seemed to tilt and spin away as she struggled to grasp the reality of the situation.

Panic flickered through her as she realized she was about to give herself in holy matrimony to this man—this bold and powerful man who towered over everyone in the garden . . . this man who looked at her with an expression that made her mouth feel dry and her pulse race . . . this man who had flatly stated he intended to exercise his husbandly rights.

Marganna had wanted to be married, but not this way! Not to a man who loathed her, who had nothing but scorn for who and what she was. It made a mockery of every dream she'd ever had.

She feared that Rath, aware of her physical response to him, would, in his contempt, use it to enslave and debase her, and the thought of their wedding night loomed large in her confused mind.

All afternoon she had waited for the pervading anger she had expected to feel as the time for the wedding drew near. She had counted on it to give her the bravado necessary for a final rebellion; when it did not materialize, she was left with a feeling of numb acceptance. That feeling helped to calm her. It saw her through the ordeal of dressing for the wedding and even through the ritual by which she was delivered to Rathburn's side before the curious stares of the onlookers. But would it sustain her through the night ahead? Suddenly she knew that if she could persuade her feet to move, she would flee the garden and look for some safe hiding place instead of merely standing there, powerless to halt the inexorable tide of events.

Marganna remembered nothing of the marriage ceremony itself. She was aware of hearing the familiar words and knew she must have made the proper responses, for eventually she heard the phrase "man and wife" as though the priest had shouted it, and, looking down, she saw a wide gold band on her left hand. Then Rathburn was turning to her with a new possessiveness in his touch, bending his head to place a warm kiss on her cold lips. Mrs. Biggins and Amelyn offered the customary congratulations, and Will claimed a kiss from the bride.

The sun was gone and a night chill crept over the garden as the party moved inside Rathburn Hall for the supper the women had prepared. Mrs. Biggins lighted the candles down the length of the tables, and amid excited talk and laughter, the guests dined on huge rounds of boiled beef and roasted squab stuffed with herbs and rice, served with jugs of the strong shearing ale brewed the previous autumn.

It seemed hours later that the wedding cake—honeycake iced with spun sugar and decorated with white rosebuds—was brought in to be cut and served. At her end of the table, Marganna looked up to find Rath quietly studying her. In the dim light, his eyes were as dark as onyx, and even at that distance, she could feel their heat. Her heart gave a queer little twist.

Will Metcalfe stood up and raised his glass of ale. "I'd like to propose a toast to my friends, the new bride and groom," he said loudly.

Marganna smiled as graciously as she could while the entire company raised their glasses, then downed hearty quaffs of the brown liquid.

Rath, an impossibly smug look on his face, got to his feet next, raising his hands for silence. As the crowd quieted, he began to speak, thanking his friends, neighbors, and workmen for making the sheep shearing a grand success.

Watching her new husband fulfill his duties as host, Marganna had to admit he was inordinately handsome. He had chosen to wear the colors of York for the occasion, and the rich sheen of mulberry velvet made his skin and hair seem darker. His clothing was of the latest style and cut, more suited for court than the wilds of Yorkshire. His doublet was short, barely more than waist length, leaving his hips and legs clearly defined in dark blue hose. Marganna swiftly looked away from the daring codpiece, which was decorated with the same pearls and gold chain as his doublet.

How could he flaunt that part of himself? she wondered testily, failing to note there were several other men present who also sported the newest court fad.

Suddenly the words Rath was speaking registered. "The musicians are prepared to oblige with lively melodies for dancing, so let the festivities begin. You have my permission to stay until dawn, if you wish. You've earned a celebration—pray, enjoy it. And now, if you will excuse my wife and myself, we will retire to begin our married life."

Marganna caught her breath as the sea of faces turned toward her.

"No." The single, emphatic word was out before she realized it.

Silence fell over the room. After a few uneasy seconds, Rath spoke.

"What do you mean by that, Marganna, my love?"

She was not indifferent to the warning behind his words; she simply could not let him make a public spectacle of her this way.

"Why, husband dear, I merely meant that I would not like to miss the dancing. Surely there would be no harm in staying for a roundelay or two?"

She could tell by the way the muscle in his jaw twitched that Rath was clenching his teeth. She marveled at the control he displayed by smiling briefly before uttering his reply.

"It has been a long day," he said, "and I am fatigued.

I should like to spend the evening resting in my chambers."

A feeling of daring overwhelmed her natural good sense, and she knew it as soon as she said her next words and saw the resulting glitter in Rath's eyes. "Then perhaps you should go on up. I will join you later."

"You are trying my patience, Marganna."

The tension in the room was nearly unbearable. No one moved; indeed, if not for the collective gasp of shock at Marganna's answer, it would have been difficult to prove those gathered there were still breathing.

"As you must know, that concerns me very little."

Rath rested his clenched fists on the tabletop as he leaned forward to impale her with a furious glare. "You are my wife and you will do as I say."

Marganna leaped to her feet. Though she knew she should not say such a thing publicly, she tossed the last remnant of caution aside. "I did not ask to become your wife!"

"Nor did I ask you! But we are well and truly married, and that gives me legal authority over you. When I command you to hasten your lovely little backside upstairs to my bedchamber, you have no choice but to do so."

A titter rippled through the throng, then was quickly stifled. From the corner of her eye Marganna saw Mrs. Biggins begin to rise from her chair and frantically signal the musicians to begin playing. But they were too engrossed in the incredible scene unfolding to pay any heed to her, and she sank back into her chair, at a loss as to what to do.

Marganna could have laughed aloud at the expression on Mrs. Biggins' face. Feeling suddenly bolder, she said, "You are mistaken, my lord. I do have a choice."

"Oh? As I see it, the only other choice you have is to fling yourself over the parapet." He moved his hands to his hips and allowed a shadow of a grin to hover about his mouth. "Goad me further and I may gladly assist you!"

Marganna offered him a sweet smile. "I agree that death would be a pleasant alternative to sharing a bed with you, but I have no need for such dramatic action."

One black brow quirked high. "Then what is your plan?"

Again the sweet smile. "I do not believe the gentlemen assembled in this room will allow you to bully me in such a manner. Your conduct is rude and unchivalrous and I am certain that if I were to throw myself upon their mercy, they would protect me from your unwelcome advances."

Marganna swept the room with a coy look, hoping she sounded more assured than she felt. The blank looks on most of the faces told her these people were spectators who did not appreciate being asked to choose sides.

Rath was gloating, his features lighted by his self-assurance. His knotted fists remained on his hips as he faced the crowd boldly. "Well, shall we see if the lady is correct? Who among you wishes to be first to protect my bride from me?"

Looking at each man in turn, Rath saw nothing but bland expressions. It seemed no one wanted to challenge him.

Marganna clamped her lips together, disgusted that not one of these burly country men dared to stand against their lord.

Rath smirked at her. "Well?"

She stamped her foot, her humorous mood gone as quickly as it had come. "You have used your influence with the king to cow these people," she declared.

"Be that as it may, at least you know you need not expect immediate salvation. Now, are you quite finished with this little rebellion?"

"No, I'm not! I will never give in to you."

"Of course you will and, I'll wager, with abandon."

Another round of smothered laughter circled the room, causing Rath to grin widely. Marganna longed to slap that expression from his face.

"If you believe that, you don't have enough brains to fill . . . to fill that codpiece you are wearing!"

This time it was impossible to disguise the laughter that sounded throughout the dining room. Marganna tossed her head, certain she had scored, but when she saw the glower on Rath's face, her breath caught in her throat. This time she knew she had gone too far.

"Madam, your slur against my mentality is only compounded by the slander to my manhood," he said slowly and distinctly, causing the guests to fall silent once again. "I have no need of *brains* to fill my codpiece, as you are in a position to know very well—very well indeed."

Her face flamed as Rath's audacity was met with uninhibited guffaws.

How could he humiliate her in this manner? It had been bad enough when everyone at Middleham was speculating on what had transpired between Rath and her, but now . . . now they would know the truth for a certainty. And not just the residents of the castle, but everyone for miles around!

Refusing to meet Rath's eyes, Marganna stuck her nose in the air and, turning, walked rapidly from the room. Behind her she heard him giving orders for the music to begin. As she gained the stairs, she started to run, knowing he would be saying his farewells to his guests. She intended to be locked safely in her room before he could catch her.

Rath swiftly followed Marganna down the hall. When he saw her rushing up the stairs, he made a flying leap, and the fingers of one hand closed around her ankle. She cried out as she tripped and fell.

"Let go of me, you brute!" she gasped.

"Not a chance, my dear."

There was a note of levity in his voice, and she realized he was actually enjoying himself. She kicked out with her free foot, but he seized it also, and with a twisting motion, turned her onto her back. Instantly he flung his body over hers, pinioning her there.

"You're hurting me," she muttered, pushing at his shoulders.

"Good."

He grasped each of her wrists, holding her arms straight out from her shoulders. As she struggled against him, she saw that his avid eyes were fastened on her breasts as they heaved with her exertions, threatening to escape the low neck of her wedding gown. Incensed by his lechery, she butted her head, striking him in the nose. With a howl of pain, he released her and fell back against the steps, eyes watering profusely.

Taking advantage of his incapacitation, Marganna scrambled higher up the staircase, hampered by her long skirt. She had nearly reached the top step before Rath came after her again, throwing both arms around her hips and bringing her down with the weight of his body.

"Damn you, Marganna, you nearly killed me!" he gasped.

"I'm . . . glad!" she said, panting and wriggling beneath him. "I meant to—"

He caught her shoulders in his large hands and, despite his tear-filled eyes, grinned. "If you don't hold still, I swear I will ravish you right here on the stairs."

She was properly horrified. "In the front hall? Anyone might come in."

"Exactly. That is why I suggest we continue this in our private chambers."

He jerked her into a sitting position, straddling her legs.

"I have no desire to go into that room with you," she protested, attempting to pry his hands from her shoulders.

"I realize that, my love. At this moment it seems I am the only one feeling any sort of . . . desire at all." With a rapid and forceful movement, he thrust her back against the stair railing, his mouth coming down on hers. The pressure of the spindles against her back was less noticeable than the equally hard pressure of his body. "But with a bit of cooperation from you I can remedy that quickly enough," he added.

Her reply was lost against his searing kiss, and her hands dropped ineffectually to her sides. She couldn't think with the blood drumming so loudly in her ears.

At last he lifted his head; drawing a deep, unsteady breath, he got to his feet and stood over her. She felt like a large cloth doll sprawled against the steps, her neck too limp to support her head, which rolled back against the banister.

"This marriage will be consummated, Marganna," he stated in a cheerful voice. "You may have your choice of whether it will be here or in our bedchamber."

"You callous beast," she said, her voice faint instead of bitter, as she'd intended.

He reached down a hand to pull her to her feet. She swayed momentarily, and he draped an arm around her waist.

"I take it you've made your decision?" he queried, a strange light in his green eyes.

Seemingly resigned, she nodded.

He had just opened the arched wooden door leading to the master bedchamber when Marganna uttered a dismayed cry. "Oh, no—my ring!" She held out a bare hand. "I must have lost it on the stairs."

"How in the name of the saints could you lose a ring? Oh, never mind—I'll look for it. Go inside and wait for me. I won't be long."

As soon as he was gone, she turned the key in the lock and leaned against the door, weak with relief. She had not expected it to be so easy to fool him.

When Rath returned and found the door locked, he bellowed in rage. He cursed and threatened until Marganna covered her ears with her hands. She did not relish the thought of meeting him face to face in the morning.

When he finally gave up and went away, she found she had been clenching her hands so tightly they were cramped. Now she rubbed them together and gazed around the room, wondering what she should do next.

The first feeling of elation at outwitting Rath faded rapidly, leaving her with the somber realization that she was a bride alone on her wedding night. She sighed deeply. If the truth were known, she admitted to herself, the trembling upheaval she felt inside was the result of her inability to quell the desire to experience Rath's lovemaking again. Her silly wounded pride and worry over an uncertain future—all caused by Bronwyn's angry words that day at the falls—were the actual reasons she had spurned Rath. Deep down, she knew she wasn't as opposed to this marriage as she pretended, and now she must pay for her childish refusal to face the truth. She felt empty, defeated . . . lonely.

Only one candle had been lighted, but it was enough to

enable her to see that Lilibeth had laid her night clothing on the turned-back bedclothes. Slowly Marganna crossed the carpet and stood looking down at the sheer white lace, a symbol of all she had hoped marriage would be. Sadly she realized it could never be those things now, not after the way she had treated Rathburn.

"Put on your bride's nightgown, Marganna. I would like to see you in it."

She whirled at the sound of Rath's voice, so close.

A section of walnut panelling beside the fireplace gaped open, and Rath stood in front of it, eyeing her sardonically. Her hand flew to her mouth as she raised astonished eyes to his triumphant gaze.

"Most of these old manor houses have secret passages of one sort or another. Isn't it fortunate I happened to know about this one?"

He touched the wooden panel lightly and it slid silently back into place, leaving them locked within the intimacy of the bedroom.

Rath shrugged out of his doublet and dropped into the nearest chair, crossing his long legs at the ankle.

"Do you know, I think this is the first time I have ever seen you speechless."

She lowered her shocked gaze, knowing his words were true. She could not have spoken if her life depended on it. But she was suddenly filled with happiness, a pure burning joy, because despite her stubbornness Rath had not given up.

"You may undress now, Marganna."

She looked up quickly, but he seemed quite serious. He raised a warning hand.

"No more arguments, if you please. I am in no mood for them. Just take off your clothes and get ready for bed."

Presenting him with her back, mainly because she did not want him to see her pleased smile, she began unlacing the white woolen dress, letting it drop to the floor at her feet. He admired the slim line of back and hips as she stepped out of the gown, folding it carefully and placing it on the chest at the foot of the bed. Next she removed her slippers, meticulously placing them side by side. Sitting on the edge of the chest, still turned away from him, she unrolled and removed her stockings.

"Come here, Marganna."

She glanced cautiously over her shoulder, and he beckoned. "Yes, here . . . by the fire."

Slowly she approached him.

"There," he said softly. "Stand there."

Like a pale statue, clad only in her undergarment, she stood obediently, bathed in the red-gold light of the fire. His eyes intent on hers, Rath rose to his feet and began unlacing his shirt. As he pulled it over his head, she watched him through lowered lashes, her pulse racing riotously as he began removing his hose, the last piece of clothing he was wearing.

"Now, Marganna . . . wife," he said hoarsely, "take off your smock."

She hesitated only a second before grasping the hem of the garment and pulling it over her head; his sharp intake of breath compelled her to look directly into his eyes.

For a long moment they stared at each other.

Marganna thought he was . . . so male—so virile in some mysterious, primitive way. His smoothly muscled body was gilded by the faint wash of candlelight, and for a brief instant she remembered what it had been like to touch him; the memory caused her fingertips to tingle restlessly.

Rath knew he would never again behold beauty that affected him in the same way Marganna's did. Though she might still be suffering an agony of conflict, she stood before him with a calm, natural grace. To him she was perfect, from the tangled top of her rusty brown hair to her slender ankles and feet. His eyes caressed the regal column of her throat, the slant of her slim shoulders, the enticing fullness of her breasts, and the womanly swell of her rounded hips. It was utterly impossible to remain at a distance from her.

As he moved to stand before her, he held out his open palm; her wedding ring shone in the dim light.

"A clever trick, my love, but thank God, one that did

not work." His white teeth gleamed. "Put this back on your hand and don't ever remove it again—is that understood?"

With a brief nod, she replaced the ring, keeping her eyes on it. She felt Rath's fingers in her hair, loosening the pins until the tresses fell in a shining curtain, swirling sensuously around her naked body.

Placing one hand on the nape of her neck, Rath drew her face close and brushed her lips with his, tracing their contours with his tongue, leaving a trail of liquid flame that ignited other fires deep within them both.

His mouth moved along her cheekbone, his breath stirring the tendrils of hair near her ear. She shivered.

"Ah, Marganna, I hope I do not have to woo you so vigorously every night." He chuckled softly. "Remember the night of the storm? You didn't object so strenuously to my attentions then."

"You," she whispered, "are a cad to remind me." The kisses he now pressed into the sensitive skin at the side of her neck were making her feel weak and dizzy, incapable of lucid thought.

"Come to bed, sweetheart."

Ignoring her indecision, he lifted her into his arms and carried her to the canopied bed.

Stretching out beside her, he began stroking her with his fingertips, from the taut skin along her collarbone to the softness of her thighs. She whimpered and moved closer, causing Rath to clasp her around the waist and pull her against him for a kiss that caused her heated blood to sing. She was overcome by his loving persuasiveness, and placed a feebly detaining hand on his chest.

"Don't fight me now, Marganna," he breathed.

His arms became tight bands, binding her to him. His mouth sought hers again, his kiss made more frantic by the fear she might yet withdraw from him. Strong sensations of pleasure coursed through his body at each point of contact with hers, and he knew he would not, could not stop now.

His senses were stirred beyond belief by the feel of her hardened nipples against his chest, the softness of her belly against his hips, and the gentle caress of silken hair as it swept over them. Once again she murmured a protest but snuggled against him, and his mind exploded with an overriding need.

His hands grasped her hips, guiding her firmly beneath him. Even though he felt strengthened tenfold by his passion, he remained cognizant of the need for tenderness with her. He vowed silently that, if he saw her eyes darken with sudden pain or accusation, he would draw away, no matter what it cost him. As much as he wanted her in that moment, he would only take her if she was a willing partner. He forced himself to look down at her, relieved to see that her eyes, liquid with emotion, reflected nothing but seductive pleasure, and he was satisfied that her surrender was willingly offered.

She ran her hands upward along his arms, linking her fingers at the back of his neck and raising her mouth for his kiss. At the same time, she raised her hips to grind her softness against him, delighting in the feel of his weight pressing back.

"Marganna . . . oh, love!" he cried, his mouth against her throat.

She gave herself up to the shattering sensations coursing through her, and as Rath shuddered and strained above her, murmuring her name over and over, she was caught up in the same ecstasy he felt—an ecstasy they each took and, in taking, gave.

Afterward, Rath cradled her in his arms, keeping her body next to him. She lay so quietly that he suspected she was attempting to sort out the tangle of emotions she must be feeling. For the moment, his own emotions were calmed, leaving him wonderfully sated.

He could not control the urge—an urge he fully recognized as self-indulgent—to lay a possessive hand on the curve of her shoulder and let it drift slowly down her arm to curl around a fragile wrist, which he lifted to his lips for a lingering kiss. Marganna stiffened slightly, and her chin tilted against the pillow, though she said nothing.

It was evident to Rath that she had not yet made up her mind about their marriage and that, in spite of her fevered response to his lovemaking, she still had reservations about him. Nevertheless, he felt confident she already regarded the situation as less disastrous than it had first seemed.

It was not many minutes before his eyes closed and he drifted into a peaceful sleep, but long after his breathing had evened and slowed, the smile on his face remained.

Chapter 14

Rath paced back and forth along the rock wall at the back of the garden, kicking stones with one booted foot. Occasionally he glanced upward toward the bedroom window, wondering if Marganna still slept.

A glorious morning sun struck the rocky fells behind the farmhouse, driving the mists from low-lying places to disperse in the clear air. Rath stopped to gaze into the distance as though he'd never seen the sight before, but actually his mind's eye was recalling Marganna as he had first seen her—so haughty and self-righteous. Since that time, he'd observed her in various emotional states—proud, angry, sad, defiant . . . and sensual. Each mood was a separate, vital part of her personality and, with a wry smile, he realized it would take a lifetime to discover all there was to know about Marganna Tudor, the new Lady Rathburn.

Moodily he wondered if he shouldn't have been more patient with her last night. He'd meant to woo her gently, to stir her to the same fever pitch of sexual tension he had felt since the storm. Instead he had fallen back on anger and teasing banter because he was, in the final accounting, too stubborn to admit the truth—too afraid of being unmanned by his feelings to let her know how much he wanted her . . . how thankful he was to Richard for finding a way to bind her to him forever.

He ran a distracted hand through his hair. He did not want a wife who detested him. He almost laughed aloud thinking that just a few short weeks ago he would have said he did not want a wife at all. Now not only did he have one, but he wanted her fiercely.

He stopped pacing and took a deep, relieved breath. It felt good to stop fighting himself, to view the reality of the situation and recognize his dilemma for what it was. He wanted Marganna, and he wanted her to want him. He . . . loved her. Yes, by God, he loved her . . . no doubt had always done so . . . and before this day was over, he vowed to find a way to tell her so.

He glanced up at the empty window once more. He intended to start their relationship anew. He had to be willing to do whatever it took to ensnare her heart the way she had so easily captured his.

He lifted his face to the warming sun and grinned, feeling rested and refreshed. All at once he didn't give a damn that she was a Tudor or that she had been accused of treason. She was his wife—his!—and beginning with today, he was going to win her love. He was determined to make up for the way he had treated her since Richard entrusted her to his care. He was going to woo her in all the ways a husband could woo a wife. And each time he held her in his arms and kissed her, he would strive harder to banish any doubts and fears she still had about him.

He was going to give her the courtship she had missed, the courtship she deserved.

Marganna was relieved when Rath quietly opened the door to the bedchamber and seeing she was awake, asked if she would like to spend the day with Ned and Dickon. Knowing he had temporarily dismissed all but two or three of the staff at Rathburn Hall, including her own maid, she was a little uneasy about passing the day alone there with Middlehim, and readily accepted his invitation to go to Nappa Hall, all the while trying not to show too much enthusiasm. Surely the day would go more smoothly if they were in the constant company of others; as for the night . . . well, she would just have to think of a way to deal with that later.

And deal with it she must. Rath could never know how close she had come to abandoning all her fine pretenses last night. The combination of his sweet gentleness and male aggressiveness had very nearly undone her, and it had taken her last ounce of determination to deny the conflict of emotions he was raising within her. Now more than ever she could not afford to let him guess her true feelings. She knew he had been with many women. What if his sweet, loving words meant nothing? What if he had spoken them to the others? If she let herself believe he truly cared for her, she would be destroyed should he cast her aside. Her only protection lay in never letting him know how much she loved him. She would have to hide her vulnerability, keeping up the spirited sparring so he would never guess the depth of her feelings.

Suddenly feeling reckless, she threw open the coffer filled with her clothing and took out a wooden box containing the few pieces of jewelry she owned. She had already promised herself she would not resort to verbal abuse again, but wearing some small token of her identity would surely be in keeping with her current mood. She selected a gold chain from which dangled the unmistakable symbol of Henry Tudor—the red dragon of Wales. Though its tail was curled gracefully around its body, its head was reared as if to attack.

Let it be a warning to him, she thought daringly. I am not prepared to abandon my family just because I am now his wife. It will take more than forced submission to the base desires of a Yorkist boar to conquer me!

For a moment she was lost in reverie, thinking how very unforced her submission had in reality been.

When Rath came to fetch her, his eyes went immediately to the pendant and the innocent smile on her face. Without a word he stepped to the cupboard and, eyes twinkling, reached inside to pull forth a soft blue velvet hat, which he clapped upon his head. The hat had a mulberry-colored plume that curved along one side of his face to tickle his cheek; securing the feather to the velvet was King Richard's badge.

Let her see, he thought as he escorted her downstairs, that I will not back down from any Tudor threat. I will be amenable but not weak.

The journey to Nappa Hall had never seemed so long. By the time they were within sight of its twin towers, Marganna was nearly frantic in her desire to be off the palfrey and away from the awkward silence that enclosed them.

As Rath lifted her from the horse, she darted a swift look into his eyes, and what she saw there both puzzled and surprised her. She had avoided his gaze all morning, dreading what she would glimpse within its green depths, but whatever it was she had expected—contempt, disgust, ire—nothing prepared her for the startling warmth she saw there. It was almost as if he approved of her, as if he did not recall her spiteful treatment of him yesterday.

Rath lowered her to the ground, but in so doing casually let her body slide down the length of his, causing her to catch her breath—and not just in apprehension that the stable hands might have noticed, she realized. Sudden images of the night before came to life, and try as she might, she could not stifle them. By the time she dared look at Rath again, there was nothing about his composed expression to suggest the action had been more than accidental. She hastily busied herself shaking out her skirts and straightening the cuffed sleeves of her gown.

She was anxious to see the princes again; she thought they would be surprised to learn she and Rath were married.

James Metcalfe met them at the door with a welcoming smile. "Ned and Dickon have been asking about you," he informed them. "Certain . . . rumors have reached our ears."

"Oh?" Marganna murmured faintly.

"Yes, but I'll leave the lads to ask you about that. Come along; they're in the garden."

Five children were seated around a wooden table placed in the shade of an apple tree. Ned was engrossed in writing on a parchment spread before him. Three younger boys, a sober-looking Dickon included, were reciting mathematical equations under the direction of their tutor, a thin young man. Metcalfe's daughter, a girl about ten years old, was busily creating a watercolor painting, so lost in concentration that her tongue protruded inelegantly from the corner of her mouth. Her ginger-colored hair was tortured into corkscrew curls that bounced off her shoulders as she turned her head this way and that as she admired her artistic efforts.

As soon as Dickon saw Marganna and Rath, he leaped to his feet to hug them both. Ned quickly laid aside his quill and rose to clasp their hands, his sallow face lighting with pleasure.

"Is it true that you've gotten married?" Dickon burst out with a wide grin.

"How did you hear the news so quickly, Dickon?" Rath inquired, amused by the child's excitement.

"Our groom's brother attended the sheep shearing at Rathburn Hall," Metcalfe explained, "and stopped by this morning to spread the news." He favored both Rath and Marganna with a bland look. "Not only was he surprised to find there was to be a wedding after the shearing, but it seems he also had . . . er, certain tales of rather irregular events, shall we say, at the wedding banquet."

Marganna lowered her head quickly, a flood of color washing over her face.

Rath chuckled. "And I suppose you wish to hear all about it?"

"I know *I* do," interrupted Ned. "I didn't get to hear those tales."

"It's probably just as well," Rath said. " 'Tis best to ignore gossip, for it is often distorted beyond belief."

Metcalfe's eyebrows flew upward. "Indeed? Well, perhaps we can discuss it later. Right now I think it would be a good idea to dismiss the children's tutor for the rest of the afternoon and speak to my wife about having our meal outdoors, here in the garden. How does that sound?"

His suggestion was met with such a chorus of approval that he took himself off immediately, leaving Rath and Marganna with the children.

"You'll never guess," exclaimed Dickon, his hazel eyes round and shining. "Edward has written a play for us. It's about Robin Hood and his band of merry men."

"Ned, how wonderful," cried Marganna. "I didn't know you wrote plays."

The older boy smiled shyly. "This is my first effort, actually, but it has come along fairly well. I mean, it should be a decent production—if William and Talitha can remember their parts." He cast a severe glance at the two younger Metcalfe children.

"I know my part." Talitha grimaced, displaying a gap where a front tooth should have been. "I just can't shoot that stupid bow and arrow." The little girl shook her head, causing her curls to jounce emphatically.

"She has the part of Will Scarlett," Ned explained. "It's really not a part for a girl."

"I wanted to be Maid Marian," she announced sourly. "Who cares about being a silly outlaw?"

"We've already taken a vote and decided Will Scarlett was more important than Maid Marian," Ned stated calmly.

"I was outvoted because I am the only girl. It's not fair!"

"I'm sorry, Talitha, it just can't be helped. Anyway," Ned turned back to Rath and Marganna, "William is playing the part of the sheriff of Nottingham, but he always forgets his lines." He indicated the older of the two Metcalfe boys. "On the other hand, Charles makes a very good Robin Hood. He got that part because he is an excellent archer."

Dickon spoke up. "I am to be Friar Tuck. I have to wear a pillow tied around my middle so I will be plump enough."

Marganna laughed. "I'd love to see your play."

"Perhaps we might watch it after we eat," suggested Rath.

Ned looked pleased. "Yes, indeed, though I'm not so sure my cast is ready for an audience," he warned.

"At least it will be more fun," retorted Talitha, "than going over and over it in the attic."

Marganna immediately liked James Metcalfe's wife, Elizabeth. A serene and practical woman, she skillfully supervised the serving of the outdoor meal, all the while chatting cheerfully with her guests and keeping a close eye on the children. She questioned Marganna about herself without appearing merely curious or prying.

For the first time since coming to Yorkshire, Marganna found herself talking and laughing naturally, feeling as if she had found a friend for life.

Rath viewed her from across the table, thinking how pretty she looked with the shade dappling her skin and darkening her eyes. This was the way he had often wished to see her, animated and happy—though he had to admit to a small twinge of jealousy because he had imagined her smiles would be for him alone.

After the meal Marganna sat beside young Edward as she read his play, while he self-consciously explained various parts to her. Dickon and Talitha were standing close by, their heads next to hers, and the other two boys sat on the ground at her feet. Each time she smiled or made a comment, the children shared pleased looks, proud of her interest in their project.

Rath, arms crossed over his chest, was leaning against the apple tree watching. For the first time it occurred to him what a wonderful mother Marganna would someday make, and he found the thought both intriguing and satisfying.

Rath himself was being observed by Elizabeth Metcalfe from the shady spot where she had settled with her needlework. Leaning close to her husband's ear, she whispered, "Rath may look casual standing by that tree, but there is nothing casual about those wonderful eyes when he turns them on Marganna. They look as if they are smoldering. It makes one think they will burst into flame."

"Come now," teased Metcalfe. "You have not been married *that* long, my dear."

For the space of a few seconds it was obvious she was giving rein to her imagination, but in another moment she found it necessary to appeal to her husband. "James, darling, would you mind fetching my lace fan from the parlor? I feel quite overheated."

As her husband dutifully obliged and presented her with

the fan, she murmured, "I am so glad you are such a mild-mannered man, safe and predictable. I am not at all certain I envy Marganna, having to deal with the dark and dangerous Lord Rathburn."

Soon Rath called for an enactment of the play, and with whoops of glee, the children dashed away to dress.

James Metcalfe, watched them go and then turned to Rath, saying, "I hope you don't think we indulge them too much, letting them spend time on activities such as this."

"Not at all," Rath replied. "Children need education in every field, not just mathematics and language." He flashed a smile at Edward. "Who knows? You may have a fledgling playwright living here at Nappa Hall—mayhap another Sophocles, eh, Ned?"

The boy beamed with pride, and Marganna silently blessed Rath for his kindness.

"Mother!" bellowed Talitha from an upstairs window. "I want to dress as Maid Marian and the boys won't let me!"

"Oh, dear, that child." Elizabeth sighed and prepared to lay aside her sewing. "She is such an independent little mite."

"I'll go in and see to their problems, shall I?" offered Marganna.

"Why . . . if you'd like to," Elizabeth said, surprised. "But you will have to be firm, I'm afraid."

"Don't worry—I will be."

"We'll be waiting at the bottom of the garden, then," James Metcalfe called after her. "That is where Ned and I have set up the stage."

Edward had just asked Rath if he would consent to play the role of Little John when the others began trooping down the path from the house. Dickon, rotund in a monk's robe that trailed after him, led the way, followed by the Metcalfe boys, very presentable in the guises of forest outlaw and villain. Charles, resplendant in green, sported a false goatee and a pointed hat adorned with a feather, and

William, though his clothing was baggy, looked threatening as the black-clad sheriff.

"I must say, Talitha, you are a somewhat feminine-looking Will Scarlett," said her father, laughing as the little girl appeared dressed in a pink brocade gown, her hair and shoulders draped in a lace cloth.

"I'm not Will Scarlett!" she said emphatically, unable to resist a smile. "I'm Maid Marian. Marganna said she would be Will so I could wear my pretty gown."

Rath's head came up as he heard the words, and an incredulous expression masked his features as he saw Marganna coming slowly down the walk.

"I hope you don't mind, Ned," she was saying, her cheekbones streaked with vivid color. "I knew how much Talitha wanted to play Maid Marian, but I must admit I didn't know how ridiculous I was going to feel in these clothes."

Despite her embarrassment, Rath thought she looked utterly delightful. She was wearing a full-sleeved white shirt, probably belonging to Charles, a leather jerkin that just cleared her hips, and a pair of crimson tights. Her hair had been pulled back and tied with a leather thong at the nape of her neck, but neither her hairstyle nor the cudgel in her hand made her look anything like a boy, Rath decided. Suddenly he found himself entertaining an overwhelming interest in theatrics.

"Are we ready to start?" Ned asked, and his players chimed their assent. "Well, since we have someone to play Little John, I think we should go back to our original opening scene—where the outlaws first meet. Robin Hood and Little John both try to cross the footbridge at the same time, remember? And Little John challenges Robin to a match with their quarterstaves."

A footbridge had been cleverly constructed from a log placed across two kegs, with piles of fresh straw strewn beneath it to simulate the stream. Robin Hood and Little John took their places on the log and were handed long staffs such as the one Marganna held.

Playing the part of the outlaw leader, Charles had to shout his lines above the clash of the staffs, with Ned providing ample prompting from his vantage point. The two dodged and parried, with Rath taking care to avoid striking Charles' fingers. Marganna was fully appreciating the sight of Rath's lean, athletic body balanced on the log when he unexpectedly slipped and went down on one knee. As he did so, his quarterstaff wavered and neatly swiped Robin Hood from his feet and into the straw below.

The adults laughed at the look of chagrin on Rath's face as he reached down to pull the scowling youngster to his feet.

"Are you all right, lad?" Rath asked.

"I'm fine, but this isn't the way the play is supposed to go."

"Never mind," Elizabeth Metcalfe said soothingly.

"Surely someone else wishes to challenge the noble Little John?" Metcalfe said. "How about you, Sheriff?"

William ducked his head and grinned shyly, but after a bit of urging was up on the log, battling as fiercely as ever a villain could. The boy's energetic attack took Rath by surprise, but he smiled, his white teeth flashing, as he defended himself against the swinging staff that stirred the air only inches from his head.

"Take pity, my lord sheriff," Rath cried in mock terror, his knees quaking. William burst into a fit of giggles at the sight, his eyes squeezing shut in mirth. In the next instant, he had landed squarely on his backside in the thick straw.

"Foul!" cried Marganna. "Sir, you used unethical tactics to unarm your opponent. It wasn't fair to make him laugh."

Rath slanted a bright green look in her direction. "Who accuses me of treachery? Ah, the noisy Will Scarlett! Are you brave enough to come up here beside me and do battle? I'd welcome the chance to unarm *you!*"

James and Elizabeth could not control their discreet laughter, and Marganna's chin rose stubbornly.

"Afraid to accept my challenge?" Rath said loudly. The play forgotten, the children entreated her to climb onto the log and silence his disrespectful tongue. After a moment's hesitation, Marganna agreed, and allowed Charles and his father to lift her onto the footbridge.

Rath raised his cudgel chest high, his eyes intense in his tanned face. "Strike the first blow, stripling."

"Cease your mindless prattle, varlet," Marganna cried dramatically, gripping her staff by one end and swinging it forcefully, so that Rath had to scramble backward. A rousing cheer greeted this maneuver, and she took a moment to throw a look of gratitude over her shoulder.

"Look out!" shrieked Talitha, and Marganna whirled to see Rath rapidly advancing. She ducked back, raising her staff to parry the light blow he landed. As their quarterstaves met and held, his face came close to hers.

"You look most fetching in that garb," he said, his voice low and caressing, reaching her ears only. "I think you should dress like a boy more often."

She withdrew her cudgel, then put all her strength into an answering thwack. Rath grinned as he caught her off balance with a light tap behind the knees.

"Oh!" she gasped, arms flailing. "You brute!" She swayed dangerously and the staff dropped from her fingers, bouncing end over end as she teetered this way and that.

Seeing she was going to tumble from the log, Rath tossed aside his own quarterstaff and threw his arms around her, attempting to steady both of them. Instead, as she toppled, she clutched at his shoulders, causing him to fall with her. Just before they struck the ground, Rath twisted his body to cushion her fall, and in another instant they were lying in the straw, legs and arms tangled.

Marganna, sprawled atop Rath in a most unladylike way, struggled to get up, but he wrapped an iron-muscled arm around her hips, pressing her firmly against him.

"Rath!" she exclaimed, laughing. "What do you think you are doing?"

Before he could reply, they were surrounded by chattering children, each voicing a different question.

"Are you hurt?" queried Charles, leaning over them.

"Who won the fight?" shouted Dickon, appealing to the Metcalfes. "Is it a draw?"

"Little John struck the last blow," William pointed out.

"But he cheated," argued Talitha.

"Did not!" exclaimed Dickon.

"He struck her legs!"

"That's perfectly acceptable, isn't it, Father?" Charles appealed to his parent.

"Perhaps we should help Rath and Marganna up and then decide," said Elizabeth, peering over her sons' shoulders at the couple lying half covered with straw.

Marganna made a feeble attempt to rise, almost regretting having to remove herself from the broad expanse of Rath's chest and the comforting thump of his heart. As she stirred, he placed a stealthy kiss beneath her ear and moved his hips in a boldly suggestive manner. She stared at him, her eyes moving from the wisps of straw in his black hair past his mocking green eyes and down to his finely chiseled mouth, which curved into a smile at her perusal. The anger she usually managed to summon vanished completely, and she found herself quite tempted to kiss him.

Just then two strong hands gripped her waist, and James Metcalfe lifted her to her feet. Suddenly aware of the staring faces all around them, Marganna busied herself brushing the dust and straw from her borrowed clothing, and when Rath again stood at her side, she kept her head lowered, refusing to look at him.

James winked broadly at his wife, then cleverly distracted the children by suggesting an archery tournament. As the boys skipped away to find their bows and arrows, Marganna dropped down beside her hostess, breathing heavily.

"Whew!"

With a knowing smile, Elizabeth handed her the fan. "Here, use this. You look rather overheated."

Later, when Dickon insisted Rath demonstrate his abilities as an archer, Marganna found pleasure in simply watching this man to whom she was married. As he drew the bow taut, muscles flared along his shoulders and arms, and his long legs tightened in an archer's stance. There was an aura of dangerous physical strength about him, and though it was ordinarily kept in check, Marganna knew very well he would not hesitate to unleash it when necessary. As she vividly recalled, there had been times when he had used some part of his physical power against her, though she knew he had never shown her the full force of the strength he was capable of exerting—not even at Will's house when he had plucked her out of the ivy vines or last night on the stairs.

"I'll wager Rath could teach Will Scarlett how to handle a bow," she heard James Metcalfe suggest wickedly.

Marganna laughed. "I'd much rather watch."

"Oh, please!" the younger children pleaded in unison.

"I'll write a larger part for you," bargained Ned.

"It isn't that. It's just that . . . well, I've never shot a bow either. I'd make a very poor outlaw."

"Rath could teach you," William insisted. "Couldn't you?"

"But of course." The dimples came and went in his cheeks. "Come here, Will Scarlett, and I shall oblige with your first lesson."

As she stepped to his side, Marganna threw Rath a wary look. "Just how dangerous is *this* going to be?" she asked in a low voice.

"That depends," he replied softly. "It could prove very dangerous indeed."

Rath handed Marganna a curved wooden bow, then instructed her in the correct positioning of her feet. "Now, raise the bow . . . no, higher—here, I'll show you." He came up close behind her, arms curving on each side to grasp and steady the weapon. As his hands covered hers, he said, "Pull the bowstring back like this . . ."

He shifted his stance to move even closer, and Marganna felt him along the length of her body. She knew the contact was even more intimate than it would have been had she been wearing her long skirts.

"Good," he whispered, his mouth grazing her ear, and a shudder went through her as she contemplated his meaning. For the benefit of those watching, he spoke more loudly. "You're doing fine, Marganna. Now we'll attempt a shot." He reached for an arrow from the quiver on his back, and quickly fitting it, assisted her in drawing back the bowstring a second time. Situated snugly within his embrace, with his breath warm on her cheek, Marganna was not able to think of the task at hand, and when the arrow was released with a resounding twang, the recoil of the bowstring snapped it against the inside of her arm, painfully burning the skin below her wrist.

"Ouch!" she cried in surprise.

Rath tossed the bow aside. "Damn, what was I thinking of?" he muttered, pulling back her sleeve to examine the injury.

"It's nothing, really," she assured him. "I was startled, that's all."

"I should have known better." He raised her arm and placed a kiss against the reddened skin. The touch was so gently soothing that it sent a spiraling thrill through her, and for an instant her breath caught in her throat. She stared into his eyes, her own darkened by inner turmoil.

Rath's grim look was replaced by a slow smile. "I think you have had enough lessons for one day, Will Scarlett. To save you further injury, mayhap we should start back to Rathburn Hall."

Something in his gaze caused the thrill to flutter to life again and streak through her with devastating effect. Fearing her knees might buckle, she merely nodded and turned away.

Marganna had never been so aware of Rath; she hung on his every word and savored his smallest movement, powerless to stop herself. She tried to dredge up a bit of self-disgust, but for some reason, this new turn of events was too intriguing and she was too fascinated by the fresh influx of feelings she was experiencing to succeed.

She knew he sensed her change of attitude as well, for he dared small intimacies she would once have scorned: his hands lingered far longer than necessary as he lifted her onto horseback for the return trip to Rathburn Hall, and he casually caressed her knee as he turned to bid the Metcalfes and all the children farewell. Instead of irritating her, his actions, proprietary and possessive as they were, seemed only an indication of things to come. A soft, anticipatory smile lighted her face and lingered all the way across the moor.

Rathburn Hall awaited them, its profusion of white roses gleaming like stars in the gathering dusk. For the first time Marganna thought of it as home and found the idea inordinately pleasant.

She waited on the lawn while Rath stabled the horses. When he returned and held out his hand, she unhesitatingly put hers in it, letting him lead her into the house.

Pausing just long enough to inform the cook they would not be wanting supper for some time, Rath and Marganna hastened up the curving flight of stairs to their bedchamber.

As soon as the door was secured, Rath closed the distance between them with three long strides, his arms going around Marganna.

"It has been a most . . . enlightening day, sweetheart," he murmured with his lips against her hair. "I thoroughly enjoyed it."

"As did I."

One large hand slid beneath her tumbled hair to close around the nape of her neck; the other moved to the small of her back, pulling her tightly against him. Rath lowered his head and, sensing no resistance in her, rested his mouth against hers for a long moment. As his lips began to warm hers, to shape and mold them, he felt the acceleration of her pulse beneath his fingers that lay along her neck.

Despite her shock at her own lack of self-control, Marganna arched against him and slipped her arms around his shoulders. His dark head dipped so he could place swift, hot kisses along the base of her neck; her head fell back, and her mouth was open in unashamed abandonment. Rath kissed her lips, absorbing her moan of passion.

When his eager hands went to the fastenings of her gown she helped him, her fingers trembling with a growing urgency, and she made no protest when he carried her to bed.

The darkened room was filled with an evening chill, but she didn't feel it, for it seemed Rath's burning hands were touching her everywhere, heating her flesh and blood to a point near boiling.

"I know you have been . . . teasing me all day long . . . oh, Rath!"

Her words were cut short by the intense pleasure of his mouth on her breast, kissing, pulling, playfully nibbling. She caught her breath and writhed beneath him.

His mouth moved to hers again, his kiss wildly ravaging, leaving her aching and breathless, longing for the feel of his hard body against her.

"Rath, I want you," she confessed. "I just can't help myself."

Marganna fell silent, relinquishing herself to him, to the undeniable mastery of his body as he claimed her and took her with him to some thrilling, secret place she had never dreamed existed. Rath had become a part of her, the most important part. No longer capable of reason, Marganna could only cling to him, letting him guide her through the myriad of sensations and feelings that assaulted her, that washed over her in blinding waves of ecstasy.

"Marganna!" he shouted—or whispered—she couldn't tell which. And then it didn't matter anymore, for they were both drowning, lost together—sinking into the black depths, then just as suddenly tossed high on the crests of relentless waves of shattering release, which left them lying on a distant shore, sweetly tired, battered but satiated.

Eventually the last remnant of sunlight crept from the room, leaving the two figures still entwined on the rumpled bed, alone in the darkness.

Alone, but never again lonely.

Chapter 15

A midnight moon rode high in the strange light of the northern sky when Marganna awakened. For a moment she was afraid she had been dreaming; then she turned her head on the pillow and saw Rath asleep beside her, his peaceful features bathed in moonlight. It hadn't been a dream after all . . .

He sighed and snuggled deeper into the bedcovers, one hand groping sleepily toward her side of the bed.

She watched him, thinking how vulnerable he looked lying there, every trace of stern arrogance erased by slumber. So many times in their stormy acquaintance she had seen his mouth set in a grim line or his brow scarred by a slashing frown, but never had she seen him look so serene and untroubled. Now that she knew the vibrant texture of his skin, she longed to touch him again but contented herself with easing back down beside him.

"Rath," she breathed in a whisper so soft it barely stirred the air. "I wish I dared tell you how much I love you."

She only meant to experiment with the words, to see how they sounded, and her eyes widened in surprise when he turned onto his side and regarded her with a devilish smile.

"Why can't you?" he asked.

"Oh!" She blushed faintly. "I didn't mean to wake you."

"No matter. Now, answer my question."

She dropped her head, but he put a finger beneath her

chin and gently raised her face, forcing her to look into his eyes.

"Is it true?" His gaze was intent. "Do you love me?"

She sensed he was risking a great deal to ask the question, and she found she could not deny him the answer. "Yes," she murmured, brushing her fingertips across his firm mouth. He smiled beneath the caress, kissing her fingers.

The deviltry was still in his voice. "And did you just decide that at this moment?"

"Yes, seeing you asleep—looking like a harmless little boy." She couldn't resist the jab.

He rose above her, eyes twinkling. "I'll show you how harmless I am," he threatened. His mouth sought hers in a wildly sweet kiss as he threw one bare leg across her thighs, reminding her they were naked beneath the linen sheet.

"So, you love me, do you?" he teased. "Lord, I never thought to hear those words from you."

She laughed softly, wonderingly. "I don't know how or why, but I do . . ." Her face grew sober. "I love you."

He dropped another kiss on her lips. "Why do you look so distressed when you say it?"

"I didn't know I looked distressed . . . but if I did, it must be because I never wanted to love you. You know that."

"Why not?"

"Surely you are as aware of the reasons as I am," she murmured. "Our loyalties—"

"Our loyalties are in London. That's a long way from Middleham." He lifted a hand to brush the hair from her forehead and twined his fingers through the shining strands cascading over her pillow. "As long as we stay here, away from court and politics, what will it matter? Plots and rumors and intrigue can't reach us, can't hurt us."

"I hope you're right."

"Come, love, tell me the rest of it."

"What do you mean?"

"There's something else, isn't there?"

Marganna was amazed at the depth of her hurt. Why

should he force such confessions from her when he had said no word of love himself? Couldn't he guess that she needed and wanted to know the extent of his feelings for her? But if he would not reveal them freely, she would not attempt to make him do so.

Seeking a diversion, she glanced toward the window and saw the brilliant moonfire spilling into the room. She moved from his arms and threw her legs over the side of the bed.

"Marganna? Where are you going?" he asked softly.

"I wanted to look at the moon, but I just realized I . . . I can't walk across the room with no clothes on."

"I assure you I wouldn't mind in the least."

"No, perhaps not . . . but I find I am unable to do it."

"A problem easily solved, my love." He chuckled as he slid out of the bed and scooped her up, sheets and all. In a few steps, he had crossed the room and settled himself in the cushioned window recess with Marganna on his lap. He unlatched the window and opened it to admit a chilly breeze as well as the sounds of night birds and the faint bleating of sheep.

He pulled the sheet high around Marganna's shoulders, and she snuggled closer to his warmth. His hand moved to gently massage her back.

"I want to know why you are so displeased to find yourself loving me." His reminder was quiet but firm. She knew he would not rest until he had the answer.

It took her a long moment to summon her courage. "No woman wants to be in love with a man who . . . well, one who doesn't love her," she finally blurted out. "You yourself told me the only marriage you wanted was one like Anne and Richard's. A marriage such as ours could never be so ideal. It's as simple as that."

"Ah." He leaned against the wall and pressed her closer to his bare chest. "You know, Marganna, simple is not a word I would have chosen to describe any facet of our relationship. It has been hopelessly complicated from the first."

"And it promises to get worse," she said gloomily.

"So that is how you view married life with me?"

She drew back to look at him in surprise. "Why, no. I mean . . . well, I did not suppose . . . we would ever even . . ."

"Live as man and wife?" he finished for her.

She nodded.

"My dear, I don't believe I am going to be able to measure up to the image of knavery you have created for me."

"What do you mean?"

"I mean I am your husband, you little idiot, and I intend to remain your husband. That, of course, entails living in the same house as you, eating at the same table as you, and . . ." He put his mouth to her ear, his heated breath sending shivers skittering through her body. " . . . sleeping in the same bed as you. Did you expect me to tire of a wife as soon as the wedding night was over?"

"I didn't know what to expect. After all, you never wanted a wife."

Her words were so forlorn, he could not hold back a deep, rich laugh. "Poor Marganna! I know that is how it must have seemed to you. God knows I tried often enough to make you think I despised you—remember that night we slept manacled together?"

She tossed her head. "How could I forget? Nothing in my proper upbringing prepared me for that."

"Nor in my improper one, if you must know. Did you think I hated you that night?"

"Yes, I did. You were so cold."

"Hardly that! But the truth is I had never met a female like you—I didn't know what to do with you. You were obviously leading me on a merry chase and enjoying every minute of it."

"Well, you made up for it when you were bargaining with that horrible peddlar." She sniffed, tilting her head to look up at him. "You liked humiliating and insulting me, admit it."

"I wasn't insulting you, love—quite the opposite, if you can believe it. Oh, I don't deny there was a certain element of revenge in my actions. I was furious you had eluded us so easily, and I wanted to repay you for some of the worry I'd been through. But mostly I was just curious."

"Curious?"

"Naturally. From the first moment I saw you at Nottingham—even during those times you were hurling insults at me—I felt a compelling need to learn what lay beneath that unruffled surface. Imagine my delight when I discovered what treasures that dull traveling gown was hiding."

"You told the peddlar I was barely adequate, if I remember correctly," she said, the corners of her mouth lifting. "You called me skinny . . . and . . . and . . . said I would barely fill a man's hand . . ."

"I did it to rankle you, sweetheart." He grinned. "How could I possibly announce that I found you much more than adequate? Think how my pride would have been compromised. No, it wasn't the right moment to display pleasure because you seemed made for my hand alone. You look surprised—I'll demonstrate, shall I? See . . . every bend and curve of your leg fits my hand perfectly."

His broad palm curled around one ankle, then slid upward along the calf and knee, coming to rest on her thigh and shifting her even closer to him.

"As for the part about not filling a man's hand . . . well, perhaps I misjudged. After all, I couldn't measure properly with so many eyes on us. Perhaps your clothing was misleading."

His hand crept upward from her thigh, over her hip, and along her ribcage. Gently he brushed the back of his knuckles against the underside of her breast, then turned his hand to cup her flesh. As he did so, she took an unsteady breath, finding the contrast between his tanned skin and the fairness of hers subtly exciting.

"See, love? You fill my hand completely . . . wonderfully. I apologize for underestimating you."

He placed a feathery kiss on her lips, then a second at the base of her throat, and a third just above the breast he still held captive.

"I accept your apology with gratitude. But what about the night at Moor's End when you found me trying to escape over the roof? Your actions proved then that you hated me.''

''You sweet little innocent,'' he chided. ''All that was proved that night was how much I had already lost to you—my reason, my self-restraint, my self-respect.''

She raised a darkly winged brow, fascinated by his confession. ''Then, you didn't . . . hate me?'' she prompted.

''Not even when I wanted to most.''

''When was that?''

''On our wedding night, when you made it clear to every one of our guests that you couldn't stand the thought of going to bed with me.''

''Oh!'' She looked shamefaced. ''It truly wasn't that, Rath. I just hated Richard ordering us to marry when I thought you despised me because I am a Tudor. Perhaps,'' she said in a considering tone, ''I only defied you to test you. To try and learn your real feelings.''

His mouth was agonizingly tender as it moved over hers and awakened a trembling response deep within her.

''I understand your reasoning, Marganna, but sweetheart, your defiance was what drew me.'' His eyes danced as he put his hands on either side of her face and said, ''Listen to me. I knew you were an extraordinary woman when you stood in front of a roomful of people and sang a bawdy song meant to put me in my place . . . and when you made the trip to Yorkshire without complaining, even when you thought I was going to lock you in a prison somewhere. I had to admire your courage when you dared everything to escape me, and when you lifted that stubborn chin of yours and glared right back at Bronwyn, never actually knowing what she would try next. I started each day hoping something would destroy the attraction I felt for you and went to bed each night only loving you more.''

''L-loving me?''

''You must have known. From what Will tells me, everyone in the castle did.''

''Well, *I* had no idea.''

''I was stupid enough to deny it, to think that if I could make love to you, the fascination would finally be over. There'd be no more mystery. But too late I found it wasn't going to be that easy, and now here I am, well and hopelessly entangled, knowing the fascination will never end."

He pulled her face to his and kissed her again. "Dear God, I love you, Marganna. And with any luck at all, I believe we can have a marriage to rival even that of Richard and Anne."

"Oh, Rath," she whispered incredulously, her arms going around his neck. As they clasped each other, the rumpled linen sheet dropped from Marganna's shoulders and fell unnoticed to the floor.

Outside the pale summer moon—the moon she had come to the window to see—burned on, also forgotten.

Later, clad in dressing gowns, they sneaked down to the kitchen where, to their shame, they found the exhausted cook asleep with her head on the table. Their supper was being kept warm on the hearth, and after apologizing profusely to the groggy cook and sending her off to bed they took the food upstairs and shared it, sitting upright in the middle of the huge canopied bed, laughing and chatting.

They spoke of many things that night, but Marganna's family was never mentioned, nor was the king, nor even the princes. They talked about their childhoods, something neither of them had ever done with such honesty or in such detail; they laughed about their fateful meeting and all the events that followed; they even spoke of a future together, albeit tentatively and with a certain shyness.

Dawn found them snuggled together under the covers, her head on his shoulder, his arm possessively around her waist. The first fevered passion had gone, leaving them tired but replete, secure in their newfound happiness. The misty dampness of a midsummer morning swirled into the chamber through the open window.

Their week at Rathburn Hall passed swiftly. They spent the days walking or riding, reading to each other in the garden, exploring every nook and cranny of the manor house, or cooking their own meals in the kitchen.

The nights were long and precious, filled with passion and tenderness. Every evening they shared candlelit dinners in the privacy of their bedchamber, and sometimes Marganna would play the harp and sing old Welsh love songs, while Rath sipped wine in front of the fire. At those times he would watch her as he sat quietly for an hour or more, his green eyes reflecting the flames in the fireplace, until suddenly the wineglass he held would be set down unheeded on the table next to him and he would rise from his chair to bear her away to the shadowy recesses of the curtained bed. There, whispers and intimate laughter interspersed with long, intense silences would be repeated until the wee hours of the morning.

On their last full day before returning to Middleham, they rode out onto the moor. Rath had awakened Marganna with a kiss and the announcement he was taking her on a picnic to a special place.

Rathburn Gill, as he called it, was a wooded glen hidden in a crevice on the moor and impossible to see until the trail topped the rim of the hills surrounding it. Running through the heart of the leafy oasis was the gill, a rock-tumbled stream that twisted through the woods, pausing to form a deep pool before trickling out the lower end of the crevice onto more barren ground.

Marganna was enchanted, for she had not suspected such a place existed. They walked over every inch of it, Rath pointing out wildflowers and naming the plants and herbs he had gathered as a child under Clovelly Biggins' supervision. Later, as they sat on blankets spread under an oak tree sharing the meat pies, wine, and cheese the cook had packed for them, he amused her with stories of swimming in the pool or, with the other boys, pretending to be pirates on a raft built of willow saplings. All the while Mrs. Biggins sat on the bank, sorting her herbs and keeping a stern eye on them.

After lunch, Rath and Marganna lay back to stare at the scene overhead, playing the child's game of looking for images in the masses of white clouds that foamed across a sky the color of robins' eggs.

"I see a castle," Rath said, pointing upward. "See? And there's an old lady with a dog."

"Oh, Rath, I don't see any such thing. Oh, wait . . .

yes, I do." Delighted, she brushed a kiss on his cheek. "How clever of you."

"Now you find something," he prompted, realizing she had probably never done this sort of thing before.

Obediently she gazed at the clouds, feeling small and insignificant as they swept rapidly across the endless sky.

"Look! I see a dragon," she exclaimed, pointing out the grouping of clouds that really did resemble such a creature.

"A dragon?" Rath murmured. "Is that beast going to rear its ugly head again?"

Suddenly understanding that she'd made him think that Henry Tudor and his cause were never far from her mind, she threw an arm around him and rested her head on his shoulder.

"Never again, my love," she whispered. "I promise, never again."

Later Marganna realized she must have fallen asleep, for she was awakened by an odd, rustling noise. Turning on her side, she looked up to see her husband unashamedly shedding his clothing.

"What are you doing?" she cried, smiling in spite of herself.

"I can't come to the gill and not go for a swim in the pool. Care to join me?"

He sounded so reasonable that she considered it, but only for a moment. "No, thank you. The water is no doubt icy cold . . . and besides, what if someone should see us?"

"The water is not cold, merely invigorating," he replied. "And no one will see us. Even if someone did venture this way, which is unlikely, we would hear their approach and have time to dress before they saw us."

"No, Rath, really . . . I think I would prefer to watch."

His smile broadened at that, but he tugged at her hand, insisting she come in too.

"At least wade into the water," he said coaxingly. " 'Twill be more enjoyable than your experience at Aysgarth, I guarantee."

"Oh, all right," she conceded, "but I'll only go wading. And you go on with your swimming. There's no need to watch me undress."

Reluctantly he agreed, and as she began loosening her gown, she heard the splash of his dive into the pool. He surfaced with a loud whoop and, shaking the water from his hair, swam vigorously from one end of the pool to the other, then back again.

Clad only in her smock, Marganna tentatively approached the edge of the water; seeing her, Rath swam toward her. She watched fascinated as his feet touched bottom and he rose, water streaming from his body.

Marganna thought he looked magnificent and experienced a surge of pride as her eyes moved lovingly over the breadth of his shoulders, the narrowness of his waist and hips, the length of his strong legs—the pure, masculine beauty of him. She recalled the notion she'd had the night of the storm that he was a pagan, and at this moment, in this setting, it seemed even more likely.

"Here, love, let me help you," he said, reaching out to take her hand. Before she realized his intention, he had swung her up into his arms and was striding out into the deeper water with her.

"Rath!" she exclaimed. "I intend only to go wading. Don't you dare!"

His eyes gleamed with devilish glee. "You can't come to Rathburn Gill and not go swimming, Marganna."

"I can."

He lowered his arms, dipping her bottom into the cold water. She screamed and struggled within his grasp, her feet churning and splashing.

"I'm warning you," she threatened, trying not to laugh. "I will not tolerate such treatment."

"All right. Give me a kiss and I will return you to shore."

She eyed him doubtfully, but when he maintained a sober face, she slipped her arms around his neck and lifted her lips to his. The dampness of his body quickly soaked through the skimpy undergarment she wore, and the resulting chill caused her to burrow deeper against his chest. As they kissed, his exciting masculine scent filled her nostrils, inspiring her to trail the kiss down the side of his neck. Mischievously she traced the outer rim of his ear with her tongue and felt his start of surprise. In the next instant his arms relaxed and she plummeted into the pool, her scream swallowed up by the water closing over her head. She came up splashing and spluttering, dashing water from her eyes.

"Damn you, Rathburn! This water is cold!"

"I'm sorry, love, but you distracted me so much, I forgot what I was doing."

"Oh, hellfire!"

He cocked his dark head to one side, grinning. "You know, for someone raised in a convent, you certainly swear a great deal."

"Only in your presence," she retorted, turning her back and swimming toward the opposite bank.

"Where are you going?" he called after her.

"As far away from you as I can get!"

"Oh, no you don't!"

He dived beneath the water, groping with one hand until he clutched Marganna's ankle, with which he dragged her back to him.

His actions were arrested as he looked down on her upturned face, and he could not prevent a smile as she grimaced at him. She moved her arms to keep afloat, her long hair streaming out behind her. "I suppose you think this is amusing?" she asked.

"Amusing is hardly the word I would have chosen," Rath replied. "You look remarkably like a lovely mermaid tempting her lover . . . " He clasped her waist with both hands and pulled her against him. "And, sweetheart, I was never one to resist temptation."

He brought his mouth down upon hers, and very soon her hands crept upward along his arms to lock behind his neck. Marganna welcomed his warmth in the cool water and entwined her legs with his, bringing them even closer together. He caught his breath and took her lips again in a fiery, demanding kiss. Then he lowered his mouth to capture the tightened peak of one breast as it strained against the soaked fabric of her smock. This time it was

Marganna's turn to gasp in pleasure, and as his mouth moved to caress the other breast, her fingers curled in the thick dark hair at the back of his head.

Rath's hands slid down to cup her buttocks, pressing her closer to him, making her intensely aware of his intentions. She had no thought of denying him now, and urged him on by moving her hands to knead the powerful muscles spanning his broad back.

Their bodies seemed weightless as they floated in the water, surrounded by billowing strands of Marganna's hair. The crystalline liquid swirled around them, lifting and supporting them, as their bodies merged. Time ceased to be as they moved together, losing themselves in some other world of exquisite pleasure—a world where only they existed and all that mattered was the sharing of their fevered passions.

They were slow to return to their senses, drifting languorously together. It was only the iciness of the water, finally penetrating their bodies and minds, that roused them and sent them back to shore to wrap themselves in the blankets.

"Didn't I tell you it would be an enjoyable experience?" Rath asked as they huddled together. She nodded, smiling contentedly.

"You know, from this day forward, I think we should call this 'Marganna's Pool.' We could start a new tradition: every time we come here, we could . . ." The rest of his words were whispered into her ear, and her soft laugh drifted gently on the warm summer breeze as she turned her face to his.

Middleham Castle was just as they had left it. Though Marganna looked forward to seeing its residents again, she was well pleased when Rath suggested they stay only a week or so until he could put some business affairs in order and then return to Rathburn Hall. Feeling a happiness, a security, she had never before known, she began to believe the moorland farm could become the home she had always wanted. Sometimes at night or on stormy days, the sound of the wind still had the power to chill her to the bone, but she told herself she would become accustomed to it. With Rath beside her, she vowed, nothing seemed too difficult or discouraging.

During the first few days they were back at Middleham, Rath was forced to spend long hours away from Marganna, attending to business matters that needed his immediate attention. Marganna filled her days by helping Mrs. Biggins and learning all she could about the running of a large household. On one such day she had lingered overlong in the kitchens and was hurrying down the hallway to her chamber to change clothes before dinner when, abruptly turning a corner, she saw a couple wrapped in each other's arms, lost in a passionate kiss. The woman's black hair fell in tangled curls down her back, making her easy to identify, and the man was so huge, he could be none other than the Norseman, Erik Vogelman.

Marganna must have made some small sound, for the couple hastily moved apart, and Bronwyn whirled to face the intruder.

"I'm . . . I'm sorry to disturb you," Marganna said, hoping to forestall Bronwyn's anger.

Instead of the response Marganna expected, Bronwyn favored her with the first genuine smile of their acquaintance. Even Vogelman smiled, stepping out of the shadows to lay an arm across Bronwyn's shoulders.

"Congratulations on your marriage, your ladyship. May you and Lord Rathburn be very happy." Then, with another nod, he squeezed Bronwyn's shoulder, and she nodded as if in agreement.

Marganna was surprised to find the other woman so docile. Could it be the fierce Vogelman was having a greater influence on her than anyone had suspected?

"Bronwyn, I haven't had an opportunity to tell you how very much I appreciate what you did for me that day at the falls. Rath tells me you saved my life."

Bronwyn considered the words carefully, her black eyes intent on Marganna's face. "You are welcome." Suddenly, she grinned. "Of course, I must confess I did consider letting you drown."

Marganna smiled back, finding no trace of enmity in Bronwyn's expression. "I'm certain you did. I'm only grateful you decided against it."

"Yes . . . though my motives weren't entirely unselfish. When I saw the look on Rath's face, I knew I had best save you. I didn't want to have to answer to him."

Rosiness tinged Marganna's cheeks. "Yes, I know how formidable he can sometimes be."

For a long moment, the two women regarded each other, sensing the end of old hostilities and the beginning of a mutual respect.

For an instant, Bronwyn's face softened and she allowed herself a thoughtful smile. "I suppose I must thank you for something too. Had I not been so insanely jealous and filled with hatred for you, Rath would never have ordered Erik to guard me."

"Then everything has turned out well?" Marganna asked quietly.

"For all of us," spoke up Vogelman, his golden leonine eyes caressing Bronwyn's upturned face.

With a small thrill of wonder, Marganna realized he was right.

When they parted, she watched until Erik and Bronwyn had disappeared around the corner, then continued on her own way with a much lighter step.

Chapter 16

Pinning the last braided coil of hair into place, Marganna studied her reflection in the mirror. Even she could find no fault with her appearance today, for her wide brown eyes were shining, and her cheeks were flushed a becoming rose color. Her mouth looked soft, the corners tilted upward, as though she were about to smile. She told herself her new gown was responsible for her heightened color, but even as she admired its flowing moss green skirts, she knew the truth.

The change in her appearance, in her entire life, was due to Rath and the love she had discovered with him. The walls of her world could shrink to the size of this bedchamber and she wouldn't care a whit, not so long as Rath was confined within that space with her.

She glanced around the room, seeing nothing of its neat, daytime arrangement; rather, she was reviewing the firelit scene that had taken place the night before. Even now a smile broke over her face as she remembered Rath's playful antics. She had been sitting before the fire half dozing when suddenly he'd emerged from the garderobe and started toward her, wailing maniacally like the Mad Monk.

Protesting the noise, she'd backed away; then, finally giving way to her delighted terror, she had fled from him, uttering small, laughing shrieks as she dodged chairs, edged around corners, and leaped onto the bed to escape his clutching hands. In the end he'd caught her easily, of course, and pulled her down onto the hearth rug with him. As he rolled her into his arms, his face had suddenly sobered, an oddly serious light filling his eyes. He'd looked at her for long seconds, then crushed her to him almost desperately, capturing her mouth in a kiss that left little room for further thought.

"Oh, God, Marganna, I adore you," he'd whispered harshly. "I adore you so damned much it scares me."

She knew exactly what he meant, for she felt the same way about him. One couldn't trust happiness this complete, this fulfilling.

Now, shaking her head to clear it of such thoughts, she hastened from the room, gently closing the door behind her. She had promised to help Amelyn with the marketing that morning and knew her friend was probably waiting impatiently belowstairs. There was no time to entertain any more of this silly morbidity.

The town of Middleham was busier than Marganna had ever seen it. Throngs of people filled the narrow streets, pushing between the market stalls and bargaining noisily with the hawkers and sellers. Church bells rang, dogs barked, children ran and shouted. It was a confusion of color, sound, and smell, not always pleasant but exhilarating nonetheless.

The fact that she was allowed outside the castle with no escort other than Amelyn was, to Marganna, an indication of the new trust Rath had in her. Ruefully acknowledging the strain her marriage had put on her friendship with the other woman, she had gone to Rath for his permission, which he had willingly given, and now she hoped a day spent together would set everything right between her and Amelyn.

As they wandered through the marketplace, under the benevolent shadow of Middleham Castle, Amelyn had seemed more herself, talking and laughing without the restraint of the past weeks.

Marganna had paused to look at some beautifully woven shawls when she realized she was becoming separated from Amelyn, who had walked on ahead and was examining the contents of a fruit stall. Glancing regretfully at the shawls, she decided it would be best to keep pace with her companion.

"Marganna!"

At the sound of a familiar voice close behind her, she whirled.

"Donal FitzClinton," she gasped, sudden joy blazing through her. He had come to rescue her! Just as suddenly her elation faded. She no longer needed or wanted to be saved from Rath.

As if seeing her conflicting emotions, he laughed softly. "You are glad to see me, aren't you?"

"Well, yes, of course," she faltered.

He was, she noted, as elegant as she'd remembered, with his shining waves of golden hair, his perfect, imperious features, and his fashionable clothing. Still, why had she not noticed before how dandified and preening he seemed?

With an inward smile, she knew she was comparing him to her husband, and the last weeks had taught her an appreciation of Rath's aura of male strength, his ruggedness, his hardness of mind and body. No courtly manners or pretenses for him, she thought with satisfaction.

"There's a great deal we must talk about, Marganna," FitzClinton was saying. "Will you come with me now?"

"But where? What about Amelyn? Why don't you return to Middleham with me?"

"No, that wouldn't be safe. Your . . . husband has been less than welcoming in the past."

"Things have changed," Marganna began, but he interrupted somewhat impatiently.

"What? Just because you've married the rogue? Don't be foolish. That won't make him any happier to see me."

"But you could discuss the situation with him, couldn't you? And I'd like to send a message to my aunt."

His arm snaked unexpectedly around her waist; as she tried to draw away, he jerked her close to his side.

"I don't have time to stand chattering. We must talk in private. Come along."

"What do you think you're doing?" she cried, struggling. The basket she was carrying dropped to the ground, its contents spilling onto the cobblestones, but in the over-crowded street only a few people seemed to notice, and they appeared unwilling to interfere in the matter. She cast a desperate look over her shoulder, but Amelyn was still moving away, her back turned.

"Don't make me hurt you, Marganna," FitzClinton said in such a menacing tone that she felt the hair at the back of her neck stir in response. What had happened to the soft courtier? Who was this cold stranger in his place?

She had no time to formulate answers before the man was half dragging, half carrying her from the market square. She tried to kick out at him but staggered, causing him to yank her arm viciously. He held her close to his side, nearly crushing her ribs, and she felt the bruises his fingers were inflicting on her wrists as he gripped her.

He managed to carry her beyond the thickest part of the crowd to the entrance of a narrow alley, and now they were flanked by two other men, obviously in league with him. Knowing she had little time left to summon aid, Marganna raised her head to scream. Instantly FitzClinton's arms were like steel bands around her body, and his mouth came down on hers, swallowing her cry for help. At the feel of his moist lips shutting off her breath, Marganna felt sick, and her knees buckled. She wrenched away, wiping her face with the back of her hand, and he laughed, enjoying her disgust.

"Don't attempt anything like that again," he warned, shoving her ahead of him. "There, go through that doorway." He indicated a darkened staircase leading to the upper story of a blackened stone building.

Marganna found herself in a small, square chamber, dark except for a candle burning fitfully on the sagging table in the middle of the room. There was one long window, and she stumbled toward it, trying to determine where she was. All she could see were other rooftops until she raised her eyes; there were the jutting towers of Middleham, and she knew the house must be directly beneath the west wall of the castle.

Oh, Rath, she thought wearily, why didn't I stay there with you?

"Now, Marganna, let's make this as simple as possible. Where are the princes?"

"What?" For some reason she had not foreseen that question.

He advanced on her while the two other men stood guard at the door. "I don't have time to persuade you gently, you know."

"Listen to me," she said, holding out a hand to ward him off, "there is something my aunt doesn't know. The boys are all right. They're in no danger from the king."

FitzClinton looked puzzled. "What are you talking about?"

She stared at him, wondering how she had ever thought him handsome. Cunning and cruelty were plainly written on his aristocratic features.

"Aunt Margaret had to know the boys' whereabouts so that Henry Tudor could attempt their rescue. But since coming to Yorkshire, I have learned they are well and in absolutely no danger from Richard. In fact, my husband has always maintained Richard is trying to keep them safe from . . . others who want to harm them."

Her eyes darkened with the pain of her own stupidity. She should have listened to Rath all those weeks ago!

She backed as far away from FitzClinton as she could. "You . . . Aunt Margaret . . . Henry Tudor—you're the ones who want the princes dead, aren't you? She lied to me from the beginning."

"You thought she wanted to protect them?" he jeered, an ugly smile pulling at his mouth.

"I see now that a lifetime of obedience made me very naive and trusting where my aunt was concerned," she said crisply. "But at last I know the truth." She raised her chin bravely. "I won't tell you where they are, you know."

"What difference would it make to you if we find them?"

"I have gone through too much in my efforts to help those boys just to give up. I vowed they would never come to harm because of me, and I meant it."

FitzClinton's pale eyes narrowed, and his hand shot out

to grasp the front of her gown, ripping it to the waist in one savage motion. Marganna cried out and ducked into the corner, arms crossed to cover herself.

With an angered snarl, he closed the space between them, seizing her wrists and pulling her upright. He dragged her arms behind her back and held them there with one hand; with the other he began caressing her breasts.

"Tell me what I want to know, Marganna, or you'll regret it," he said casually, noting the way she flinched as his fingertips moved over her.

"Why are you doing this?" she gasped. "Why do you want to kill those innocent boys?"

He ignored her question, a bemused look settling over his face. "You're lovely, my dear," he said softly, moving his palm over the rounded side of her breast. Suddenly, viciously, he pinched the flesh beneath his fingers, and she bit her lips to keep from crying out in pain.

"Where are they?" he thundered.

"I . . . won't . . . tell you!"

"Stupid wench!"

Again and again his frenzied hand moved over her, pinching the tender skin, twisting it with maliciousness. Each time he hurt her, he repeated the question, and each time, she shook her head and forced back the screams.

"Damn you!" FitzClinton swore, striking her across the chest with the back of his hand. The ruby ring he wore cut a thin, jagged line that immediately beaded with crimson, bringing such a look of horror to his features that Marganna realized he could not stand the sight of blood.

With a shudder of distaste, he threw her to the floor where she lay, shaking with silent sobs. Unexpectedly he kicked her, the hard edge of his boot slamming against her hip. She curled her body, but he kicked out again, catching her in the ribs. For a moment, as the breath was knocked from her lungs, she felt as though she would faint, but she was not to be granted that mercy. She rolled onto her side, trying to ease the pain, and with a curse, he kicked her again, his boot bruising the softness of her thigh.

"For the last time, are you going to tell me where those boys are being kept?" he demanded, bending over her.

"No." She moaned, trying to twist away from him.

"Then I have no choice but to kill you," he muttered, dropping to one knee and locking his hands around her throat. "Either you tell me what I must know, or I will strangle you and go after the woman with whom you came to the market."

"She . . . she knows nothing," Marganna rasped out as she felt his thumbs press deeply against her windpipe, closing off the air.

"No, she probably doesn't, but I can use her to lure your husband out of his castle. A message that you are hurt or in danger should do it, wouldn't you think?"

She groaned inwardly. Rath wouldn't be gullible enough to believe such a lie, would he? But she knew he would. In his concern for her, he would abandon his usual caution—and, like her, he'd had no opportunity to witness the person FitzClinton really was. Panic gripped her in its cold hands, chilling her very blood. She didn't want Rath to die.

"Well?" FitzClinton's hands tightened about her neck. "Are you willing to sacrifice Rathburn to save those wretched boys? Or will you tell me what I want to know?"

She was surrounded by swirling darkness, and his voice seemed to echo from some great distance. She had been clawing at his fingers, but now her nerveless hands dropped to her sides and her head began to loll. He roused her with a hard shake, loosening his hold briefly. Marganna choked on the air flowing back into her throat.

"Ahh, God!"

Her eyes flew open as she heard FitzClinton's exclamation of distaste, and she saw him staring at the lace cuffs that had trailed over her breast, soaking up the trickling blood. Taking advantage of his distraction, she tried to scuttle away from him, but he lunged after her, strong fingers encircling her neck as though he was sorely tempted to break it.

As his heavy body pinned her down, she heard herself

whimpering, "Don't . . . please! I'll . . . I'll tell you where the boys are. Just don't hurt Rath."

Triumphantly, FitzClinton got to his feet, pulling her into a sitting position. "All right, give me those little bastards and Lord Rathburn is safe."

She drew a shaky breath. "They're . . . they're being kept at Rathburn Hall."

"Your husband's manor? Damn, I never expected Richard to chose an unfortified hiding place! A clever ruse. I've been wasting time loitering around these northern castles." He turned to his companions. "Jack, you stay here with her until we make certain she's telling the truth. Gibson and I will join the others and ride to Rathburn Hall. When we've dealt with the boys, we'll meet back here before setting out for London."

"Then what happens to her?" asked the man named Jack, jerking his head toward Marganna.

FitzClinton's smile was nasty. "I haven't decided yet. I may want to take her with me." He observed the other's avid gaze on her bared breasts. "When I tire of her, Jack, you're welcome to her. But until then, keep your hands to yourself, or rest assured, you will live out the remainder of your life as a eunuch."

When they had gone, Marganna stirred cautiously and opened her eyes to look at the man left to guard her. He was nondescript in every way—no doubt some nameless wretch willing to hire himself out for a few coins. In that case, it was unlikely he would be motivated by political reasons, so she hoped he might prove kinder than FitzClinton. She sent him a pitiful glance, holding her side as if trying to ease the very real pain she was feeling.

"Will you help me up?" she asked in a halting voice. "Please . . . I want to . . . sit in the chair. My side hurts so badly."

It was obvious that although the man was nervous, he saw no reason to leave her on the floor. Grasping her by the armpits, he lifted her up and supported her as she limped slowly to the table. He pulled out the chair that sat there and eased her into it, his avaricious eyes drawn again and again to the gaping front of her torn gown.

Just as he straightened up, Marganna seized the candle in front of her and thrust it against the side of his head. Instantly the room was filled with the odor of burning hair, the acrid smell clearing her own head somewhat. She lowered the candle, swiping it across the front of his greasy shirt. A line of flame streaked over his chest and down one arm as his scream of terror made her ears ring. As he slapped at his clothing and hair, she dashed out of the room, flinging herself down the stairs and out into the alley.

She never knew how she summoned the strength to run all the way to the castle, shouting for help as she crossed the drawbridge and stumbled through the main gateway.

A vision of Rath, strong and capable, had risen in her mind, remaining before her as she ran in distraught haste down the crowded street of the town. Now that same vision came to life in front of her as he ran down the castle stairs, three at a time, to catch her in his arms.

"Marganna, what in God's name—?"

"Rath, listen to me! FitzClinton is . . . is here after Ned and Dickon." Beneath her shielding arms, her chest heaved with the effort of breathing. "You've . . . got to . . . get to them first!"

"Where is he now?"

"I sent him . . . to . . . Rathburn Hall," she said, panting. "I thought it would give you time—"

Rath's anger exploded all around her. "You did what?" he shouted, grabbing her upper arms and shaking her fiercely. "You sent him to *Rathburn Hall?*"

She nodded, uncomprehending.

"Damn you to hell!" he exclaimed. "I moved the boys to Rathburn Hall yesterday."

"Oh, my God!" she whispered. "What have I done?"

He pushed her aside and, turning away, started bellowing orders to the men who had gathered around them in the courtyard.

Marganna stumbled to her knees and remained crouched there, only vaguely aware of the noise of the rapid departure taking place on every side of her.

Coldly, numbly, she prayed he would reach Rathburn

Hall before FitzClinton. She could not bear to think what would happen if he didn't.

"Come, lassie," a soft voice urged, and Marganna felt a strong, wiry arm around her shoulders. "Ye can't stay here. Let me help ye oop ta yer room."

"Mrs. Biggins, I . . . I didn't know the boys were at Rathburn Hall."

"Aw know, Aw know. How could ye? Ned has been ailin' all week, and Johnny just decided instead of takin' the doctor ta the boys, he had ta move them closer ta the doctor."

"It was awful!"

"Shh. Ye can tell me all aboot it later."

Leaning on the older woman for support, Marganna managed to climb the long staircase into the castle. Mrs. Biggins steered her to the small bedchamber she had first used at Middleham, not the larger, adjoining room she had been sharing with Rath. The maid Lilibeth was there, pouring steaming water into a wooden tub set before the fire.

"Noo, let's get ye oot of this ruined gown and inta a hot bath."

Marganna stood quietly, allowing them to unlace and remove her torn dress. Both women caught their breath as they pulled the gown from her shoulders and saw the masses of bruises covering her body.

"Saints preserve us, Marganna!" Mrs. Biggins gasped. "What has happened ta ye, lass?"

She made no response but climbed into the wooden tub of water and huddled there. Over her head, Mrs. Biggins and the little maid exchanged worried glances.

"Aw'm going ta find Amelyn," Mrs. Biggins announced, "and see what she can tell me. Aw will come back later, child, with some balm for those bruises."

Marganna nodded, reaching for the scented soap Lilibeth was holding. Despite the pain it cost her, she scrubbed her skin ruthlessly, trying to erase the memory of FitzClinton's thin, cruel hands. As she worked, she realized the mundane chores of bathing and washing her hair were helping to keep her mind from dwelling on the possible disaster now taking place at Rathburn Hall.

When she had finished her bath, she stood on the hearth rug and let Lilibeth dry her with tentative pats of linen toweling, accompanied by indignant clucks of the tongue and sympathetic sighs. Then, slipping into a warm dressing gown, Marganna curled into a chair by the fire to stare at the flames and wait. Sooner or later, she knew Rath would be coming.

It was late afternoon when the door to the chamber was thrown open to admit Rath. He was disheveled and breathing heavily, his hair tumbling across a dirt-streaked forehead. Marganna sprang to her feet, prepared for the worst.

"Ned and Dickon?" she whispered, one hand clutching the neck of her robe.

"Safe," he said tersely.

She sank back into the chair, filled with relief. After a long moment, she spoke again. "And . . . FitzClinton?"

It seemed to her his face twisted in contempt, and her heart twisted with it as she realized it was a question she shouldn't have asked.

"No," she said quickly, faintly. "Don't tell me—I don't want to know."

"Are you afraid he's dead?" His voice was low.

"No . . . I mean, it's not that I don't want to know," she amended. "It's that I don't care."

"I wish I could believe that, Marganna."

Her startled gaze flew to his face, tracing each stony feature. She had seen Rath furious with her many times, but never had she seen him like this. Always before, he had raged and shouted, just barely managing to keep his fierce temper in check, but at this moment he exuded an air of weary desolation that was much more forbidding.

"At any rate, he managed to elude us and escaped with only an injury. He must have familiarized himself with the area well enough to have had some sort of hiding place on the moors, should he need it."

Marganna remained silent.

"Can you deny you have been in contact with Fitz-Clinton?" he asked suddenly.

"Yes."

"Do you deny that somehow you arranged to meet him at the market?"

"Yes."

"Do you deny you told him where the boys were?"

"Yes!" she cried. In her anxiety, she had clasped her hands tightly together. Now she flung them wide, silently pleading for his understanding. "No! I did tell him, but I thought I was misleading him. How was I to know they actually were at Rathburn Hall?"

"That is exactly what I would like to learn," he said forlornly. "How did you get that information, Marganna? Who told you?"

"No one. I swear, I didn't know. It was just . . . just a horrible coincidence."

He walked to the open door. "Amelyn, you may come in now."

Amelyn stepped onto the threshold, looking hesitantly from one to the other of them.

"Mrs. Biggins has related your story, but I would like to hear it directly from you. Besides, I feel certain Marganna will find it enlightening."

Amelyn cast a quick glance across the room, and Marganna surmised she was both frightened and apologetic. She nodded back reassuringly.

"Now, Amelyn, what happened at the market?" Rath asked.

"Well . . . nothing unusual," she replied in a small voice. "Not at first, I mean. We were doing the shopping . . . laughing, talking, that sort of thing. We became . . . separated."

"How did that happen?"

"I don't know. I was looking at fruit . . . and when I turned to ask Marganna a question, she wasn't there."

Rath nodded. "Did you see her?"

"Yes, she was a . . . a short distance away," Amelyn answered.

"Alone?"

"N-no, she was with a man."

"Describe him to us."

"Well, he was fairly tall, with golden hair. Very fashionably dressed."

"The man's name is FitzClinton, Amelyn," Rath stated in a steel-edged tone. "Now please tell me what else you observed."

"What . . . what do you mean?"

"I mean, were they talking? What were they doing?"

Amelyn's distress was evident as she drew a deep breath. "Rath, must I?"

"I want to know the truth. Don't make this any more difficult than it already is."

Anxious blue eyes rested on Marganna's face. "I'm sorry," Amelyn whispered.

"Amelyn," growled Rath. "What did you see?"

"They were . . . kissing. And then they walked into . . . into the alleyway. I ran after them, but I couldn't find them."

Marganna rose to her feet. "Wait! You don't understand," she began. "I know how it must have looked to you, but he was only trying to silence me."

Rath considered her words, then said grimly, "You are either telling the truth, or you are a very good liar." Abruptly he turned away. "That will be all for now, Amelyn. Thank you for your help."

Amelyn bowed her head and fled the room.

Rath crossed the room to stand directly in front of Marganna, but his gaze was fixed on a point somewhere just above her head.

"I would like to know," he said, "what else you want to say in your own defense."

Oh, Rath, she thought sadly, how can I defend myself if you won't even look at me?

"You know, Marganna, I cannot think I was completely fooled by your affection for Ned and Dickon. You swore no harm would ever come to them through you, and God help me, I want to believe you." He turned his back and began pacing up and down the length of the room.

He stopped and looked at her. "He'd have killed them,

you know. Had we been even a few minutes later, he'd have gotten past the guards and the boys would have been dead and no longer a threat to your ambitious cousin.''

The truth of his words stunned her. Because of her, because of her family, two innocent boys had nearly been murdered. Coldly and cruelly murdered, and for what purpose? The greedy possession of a throne.

Marganna shuddered. The crime had seemed bad enough when she thought Richard was plotting against two unknown children. Now that she had become deeply involved—by meeting and growing to love the princes, learning their faults and virtues, their endearing quirks—she couldn't begin to contemplate what their murders would mean. Especially their murders at the hands of the very people she'd trusted to help them. The potential disaster of the day's events overwhelmed her, and she buried her face in her hands, unable to meet Rath's gaze.

''I will let you know what I decide to do,'' he said in a flat voice. In a moment she heard the door close quietly behind him.

As soon as Rath stepped into the great hall, he saw Mrs. Biggins and Will waiting for him. He sighed, running a hand through his still-damp hair. A bath and fresh clothes had given him time to get beyond the worst of his rage, but he had hoped to be allowed his supper in peace before having to face them. He knew damned well what they wanted, and he was in no mood to listen to them.

''We may as well get this over with,'' he said grimly. ''Where shall we talk?''

''Your bedchamber,'' Will suggested. ''Something tells me we will need the privacy.''

As he shut the door behind them, Rath said, ''Let me save you some time. I already know what you're going to say, and you're wasting your breath.''

''Be reasonable,'' Will exclaimed. ''You know Marganna did not betray those boys. She told FitzClinton where the boys were, but she thought she was putting him off the scent until she could get to you.''

"Even if that were the case, she made an extreme error in judgment. She shouldn't have told him anything."

"Did it ever occur to you that she might not have told him willingly?"

Rath's head snapped up. "What do you mean? I suppose she told you he forced her?"

"She didn't have ta tell us, Johnny," Mrs. Biggins broke in. "Aw saw for myself."

"Clovelly says Marganna's body is covered with bruises," Will said. "How could that have happened if he wasn't responsible?"

"Bruises?" Rath's expression was ominous.

Will nodded. "If I remember correctly, FitzClinton has a reputation for being something of a bully, and from the description Clovelly gave me, I'd say Marganna's injuries are exactly the sort a bully would inflict. Rath, don't you think it's possible she told him what she did just to make him leave her alone?"

"Damnation, Will! Why wouldn't she have told me?" Rath queried. "If there was any sort of excuse for what happened, why wouldn't she have let me know it?"

"Would you have listened?"

Rath studied his friend's face, seeing his disapproval. At last he shook his head.

"I . . . I don't know. Probably not." His expression was bleak as he looked from Will to Mrs. Biggins. "And anyway, it doesn't really matter now. What matters is that those boys nearly died today. A year of secrecy and planning, virtually destroyed in one afternoon because of our carelessness—mine and Marganna's."

"The lads are safe noo, Johnny," Mrs. Biggins said soothingly. " 'Tis best if ye just bear that in mind and forget the rest. Blamin' will only cause ye unhappiness, tha knows."

"I'll talk to Marganna without blaming her," Rath promised. "But it won't solve anything."

"Ye never know, laddie," Mrs. Biggins said, patting his arm. " 'Tis worth the tryin'." She held out a shallow stone dish. "Here, take this when ye go in ta see Marganna. 'Tis salve for her bruises."

Rath nodded, but after they were gone, he set the medicine aside and sank into a chair before the fire, his head in his hands.

Nearly an hour later, he opened the door to the adjoining chamber and stepped inside. The light of the dying fire barely illuminated Marganna, curled up asleep in the chair where he'd left her. He put the dish of ointment on a chest and set about lighting a candle. When he turned, he saw she was awake and watching him, her eyes huge and dark in a pale face.

"Are you feeling better?" he asked.

"Yes, I'm fine."

"That's . . . good."

He felt awkward, unsure how to proceed. He knelt to toss a log on the fire, then turned back to her.

"Clovelly tells me you . . . are injured."

"It's nothing, really."

"That is not what she says, Marganna. She thinks FitzClinton hurt you." He got to his feet, his eyes never leaving her face. "Did he?"

"I'm all right, Rath—truly." She gave a small, nervous sigh, and he thought her words lacked conviction.

"Come here," he said softly. "Please. I'd like to see for myself."

"What difference could it make?" she asked, still not looking at him.

"I was a fool to believe you could have plotted against Ned and Dickon. I think FitzClinton coerced you into giving him information and that you thought you were lying when you told him they were at Rathburn Hall. Is that true?"

She nodded.

"Why didn't you tell me?"

She finally raised her head to look at him. "I didn't think I should have to defend myself to you, of all people. If you didn't have faith in me . . ."

"You're right, of course."

He reached out a hand and pulled her gently to her feet. Marganna, having been in the chair for several hours, found her body stiff and sore, her legs cramped. She tried to take a step and stumbled against him.

Rath's arm shot out to steady her. "You *are* in pain," he murmured.

His fingers unhooked the front of her robe, opening and sliding it off her shoulders. His indrawn breath sounded loud in the room. "Jesus Christ and all the saints," he exploded in quiet fury. "FitzClinton did this to you?"

Her breast and shoulders were covered with small, blackened bruises, and as the robe fell away to crumple at her feet, the larger bruises on her hips and thighs were revealed.

Gently he traced the angry cut left by FitzClinton's ring. "My God, what kind of a bastard would do something like this."

He raised his hands to lift the heavy fall of hair from her neck. Gingerly he laid his fingertips over the purpling marks on her throat. A low groan issued from his own throat. "He tried to strangle you?"

She bowed her head.

"Marganna . . . look at me."

She obeyed, clenching her hands at her sides, shaken by the cold hatred in his eyes. Even knowing the hatred was for FitzClinton did not ease her mind.

"You know I will kill him for this, don't you?"

His voice was so low she could barely hear him.

"I know. But if you kill him, it should be for what he tried to do to Ned and Dickon—for what he would do if given a second chance. They are the ones to be avenged."

"No man could see such treatment of one he loves and not feel an overpowering bloodlust."

"I don't care about what FitzClinton did to me," she whispered. "All that matters is that despite everything between us, you had the same doubts and suspicions."

"I'm sorry," he said quietly.

Suddenly he bent and picked up her robe, draping it around her shoulders. "Come, let me put some of Clovelly's medicine on those bruises."

She let him lead her to the bed, where she eased her stiffening body down to rest against the pillows, grateful for their soft comfort. Rath took up the dish of salve and sat gingerly beside her.

"I must have been insane to think we could get away from . . . well, from the things that have plagued us since the beginning—Richard, the boys, the Tudors' desire for the throne." He dipped his fingers into the sweet-smelling balm and began to spread it gently over the bruises along her collar bone. "The treachery seems determined to follow us wherever we go."

His soothing hand moved lower, tenderly ministering to her battered flesh. She shuddered beneath his touch and closed her eyes.

"Marganna, I . . . I've spent the last hours thinking about this." She could hear his heavy sigh, sense his hesitation. "I've got to send you away."

Slowly she opened her eyes and looked into his. She was certain there was pain in their green depths, just as she knew an answering pain dwelt within her own. However, there was no surprise in her look—somehow, it was what she had expected.

"I am going to ask Will to take you back to London."

"London?" she whispered.

"It would be best for everyone concerned if we . . . well, if we don't live together until this has been resolved. I can't be responsible for both you and the boys. You see that, don't you?"

He put the salve aside and, placing an arm on either side of her, leaned forward to look into her face. "For the past weeks I have indulged myself in my passion for you—God, I can't deny it has been the happiest time of my life—but it can't continue. Not if Ned and Dickon are going to be the ones to suffer! When I'm with you, you're all I can think about, and I've neglected my duty to those boys long enough. It nearly cost them their lives."

"I know." She kept her voice carefully neutral. "And I realize your first loyalty must be to Richard."

"Yes, I owe him that." He paused, studying her face. "Love, if I send you back to him and explain the dilemma, he will keep you safe until this Tudor threat has ended one way or another. Then we can be together again without danger to anyone. It's the only thing I can think to do, Marganna—the only thing."

He brushed her lips softly with his.

"Do you still believe I betrayed you?" she whispered.

"No, I don't think you betrayed me."

"And you don't hate me?"

He swung away from her. "Christ, no. I *love* you . . . and that's what makes this so damned difficult. It's the reason I want you here, but it's the reason I have to send you away."

She drew a long, shuddering breath. "When must I leave?"

"It has to be right away or I won't be able to let you go."

She was silent for a long moment. "All right. I won't argue, Rath, but I would ask you one favor." She held out a hand to him. "Please, come lie here beside me."

"Marganna . . ."

"Please," she cried softly, "just make love to me one last time."

"It will only make things worse, sweetheart. I can't do it."

His features rigid with determination, he started for the door to his own chamber. But she said his name so quietly, with such despair, that he turned to look back at her, and in so doing was lost.

Slowly he crossed to the bed and lay down beside her, taking her shaking body into his arms. They clung together for a long moment; then he cursed softly and pulled away.

"Your injuries, love—it would be too painful for you."

She gripped his hands. "It would be even more painful if we parted like this," she whispered. "Rath, please . . . I need you to love me tonight."

The expression on her face caused him to abandon further argument. Kissing her gently, he stood and began to undress. Then, throwing back the bedcovers, he got into bed beside her.

As she turned toward him, she could not hide a wince of pain as her weight rested momentarily on her bruised hip.

Rath pulled her carefully atop his body, and, reaching for the dish of salve, murmured, "Lie quietly for a moment, sweet, and let me rub some of this on your hips and back. It will ease your pain."

Marganna did as she was told, nestling her head in the hollow of his shoulder. The steady beat of his heart was comforting, as was the cushioning warmth of his muscular frame, and when his arms went around her so that his hands might begin the soothing massage of her tender flesh, she felt safe and protected, surrounded by a fulfilling sense of peace and love.

Using his fingertips and the heels of his palms, Rath pressed and smoothed the muscles of her back, beginning at the base of her neck and stroking downward and outward along the curve of her spine. The aroma of the ointment filled the room with the scent of sun-warmed herbs and wildflowers as he spread it, the heat of his hands turning it to liquid against her skin.

He spanned her ribcage, his fingers gently manipulating the discolored area, then sliding lower to massage her hips. Next, cupping her buttocks, he moved his thumbs in a circular motion, alternately pressing and releasing the soft mounds of flesh. As her hips shifted against him, Marganna could feel the answering response of his body. Stirred, she turned to kiss his neck and jaw; presently, he moved his head for a slow, deliberate exploration of her mouth.

When his lips traced a path from the corner of her mouth down the slender column of her throat, his hands came up to raise her slightly above his chest, so that he could kiss each of the small bruises that disfigured the ivory skin of her breasts. Marganna arched her back, reveling in his touch, which healed and erased the pain and shame of FitzClinton's savagery.

She settled back against the furred breadth of his chest, lifting her face to express her gratitude with a kiss that surprised him with its intensity. Stimulated by her show of passion and emotion, Rath let his hands move to her hips, to grasp and guide them firmly down over his suddenly impatient body. His fingers massaged the backs of her thighs, pressing and rocking her body against his. Her gasp sounded loudly in the silent room, and he grew still, opening his storm-dark eyes to look into hers. Seeing nothing but unguarded pleasure on her glowing face, he kissed her gently, thoroughly, as he returned to the sweet torture of their slow-paced and leisurely lovemaking.

Forgotten were the events of the day—the anger, the distrust, the threat of separation. All that remained was the solace each gave the other . . . Marganna's cries of fulfillment muffled against his chest, Rath's fingers lovingly entwined in her long, flowing hair.

Dawn was tinting the moorland skies with pale rose and gold when Marganna awoke, filled with new determination. Surely after last night, Rath would not be able to send her away.

She turned to meet his gaze, but when he returned her tremulous smile with sober regard, her hopes crumbled.

"Last night was wonderful, sweetheart," he whispered, drawing her close, "but it cannot change anything. I made that clear."

Miserably she nodded. As usual, he had been right. Experiencing his tenderness was only going to make the inevitable parting more bitter.

She felt confused—almost betrayed. After the last week, how could she doubt his love? Yet, if he loved her as much as he claimed, why couldn't he find a way to keep her with him?

"For God's sake, don't cry," his voice hoarse and pleading.

"Don't worry," she said softly, "I remember how you despise tears. I despise them too. No, I won't cry."

His sigh of relief hurt her so much that she pulled away from him and turned her back, vowing he would never know that she had lied.

Chapter 17

Marganna stood at the long windows in the great hall, looking out at the rain that made the late July day seem like autumn. All around her were piled the chests and coffers containing her possessions. In just a few short minutes she would be leaving Middleham Castle forever.

As she had done so many times in the past two days, she straightened her shoulders and renewed her silent vow to conceal her real emotions. Rath had announced he was sending her away for her own protection until England's civil strife had ended, and while she didn't know whether other people believed him, she knew she did not.

Although she felt he was sincere when he said he loved her, hours of thought on the matter had brought her to the only possible conclusion: he did not trust her.

"No, Ned! Damn it! Dickon, come back here!"

At Rathburn's enraged shout she turned to see two slight figures hurl themselves across the wide stone floor toward her.

"Marganna," Dickon cried, throwing his arms around her waist, the force of his hug bringing her to her knees. "We knew you were here somewhere!"

"We've been searching for you," Ned explained, embracing her despite the embarrased blush on his cheeks. "We knew you were at Middleham, but Rath wouldn't tell us where."

Marganna looked up as Rath approached, scowling blackly. "And this is the very reason I didn't. I saw no need for a scene of this nature," he said, eyeing the princes coldly.

"But you're sending Marganna away," accused Dickon, "and you weren't even going to let us see her."

"What purpose would it serve," Rath queried, "other than to make all of you feel worse?"

"Mrs. Biggins says you are angry with Marganna, but we're not," Ned began.

Rath interrupted with a gusty sigh. "I am not angry with Marganna!"

"Then why does she have to go away?" demanded Dickon.

"For your safety . . . and for hers."

"You think she is a spy, don't you?" Ned inquired quietly, more composed than the older man. "I overheard Amelyn and Clovelly talking. I know who Marganna really is, but I don't understand what difference it makes. She has proved herself our friend."

"Oh, for God's sake," Rath ground out, teeth clenching in agitation. "This is precisely what I hoped to avoid by not allowing you boys to talk to Marganna. Now listen to me. For the final time, I am not angry with Marganna. I am only sending her away because her connection with the Tudors makes her a threat to your safety. And if she repudiates her family, she herself is in danger. I want to place her under your uncle's protection."

"But Clovelly says Uncle Richard sent her to Middleham in the first place," Edward pointed out, reasonable as always. "Perhaps he will not want Marganna to come back to London."

"He will understand when I send word about FitzClinton."

"And that's another thing," Ned went on. "FitzClinton. If he was only injured at Rathburn Hall, what is to prevent him from overtaking Will and Marganna on the way south? Won't she be in greater danger if you make her leave Middleham?"

"Don't you think I've thought of that?" Rath's reply was directed at Ned, but his eyes were on Marganna, as though anxious for her to understand. "I am sending an armed escort with them, so they will be safe enough. After all, FitzClinton had only six or eight men with him."

"Why can't she stay?" Dickon asked. "We have to live here now, and if Marganna is gone, we won't have anyone to play with."

"Look, Dickon, Ned, I'm sorry, but you both knew the day might come when events would force us to confine you to the castle. As long as there was no threat, we could indulge your uncle's wish that you have as normal a life as possible. You enjoyed a long stay with the Metcalfes, but now circumstances we can no longer control make it necessary to safeguard you, even if it means you are not as happy as before. It cannot be helped."

"How can it be unsafe to have Marganna here?" Ned asked. "We are all locked inside Middleham; no one can get in."

"I'd rather you didn't argue, Ned. I don't like this any more than you do."

"Then why are you being so hateful?" Dickon was beyond fear of the tall man towering over them. Marganna, sensing the scene about to erupt, got to her feet and laid a restraining hand on Dickon's shoulder.

"Perhaps Rath will permit us five minutes in private," she said, "and I will try to explain why I must return to London."

"I don't think it would be wise, Marganna," Rath interjected. "Right now, these boys are not going to listen to anyone. 'Twould be best just to get the parting over with."

Stung, she regarded him in disbelief. His haste was hardly flattering.

"I see," she said, her voice faltering as she felt Dickon's shoulder stiffen beneath her touch.

"You can't send her away," Dickon said on a rising note. "We aren't going to let you."

"You can't stop me, young man," returned Rath. "It's for your own good."

"No!" Dickon bellowed, stamping his foot. "If you send Marganna away, I'm going with her!"

"Please, Dickon, you must—" Marganna's plea was lost in the confusion that followed.

As Rath reached for the youngster, Dickon shouted angrily and eluded him by running across the room. Ned, trying to reason with his brother at the top of his lungs, started after them and nearly collided with Mrs. Biggins, who, drawn by the din, came into the room wiping her hands on her apron and muttering under her breath. Suddenly the door to the great hall was thrown open and a group of people entered, to stand staring at the scene before them.

"What the devil is going on here?" a low voice demanded, and the small knot of people separated to let the speaker through. The man, dressed in the rain-soaked garb of a traveler, pushed back the hood of his cape and swept the room with a piercing gaze.

A series of gasps sounded—from Rath, from the boys, and from Clovelly Biggins, who immediately bent her knees in a clumsy curtsey.

"Your Grace," she murmured.

"Uncle!" Ned and Dickon cried in unison.

"Richard!" exclaimed Rath, his features etched with shock.

Marganna blinked her eyes and took a closer look at the man standing before them; then she, too, dropped into as graceful a curtsey as she could manage.

Though she did not know what circumstances had brought about such a thing, she knew they were unmistakably in the presence of Richard III, king of England.

Richard was weary. Every line of face and body showed his fatigue. Watching him, Rath knew instinctively it was more than just the tiring journey from London. It was as if a pall of gloom had settled over the man, graying his features and clouding his eyes; his thoughts seemed turned inward to view the past, in some strange way trying to deny the future.

With his usual calm efficiency, Richard dealt with the boisterous scene in the hall, restoring order within a few moments of his arrival. He had greeted his nephews with affection, listening seriously to their complaints against Rath. Promising to investigate the matter thoroughly, he sent the boys and Marganna upstairs, then turned to Rath with the ghost of a smile.

"Why is it I always find you in the midst of controversy, Rath?"

Rath looked sheepish. "It seems to be my lot these days," he agreed. Then his expression became sober. "But what are you doing here at Middleham? Why did we have no advance warning of your arrival?"

"Coming here was a sudden decision," Richard explained. For a long moment he was silent, lost in thought, his gaze wandering over the huge room in which they stood. "My agents in France sent word that Tudor is preparing a fleet at Harfleur. The invasion will not be delayed much longer."

"So he's really coming?" Rath murmured.

"I've never doubted it. His ambitions run high. Too high." Richard sighed. "The truth of the matter is that he is being backed by a great many other ambitious people."

"You're not worried?"

Richard began pacing the room, and Rath fell into step beside him. "Only a fool would be otherwise. That's one of the first rules of warfare, my good friend—never underestimate your opponent. I have the crown, the government, and the army, but Tudor has something much more formidable—the desire for all those things. He wants to be king."

"And you don't?" Rath asked softly.

"I'm tired, Rath. Sometimes I think all I really want is rest."

Before Rathburn could frame a reply, Richard went on. "That's why I came to Middleham secretly. If I can find even a few days away from the clamor at court—the petitions, the complaints, the rumors—perhaps I can rest and prepare myself for this meeting with Henry Tudor." Stopping before the fireplace, he traced the smooth lines of the boar's head carved there. "It has been an age since I was last at Middleham." Both he and Rath knew the last time Richard had traveled north had been for the burial of his eight-year-old son. "I had a notion I wanted to walk the moors again."

For the last time . . .

The words seemed to echo through the room, though Richard did not speak them. Rath attempted to shrug off his uneasiness.

"Then no one knows where you've gone?" he asked.

"Just my closest advisors. Sir Francis Lovell, old comrade that he is, offered to accompany me, but I thought it best for him to remain behind. He is one of the few people I can trust completely these days. Of course my secretary, John Kendall, is very capable also. If something should go amiss, he would get word to me in a day's time and I would return."

"I see. Tell me, what is the general mood at court after this latest news of Tudor?"

"Apprehension. It's as if everyone is waiting. Waiting to see what will happen, who will emerge victorious. The only one to make any sort of move is Lord Stanley. He has asked permission to leave court to return to his estates on business."

"His timing seems questionable, what with his stepson's imminent invasion of England. Good God, does the man think you don't recognize his motives?"

"He knows there is little I can do about them. If I had refused to let him leave court, he could have pointed to that as an obvious reason to back Tudor. I didn't want to hold the man prisoner. No, I had to let him go, with the hope that when the invasion comes, he will honor the allegiance he once gave freely."

"Honor?" exclaimed Rath. "A strange word to use in connection with the Stanleys. They have long been known for their propensity for waiting to see which way the battle goes before casting their allegiance. It won't be any different this time. Lord Stanley is like a rotten apple, clinging to the tree as long as possible before deciding on which side of the fence to fall."

"True. But at least we know what to expect from the man, and I've done all I can to insure his loyalty. I granted him permission to leave court so long as he was willing to send his son, Lord Strange, to stand in as his deputy. Stanley knows Strange's life will be forfeit if he makes any overt move to side with Tudor. Surely even a self-serving wretch such as he has proven himself to be could not sacrifice his own son's life for ambition."

"Who knows? With that sharp-tongued wife of his nagging into his ear day and night . . ."

Richard cocked a dark eyebrow. "Oh? It would seem you have a sour view of marriage—or at least of Sir Stanley's. I hope you don't feel so strongly about marriage in general after such short experience with the state yourself."

"As you witnessed, my marriage has its problems."

"You mean that melee with Ned and Dickon? Yes, I suppose you had better tell me about that. Come, walk with me to my chambers. My escort and I rode through the night, and I find myself in need of some sleep."

As they proceeded to Richard's room, Rath told him the details of the boys' peril at the hands of FitzClinton, Lady Margaret Stanley's envoy. He spared himself no blame, nor did he deny the bearing Marganna's relationship to the would-be king had on the subject.

"When you discovered Marganna's attempt at spying, you inadvertantly crushed a large part of Margaret Stanley's plot against me, Rath. I have learned she brought the lovely Marganna to court as a candidate for Tudor's wife."

"What?!"

"Why should that surprise you? Think about it for a moment. Though illegitimate, the girl is a Tudor, after all. To Lady Stanley's way of thinking, the combined blood of her son and his cousin would have produced an admirable line of kings for this country."

"But I thought Tudor vowed to marry your niece, Elizabeth."

"Up to that point, I suspect it was sheer political bargaining. Tudor wanted to win the approval of the Woodvilles. What better way than to offer them a throne? And he may never have known of his mother's plan to marry him to Marganna. It does seem likely the two have not met. At any rate, it matters little now. Marganna is your wife, which puts her out of Henry Tudor's reach. When you brought her north, her virginity could no longer be ensured, which immediately made her less than ideal as a possible wife for Lady Stanley's son. That straitlaced soul would never take the risk of marrying the future king to a woman who might already be carrying the child of the enemy. Now they are considering young Elizabeth again, which is the primary reason I have moved her and her sisters to the castle at Sheriff Hutton."

"Did Marganna know she was to marry Tudor?"

"No, our informer seemed to think she had no idea. Apparently she was an innocent victim of her scheming aunt. First she was to be used as a spy—sacrificed only if necessary. Had all gone according to plan, she would have been married to Tudor and encouraged to start breeding heirs."

"Damn that old woman," Rath muttered darkly. "She's the most conniving, manipulating—"

"Easy, lad." Richard chuckled. "Her influence over Marganna has ended. If you can heal the rift between yourself and your wife, Marganna will be far safer here at Middleham than she would be in London."

"Even if it were possible to 'heal the rift,' as you say, what about the boys? And FitzClinton?"

"I have plans for Ned and Dickon," Richard answered. "As for FitzClinton, if I understand what you tell me, he will soon be run to ground. With your men combing the moors for him, they can't help but rout him. After all, he cannot know the area as well as they do. In the meantime, your wife and my nephews are as safe here in the castle as they would be anywhere else."

"While that may be true, I'm not certain Marganna would be willing to remain with me."

"What?" Richard paused, smiling. "Surely you can't think your bride is disillusioned with you already."

"I believe she may be."

"Why do you think that?"

"She was willing to return to London, don't forget."

"Good lord, man—you ordered her to go!"

"But she didn't argue. In fact, she acquiesced so quickly, I have no choice but to think it was what she wanted."

"Perhaps she was trying to make it easier for you by being compliant," Richard suggested. "Rath, for all your experience with women, I'm beginning to think you don't know much about them."

Rath grinned. "Aye, you are right. At least in Marganna's case."

"Do you love her?" The sudden question was quiet, but Rath discerned the other man's need to know.

"Yes, I love her."

"Good. Then I believe everything will be all right. I'll have a talk with Marganna and see what I can learn. But Rath, I'm willing to wager—just as I was in the beginning—you and she were meant to be together."

As they approached Richard's chamber, Mrs. Biggins and one of the young maids came out of the room.

"We've been tidying yer room, Dickon . . . er, Yer Gr—" The woman's broad smile beamed. "How can Aw call someone Aw've known since he was a bit of a lad 'sire'?"

"You can't, Clovelly. And anyway, while I'm at Middleham I want to forget I'm king."

"Then Aw'll forget it too. Noo, Aw've lighted the fire and turned back the bed. Would ye like sommat ta eat?"

"Later, perhaps. Right now I just want to rest."

Mrs. Biggins looked disapproving but said nothing.

When she had gone, Richard stepped over the threshold and stood looking around him, the half smile he'd worn while speaking to Rath slowly fading. His eyes were drawn immediately to the portrait of Anne.

After a few seconds he spoke, his voice barely audible. "God, I'm bone weary, Rath."

He almost seemed to stumble toward the bed, and Rath knelt quickly to assist him with his boots.

"I'll leave you alone for now, Dickon, and come back when you've slept."

"No, stay a few minutes more. At least until I'm asleep." Richard settled back against the pillows, not even bothering to remove his cloak. His face seemed gray and lined in the firelight. "I'm not certain I can find rest in this room anymore. Strange, isn't it? A room that once afforded me refuge."

Rath was at a loss for words. He had never seen Richard in such an introspective mood; it did little to alleviate the unease he'd experienced earlier.

"I miss her, Rath," the other man stated simply. "The hell of it is, it has been over four months and I miss her more every day."

"I know. Anne was wonderful. We all miss her."

"I thought I might find her again here in this room we shared, but now that I'm here, I'm almost afraid to try." He rubbed his fingers across his eyes, and Rath saw the death's-head ring he wore—had worn since his son's funeral. "I think it would be tempting just to let myself give up."

"Dickon, don't talk like that. You're not yourself right now. You're tired."

"What is my 'self' these days?" he asked, his words tinged with bitterness. "I swear sometimes I don't know. When I hear the rumors people are spreading about King Richard, I wonder who he is. Who *I* am." He sighed. "You're right, of course. I'm just tired. Go on, if you wish. I'll speak with you at dinner this evening."

"You don't mind being alone?"

"No . . . I don't mind."

As he slipped out the door, Rath noticed Richard's gaze was once again fastened on the portrait of his wife.

Marganna's thoughts had been thrown into turmoil by the arrival of the king earlier in the day. He had not seemed inclined to let her leave Middleham—had sent her upstairs with the lads and ordered her luggage returned to her chambers, in fact. But what did he intend to do with her?

Her hands grew still above her needlework, and she leaned over the wooden tapestry frame to peer out the solar window at the roofs of Middleham, gilded by the dying sun.

I can't stay here if Rath doesn't want me, she thought bleakly, but, dear God, how can I leave him?

It seemed a hopeless situation, and her shoulders

slumped in dejection. How could her life have changed so drastically in two short months?

She heard footsteps behind her and then a sharp, suddenly indrawn breath.

"My God . . ."

She whirled to find herself facing Richard, his face ashen.

"Oh, it's you, Marganna. I thought you were . . . someone else. Forgive me if I startled you."

He looked so shaken she could not keep from asking, "Are you all right, sir?"

"Yes, I'm fine." He stared intensely for a few seconds longer. "I suppose I owe you an explanation," he finally said.

"No explanation is necessary, I assure you."

"I want you to know what I thought I saw," he stated. "I must have looked like a man who'd encountered a ghost . . . and in a sense that is what happened. When I came into the room, I mistook you for my wife Anne. I have seen her standing at that window a thousand times, the sun on her hair exactly as it was on yours."

He reached out a hand to lift the strand of reddish-brown hair lying over her shoulder, and Marganna caught the expression of indescribable longing that crossed his face.

"Perhaps it was a mistake to come here," he muttered, letting his hand drop to his side. "I wanted to rest and . . . remember a happier time. But mayhap my beloved ghosts will distract me too much from the task at hand." He gave her a shrewd glance. "Your rebellious Tudor cousin."

Marganna dropped her head. "Yes . . ."

He raised her face with a finger beneath her chin. "Marganna, I want you to know I do not hold you at all responsible for the actions of your cousin Henry or for those of any other member of your family. Do you understand?"

She met his look. "Thank you," she said simply. "It seems I have done you disservices I didn't even realize."

"That was in the past, before you married one of my

dearest friends. Our own friendship begins here and now. What do you say?''

Marganna studied the man standing before her, wondering why she had so readily believed the worst of him.

At first glance, Richard Plantagenet seemed an ordinary man to Marganna—average height, slight build, straight, dark hair, and somber blue eyes. But on closer inspection, she saw details that bespoke the man's innermost character. His keen eyes showed intelligence and concern, as well as an empathy for his fellow man. The fine lines radiating from the corners of his eyes proved his life had been a mixture of laughter and pain; the curve of his mouth displayed an emotional control that could not always have been easy to maintain. His tanned skin indicated an outdoorsman, one unafraid of the weather, fond of hunting and hawking. His body was hard and muscular, that of a battle-scarred warrior rather than a pampered prince.

Richard was very much aware of her scrutiny, and it was to his credit that he stood so calmly before her searching gaze. That he was able to do so made a deep impression on Marganna; no one accused of the sins he was supposed to have committed could afford to be so open, so unflinching. Human nature being what it was, a man with a burden of guilt would flounder in some way—a rapid blink, a nervous smile.

''I'd like us to be friends,'' she admitted in a quiet voice. ''I'd like that very much.''

''Thank you. I believe Rathburn would like to know we have made our peace with each other also.''

She did not know what to say, since she felt uncertain of Rath's interest in what she thought or did these days.

''Have you forgiven me for my high-handed method of getting you two together?'' There was a hint of a smile in Richard's deep-set eyes as he asked the question.

''Of course. I'm certain you did what you thought was best for all concerned.''

''Do I detect a note of dissatisfaction on your part?''

''No. It's just that, well, the situation has not worked out as I think you hoped it would.''

"I take it you are referring to this latest spat between yourself and your stubborn husband?"

She nodded, wondering just how much Rath had told him.

"I understand Rathburn was sending you back to London—he told me his reasons for that decision—but I'm wondering whether you are happy to be going."

"No! I mean . . . well, I know why he thought I should go, but I didn't want to leave the boys . . ."

"What about Rath? How did you feel about leaving him?"

"I . . ." She bit her lip. "I couldn't stay here knowing he didn't want me."

"Even if it was your safety that concerned him?"

Her voice sank to a whisper. "If I believed that, I might feel differently. The truth is, he doesn't trust me, doesn't think I can give up my family loyalties."

"Surely you believe he loves you."

"I believe that he thinks he loves me. I also believe love without trust is really no love at all."

Richard smiled faintly. "So you think his sending you away is just a convenient means of ridding himself of your presence?"

She shrugged. "I'm not really blaming Rath. I'm just convinced reality will destroy his feelings, if it hasn't already. No matter what we may feel for each other, who we are and what we are makes it impossible for us to be together."

"Nothing is impossible, Marganna. Give me a chance and I will prove it to you."

"But what can you do?"

"Promise me you will wait and see." Richard smiled.

After a few seconds she smiled back. "All right, but please don't expect too much. Rath is . . ."

"Oh, you needn't tell me about Rath." He chuckled. "I'm well aware of his monumental obstinacy. But there are ways to get around that. Just leave him to me."

On the following day Richard and Marganna went walking on the moors in a gale that blew their cloaks out behind them like great, clumsy wings. It was the first time Richard seemed able to throw off the chains of depression that bound him.

He inhaled deep breaths of the fresh, damp air, lifting his head to let the fitful sun strike his features.

"At last I feel I am home!" His keen gaze swept the misted horizon, and his voice was filled with contentment. "This must be the way the crusaders who marched off to the Holy Land felt when they returned from years in the hot, dry desert. In a sense London has been a desert for me—a wasteland . . ." His dark brown hair was ruffled as he faced into the wind. "God, there were days when I thought I would never feel the force of a Yorkshire wind again, never smell the wet heather or hear the curlew's cry. But even I didn't realize how much I'd missed it."

An appealing youthfulness shone in his eyes, and Marganna smiled, caught up in his enthusiasm.

"I love the solitude of the moors," he declared, indicating the emptiness with a wave of his arm.

"Solitude?" Marganna shivered. "To me the moors seem so lonely."

Richard looked at her, surprised. "Lonely? The moors? Lord, no. Loneliness is . . . is being king, or living at court where no one has a thought for anything other than amusement. I used to agonize over my brother Edward's life-style. I couldn't understand why he indulged himself by drinking too much and taking mistresses, but now I know. Temptation is thrust at you from all sides, and eventually it simply wears you down." He sighed heavily. "Of course, it's all the same whether you battle against it or let yourself succumb; either way it will destroy you and bring you to a lonely end."

Marganna silently cursed herself for her careless words, knowing they were the cause of Richard's return to melancholy.

"Life at court is distorted, unnatural. Did you know the vultures couldn't even permit me time to mourn my wife before they started parading candidates for her replacement in front of me? I'll never forgive them for that."

"I'm sorry. That must have been unbearable for you," she said sympathetically.

"I am weary of hearing about my duties—tired of being reminded a king must have a queen, must produce heirs for the throne." He glanced up at her, a twisted smile on his face. "I must sound very self-pitying and I apologize. But oh, God, I wish I didn't have to go back!"

He started off down the path they'd been following, swinging the walking stick he carried at clumps of bracken in short, vengeful strokes. Helplessly she stood and watched him stride away, a vulnerable figure silhouetted against the dark, lowering sky.

Marganna and the boys had spent an afternoon cleaning the old nursery, sweeping cobwebs from the walls and polishing the furniture. Now, with yet another summer rain beating against the tall, narrow windows, they basked in the warmth of the fire. Marganna was reading the newest version of Ned's play while its author looked on anxiously; Dickon was building a house of blocks on the hearth rug, under the puzzled scrutiny of the hound, Caesar.

Footsteps sounded in the hallway, then halted at the door. The trio looked up to see Richard, a strained smile on his face.

Marganna leaped to her feet. "Oh, sir . . . won't you come in and join us? It's very cozy here."

Richard took a deep breath, then coughed lightly. "So I see." His glance moved around the room, and for the most part he looked merely curious. It was only when his eyes fell upon the leather rocking horse in the corner or the regiment of painted soldiers marching neatly across a dusted shelf that they darkened in pain. Marganna swallowed with difficulty, only able to guess at the memories that must be assailing him. She realized the courage it had taken for him to approach this, the one room at Middleham he had not yet visited.

Ned and Dickon exchanged a quick, darting look, recalling Marganna's warning not to insist on their uncle's company. Ned's face looked immensely adult as he chewed at his lower lip, his blue eyes wide with sympathy. Dickon stood very still, waiting for Richard's next move. When the king took a tentative step inside the chamber, the boy's pent-up breath escaped with a *whoosh* and, at a nod from Marganna, he flew toward Richard, beaming mightily.

"Won't you stay and play with us, Uncle?"

Richard staggered under the force of Dickon's welcome, but his answering smile was warm. "I would be delighted," he replied. Over Dickon's tousled head, he looked at Marganna. "It's good to see this room in use once again."

"You're . . . not sorry you told us we could refurbish it?"

"No." He stroked the cracked leather of the rocking horse. Though the lines around his mouth tightened, his voice was firm. "It's time the ghosts at Middleham were exorcised. I want to remember this old place filled with happy memories, not with sad reminders of what might have been."

"Er . . . Uncle Richard," ventured young Edward, drawing close to the older man, "could you please tell us some stories about our father? Like you used to?"

Dickon danced around in his excitement. "Oh, yes! Won't you tell us about the battles you fought together? Oh, please, Uncle!"

Marganna slipped quietly from the room, pausing to look back over her shoulder. Once again the king was holding court, but this time it was in a worn nursery chair, one lad at his feet, another on his lap, both intent on the story he was telling and oblivious to the rain slanting against the glass. She knew it was a scene she would never forget.

Though Richard's visit to Middleham had been a closely guarded secret, word of his presence leaked out, and after the first days a steady stream of visitors straggled up the hill, seeking admittance to the castle. Those known to Richard were allowed an audience; most wanted only to speak a word of welcome to their sovereign.

For an hour or two each morning, Richard stood in the

great hall, meeting those who came to see him. He did not sit on a makeshift throne, but rather mingled with his old friends and tenants, clasping their hands or throwing an arm around their shoulders. He called these men and women by name, asked about their families, and calmly accepted their words of greeting or condolence as well as their advice and good wishes for the inevitable confrontation with Tudor.

Standing at the back of the hall with Mrs. Biggins during one of the daily sessions, Marganna felt compelled to say, "I think I have sadly misjudged the king. He is not the man I believed him to be."

Mrs. Biggins chuckled. "Aw would like for his enemies ta see him like this. 'Tis the real Richard Plantagenet, tha knows."

"Yes, and these people love him."

"Because they know him, lass. They know what he has done for them, what he has sacrificed ta serve them."

"I'm ashamed of the way I let myself be swayed by my aunt's opinions. And, Clovelly, I never thought I would be grateful for the night Rath caught me spying, but I am."

The older woman smiled broadly. "Aye, 'twould seem that day was a blessin' for both of ye."

"What the hell does Richard think he's doing?" Rath demanded, staring down the length of dining table.

Will Metcalfe carefully hid a grin by raising his wineglass to his lips. "What do you mean?" he asked innocently.

"Don't tell me you haven't noticed the way he has lavished his attention on Marganna throughout this interminable meal? He's scarcely spoken to anyone else."

"Perhaps he finds her a charming dinner companion," Will suggested. "After all, she is a fresh face after the jaded bawds at court. You yourself know Richard was never partial to that kind of woman. No doubt he is pleased to converse with a decent female for a change."

"It would behoove him to remember the female in question is married," snapped Rath, pushing aside his pewter trencher. "Does convention allow a man and his wife to be separated at table just so another man can satisfy his longing for acceptable companionship?''

"I suppose it does when the other man is a king,'' Will said dryly. "And anyway, Richard knows you were sending Marganna away, so he probably feels you have no objection to being apart from her.''

Before Rath could give vent to the wealth of confused emotions that statement called up, Will slipped from his seat and, with a murmured excuse, left the hall. Rath watched him go, then turned back in time to see Marganna laughing gaily at something Richard had said.

"Damn it all,'' he muttered, his scowl deepening.

It was not many minutes later that Richard stood up and announced he had prevailed upon Marganna to entertain them with music on the harp; the entire company shifted to the end of the room where a bright fire blazed.

When Marganna's fingers caressed the harp strings and her clear alto voice rose, silencing all other sound in the hall, Rath was torn between pride in her abilities and jealousy, because each time she looked up, she smiled at Richard and not at him.

Richard sat sprawled in a chair before the fire, a glass of wine in his hand, his eyes alternating between the singer and the hypnotic dance of the flames. As the evening wore on, he roused himself only twice—once to give the others permission to quit the hall for their beds, and a second time to inquire whether Marganna knew one of his favorite pastorales. She did and, though she was so tired it was all she could do to keep from nodding over the harp, she began to play, sensing his need for the solace of her music.

> *"Ah, what is love?''* she sang. *"It is a pretty thing,*
> *as sweet unto a shepherd as a king;*
>
> *"And sweeter, too,*
> *For kings have cares that wait upon a crown,*
> *And cares can make the sweetest love to frown:*
> *Ah, then, ah, then,*
> *If country loves such sweet desires do gain,*
> *What lady would not love a shepherd swain?*

"His flocks are folded, he comes home at night,
As merry as a king in his delight;
And merrier, too,
For kings bethink them what the state require,
Where shepherds careless carol by the fire."

Marganna's placid expression hid her turbulent thoughts. As she sang about the shepherd, persistent memories of Rath sprang to mind, and she was seeing him as he had been that day of the sheep washing—muscular, sun browned, wiping the barley ale from his chin as his audacious eyes sought hers. With a surreptitious glance, she looked for him now and found him standing deep in the shadows, a forbidding frown on his handsome face. She sighed sadly, knowing they had come a long way since that carefree time.

"He kisseth first, then sits as blithe to eat
His cream and curds as doth the king his meat;
And blither, too,
For kings have often fears when they do sup,
Where shepherds dread no poison in their cup.

"To bed he goes as wanton then, I ween,
As is king in dalliance with a queen;
More wanton, too,
For kings have many griefs, their souls to move,
Where shepherds have no greater grief than love.

"Upon his couch of straw he sleeps as sound,
As does the king upon his bed of down;
More sounder, too,
For cares cause kings full oft their sleep to spill,
Where weary shepherds lie and dream their fill."

Rath's constant scrutiny of Marganna forced him to admit her obvious fatigue. Though her shoulders slumped wearily, her hands and voice never faltered, and when she glanced at Richard, her eyes were kind.

Grimacing in self-disgust, Rath forced himself to take a closer look at the man he had called friend for most of his life. The gentle smile and careworn face filled him with guilt. He felt ashamed that he had ever thought Richard's interest in Marganna was other than friendly concern.

He knew how much Richard had loved his queen, how her slow death from diseased lungs had staggered him when he was already reeling from the unexpected death of his young son. After all Richard had done for him, all he had been to him, Rath hated himself for the ugly suspicions he'd let cloud his mind. The words of Marganna's song echoed in his head.

"Thus with his wife he spends the year, as blithe
As doth the king at every tide or sithe;
And blither, too,
For kings have wars and broils to take in hand,
Where shepherds laugh and love upon the land.
Ah, then, ah, then,
If country loves such sweet desires do gain,
What lady would not love a shepherd swain?"

Rath stepped to Richard's side and clasped his shoulder with a strong, comforting hand. Richard's own hand came down over his friend's, and the smile they exchanged expressed the emotions they could never put into words.

A few nights later Rath sat at the table downing one drink after another. The past days had left him so confused and frustrated he didn't know which way to turn. He wavered between love and loyalty for Richard and love and longing for Marganna. He was glad she had proven to be a comfort to the restless king, yet he envied their closeness, was jealous of the time they spent together. He kept his emotions under tight rein when they chanced to be together; later, like a spoiled child, he would curse and rage in the privacy of his room. He couldn't remember ever being so emotionally distraught.

"What ails you, Rath, my friend?" Will Metcalfe asked,

taking up the carafe to fill Rath's glass again. "You seem particularly glum tonight."

"I'm in no mood for your levity," Rath warned blackly.

"A bit touchy, aren't we?" Will chuckled, his amusement echoed by the other men of the household, who were sharing a private dinner in the sitting room next to Richard's bedchamber. "What do you suppose is wrong with him, Richard?"

The king smiled. "I think our suffering comrade is in the throes of marital discord."

Rath cast him a surly look. "You said you were going to speak to Marganna about why she was so willing to leave Middleham, Richard, but it appears you have been too busy walking with her and riding on the moor and . . . listening to that damned harp."

The princes had been allowed to attend the meal; at this bitter statement, they looked at each other, fighting the wide smiles that threatened to break over their faces.

"Don't be impatient, Rath—I will speak with your wife soon enough. In the meantime, I advise you to forget this silly battle and amuse yourself elsewhere."

"With another woman?" Rath asked, realizing his brain must indeed be clouded with drink if he thought Richard had suggested such a thing.

"An excellent idea," agreed Will. "You know, I think Richard is right. That would be the perfect way to show Marganna you are her lord and master and that if she is too busy for you, there are always other females who aren't."

"Damn, Will, I must be drunker than I thought," Rath muttered, draining the glass he held. "My hearing must be seriously affected."

Rath pushed his chair away from the table and stood up to survey them through the haze that inexplicably filled the small room. "What are you saying?"

Richard smiled benignly. "Why don't you retire now, Rath, before your condition worsens. And for treatment of that . . . er, other condition that I'm certain must be plaguing you, I will send a warm and willing wench to your chambers directly."

"A wench?" Rath repeated dully.

"Splendid," Will cried, clapping his hands. "Splendid idea. Rath, you lucky devil."

As Rath shot them one more uncomprehending look, Ned grinned and looked at Dickon, one eyelid drooping in a bold wink.

Marganna had been sitting at the open window staring out at the stars scattered across the night sky. As usual her thoughts were of her husband and the complicated marriage they shared . . . no, didn't share. These days they shared nothing, she realized—or at least nothing but doubt and mistrust.

A slight tap sounded at the door, and when she opened it to peer around the edge, she was astonished to see Ned and Dickon standing there.

"Is something wrong?" she asked in alarm.

"Yes," Dickon responded. "Uncle Richard wanted us to—"

"Tell you that Lord Rathburn is terribly ill," Ned interrupted.

"Rath?" The blood drained from her face, leaving it pale and anxious. "What has happened to him?"

"We don't know. We just know that he is very sick." Dickon had to struggle to maintain his somber expression, but Marganna didn't seem to notice.

"He's asking for you, Marganna," Ned stated. "Uncle wants to know if you will go to him."

"Oh, my God," she cried, brushing past them. "Of course I'll go to him."

They watched her dash the short distance down the hall to Rath's door. The fact that she did not bother to don her dressing robe seemed evidence enough of her haste. This time as their gazes locked, it was Dickon who winked.

Strangely the room was dark, but there was just enough moonlight to enable Marganna to rush to Rath's bedside.

She could see his dark outline against the pillow, hear his labored breathing. "I'm here," she whispered, stricken with terrible remorse.

"It's about time."

Two strong hands were clamped around her upper arms, and she was lifted bodily into the bed.

"Rath?" she gasped as he dragged her down beside him. "What . . . ?"

"Wha's your name?"

"My name?"

"Yes . . . I want to know who Richard sent me."

"Richard? Sent you?"

She stiffened in angry alarm, but Rath took her face in his hands and captured her mouth in a fierce kiss. He smelled of strong drink, and she began to struggle in his grasp. Something was terribly wrong! Apparently he thought she was someone else—someone Richard had sent. But no, that was impossible . . . wasn't it?

"You taste like Marganna," he mumbled, drawing back to peer at her in the darkness. "Damn Marganna . . . don't want to think about her now."

One hand wandered to the low neck of her smock, and she shuddered as his hard knuckles brushed her breast.

"I have a need to make love to a woman," he informed her, his lips moving unsteadily down her throat.

Suddenly the situation began to make horrible sense to her, and she was filled with blinding rage. It had been a trick! Richard was making an underhanded attempt to reconcile them. She couldn't believe he would try something so . . . so vile!

She pushed Rath away and flung her legs over the side of the bed, but before she knew what was happening, he had easily tossed her back and was half lying across her body.

"Where d'ya think you're goin'? Think you can run away from me like Marganna does?" He hooked his hands in the neck of her smock, ripping the garment with one swift motion. "I'm going to make love to . . ."

He groaned and dropped his head. "Oh, hell! Go on, go away! Jus' want Marganna. Damn her—*damn her!*"

Marganna's anger faded instantly as she heard his anguished words and felt the softness of his thick hair against her bare skin. With a smile, she slipped her arms around him and pulled him close, soothing and cradling him.

"Shh, it's all right. Lie still, Rath—everything will be all right."

"Love her, damn it . . ."

Again she smiled in the darkness. Richard was truly a wise man. He had chosen a strange way to make them both come to their senses, but it had worked—thank God, it had worked!

Tonight she would stay with this overbearing, irritating, exasperating, wonderful man who loved her too much to seek release with someone else, and tomorrow they would rectify their differences one way or another.

Richard believed they were meant to be together and he had proved it. Now it was up to them to fulfill their own destiny. Marganna would always be grateful to the forces of fate that had brought the king back to Middleham Castle.

Chapter 18

Rath turned his face away from the morning light streaming in through the windows. He was reluctant to give up sleep and destroy the dream he'd been having of lying next to Marganna with their limbs intertwined. The dream was so real he could smell the spicy clove scent of her hair, feel her gentle fingers brushing back and forth across his naked chest . . .

He opened his eyes and looked straight into a pair of wide brown ones sparkling with laughter.

"Marganna? You're really here?"

"I'm really here, my love," she replied, smiling as she ran a hand along his ribs and upward to his shoulder.

"But . . . how? Why? I thought Richard—" He quickly broke off his words and took another, more intent look at her.

"You thought your friend Richard was sending one of the kitchen wenches to amuse you, didn't you?" she asked, moving her hand until it lay against the pulse at the side of his neck. "Instead he sent your wife."

"Richard sent you? You were the woman who came into my room last night?"

She nodded and he groaned, falling back against the pillows.

"I can explain," he began, but her laughter interrupted him.

"There's no need to explain, Rath. I have seen right through Richard's plan—right to the wisdom behind it."

He grinned suddenly. "I couldn't believe I was hearing Richard suggest I bed another woman. Now I know what he had in mind. I'm just sorry I was not more capable of appreciating you last night."

"Oh, I'm not. If you had made love to me then, it would have meant you were willing to accept another in my place. But, dear heart, you turned me away, saying you wanted only Marganna. Don't you see? You paid me the highest compliment imaginable . . ." She giggled. "Even if you didn't know who I was."

She leaned forward and pressed a warm kiss against his mouth, causing him to pull her tightly against him, his mouth opening in warm welcome. She nestled closer, making him very much aware of how long it had been since they had lain together thus.

"I have missed you, love," he whispered, lips moving fiercely along her throat.

"Think how it would have been had you succeeded in sending me away," she said in a mildly reproving tone. "I think I would have died."

"Then why were you so willing to go?"

"Why were you so willing to send me?"

"You know the reasons."

"And you expected obedience. That is what I tried to give you."

He sighed. "Then we were both fools. 'Tis a good thing Richard came along and saw the difficulty."

His mouth covered hers again, and her hands began a slow, languorous massage of his back muscles. He lifted his lips a fraction of an inch to whisper, "I was actually jealous of Richard, you know."

She smiled against the renewed kiss. "I know."

"Damn him for a rogue—he knew exactly what he was doing."

She pulled his mouth back to hers. "Exactly."

His hand traveled downward only to encounter the torn edges of the smock she still wore, and he leaned away to look questioningly at her.

"You managed that last night in a burst of enthusiasm," she explained, "but fortunately your interest waned. However, if you wish, you may complete the task now."

The thin cotton garment was readily dispatched and tossed aside. Rough in his eagerness, Rath caressed her, raining kisses on the fading bruises that still marred her breasts and shoulders. Fired by his uncontrolled passion, Marganna clung to him, answering his kisses with her own, murmuring encouragement into his ear, letting her fingers tighten in his hair as she gasped in pleasure.

The frustrations of the past week were being released, their bodies communicating in ways that made words unnecessary. They rejoiced in the fact that they loved each other and were still together, but there were remnants of anger and hurt feelings to be dealt with, as well as the pent-up desires that threatened to overwhelm them. There would be time enough for gentleness later.

Rath's kisses were impatient as he pulled her beneath him, his powerfully thrusting body leaving no doubt as to which of them was the physical master. Marganna, thrilled by his dominating masculinity, nonetheless exercised her own command by murmuring a few well-chosen words, rendering him helpless in the grip of a sensual explosion that left him shuddering and gasping, chanting her name over and over.

They had lain quietly for a time, when suddenly Marganna said, "I've just thought of something important I want to get from my room."

"All right," Rath said. "Go through the adjoining door, if you like. I think it's time we unlocked it again."

Marganna dashed across the carpet to unlock the door, wearing not a stitch of clothing to cover herself. Arms folded behind his head, Rath watched with admiration, enjoying completely the sight of rounded buttocks and long, slim legs.

When Marganna returned, she held out her hand. There, lying on her palm, was the dragon pendant she had once worn to aggravate Rath. He stared at it, raising one eyebrow in question.

"Once and for all, let's have an end to this business of loyalties," she said firmly. "I want you to forget my name was ever Tudor, and I want your promise you will trust me henceforth . . . that you will never again doubt my words or motives."

"Very well—I promise," he said slowly. "And in return, I want you to admit you were wrong about Richard."

"That will be my pleasure," she said. "I have learned a great deal about your king since he has been at Middleham. I understand your affection and regard for him. In truth, I have come to admire him very much myself."

"Oh?" Rath growled, his query not entirely in jest.

"As a friend and as a king. Your Richard is as wonderful as you have always said."

"Well, I'm glad you think so, love. Does that mean we are of one mind on the subject now?"

"It does. Let's make a pact that we will be loyal to the same king . . . and to each other."

He rose from the bed and, pulling the sheet with him, wrapped it around both of them, binding them together.

"It's something we should have done a long time ago," he agreed, kissing her soundly. "But why did you need the pendant?"

"To seal our bargain," she said. "This is a symbol of my tie to the Tudor family. I want to throw it in the fire or something equally drastic, just to prove to you I mean what I am saying. I will never wear it again."

"And I assume I am supposed to do the same with some belonging of my own?"

"No, I don't expect that. After all, you aren't giving up your allegiance to Richard or the Yorkist cause."

"But it wouldn't be fair to let you make the gesture alone, love. Wait here."

He left her and crossed the room to the wardrobe, this time permitting her the pleasure of watching his unclothed body. When he returned, he held the velvet hat he had donned the day she'd worn her pendant to the Metcalfes. Swiftly he unpinned the boar badge fastened on it.

"I'll sacrifice this badge," he declared.

"Oh, no, I can't let you do that!" she cried. "I know you value it tremendously."

"I do, and that is what makes the gesture worthwhile. Richard ordered these badges to commemorate his son's investiture as Prince of Wales. Anything less valuable would make my oath pointless."

"But, Rath, I don't want—"

"I know you aren't asking me to do this, Marganna—it's my choice. I want you to know that while my life is and always has been pledged to Richard, I will never feel a greater love than that I feel for you." His hand came up to stroke her cheek. "No matter where my other loyalties may lie, my love for you will always be strongest. I am bound to you . . . forever."

Solemnly he kissed her, bringing a shimmer of tears to her eyes. She rested her head against his chest, whispering, "I love you, Rath . . . so much."

"Come to the window," he said. "Let's seal our bargain by tossing the pendant and badge into the moat."

Awkwardly, still wrapped together in the sheet, they moved to the window, which Rath unlatched and opened wide. With a last look at the thin brass badge he held, he leaned far out and threw it in a shining arc into the blue waters of the moat below. Marganna did not spare her pendant a last look; she simply leaned forward, her husband's arm around her waist, and gave it a careless toss. It swiftly followed the badge, sinking beneath the surface.

Rath and Marganna faced each other triumphantly. "This is a new beginning for us," she vowed, "and this time we aren't going to make the same mistakes."

Rath stooped to swing her up into his arms and carry her to the rumpled bed. Dropping her gently, he stretched and yawned.

"After all I drank last night, I should feel hellish this morning, but I don't." He leaned forward to give her a kiss full of loving promise, and she looped her arms around his neck, allowing the sheet she was clutching to drop to the floor. His white teeth flashed. "By all the saints, I never felt better!"

Richard left Middleham the same way he had arrived—secretly, dressed in the travel-stained cloak and accompanied only by four armed bodyguards.

In the courtyard he said an affectionate farewell to his

nephews, who clung to him until the last possible moment. Then, humor shining in the depths of his dark blue eyes, he turned to Rath and Marganna, a smile curving his mouth.

"I'm pleased to see you both looking so content," he said, "and even more pleased to think I had a hand in it."

Putting an arm around Marganna's shoulder, Rath nodded. "We'll be eternally grateful to you, Dickon, for your devious measures."

"Yes," Marganna agreed. "We can never thank you properly."

"If you manage to do what I have asked of you, it will more than repay anything I may have done for you." The expression on Richard's face was serious, bringing to mind the request he had made of them only the night before: "I will send you word as soon as Tudor has landed, and when I do, I want you to take the boys to Scarborough Castle on the coast and wait for news. If I am victorious when I meet Henry Tudor, I will send for them. If not, they must board the ship I will have waiting in the harbor and set sail for the Low Countries." He had fixed Rath with a piercing gaze. "I trust you and Will to see that the princes arrive at Scarborough safely. Once there, they should be secure enough until . . . until the skirmish is over."

"You have no need to worry about them," Rath assured him.

"I know." Richard clasped Rath's hand. "I have great faith in you, my friend. And in your beautiful wife." He took Marganna's hands and kissed her on the forehead. Stepping back, he took one more look around the courtyard, raising his eyes to the heights of the great central keep.

"This visit to Middleham has done me good," he declared. "It has set my mind at ease."

And indeed he did look more rested, more prepared for the days ahead.

"Well, I must go. I have to stop at Sheriff Hutton before heading south, so I dare not tarry any longer. Rath, Marganna . . . I pray we will meet again soon."

Marganna seized his hand and knelt before him. "Our

thoughts will be with you daily." She raised her eyes to his. "As will our hearts and our loyalties."

Richard smiled gently at Rath. "Would I had more subjects as faithful as your reformed spy."

"Aye, the rest of the Tudors could take a lesson from her."

Marganna blushed as Rath drew her to her feet and into the curve of his arm.

Together they watched as Richard rode from the courtyard, pausing at the main gate to turn and wave a gauntleted hand. As he passed through the gateway, they heard the cheers of the villagers who had somehow gotten news of his departure and had gathered along the castle hill.

"Richard must be heartened by their love," Marganna said. "There is no lack of support for him here in the north."

"If only it could be that way throughout the rest of the country," Rath murmured, his eyes on the portcullis now being lowered again. A faint frown appeared on his forehead. "Godspeed, Dickon—Godspeed!"

Less than two weeks later, Henry Tudor landed at Milford Haven and began a march across the Welsh countryside that would bring him at last face to face with the man from whom he sought to wrest the crown.

Word of his arrival was received at Middleham with mixed feelings—disbelief that the long-awaited event had actually taken place, anger against the Tudor upstart for daring to embark on such a mission, and fear for the lives of Richard and his supporters.

Before leaving Middleham, Richard had named two dozen trustworthy men to act as an armed guard when the time came to move the boys across Yorkshire to Scarborough. Now these men were summoned and given their orders; Rath and Will intended to leave the castle at the earliest possible moment.

The trip to Scarborough would be relatively easy, and hoping to avoid alarming the princes, Rath tried to maintain the normalcy of their everyday existence by putting them in Clovelly Biggins' charge. Because Edward's health was uncertain, Dr. Coombs would also be present, and since the entourage would be spending at least one night on the road, Amelyn and Bronwyn were to go along to assist with the cooking.

Rath and Will felt such a large force of armed men would be far too conspicuous at an inn; therefore, the night would be spent in the open, in a place that afforded shelter as well as an unencumbered view of the surrounding countryside. They planned to take no chances on FitzClinton slipping into their midst. He had not yet been apprehended, and there could be no mitigating the danger he represented.

Ned and Dickon were excited about the journey, especially since they were to be accompanied by the hound Caesar, who now followed them as freely as he once had his former master; in addition, each of them was allowed his own mount and a weapon. Before many hours had passed, however, Ned became increasingly pale and tired, and by early afternoon he had to be placed in a wagon where, it was hoped, he would be more comfortable. Marganna rode with him, alarmed by his pallor and the sudden shifting of his mood.

"Something dreadful is going to happen, isn't it?" he asked, lying back on a makeshift bed.

"Ned, you mustn't feel that way. Everything is going to be fine," she insisted, even though she, too, was aware of a sense of doom hanging over them.

Because of Ned's uncertain condition, the travelers made camp early that night. Rath carried a weary Dickon to the wagon, helping him inside so that he might rest with Ned until supper was ready.

"Wait, Rath, let me walk back with you," Marganna said, stepping down from the small vehicle. "I can help the others with the cooking while the boys are resting. Dr. Coombs is with them, so they should be safe enough here, don't you think?"

Leaving nothing to chance, Rath signaled to several nearby men, requesting they stand guard over the princes.

"I feel better about camping here than I would if we were in some cramped inn somewhere. FitzClinton could easily rout us with a fire or some other ruse. At least this way the only means he has to get to us is open attack, and I doubt he has enough men to try that."

"But I feel so . . . uneasy," she confided. "Do you feel the same?"

He nodded. "I think everyone's nerves are on edge. We've all spent a long summer waiting for something to happen, and now that it has, no one knows quite how to react."

Mrs. Biggins and Amelyn were standing over the two cooking fires, stirring pots of stew. Rath sniffed appreciatively. "That smells wonderful, Clovelly, my love. I hope you are about to start serving it up."

"Be patient, Johnny. 'Twill be only a few minnits more."

"Is there anything I can do to help?" Marganna asked, approaching Amelyn.

The woman's gaze shifted from Marganna's, and she busied herself with tossing more sticks onto the cooking fire. Mrs. Biggins, noticing Amelyn's puzzling behavior, hastened to reply.

"Ta be sure! Ye might fetch the wooden bowls from the supply wagon. Johnny, ye can help by bringing me that basket of bread."

"Will I ever be too old for you to boss me about?" Rath teased, placing the basket at her feet.

"Not ye, my lad! Besides, we can use the extra hand, tha knows. That witch's daughter Bronwyn was supposed ta be here ta help us, but 'twould seem she has seen fit ta wander off inta the woods with her burly Viking. Doon't think Aw won't be givin' her a gooid tongue-lashin'!"

Except for the six guards posted at intervals around the perimeter of the camp, the men at arms came eagerly when called, grateful for the brimming bowls of stew and the crusty bread. Most of them wolfed down the food and returned for another helping. Rath and Marganna each carried two steaming bowls back to the litter to share with the boys, releasing the guards to go to their own dinners.

"Here, Doctor," Marganna said, proffering one of the bowls she was carrying. "I brought this for you. I'll have mine when the boys are through. Ned, how would you like something to eat?"

"I don't feel very hungry," he replied listlessly. "I have a terrible headache."

The doctor set his meal aside and began searching through a small chest for a headache powder.

"Well, it looks as if *you* are starving, Dickon," Rath commented, watching the younger lad spoon up the savory stew. Dickon nodded sleepily, dripping broth on his round chin and across the front of his doublet.

Several voices rose noisily outside the wagon; there was a muffled shout and a particularly foul oath, which trailed away into silence.

Dickon grinned. "You know, I've never camped outdoors before. May I sleep by the bonfire tonight?"

"It's too damp for you to stay out all night, I'm afraid," Rath said. "However, I don't see why you can't join the men around the fire until bedtime. Does that meet with your approval?"

"Yes! May I go now?"

Rath chuckled as he lifted his own spoon. "As soon as you finish your supper."

"I'll get some water to mix with that powder, Doctor," Marganna said, stepping to the back of the wagon, "I won't be long. Ned, shall I dampen a cloth to put over your forehead? Perhaps that would help ease the pain of your headache."

"Yes, please . . . if it's no trouble."

"It's no trouble at all."

Marganna's words trailed away as she alighted from the wagon and looked around her. It was the eeriest scene she had ever witnessed. Instead of the bustling camp she had expected, all was still. The area around the fires looked like a battlefield, littered with unmoving bodies. The men at arms were slumped over their suppers, some having fallen to lie face down in the grass. Near the cooking fires she could see Clovelly Biggins, sprawled awkwardly, one arm flung above her head. Amelyn was propped against the wheel of the supply wagon as though she had just fallen into a momentary doze.

One brawny fellow stumbled from the shadows, his mouth open in silent appeal, his hand reaching out to her. As she watched, his face went lax and he fell forward, unconscious.

Marganna's hand went to her throat. "Oh, my Lord!" she cried, throwing open the canvas at the back of the wagon. "Rath, something has happened! I think the entire camp has been poisoned!"

"Poisoned?" echoed Dr. Coombs. "What the—"

"Wh . . . what?" Rath blinked owlishly, then yawned. His head lolled forward, but he roused himself with an effort. "What's . . . wrong, love?"

"Look at Dickon!" Ned raised himself onto his elbows, a frightened look crossing his thin face. "Is he . . . dead?"

"No. He appears to be sleeping." Dr. Coombs knelt over Dickon's slouched form for a long moment. "I think he has been drugged . . . Rath too."

"No! I'm . . . all . . . right."

Rath heaved himself to his feet and lurched forward, teetering in the doorway. Another jaw-cracking yawn issued from his mouth and his eyes became glazed. He shook his head fiercely. "Mar . . . ganna . . . my God, I . . . can't . . ."

He suddenly pitched forward, crashing to the ground at her feet and lying there as though dead.

"Oh, no!" she whispered, kneeling by his side and shaking him. "Rath . . . oh, God! Wake up!"

"What shall we do?" Ned leaned out of the wagon, his frightened eyes taking in the still figures around the fire. Behind him the doctor said, "Marganna, we are the only ones still awake."

At that moment they heard the thunder of horses' hooves, and the firelit clearing began to fill with riders.

"Ned, quick," warned Marganna. "Get back in the wagon and hide. Don't show yourself, no matter what."

Her heart lurching wildly, she rose and faced the newcomers, aware of Dr. Coombs climbing down to stand at her side. They were surrounded by seven men on horseback.

"Well, Marganna, how pleasant to see you again."

"You!"

Donal FitzClinton laughed harshly. "You look surprised to see me. Surely you expected me to make some attempt to halt your progress to Scarborough."

"How did you know where we were going?"

"I have an informant, naturally. Quite a reliable one, as it turns out."

"Who?"

"That, I'm afraid, is none of your concern."

"How did you manage to get past the guards?" Dr. Coombs demanded.

"My men are Welsh, sir—used to fighting under difficult conditions. It was a simple matter for them to slip up behind each guard in the darkness and slash his throat."

"And you knew you'd be free to ride into camp undisturbed because your . . . informant had drugged the evening meal." Dr. Coombs drew himself up to his full stature. "Am I correct?"

"Entirely. Now, I have a question. How is it you and Marganna remain on your feet?"

"Because neither of us has eaten yet."

"And the boys?"

"They're . . . they've been taken on ahead," Marganna spoke up, knowing as she said the words that the lie was useless.

"You dissemble with such ease, my dear"—FitzClinton smiled—"but I have learned not to trust you. This arm is a daily reminder."

He indicated his left arm, which Marganna noticed for the first time was held stiffly at his side.

"I believe the boys are within this very wagon from which you alighted. Shall I have my men conduct a search to verify my theory?"

"What are your intentions?" asked the doctor, slowly backing toward the wagon. "Surely you would wish the princes no harm?"

"*I* don't, certainly, but the lady who hired me has an aversion to the bastards and wishes to see an end to their miserable lives. The gold she is willing to pay is more than enough to overcome any conscience I might have in the matter."

Turning to the men behind him, FitzClinton suddenly began issuing orders.

"You two, search the wagon for the boys. You—and you! Seize the woman! We'll take her with us."

Four of FitzClinton's men leaped from their horses as Marganna cried out in alarm. Dr. Coombs dropped to one knee to pull Rath's sword from the scabbard strapped to his unconscious body. With a snarling curse he scrambled back into the wagon and waved the weapon wildly.

"I'll kill any man who attempts to enter this wagon!"

The attackers fell back, looking askance at FitzClinton, but he merely snapped impatiently, "Have done with the fool."

The first man drew his own sword and advanced, but just as he prepared to hoist himself into the canvas-covered vehicle, Dr. Coombs thrust the sword he held, piercing the man's chest. Marganna hid her face, shuddering horribly as she saw the dripping blade pulled from his body as he fell. Suddenly there was a hoarse cry and her hands dropped from her eyes in time to see the second man throw himself at the doctor, driving the Welsh dagger he clutched into the side of Coomb's neck. The doctor fell backward, moaning in pain.

"No!" Marganna cried, still restrained by FitzClinton's henchmen. Frantically she sought Rath, but he remained unstirring. "Rath!" she screamed, her words echoing through the trees. "For God's sake—wake up!"

The Welshman wiped the dagger on his sleeve; slipping it back into its sheath, he began to climb into the wagon. Immediately a pale, pointed face appeared above him and Ned exclaimed, "Stop, or I will kill you!"

The young Plantagenet prince was standing over Dr. Coombs holding the bloodied sword. The man took a step away from the wagon and looked uncertainly at the mounted riders.

FitzClinton sneered. "Good God, man . . . surely you don't intend to be put off by a mere child." He threw a triumphant smile at Marganna. "At last we have bagged our quarry. And this time, without your clumsy lies and your husband's untimely intrusion, we shall be successful in dealing the death blow."

"How did you know I lied?" she asked slowly. "I told you the boys were at Rathburn Hall and they were. Who told you what really happened?"

"I grow weary of repeating myself, Marganna. I am not at liberty to divulge that name."

Marganna raised her chin defiantly and looked directly at FitzClinton. "I will do anything you ask in return for the lives of the boys."

"What?" FitzClinton said mockingly. "Am I to understand you are offering your virtue in exchange for their freedom?"

"If that is what it will take," she quietly replied. "After all, there is no need to slay them. They are not a threat to Tudor."

"They are direct heirs to the throne."

"But Richard has named his sister's son as his heir."

"True enough. However, when Henry Tudor becomes king, he wants no Plantagenet survivors left for misguided patriots to champion. They must all be eliminated."

"But how can you assume Richard will be defeated?"

"Enough. I am tired of arguing the matter. As to your spirited offer, I find it pointless. It has already been established that the princes must die, and since you are now in my possession, it is facetious for you to so nobly offer what is already mine for the taking."

"What are you saying?" she stormed. "If you think—"

"Silence!" FitzClinton shouted. "Bind her hands and throw her across Gibson's horse," he directed the men who held her. "I have no desire to stay while the lads are killed, so I will take the woman and these two men and return to the spot where the road forks south. We will wait there with the gold owed you. Once you have put the princes to the sword, join us and I'll have your money. Then we can disperse." He wheeled his huge mount around; as he did so, his gaze fell on Rath's prostrate form. "Oh, by the way, I think it would best serve my purposes for Marganna to become a widow, so be certain you kill Lord Rathburn before abandoning the encampment."

No!

The silent cry ripped through Marganna's mind; even as it did, it was followed by a very real echo.

"No!"

All eyes shifted to the slender blond woman by the campfire. Abandoning all pretense of being drugged, Amelyn rose to her feet and rushed across the clearing toward them. "No, damn you! You promised!"

FitzClinton smiled coldly. "It has become unwise to honor that promise, my sweet. I'm very sorry." He shrugged. "It cannot be helped."

"Amelyn," Marganna gasped. "What are you talking about? What promise?"

Amelyn whirled to toss a scathing look at her. "FitzClinton vowed that if I gave him you and the boys, he would leave Rath unharmed."

"You? You're the one who aided this vermin? My God, Amelyn . . . why?"

"It was your fault!" the other woman cried, her pale eyes shining with tears. "If only you had never come to Middleham!"

"But what does that have to do with it?"

FitzClinton's laugh was harsh. "The bitch has lusted after your husband for quite some time, Marganna. Didn't you know?"

"I *love* him!" Amelyn screamed at the man on the nervously prancing horse. "It was never a matter of lust. That is all he has ever felt for any woman . . . including you, Marganna, but if you had never come into his life, he would have loved me by now."

"How could you betray Ned and Dickon this way?" Marganna whispered. "How could you turn against the very people you've lived with?"

"Rath is all that matters to me." Amelyn straightened her shoulders and raised her chin. "When he finds you gone and the boys dead, he will turn to me for comfort. I had to do it."

"He will never love you when he finds out you are the one who conspired with FitzClinton."

"How will he find out?" Amelyn countered. "No one but FitzClinton and his men know, and they will be well on their way back to London."

"If your husband didn't suspect her that first time, there is no reason to think he will now. Amelyn has been very clever, I must say. She and I met several times within the shadow of Middleham with no one the wiser. She led you to the marketplace to meet me, and later, when I was wounded, found a safe place in the village for me to hide. She brought me word of Richard's visit and the plan to move the boys to Scarborough. Indeed, she was so useful that I planned to reward her with the only thing she ever asked—Lord Rathburn. Alas, that now becomes impossible."

"But what has changed?" Amelyn asked, her voice shrill. "Once the princes are out of the way, he can do nothing."

"Let's just say I've reconsidered, shall we? It simply isn't wise to leave the man alive."

"I won't let you kill him!" she shrieked.

"You can't stop me," FitzClinton said deliberately.

At his signal, the men holding Marganna dragged her forward and lifted her up to one of the riders beside FitzClinton. He settled her across his thighs with her head dangling. As she struggled, cursing and crying, he grasped a handful of hair and yanked painfully. Loosened from its knot, her hair streamed downward, blinding her to everything but the ground beneath the horse's feet. At his command, the animal sprang forward and the earth became a blur as they began moving.

FitzClinton cast a final command at the men he was leaving behind. "We'll be waiting—make haste!"

He spurred his mount, but Amelyn cried out and ran alongside, reaching for the bridle. "Stop!" she shouted. "Don't let them kill Rath."

"Get back, you little fool."

FitzClinton's warning came too late as Amelyn's skirts became tangled with the stallion's powerful legs, dragging her beneath its slashing hooves. Hearing Amelyn's last, strangled cry, Marganna was thankful her hair had shielded her from the sight of anything but the ground passing swiftly below.

Ignoring the crushed body lying in the dust, the riders galloped from the camp, disappearing into the blackness of the night beyond. Behind them was deadly silence.

The long silence was broken by a groan as Rath stirred and attempted to lift his head. With a muffled oath, he let it drop back onto his arms.

The three assassins were immediately spurred into action. Two of them advanced on the wagon where young Ned still stood, frozen in shock, the sword hanging limply from his fingers. The third drew his own sword and raised it above Rathburn's prone figure.

"No!" screamed Ned, suddenly bringing the sword he grasped upward and jabbing it at the first man. It caught the Welshman in the throat, and he fell back, blood pouring from the fatal wound. Now bereft of his weapon, the prince could do nothing but face his next attacker, and this he did with an expression of calm valor on his pallid features. He did not flinch as the man raised his sword.

"Aiiiigh!" A sound resembling an ancient Norse war cry rang through the clearing, and two figures sprinted from the dark underbrush. The smaller of the two hurtled through the air, leaping onto the wagon and driving a dagger deep into the back of the man who threatened Ned. The other, casting a huge, menacing shadow, threw a brawny arm about the neck of the man standing over Rath and dragged him backward. As the viselike arm muscles tightened, the terrified man's pleas for help were choked off, his raspy breathing abruptly silenced as his windpipe was crushed.

"Bronwyn! Vogelman!" cried Ned in relief, leaning out of the wagon. "Where did you come from?"

"We've been hiding just out of sight," said Bronwyn, panting as she cleaned her dagger and slipped it back into the sheath hanging from her leather girdle. "We thought it best to wait until FitzClinton had gone before showing ourselves."

"But they have Marganna!" At that instant, there was a movement near his foot and Ned looked down, startled. "Dr. Coombs . . . I thought they had killed you!"

The physician tried to sit up but slumped weakly. He was covered with blood and his face was ashen. "I'm . . . all right. You . . . you'll have . . . to . . . wake Rath."

"Let me have a look at the doctor," Vogelman said, swinging up beside Ned. "There may be something we can do."

"No . . . need. My wound is . . . not serious."

As Vogelman peeled the layer of clothing away, it could be seen that the stab wound, now just oozing blood, was in the curve of shoulder and neck, missing the vital artery. "He's right," the big man announced. "This won't prove fatal."

"Go . . . get Marganna," the doctor whispered hoarsely. "Rath . . ."

"Was Rath drugged?" Bronwyn asked Ned.

He nodded. "But I don't think he had more than a few bites of the stew. Dickon was greedy and ate all of his." He indicated his younger brother, still sleeping soundly at the rear of the vehicle.

"What should we do for Rath?" Vogelman asked the doctor.

"Take him . . . to the . . . river. Douse him . . ."

Vogelman leaped from the wagon and, with Bronwyn's aid, managed to toss Rath's body over his shoulder. With a grim look on his harshly carved features, he began striding toward the narrow river at the edge of the camp.

Barely conscious of what was happening, Rath had just become aware of bumping painfully against hard sinew when he experienced a feeling of being catapulted through the air. He hit the water with a resounding splash and felt its iciness close over his head; it gradually revived him and restored his senses. As he surfaced and shook the cold water from his face and hair, he was stricken with dreadful anguish.

Marganna!

* * *

Marganna was surprised when FitzClinton gave the order to halt and the agonizing ride came to an end. She had fully expected to die, if not from the painful jarring and the blood thundering in her head, then from the dust swirling up to clog her nose and throat, making each breath an effort. She had, in fact, resigned herself to death, having no wish to survive if Rath and the princes did not.

She was allowed to slide from the horse and fall to the ground, where she lay with her face in the damp grass, its sweetly familiar scent welcome after the choking dust. Despite herself she drew in long, deep breaths of the fresh night air, knowing she was only delaying her inevitable death but unable to suppress her body's natural attempt to sustain life.

A few curt words from FitzClinton sent one of his men scrambling up onto a nearby outcropping of rock to act as a sentry and the other to lead the horses to water and ready them for the long ride ahead. FitzClinton himself dismounted, walked to where Marganna lay, and stood over her.

"Well, Marganna," he said in a thoughtful tone, "your circumstances seem to have changed again. I wonder what you think of this latest development?"

"I'm not afraid to die," she replied stoutly.

"Die? Oh, my dear, who said anything about dying?"

"But I thought . . ."

"Oh, surely you didn't think I would let you be killed."

"If my husband is dead, I would gladly welcome death myself."

"Exactly the reason I intend to see that you remain alive, my pet. I feel it will be a much more fitting punishment for you than oblivion."

"Then what will you do with me?"

He smiled, and even in the dim moonlight she could see the perverse evil of his expression.

"Do you recall that night at Nottingham Castle when you gazed across the dining table at me with such promise in your eyes? Well, Marganna, I want to know more about the things your eyes promised. It occurs to me you must be a passionate female, given the way you so easily brought Rathburn to heel. His reputation was such that I cannot believe an ordinary woman would have been able to so entangle him in two short months.'' He reached out a gloved hand and grasped her arm, pulling her to her feet. She stared at him with wide, shocked eyes. ''Are you a wanton, Marganna? Is that the secret you hide behind that innocent face? Is the angelic niece of the good Lady Stanley really a whore at heart?''

She took a step backward. ''I think you must be mad,'' she whispered.

He threw back his head and laughed in delight. ''Indeed! Mad to find out what kind of mistress you will make.''

''What are you saying?''

''That with a bit of cooperation from you, the journey back to London can be most enjoyable. Then, if you have pleased me well, I will intercede with your aunt on your behalf. She is very angry with you, you know. I wager you would much prefer remaining in my company than being left at the mercy of Lady Stanley.''

''You forget the king! Do you think Richard would stand by and see me at your mercy?''

''Richard? My dear, what must I say to convince you that he will be king no longer? Henry Tudor, on the other hand, should be quite willing to give you to me, after the service I have performed on his behalf.''

''Richard is going to kill Henry Tudor,'' Marganna cried angrily. ''My God, he has an army of soldiers—all Tudor has is a mismatched band of French criminals and a handful of dissatisfied, war-minded Welshmen.''

''Believe me when I tell you there are more ways than one to depose a king. Plantagenet may lead an army, but who is to say that army is entirely . . . faithful? What if one or two divisions decide to go over to the other side . . . even in the midst of battle? Who could prepare for such a contingency? Indeed, who could survive such mass treachery?''

''I don't believe it! No one could be so traitorous!''

"Don't be naive. Kings can be bought and sold just like anyone else. And your beloved Dickon is going to fall, mark my word. Too much gold stands against him."

"Meaning that this plot against Richard has been contrived by people like my aunt and her husband . . . people who hunger for power, people who don't care anything at all about what is best for England."

"People who can pay for what they want," FitzClinton reminded her.

"God, I wish I could do something to stop them! I hate them for what they are trying to do to Richard and for what they have already done to Rath and the boys." Her voice broke and faded.

"Come now, don't waste your tears on insignificant matters. You can't help anyone but yourself, so you'd best begin to think of how you are going to make amends to me."

"I won't be your . . . I won't let you touch me," she declared. "You would have to kill me first!"

"Proud to the last, eh? I expected nothing less." He smiled as though pleased by her resistance and moved a step closer. "But be assured, I can and will take you anytime I please . . . and there isn't a thing you can do to stop me. You can only make the experience more pleasant for—"

"Don't touch me!" she snarled, backing away. Her hands, still bound behind her back, arched into claws, which she longed to rake down his handsomely arrogant face.

His laugh was harsh. "You have nothing to fear at this moment, my dear. I prefer to wait until you've bathed and washed your hair. There's an inn a few miles down the road where I plan to spend the night with you."

A faint cry from the sentry reached their ears. "They're coming!" he called out, making his way down from the rock.

Marganna realized she did not have more than a few seconds in which to make an attempt at escape. Once the others joined them, she would be tossed over another horse and borne away, irrevocably trapped in FitzClinton's plan.

She could think of nothing more degrading or horrible than sharing a bed with the man responsible for killing her husband.

Oh, Rath, she thought, fighting back the tears that welled into her eyes, what have they done to you? If only . . . if I thought there was any chance you might be alive . . .

But no, what chance could there be? FitzClinton's ruthless hirelings would have struck swiftly, brutally.

While her captor's attention was on the sentry, Marganna turned and began a stumbling run into the darkness of a nearby copse of trees. She knew there was virtually no chance of eluding the men, but perhaps her flight would provoke them into killing her quickly, thus putting an end to FitzClinton's threats.

"She's getting away!" the sentry yelled, pointing at Marganna's fleeing figure.

With a nod from FitzClinton, he followed her, thrashing through the underbrush. He caught her easily and dragged her back into the clearing, shoving her toward FitzClinton with a satisfied grunt. She staggered against the courtier and, as he righted her, swung an elbow into his ribs. Instantly the sentry was beside them, his sword drawn and raised high.

"No," FitzClinton gasped. "Don't kill her. Can't you see? That is what she wants."

Marganna kicked out, and he bent over in pain as her boot grazed his shin. Quickly she whirled, lowered her head, and butted the sentry in the stomach. His groan of pain was lost in a deeper, louder cry.

"Aiiigh!"

Two riders had entered the clearing and now flung themselves from their horses. Marganna was stunned to see Erik Vogelman stride forward to pick up the sentry bodily and toss him against a boulder as if he weighed no more than a child. Before he could move, Vogelman had slashed the man's throat with his own dagger.

"Marganna, love—are you all right?"

At the sound of the beloved voice she had thought never to hear again, Marganna turned to the second man.

"Rath!" she cried joyously. "Oh, my God! How can it be?" He was quickly at her side, an arm around her waist, his lips on hers for a brief instant.

"Rath, I thought you were dead."

"I know," he said soothingly, kissing her again. "I know."

"Indeed, you should have been dead," stated FitzClinton, drawing his sword from its scabbard. "Tell me, how is it you managed to evade death until this moment?"

Rath's own sword glinted in the pale moonlight. "It doesn't matter. Just know that I did, and now I intend to take pleasure in killing you." He gave Marganna a light push. "Stand back, love—this shouldn't take long."

"You're very confident." FitzClinton smirked. "Perhaps it is because you think I am maimed. Let me assure you, my sword arm suffered no injury."

Without warning his blade sliced the air, but Rath dodged with agility and answered with a dangerous parry of his own.

Marganna, watching anxiously, was scarcely aware that Vogelman had stepped up behind her to cut the cords still binding her wrists. As her arms were freed, she experienced a wave of crippling pain. With gentle hands, Vogelman led her to an outcropping of rock where she sank down onto a low boulder.

Rath and FitzClinton circled warily around the clearing; this was no tidy, formal duel but rather an intense, primitive fight to the death. FitzClinton seemed the more refreshed of the two, only slightly hampered by his stiffened arm. Rath's movements grew imperceptibly slower, and Marganna thought he looked haggard and drawn. It was evident he was tiring rapidly. She glanced at Vogelman and saw his hand tighten on the hilt of his own sword. No doubt he would step in should Rath begin to falter.

Just at that moment, in a flurry of hoofbeats, the third Welshman, who had been hiding along the riverbank where he'd taken the horses, rode past, skirting the clearing to take flight. Before Rath could shout the order, Vogelman leaped onto the back of his own mount and went galloping madly after the fleeing man.

Taking advantage of Rath's distraction, FitzClinton swung his weapon in a deadly arc that would surely have decapitated his opponent had Rath not swiftly fallen back.

Feeling his physical powers waning, Rath forced himself to recall each and every one of FitzClinton's crimes, using the hatred he felt to sustain his strength.

"I only wish I could kill you more than once," Rath panted, his blade gleaming silver in the faint light. His mind filled with rage, and he began furiously driving the courtier backward. "I'd like to kill you for what you tried to do to the boys . . . for what you are attempting to do to the king . . . for all the others you've hurt . . . Dr. Coombs, Amelyn. But since I can kill you only once . . ."

FitzClinton's boot struck a loose stone and he slipped, falling to one knee, his sword arm swinging wide in an effort to maintain his balance. The tip of Rath's sword sharply pressed his chest.

"I will kill you for what you did to my wife!"

FitzClinton's fear was evident in his eyes, but he managed to summon his usual sarcasm. "The Tudor trollop?"

Rath's mouth tightened. "Guard your tongue, damn you. I may be able to slay you only once, but I can make it slow and painful. As a matter of fact, I believe I would enjoy carving you up bit by bit . . ." He lowered his blade considerably. "Shall I start by gelding you?"

The insistent prod of the blade brought forth a sharp cry of alarm from the kneeling man.

"Rath, please!" cried Marganna. "There is no need for—"

"Cruelty? When did he ever worry about *his* cruelties? But I suppose you are right. A civilized Englishman would never commit such an atrocity."

FitzClinton nearly sagged in his relief, but again Rath's sword threatened him. "Of course, in addition to being an Englishman, I am one of those crude North Country men. Mayhap I shouldn't hesitate to mutilate him. Think of all he did to you, Marganna, and of what he no doubt planned."

"Kill me and be done with it!" FitzClinton cried shrilly, suddenly leaping to his feet. His knee came up, striking

Rath in the chest and toppling him backward. With a triumphant cry, FitzClinton swung his sword downward.

Utilizing his last ounce of energy, Rath rolled to one side, barely avoiding the blade; then he swiftly thrust his own blade upward, meeting flesh and angling the sword into FitzClinton's heart.

A gurgling sigh of air was expelled from FitzClinton's lungs as his body sagged, then pitched forward to lie at Marganna's feet. A smile flickered over his elegant features and his eyes began to dull, staring lifelessly upward. As his head rolled gracefully to one side, Marganna's horrified gaze caught sight of a flash of fire from the single diamond earring he wore.

She could not control a shudder of disgust as she stepped away from the courtier's body. Then, seeing Rath stagger to his feet, she felt an overwhelming surge of relief and fierce pride, and she approached her weary husband to take him into her arms.

"Thank God you're safe!" she murmured. "Thank God."

In a few moments, Erik Vogelman returned, leading a second horse over whose back was thrown the body of the man who had tried to escape. After one dispassionate glance at the dead FitzClinton, he spurred his mount onto the road that led back to the encampment, leaving Rath and Marganna to follow.

Rath rode silently astride the huge war-horse, Marganna once again secure in his arms.

When they reached the camp, they found that Bronwyn had tended the doctor's wound and was following his instructions in reviving some of the others. A groggy Clovelly Biggins stood over the fire, stirring a kettle of evil-smelling brew, which she declared would expunge the effects of the drug Amelyn had put into the evening meal.

"Aw'm ashamed ta say she sneaked the herbs from my own cupboard." She shook her gray head, wincing at the pain. "Thank the Lord, Aw've always kept the poisons locked oop or Aw've no doubt we'd all be daid by noo!"

"I can't believe Amelyn was the one who betrayed us." Marganna signed, averting her eyes as the woman's battered body was removed from the camp for burial. "I . . . I thought it was you, Bronwyn. I mean, you were so obviously missing from the encampment."

For the first time since Marganna had first met her, the black-haired beauty blushed as she cast a sidelong glance at Vogelman. He threw back his curly head and roared with laughter, pulling Bronwyn tightly against his massive chest.

"Aye, 'tis certain it did look odd." He chuckled. "But 'twas a good thing my woman desired a . . . walk in the woods. Otherwise we'd have been drugged like the rest and no help to ye at all."

Rath smiled tiredly. "I owe you everything, Vogelman. God, I've never heard a more beautiful sound than that damned Viking war cry of yours!"

Later, when everyone else was finally settled for the night, Rath and Marganna walked quietly through the camp. Marganna recounted FitzClinton's boast that there was an assassination plot against Richard, knowing as she did so what her hushand's reaction would be.

"We've got to warn him. In the morning I'll send two men south with a message for him." He ceased walking, put his hands on her shoulders, and looked intently into her eyes. "As soon as I've seen the lads safely to Scarborough, I'll have to go to Richard myself. He's not likely to take this threat any more seriously than any of the others."

His hands slid down her back, pressing her close, and she clung to him.

"Marganna? For an argumentative wench, you have very little to say. I thought you would try to persuade me not to go." He pulled back to look at her again.

"I'd like nothing better than to keep you here where you'll be safe," she admitted with a sad smile. "But we made a vow, remember? I know you must go."

She recognized the relief on his face and was gratified

she had chosen not to complicate his decision. His ardent kiss warmed her, momentarily dispelling the chill creeping inexorably into her soul.

Why did she feel the nightmare had yet to end?

Chapter 19

Two weeks later, Marganna realized the nightmare had, in fact, only begun.

Richard III, the last of the Plantagenet kings, fell in battle on August 22, 1485, at Bosworth Field in Leicestershire.

Word came to Scarborough Castle in the early morning hours, and by the time the princes had arisen for the day, plans for their removal from England were already being carried out.

Shocked by the king's death, a grieving Clovelly Biggins asked that the boys be spared the news until after they set sail. She would, she promised, tell them about it later.

"Poor lads, they will have enough ta worry aboot, just leavin' England behind."

Carts containing the boys' possessions were trundled down the steep hillside to the harbor below, where they were loaded onto the small merchant ship waiting there.

From a window high in the castle Marganna watched, gripped by icy numbness. She could not believe Richard was dead—poor, sad, tragic man! And if he had not known of the plot against him, did that mean Rath who had left one week ago, had not reached him, or only that Richard had refused to believe the worst? Since the day they'd arrived safely at Scarborough and Rath had kissed her goodbye to ride in search of his friend and king, she had had no word of him. Where could he be? Dear Lord, not dead like Richard . . . please!

The time she had dreaded came at midafternoon, and too soon it was time to say farewell to the princes.

Ned was his usual serious self, wearing plain clothes covered by a dark blue cloak. Dickon, excited by the thrill of a sea journey, raced with the hound Caesar along the beach, his scarlet cloak left forgotten in a heap on the stone quay, not far from where the others stood murmuring in low tones.

Marganna looked at the faces of her friends, trying to memorize each one in the event she would never see them again. The ship would carry them across the North Sea to the Low Countries, where the princes would be put into the capable hands of a Flemish merchant family, members of the same family that had been so loyal to Edward IV when he and Richard had been forced to flee England and live in exile. The boys were to reside with this large, well-to-do family, though they would be under the constant surveillance and invisible protection of their aunt, the duchess Margaret of Burgundy. Should their existence become threatened in any way, she had assured Richard she would move swiftly to have the boys brought to her.

Marganna sighed wearily. God only knew what future lay in store for Ned and Dickon.

Her somber thoughts returned to the stone quay and Scarborough's breezy harbor. A short distance away stood Erik Vogelman and Bronwyn. As Marganna gazed at them, she was reminded again of what a magnificent couple they made. He was so massive and fair, she so feminine and dark, his savage strength making a perfect foil for her wild, spirited beauty.

After the weary group's arrival at Scarborough Castle, Bronwyn and Vogelman had approached Rath to seek his permission to accompany Mrs. Biggins and the boys on the journey to the Continent. Their valor had won them Rath's complete trust, and he gave his unstinting approval.

Now they stood ready to leave their homeland without any apparent apprehension.

Seeing Marganna's grave expression, Vogelman spoke. "Do not worry about Ned and Dickon. We will stay close to the lads, and I swear, no one will harm them as long as I am alive to prevent it."

"I wasn't worrying about the boys," Marganna replied.

"I was just wondering if you were not . . . well, a little sad about leaving England."

"Not an England under the rule of that cold-blooded son of a whore," Vogelman said in a soft voice. "And besides, everything I deem important goes with me." One powerful hand fell to the hilt of his sword, the other slipped beneath Bronwyn's sea-blown tresses to rest lightly on her neck. She turned her face up to him, the incredible loveliness of her smile making Marganna's breath catch in her throat. She had never seen the fiery northern woman like this!

"You leave behind no family, then?" she asked.

"Nay. Bronwyn is my family now."

"And Clovelly and the princes," Bronwyn reminded him gently. She turned to look at Marganna, and her black eyes were serene. Gone was the restlessness that had once marked her. "And I think you should know, it begins to look very much as though we are going to have a child of our own by springtime."

"How wonderful! But what about this journey? It won't be too much for you, will it?"

"I am strong enough to withstand it," the other woman replied, and Vogelman nodded his proud agreement.

"Besides," he said, " 'tis one of the reasons we asked to accompany the lads. We do not want our children raised in a country upset by such strife as there will be in a Tudor-ruled England."

"Erik's family came from Norway," Bronwyn informed her. "Perhaps someday, when the princes are older, we will leave them and travel north to live. I do not believe there is an entire race of people who look like this beautiful man." She nudged Vogelman in the ribs with her elbow and gave him a loving smile.

Marganna had to smile too, still marveling at the change in this woman who had once been her bitter enemy. Though there was much between them that no longer needed to be discussed, there was one thing she could not leave unsaid.

"Bronwyn, I . . . I want to thank you for saving Rath's life, as well as the boys'. Ned told me what you and Vogelman did, and . . . well, there are no words to express my gratitude. Thank God you were there."

"Yes, thank God." Bronwyn's smile became slightly ironic. "You know, Marganna, there was a time when I hated you."

Marganna returned the smile. "I remember it well."

"Back then I never thought I would ever consider you a friend. Isn't it amazing how things can change?"

"Yes, it is. And I'm glad we can be friends. We won't ever forget you or what you have done for us, you know." Impulsively she leaned forward to give Bronwyn a hug, and with emotion thinly disguised by a growl of laughter, Vogelman threw his arms around them both and squeezed tightly.

"Will we see you again?" he asked.

"Of course! Rath and I will come to visit when it is safe to do so. We must pray it will not be long."

"Yes." Vogelman released Bronwyn and Marganna and stepped back. "We will leave you to say good-bye to Clovelly and the boys, then. Good fortune to you and to Lord Rathburn."

"Thank you, Vogelman. Good fortune to you also."

" 'Twould seem Aw have some apologizin' ta do ta Bronwyn, tha knows," said Mrs. Biggins, standing at Marganna's side to watch the couple embark. "Aw was wrong aboot her, purely wrong."

"I think we all were, Clovelly. None of us realized how different she could become. She seems happy now, don't you think?"

"Aye. Methinks she has changed from a kestrel ta a nesting dove. Sometimes that happens when a woman finds the right man, ye know."

She favored Marganna with a keen look, and the younger woman had to laugh. "Don't look at me that way, Clovelly. Perhaps I am not the type to be a nesting dove."

"Are ye sayin' ye haven't found the right man, lass?"

"No, I'm not saying that. I'm not certain Rath is the *right* man for me . . ." At Clovelly's frown she hastened to add, "But I do know he is the only man I will ever love."

Clovelly Biggins beamed. "Aw'm proud ta hear ye finally admit it. Lord, but the two of ye took yer precious time decidin' ta get over yer stubborness!" Her expression sobered. "Ye'll take care of Johnny fer me, won't ye, Marganna?"

"You have my word on it. As soon as you are safely underway, I am going to ask Will to take me south to find Rath. I'm worried about him, Clovelly. He could be hurt . . . or worse."

Clovelly patted Marganna's hand. "Doon't concern yerself that the lad is daid. Aw feel certain he is not. But, Marganna, he will be suffering—he truly loved Richard, ye know—and ye'll be the only one ta help him through."

"I'll do everything I can; you needn't worry."

"Bless ye, lass. And bless the gooid Lord that sent ye ta us." Despite the tears that glistened in her eyes, Clovelly's head snapped up, causing the loops of iron gray braids to quiver dangerously. "Here is Ned, wantin' ta say good-bye ta ye. Aw'll go fetch Dickon."

Marganna studied the gangling young man standing before her, then reached out to take his thin hands in her own. He stood as tall as she, with his fair hair ruffled in the breeze and the ocean chill painting his cheeks with an unaccustomed rosiness. There was a new maturity in his eyes, and Marganna silently cursed the events that had put it there.

"I feel I should be kneeling before you, Edward," she said softly. "At this moment, you look every inch a king. I am so very proud of you." Her voice broke and she struggled for control. "You were wonderfully brave when FitzClinton's men attacked the camp. You proved yourself as able a warrior as ever your father or uncle did."

His smile was wan. "I want to ask you something. Please don't lie to me." He drew a deep breath. "Uncle Dickon is dead, isn't he, Marganna?"

Swift pain shot through her, and tears gathered in her throat. With an effort she held his gaze steadily.

"Oh, Ned, yes. I'm afraid he is. He died at Bosworth Field."

The boy drew himself up stiffly. "Did Tudor kill him?"

His gaze had moved to a point on the distant horizon, but his hands gripped hers tightly.

"No, he didn't. The messenger told us only that Tudor's bodyguard was responsible for Richard's death."

Edward's eyes came back to hers. "His bodyguard? I don't understand."

"Nor did we, Ned, but I intend to find out what happened, and I promise I'll write you a letter to explain the details. It will be . . . painful for you, but you have the right to know."

"I want to know," he said harshly. "My uncle was an exceptionally fine warrior, Marganna—I cannot help but think there must have been treachery of some sort involved."

At that moment Marganna thought he was as splendid as ever his father had been. There was little doubt the royal Plantagenet blood ran strongly in his veins. He would have made an admirable king.

"Mrs. Biggins did not want us to tell you about your uncle just yet. She thought it wisest to wait until you were past the confusion of leaving England."

"Yes, that was probably for the best. It's just that . . . somehow . . . I knew what must have happened. It seemed the only reason we would have to leave the country. Don't worry, I will tell Dickon myself. Later, when things are calmer."

"Your brother is lucky to have you to watch over him," she said. "Very lucky indeed."

"I want us to be like . . ." For the first time his young voice quavered. "Like my father and Uncle Dickon." A look of uncertainty came into his eyes. "Do you think we will ever see our sisters again?"

"I expect so, Ned. It will be up to your mother . . . and, I suppose, to the new king."

"There is no king named Tudor," Ned whispered fiercely. "My cousin, the earl of Lincoln, is king. There can be no other!"

With a muffled sob, he threw his arms around Marganna and she held him close, her own tears dampening the fur collar of his cloak. They stood for a long moment, buffeted by the rising sea wind; then, shakily, Ned pulled away and smiled.

"We cannot let Dickon suspect anything is wrong," he said, struggling to pull the newly donned mantle of manhood around himself once more.

Clovelly Biggins followed Dickon as he approached, shaking the wrinkles from his cloak and slipping it around his shoulders when he halted in front of Marganna. Squinting against the sun, he looked up at her.

"I wish you could go with us, Marganna. We could have ever so much more fun."

"I know, Dickon," she answered, laying a hand on his shoulder, "but I must stay here to help Rath. However, we will come to visit you as soon as we can."

"Is that a promise?"

"Indeed it is."

"I am going to write Uncle Richard a long letter to tell him all about our sea journey. Shall I write one to you also?"

Marganna's eyes met Edward's over the younger lad's head. "Yes, please do. I should love to receive a letter from you. I will write back and tell you how things are at Middleham and Nappa Hall."

" 'Tis time ta go, lads," Clovelly Biggins said gently.

For an instant tears welled in Dickon's hazel eyes; then he hid his freckled face against Marganna's waist and hugged her tightly. "I will miss you, Marganna," he said, sniffing.

"And I will miss you, Dickon." Her arms opened to include the older boy. "And you, Ned."

"Please thank Lord Rathburn for all he has done for us," Ned said in an oddly adult tone.

"And promise you will name your first baby after us!" Dickon dared to say, the hint of a mischievous smile shining through his woeful expression.

Marganna laughed softly. "I will be honored to do both things," she said. "God go with you on your journey . . . and I shall think of you every day for the rest of my life."

Marganna kissed both boys, then watched as Clovelly led them away, the faithful Caesar trotting close at their heels. They turned and waved once, and then the sailors were helping them board the ship.

Despite the increasing chill of the air, Marganna stood on the quay watching the ship until its sails had disappeared from sight. When she started at last to return to the castle, Will Metcalfe fell into step beside her, and with a tearful smile she clutched his hand.

"What is going to happen to us all, Will?" she asked.

"Whatever God wills, Marganna. Not always an easy thing to understand or accept."

"You speak the truth of it." She sighed, looking back once more at the empty horizon. "Will, there is something I must ask of you."

"Yes, I will take you to find Rath." He smiled gently at her look of surprise. "You are not the sort of woman to sit calmly at home when your husband might be in danger . . . and we both know it."

"I am so worried about him!"

He pressed her hands reassuringly. "We'll leave first thing in the morning."

When Will and Marganna arrived at Market Bosworth, a small village only two miles from Bosworth Field, the battle had been over for several days.

They were told that those captured after the battle had been taken to Leicester for execution, and fear gripped Marganna. She had come all this way praying every mile that Rath might not be dead. What if he was alive and they had come only in time to see him executed?

It seemed an eternity before Will located anyone in Leicester who had heard of Rathburn. "I talked to a soldier who remembers him," he told her. "He thinks Rath is being held at the church at Greyfriars. That's where they moved those who were injured."

"Rath was injured?"

"The man wasn't certain, but he thought so."

"Oh, God, Will—please, we must hurry!"

The small stone church stood on the banks of the River Soar, its entrance flanked by Tudor guards who immediately blocked their way until Will dangled a bag of coins before their greedy eyes. One of them snatched the sack and stepped aside.

"Go on in and find Lord Rathburn. He'll be there. They aren't hanging the sick ones until tomorrow."

The interior of the church was inadequately lighted by cheap candles that smoked and sputtered. Their rancid odor mixed with the smells of blood and sickness, sweat, dirt, and despair. Some of the prisoners sat on benches along the walls, their heads or limbs bandaged, their lack-luster eyes following Marganna and Will as they stepped over and around the crude beds on the floor, where the more seriously wounded had been placed. A few nuns moved silently among the casualties.

"Marganna?"

She heard his voice before she actually saw him, but when her eyes searched the shadows, she spied Rath, propped against the wall and looking like a gaunt scare-the-crow. With a cry of joy she flung herself down on the pallet beside him, throwing her arms around his thin form.

"Oh, Rath, love . . . what have they done to you?" She kissed his mouth, her tears pouring freely over his roughly bearded face. "Oh, my God, I have been so afraid we would not find you."

She rested her head on his shoulder, feeling the rasp of his whiskers on her skin and smelling the faint tang of fever that clung to him. He stirred beneath her cheek, and she lifted her head to look into his haunted eyes. Weakly he raised a hand to stroke her face.

"How did you get to Leicester? Are you really here, sweetheart," he murmured, "or am I still dreaming?"

"You're not dreaming. I'm here . . . and so is Will. We want to take you home."

Will dropped to one knee and laid a hand on his friend's shoulder. "What injuries do you have, Rath?"

Rath's hand left Marganna's cheek to rub his own fore-head, fingers raking back through the thick hair above it.

"I'm not injured, just suffering from this damned fever. I've had it ever since I left Scarborough."

Will and Marganna exchanged looks. "It could have

been the drug or the dousing in the icy river," Will muttered. "Or any of a dozen other causes."

"I never made it to the battle," Rath continued, a weary rage in his voice.

"Rath, you can't be blamed. At least you tried. There was nothing more you could have done."

"But I never got to warn Richard." His eyes darkened in pain. "They killed him, did you know? The black-hearted bastards killed him!" A sob was wrenched from deep within him. "Damn them all—may their traitorous souls rot in hell!" Tears trickled down the hollows of his cheeks, gleaming in the dim light. "Aw, God!"

Marganna cradled him in her arms, her own tears dripping like rain onto his ebony hair. "Rath . . . oh, darling . . . don't! Please don't torture yourself this way!"

He dropped back onto the pallet, flinging an arm across his face. Marganna was glad, for the suffering in his eyes unnerved her. He might have been observing hell from within its very depths.

Tenderly she stroked his forehead, hoping he would not notice how her hand was shaking. "Try to sleep for a while, Rath. We'll be here when you awaken."

Marganna's voice and the gentle movements of her fingers soothed him; it took only a few minutes for him to fall into a restless slumber. His skin felt too warm beneath her touch, and his exhaustion seemed to indicate he was far from well.

"Will," she whispered anxiously, "he is so weak. How long do you think he has been like this?"

An aging man on the next pallet half rose to look at her. "Pardon me, ma'am, but Rath . . . er, Lord Rathburn . . . was brought in the first evening after the battle. He was fairly lucid at first, told me he'd taken ill on his way south and that he'd spent several days at a farmhouse where a family cared for him. He'd been here only a day before he became feverish again. I've done what little I could for him, but . . ." He shrugged. "The guards won't allow the sisters to administer any medicine. No sense wasting it on men who are going to die anyway, they said."

Marganna's eyes clouded as she gazed down at Rath. "Do you know why my husband was arrested, Master . . . ?"

"Matthew Finch at your service, ma'am. Lately of King Richard's army." The man painfully pulled himself into a sitting position, resting his shoulders against the wall. The tattered blanket thrown over him slipped aside to reveal a leg wrapped in a stained and blood-soaked bandage. "When his lordship rode into Leicester, he heard the news from one of Tudor's soldiers. Seems the man boasted overmuch of helping slay Richard and nearly got himself killed for his efforts." He managed a dry chuckle.

"Rath tried to kill him?"

"Yes, ma'am. They tossed him in here, and I reckon they plan to hang him with the rest of us."

"Thank God Rath didn't kill the man," said Will. "Since he didn't take part in the battle, we may be able to do something."

"Of course, I think he feels he deserves to die," Finch said. "For not getting to Richard in time and for not being here to fight beside him."

"Yes, that is how Rath would think," Will agreed wryly. "But we'll just have to save him if we can and worry about him forgiving us later."

"Poor Rath," Marganna murmured, "hearing about Richard that way. It seems FitzClinton told the truth—there must have been a conspiracy."

Finch's eyes narrowed. "Aye, that's right enough. Though a dozen other men might have struck the blows, it was the Stanleys who were really responsible for our King Dickon's death."

"In what way?" Will inquired. "Do you mean they came out for Tudor?"

"No, they came out for Richard as was expected, but they held back and ignored his order to attack."

"Waiting to see which way the battle would go?"

"So we thought at first. Now, looking back on it, I believe the whoresons meant to back Tudor all the time. As did the duke of Northumberland."

"Northumberland?" breathed Will. "Good God, a North Country man?"

"He delayed so long in sending a battle summons north that the men of York couldn't make it to Bosworth in time to support the king. They were somewhere on the road when he was slain."

"That son of a bitch!" Will swore softly. "They'll never forgive him that. He'd best never go home because they will see him pay for his treachery."

Matthew Finch looked grim. "Between the Stanley brothers and Northumberland, fully two thirds of Richard's army stood idly by, never even engaging in the fighting. Finally Richard tried a desperate measure. He rode right into the enemy forces, accompanied only by the men of his household, and by God, he was cutting his way through to Tudor himself."

Finch ceased talking to turn his shaggy gray head and spit in contempt. "Tudor sat quaking in fear, surrounded by his bodyguard and watching Richard come closer and closer. I swear the king was within yards of him—and would have had him too, had not Sir William Stanley chosen that moment to make his allegiance to Tudor known."

"God damn him," Will muttered, brushing a hand over his eyes.

"Hundreds of red-jacketed soldiers surrounded Richard, closing over him like . . . like an ocean of blood. He never had a chance." Finch coughed harshly, and a single tear rolled down his leathery cheek.

Marganna, too, began to cry quietly. What must it have done to Rath to learn the circumstances of Richard's death?

"Those who loved King Dickon would have been proud of the way he faced his death, swinging his battle-ax and meeting the foe head-on. No cowering in fright for him! He gave no mercy and expected none in return."

Matthew Finch squinted against the light coming through a nearby window, but it was obvious he was seeing the scene at Bosworth Field once again. "The fiends didn't just kill Richard, they mutilated him. Tudor's men gathered around his body and kept striking blow after blow, nearly hacking him to pieces."

Marganna's small cry of anguish sounded loud in the room, and her eyes were dark with horror.

"The worst part is . . . they stripped him naked and threw his body over the back of a packhorse, then led the animal through the streets of Leicester, letting the crowd ridicule and abuse his dead body."

"No king should be so defiled," declared Will angrily.

"Has . . . has Richard been given burial?" Marganna asked.

"Aye. After his despoiled body was left on display in the square for two days. Some of the holy people took it away in the dark of night and brought it to Greyfriars. One of the nuns told me they washed Richard and stitched his wounds as best they could, then laid him to rest in the little churchyard out back. I've seen the grave from that window. 'Tis unmarked, like a pauper's grave."

"And Tudor?" asked Will.

" 'Tis said he wasted no time in putting the crown on his head. Dickon had worn it into battle, saying he would either live or die as king of England." Finch was silent for a few moments, then went on. "After the fighting ended, a page found the crown lying in a bush, bent and tarnished. It was immediately straightened so the traitor Stanley might place it on his new sovereign's head. God's vengeance on both of them!"

Rath moaned and began to thrash his head from side to side. Marganna leaned forward to comfort him.

"Shh, love . . . you are all right."

"Will," Rath said suddenly, opening eyes that were piercingly clear as they rested on his friend, "I want you to take Marganna away. I don't want her here tomorrow."

"We're not leaving you to hang!" she cried. "You've done nothing—you didn't fight against Tudor."

"It was my intention to do so," he stated. "Will you take her home, my friend?"

"John Rathburn," Marganna muttered, "you are insane if you think I came all this way just to go home without you."

"First we are going to see what we can do to get you released," Will declared. "But you may be certain I will protect your wife."

"Thank you . . . damn, I'm weak as a kitten." Rath groaned, lying back on the pallet and closing his eyes.

"Why don't you rest while we see what is to be done?" Will suggested.

Rath merely nodded, but when Marganna leaned over him, his arms tightened around her. "Good-bye for now, love," he whispered. "Don't worry about me."

Before leaving the church, Marganna turned to Matthew Finch. "What about you, sir? Is there anything we can do to secure your freedom?"

"Nay." He waved a careless hand. "Perhaps if I were a few years younger or hadn't suffered this wound. As it is, I can't think of anything more useless than a one-legged old war-horse. No, Richard was the finest man I ever served under. I won't mind dying for his cause, for there'd not be another like him in my lifetime."

Will extended a hand and Finch clasped it. "God be with you, friend," Will said.

Outside the church Marganna looked at Will with renewed determination in her brown eyes.

"I'm not going to give up, even if Rath has. God knows there is little enough we can do, but I have an idea. And I shall need your promise that you will not argue with me about the matter."

In that moment, if she could have known it, she looked every bit as ferocious and commanding as her rebellious Tudor grandfather once had.

Chapter 20

Henry Tudor had commandeered Leicester's most comfortable inn for himself and his highest-ranking officers; it was close to the river and well away from the noisy town center.

Marganna was escorted inside to a small sitting room where she waited, nervously smoothing her skirts and thinking about Rath.

Her petition for an audience having been granted, she tried to calm her breathing as she followed a guard up a narrow flight of stairs and along a corridor. It seemed her heart was beating so loudly he must surely hear it, but if so, he gave no indication, merely pausing outside a closed wooden door to knock once and announce her name. When he opened the door and gestured for her to enter, she uttered a small, silent prayer and stepped inside.

Please, dear God, let him be generous! Let him be nothing like his mother.

Henry Tudor, now Henry VII of England, stood at the end of the room near the windows. When Marganna walked across the threshold, he turned to look at her and saw her drop into a graceful curtsey.

"Here . . . no need for that, cousin," he said hastily, reaching out a hand to draw her up.

Marganna had swallowed a great deal of pride in forcing herself to make obeisance to this man, but now she was glad she had. It appeared her display of humility had made him uncomfortable.

In appearance Henry Tudor was truly his mother's son. He was only average in height and build, his body stamped with the same ascetic look as Lady Stanley's. Instead of the kingly robes Marganna thought he would be wearing, he was dressed simply in a doublet whose brown color made his skin look dull and pasty, as though he'd been ill.

Marganna searched his face looking for some clue to his temperament or mood. It was long and bony, his lips thin; the lank brown hair that brushed his shoulders was the same color as the eyes that regarded her from beneath heavy lids. Though she knew Tudor to be close to Rath's age, he looked more than fifteen years older.

Henry Tudor was pleasantly surprised by his young cousin. His mother had not told him she was such a beauty. It had cost the young woman much to come before him; he could tell it by her defiant stance. But she was lovely, wearing a becoming gown the color of the sun-warmed apricots he'd loved so much in France. The color suited her, heightening the ivory glow of a flawless complexion and bringing out the brilliant depths of her splendid eyes. Her hair was glorious, its color rich and warm, changing shades each time she moved her head—sometimes the brown of precious spices, sometimes a clear autumn bronze.

So this was the woman his mother had wanted him to marry. He'd been mistaken to assume Lady Stanley's choice would have been a plain, devout young miss with no mind of her own. What a queen this woman would have made! Of course, her unfortunate marriage to Lord Rathburn had rendered that an impossibility.

"Tell me, cousin, have you come to congratulate me on my victory?"

She bit her lip, fighting to stifle the angry, hateful words crowding her mouth.

He gave a short, cold laugh. "No, of course not. You had gone over to the enemy, had you not?"

She clasped her hands together so tightly the knuckles were white. She cleared her throat nervously. "Sire, I . . . I am certain your mother must have told you the details of my imprisonment in the north. I did not go over to the enemy willingly."

"But you did go over?"

She nodded. "Yes. I fell in love with Rathburn, you see."

"So you love the man? Did you also love his king?"

Marganna considered the truth, then decided a half-truth would serve her purposes best. No matter what she would like to say to this usurper, she had to consider Rath's well-being first. "I did not know his king. Our meeting was not an auspicious occasion, if I may remind you."

"Ah, yes, the night you were caught spying." He studied her intently. "I assume, then, that you merely followed your husband's lead in matters political, as any good wife would do?"

Again she nodded briefly.

"What about the lads?"

"The lads?"

"Yes, Edward's sons. Where were they? Mother seems to feel you had some information about them."

She shrugged. "I thought I did also, but unhappily it seems I was mistaken. If the boys were being kept in the north, neither I nor my husband ever saw them."

His eyes narrowed. "You may not have known anything of their existence, but I believe your husband did. Knowing of my certain invasion, Richard would have seen the boys protected. Has Rathburn spirited them away, out of the country?"

"I think not," she replied stiffly. "He could have had no part in doing so, as he has been ill since coming south from Yorkshire nearly two weeks ago. Even now he lies ill in Greyfriars Church . . . your prisoner."

"Rathburn? A prisoner here?"

"Yes. Scheduled to hang tomorrow," she added, feeling a sense of desperation beginning to claw at her mind.

"He fought with Plantagenet?"

"No . . . no, he didn't. He fell ill. He had no part in the battle. He has done nothing wrong, other than to threaten a soldier who taunted him about the king . . . er, about Richard's death." She spread her hands in supplication. "Please, Your Grace, that is why I have come to you—to ask for his release. He is sick. Please, let me take him home."

"Do you presume to seek favor because your name was once Tudor?" he asked sternly.

She dropped her head, unsure how to answer his question. Finally, miserably she nodded. "I suppose so. It seemed the only chance I had of securing his pardon."

Tudor dipped his head, smiling faintly. "At least you are honest in the matter, Marganna. A rare trait, I believe."

She did not look at him, fearful he would know not all of her answers had been as truthful.

Entranced by the sweetly feminine curve of her averted cheek, Tudor realized she was different from any woman he had ever met. In his life of secrecy and exile, most of the women he'd known had been camp followers and whores—bold, outspoken, none too clean—their beauty, if ever they'd had any, long since faded, erased by the hardships of the life they were forced to lead. Other than bawdy women, his experience had been with ladies like his mother—proper, austere, cold, and too holy to feel or express any real human emotion. His eyes traced the soft outline of Marganna's rose-colored mouth, and he wondered what it would feel like to kiss her. She would be warm, he sensed, pliant and giving.

He felt like a foolish schoolboy as his neck flushed with heat, heat that surged upward, bringing some spark of life to his features.

My Lord, what would it be like to actually bed a woman such as Marganna? To forget every furtive encounter in wind-whipped tents or broken-down hostels in a night of slow, satisfying, sensual discovery?

"Marganna . . ." His voice sounded strained even to himself.

At that instant the door to the room burst open and in swept Lady Margaret Stanley, her coifed head held high, her thin nostrils quivering in rage. Her cold, pale eyes shot sparks of wrath as she crossed the room and stood before her niece.

"You lying, conniving strumpet," she declared. "I couldn't believe you would have the nerve to show your face before us! You are no longer a member of this family."

"Mother, I would appreciate it if you would kindly—"

Lady Stanley whirled to impale her son with a withering glare. "What were you thinking of, Henry, even to receive this . . . this ingrate?" She turned back to Marganna. "I suppose now that we are in power, you have decided to return to the fold? To plead your innocence again? To deny your betrayal of us?"

"No," Marganna quietly replied. "I came to ask a pardon for my husband. He is ill."

"A pardon!" the older woman shrilled. "Never! If your treacherous husband has somehow fallen into our hands, we will execute him with pleasure. And it would take very little to condemn you to the same death."

"Mother," Henry Tudor intoned calmly, "*I* will conduct this interview with my cousin, if you don't mind."

"You must be harsh with her, son. You see only the pretty, feminine exterior. How could you possibly know the evil in her heart?"

"She is kin," he pointed out. "She deserves the respect of being heard."

"She deserves nothing from the Tudors. She has taken from us all her miserable life . . . and couldn't do one simple thing to repay our charity."

Marganna thought of Rath lying helpless in the dark, cramped church and held her tongue. No matter what she had to endure, she would stay here for his sake.

Henry Tudor tapped his long, thin fingers impatiently on the windowsill.

"I will listen to her request and then make my own decision. Now, if you would please . . ."

"No!" Lady Stanley stamped a foot in frustration. "I say you will not aid this woman or her traitorous husband."

Tudor's face grew mottled and he drew himself up, towering over the small, enraged woman standing between himself and Marganna. "Madam, have you forgotten just which of us is king? Since your arrival in Leicester, I have heard nothing but 'we'! 'We' think thusly—'We' will grant this petition—'We' will not grant that one. I am exceedingly weary of it, I must say. Now you have gone too far. Take yourself from this chamber before I summon my stepfather and place you in his custody. The next time I need your advice, I will seek it. Until then I beg you, remember who wears the crown."

Lady Stanley stood still for a long moment, then slowly left the room. At the door she turned to cast one last look at her niece, giving Marganna the first glimpse of humility she had ever seen in the woman's eyes.

When the door had closed silently behind her, Henry Tudor said, "I hope you will forgive that unpleasant scene. Now, cousin, perhaps you will tell me just what it is you think I can do for your husband."

She quickly raised her eyes. "I . . . I would ask that you spare his life."

"Pardon him?"

"He is guilty of no wrongdoing. True, he was Richard's man, but he didn't raise a hand against you."

"What of his property?"

She shrugged. "We would need a place to live, but that is not important right now. I want only to take him someplace where he can rest and recuperate."

"And when he has regained his health? Would he not have thoughts of stirring a rebellion against me?"

"I . . . I do not think so. Richard's men are scattered, their leader gone. It would prove too difficult to launch yet another campaign. I feel I can safely promise you Rath would have nothing further to do with politics." She smiled wanly. "We could live in the north and raise sheep."

"All right, I have one last question. If I signed a document giving Rathburn a full pardon, one that preserved his family estates and promised to leave him in peace as long as he did not engage in political activity for the remainder of his life—if I were to do all that, please inform me, cousin, what would you be willing to do in return?"

He had moved closer to her, and now he lifted her chin with one thin hand.

Marganna swallowed with difficulty, her thoughts in turmoil, but when her gaze met his, her eyes were clear and calm.

"I love Rathburn. I will do anything you ask." She did not blink or look away. "Anything."

"Would you sleep with me to gain my favor?"

Forgive me, Rath . . .

"Yes, if that is what you wish."

He released a pent-up breath. "You are a beautiful woman, Marganna."

He bent his face to hers and she shut her eyes, praying she would not flinch.

His cold, dry kiss was nothing like Rath's, but concentrating on the heated passion of her husband's affections helped steady her, giving her the strength to endure Tudor's touch without showing the revulsion she felt.

Henry Tudor stepped back and looked into her lovely, upturned face. There had not been a flicker of response in her, he realized. A shame, but he'd expected nothing else. She'd said she loved Rathburn, and though it was clear she would sacrifice anything to save him, no other man would ever possess that which was his alone—her heart, her soul . . . her love. The taking of her body without those things would be a wasted, useless gesture.

"If you'll wait belowstairs, I will call my secretary and have Rathburn's pardon drawn up."

A small, shocked gasp was torn from her rigid throat, and tears welled in her extraordinary eyes. "I can never thank you . . ." Her words trailed away suddenly.

He shook his head and gave a soft laugh. "I demand no payment, cousin—though I must say, the relief on your face is hardly flattering! No, just take your husband home to Yorkshire and live a very quiet life."

"I swear it," she cried, feeling joy rising within her. Swiftly she knelt at his feet, then began to back from the room.

"I'm leaving for London tomorrow," he said suddenly, his lips curving into a half smile. "I don't suppose we will see much of you at court."

Marganna stood in the open doorway considering him. She did not like him—Henry Tudor was not a likable man—but neither had she felt the expected hatred. She had come to the inn prepared to beg for Rath's life, to humble herself in any way necessary. Thinking to meet a cold, judgmental tyrant, she had instead encountered a kinsman. She wondered whether he would have acknowledged that kinship if it had not been for his mother's arrogant interference. Thank God she, Marganna, would never have to know.

After tomorrow, she knew, the Henry Tudor she had met this afternoon would no longer exist. As king he could not afford to be that man ever again.

"No, I don't suppose you will see us at court," she replied softly, and the parting smile she gave him was dazzling.

'Tis just as well, he thought with a resigned sigh.

When they returned to the church, Will and Marganna showed the pardon to one of the sentries at the main door. He read it quickly, then handed it back with a shrug. "Rathburn's a lucky devil. Tudor isn't pardoning many. But you can't go in now. The priests have come to hear the condemned make their last confessions. Wait here and I'll send Lord Rathburn out."

When the guard disappeared inside the church, Will turned to Marganna with a reassuring smile.

"Why don't you wait here for Rath while I ride back to the inn and get the wagon I purchased? If we can make him comfortable, I don't see why we can't start north now—today." He looked back toward the town and shuddered visibly. "I can't think of any reason to delay our departure from this godforsaken place another hour."

When he had gone, Marganna walked across the lawn toward the back of the church to the graveyard on the riverbank. The grassy yard was littered with tilted gravestones, most bright with moss and lichen; tall and somber yew trees stood like forbidding sentinels. She was drawn toward one corner, away from the stone markers, where she could see the raw earth of a new grave.

Without thought Marganna knelt, weighed down by an overwhelming heaviness of spirit. Despite the fact that

Rath would soon be free, Richard had died a horrible death . . . and nothing could ever be the same again.

Flowers and tokens had been strewn on the grave in a furtive fashion, though someone had dared to leave a bouquet of white roses, their stems tied with narrow red and white streamers—red and white, the colors of Plantagenet.

Marganna reached out to touch the white roses, thinking that beneath them lay a king, a man of royal lineage whose unmarked grave was flanked by those of common paupers. His enemies had thought to bring him to a shameful end. But because there had been glory in the man, there was glory even in the unkind death he had suffered.

No doubt Richard would have preferred this quiet resting place among the trees to a cold marble tomb in the echoing vastness of Westminster Abbey. He had been, above all things, an ordinary man, happiest during the uncomplicated years spent at Middleham with his wife and child. Richard would have wanted no pomp, no ceremony—this simple grave suited him well.

She glanced up to see Rath coming slowly across the lawn toward her. With a cry of joy, she got to her feet and ran to meet him. He caught her in an unsteady embrace, his mouth closing warmly over hers.

He pulled away to look into her face. "Marganna, what has happened? They tell me I am free."

"Yes, isn't it wonderful? Will is coming and we are going to start back to Yorkshire now."

Suddenly his eyes fell on Richard's grave, and his arm tightened painfully around her waist.

"Sometimes I think it was only a nightmare," he said softly. "That everything is still the same. Oh, God, Dickon—if only that were true! If only we could go back."

"But we can't," she whispered. "You have to go on, to meet whatever lies ahead. That is what Richard did, remember?"

"Yes."

"Rath, he wasn't happy—he'd lost everything he held dear, all for the sake of a kingdom he didn't want. Perhaps he's at peace now."

"In a way, I think this is what he wanted. As far as I

could ascertain, the men I sent to warn him of a conspiracy got to him in time, but he probably wouldn't listen to them. Now I wonder if he would have paid any more heed to me. He was through with life, I believe.''

Marganna nodded, then held out a hand to him. ''How would you like to go home now?'' she asked. ''Will should be here at any moment.''

''I can think of nothing I'd like more—and yet it puzzles me. How is it I am to be pardoned when there are others no more guilty than I who will die tomorrow?''

Marganna's eyes faltered, and she thought her heart had surely ceased to beat. She had hoped Rath would not ask these questions until they were as far from the agonizing reality of Bosworth Field as possible.

''Marganna . . . love, what is it?''

She moistened her lips. How could she make him understand?

''I think you had better tell me just how you obtained the pardon,'' he said quietly.

She raised her chin and met his gaze steadily. ''I . . . I spoke to my cousin about it.''

His face darkened. ''You went to *Henry Tudor* to beg for my life? You . . . you crawled to that sniveling, whey-faced coward asking for favors?''

Fear nearly throttled her as she cast around in her frantic mind for the words that would explain, that would make it all right. ''I didn't have to crawl . . . or beg.''

He wasn't listening. ''Why would you have done such a thing?'' he whispered, hands clenching and unclenching at his sides.

''Because I couldn't just stand by and watch you die. I had to do something . . . and I didn't know anything else to do!''

''I would rather you'd have let me die than know I'd gained a pardon at the expense of your pride—of my pride!'' He ran an agitated hand through his hair. ''My God, Marganna, he's the one who killed Dickon! Doesn't that mean anything to you? Did you have so little love for Richard? And what about the boys? I thought you loved them!''

"Yes," she shouted tearfully. "Yes, I loved them all! But, Rath . . . damn it, I love you more! I didn't care what I had to do, I only wanted to save you!"

Rath stepped away, moving so that Richard's grave was between them. A breeze had sprung up from the river, ruffling the petals of the roses and causing the red and white streamers to unfurl gracefully.

"What price did your cousin exact?" he asked in a weary voice.

"What do you mean?"

"Did he demand the usual favors of war? Did he ask you to sleep with him?"

"Y-yes." She raised miserable eyes. "He asked, but . . ."

He turned away, his shoulders slumped. He took a few slow paces, then stood staring upward through the trees. "I can't believe you would go to Tudor. Was I worth so much?"

"Rath," she began, starting around the grave toward him.

He shook his head. "No . . . stay where you are."

She stopped short. "So, even though Richard is dead you intend to keep him between us?" Her words were so low she was not certain he could even hear them.

"He has always been between us," Rath stated bleakly, "as have the Tudors. We should have known we couldn't change that."

"Perhaps we haven't tried hard enough."

"I'm tired of trying, Marganna. Damn it, I'm tired of everything."

She felt numb as she let her gaze move over him. He was so thin, so ill-looking. There was no doubt it would be a long time before he was the vigorous, healthy Rathburn of old.

"Nothing ever changes between us, does it?" she asked dully. "Each thing I do turns out wrong, only making you suspect me more."

He looked at her then, but there was desolation in his eyes, not the anger or contempt she expected. His exhausted sigh fell heavily on the afternoon air.

After a long moment he said, "Somehow, if we just

simply go on with our life together, it will seem more a betrayal of Richard than ever. I don't think you should go back to Yorkshire with us, Marganna. It will be better if we spend a few months apart."

Marganna steeled herself. She would not make a scene by crying or pleading with him.

"If that is what you wish."

"It is. I'm tired and confused. I just want to be alone."

"Is there nothing I can say or do?" she asked, glad her voice remained steady.

"No, nothing." Then, in a tone of firm dismissal, he added, "Now, if you'll excuse me, I'd like a moment to say good-bye to my king."

She nodded once and began walking stiffly across the lawn. She saw Will coming toward her, the wide grin on his freckled face slowly dying as he looked first at Rath, then at her.

"What is it, Marganna?"

She glanced back to where Rath knelt by the grave. She saw him take one of the white roses from the bouquet and hold it in his tanned fingers. The gesture transported her back in time to Rathburn Hall, and she was remembering the night he had picked the rose and tucked it into her bodice. *In Yorkshire, when your sweetheart gives you flowers . . .*

"He's upset with me for going to Tudor," she said flatly. "He doesn't want me to return to Yorkshire with you."

"I'll talk to him, Marganna. He's not himself. You may have to give him a little time."

"You didn't see the look in his eyes, Will. I'm afraid."

Rath approached them, purposely avoiding her gaze.

"Marganna is remaining here. Don't worry, Will, I'll send her money, but in the meantime, I'm certain she'd be welcome to stay with her family."

He began walking away unsteadily, as if he were very weary.

Marganna's eyes clung to Rath's proud back, and when he stopped in midstride, her heart lurched wildly. But she realized he was only pausing in the shadows of the yews to wait for his friend.

She turned back to Will. "Here, take the pardon. He may need it later." She thrust the rolled document into his hand. "Please take care of him, he is so ill."

"What about you?" Will's face was pale, his expression agitated.

"I'll stay here until I hear from you. Maybe he will change his mind when he is better. If not . . ."

"Let me give you what gold I have with me. That way, at least you can keep lodgings in a decent inn. And I'll leave two of my men at arms with you. It's no time for a woman to be on her own." He looked at her for another moment, clearly at a loss as to how to comfort her. Finally he enfolded her in his arms and kissed her cheek. "I will write to you as soon as I can."

Marganna watched as Will walked away. When he reached the waiting man, she heard Rath say wearily, "Let's go home, friend."

Will braced Rath with a sturdy arm, supporting him as they made their way to a nearby wagon. Soon the small entourage was gone, leaving her alone except for two guardsmen standing at a respectable distance, their eyes politely averted.

The graveyard was becoming shadowed by the dusk of evening, but she had no desire to leave it. Indeed, it seemed an appropriate setting for what she feared had just occurred—the death of Rath's love for her.

Chapter 21

Marganna stepped to the window in her room at the Leicester Arms and pulled back the draperies to peer out into the darkening gloom of a rainy, late October day. She leaned her forehead against the thick glass and sighed. It had been two long months since she had last seen Rath, and just as she had a thousand times before, she wondered where he was, what he was doing.

There had been only one letter from Yorkshire, and it had contained so little mention of Rath that Marganna knew her husband had probably forbidden Will to write of him. At least she knew he was back at Rathburn Hall, his health much improved. The letter dealt mainly with news about Ned and Dickon, with Will using a careful code to safeguard against damaging information falling into the wrong hands. Marganna was relieved to know the boys had arrived in the Low Countries safely and were settling in with the merchant family as well as could be expected. Ned, feeling fine, was learning the new language, and Dickon was busy trying to teach Caesar to track wild pigs. She had laughed at that, but all in all, the letter only left her feeling more miserable.

It was obvious Rath hadn't forgiven her and didn't want her back. He'd sent the money he'd promised, but hadn't even been concerned enough to inquire as to her well-being.

She used the money to pay Will's two men at arms a handsome wage, for they were growing restless, tired of inactivity and chafing for the time they would be released from her service and sent home.

She supposed she had kept them with her in the hope Rath would reconsider and send for her, but she was being selfish and she knew it. It was past time to let go of her last tenuous hold on the North Country.

She often longed for Owen Tudor's harp, knowing it had always had the power to soothe her. The harp, along with most of her clothes and personal possessions, had been left at Middleham to await her return from Scarborough. Again, she had delayed sending for those things because she'd hoped so fervently it wouldn't be necessary.

The rain beat a dull, steady tatoo on the window pane, and from somewhere in the distance came the low rumble of thunder.

Suddenly, with a clarity that took her by the throat, Marganna was remembering the storm that had driven her and Rath to seek shelter in the shepherds' hut on the moor. Images of that night washed over her with startling vividness—the sound of the wind and rain, the scratchy wool blanket, the heady odor of heather ale.

Lost in reverie, she felt his hard, warm hands moving over her body, heard his voice grow husky with passion, saw the look of dawning love in his eyes.

How could the strong emotions stirred to life by the raging storm die so weak and pitiful a death?

They couldn't . . . it simply wasn't possible.

Marganna's pulse began to race as she considered the situation. Rath had loved her, she knew he had. And with a love that had been all the more powerful because of the weeks spent denying it. She understood enough about Rath's innate stubbornness to know he did not pledge his love easily. Surely he would not withdraw it with haste either.

There must be some way to make him see she had only been thinking of him when she turned to Henry Tudor for help. In her love, her desperate worry, she had—at least in Rath's eyes—made a grievous mistake. She would never feel it was so, because her actions had preserved the life of the man she would always cherish. But even if they could never agree on the matter, there had to be some means of reaching a compromise. If only she could convince him to forgive her enough to allow her another chance.

With a heartening blaze of determination, she began to make plans. She nearly laughed outright as she imagined the expressions on the faces of the men at arms when she announced they were to journey to Yorkshire.

She turned back to the rain-streaked window and this time the smile didn't fade. She was going back to Yorkshire!

Yorkshire . . . and Rath.

The trail they had been following suddenly topped a steep ridge, and there below them was an incredibly lovely view of the River Ure. Marganna remembered seeing the same scene on her first journey north, though now the deep greens of summer had given way to the richer shades of autumn. The golds and russets and umbers glowed jewellike in the frosted air, and the river itself was a pure slate gray.

The damp wind was invigorating, chill and clean, fragrant with the tang of dying bracken and old heather, releasing her soul from the pain and regret she had suffered.

She reined in her horse and sat quietly for a moment, tilting her head to listen.

Coor-lee!

With the anticipated sound came the sight of the graceful curlew, wheeling through the sky, pitting its strength against the gale.

Coor-lee!

And to think, Marganna mused, an expression of delighted wonder filling her eyes as she scanned the horizon, I once thought the curlew's cry the most melancholy sound I'd ever heard, and in my ignorance, I believed the moors were lonely and desolate.

The bleakness of living alone, the unhappy days and nights without Rath, had taught her the true meaning of desolation and heart-crushing loneliness.

Joyously she raised her face to the cool autumn sunshine and laughed aloud. My God, how she had missed this.

How her spirit had longed for the freedom of the vast, unadorned, windswept reaches of the moor.

The journey was nearly done—the next sight she could expect to see was that of the towers of Middleham rising against the bruised sky. Her heart started to pound exultantly and she leaned forward, spurring her horse into a gallop that carried her swiftly over the rocky ground, leaving the two smiling men at arms to follow.

Rathburn flung open the doors to the balcony and strode out into the pale afternoon sunshine. Leaning against the stone balustrade he surveyed his property, which stretched out as far as the eye could see, clear to the line of low blue hills in the distance.

He had been granted his life and continued ownership of his property, and for that he was grateful, though there were still times when he nearly choked on the gall of broken pride. There were nights when he sweated and shouted through unbearable nightmares, and sometimes whole days when he stared unseeing into the fire, unable to forget his inability to reach Richard in time. It was certain some part of the guilt would remain with him for as long as he lived, but even so a healing of sorts was beginning to take place.

He frowned, looking around him—the autumn garden below, the neat stone outbuildings beyond. Everything seemed just as it always had. Despite the upheaval, normalcy was returning to the countryside. Yorkshire had not, would not, forget Richard, but as in all matters human, life went on, and eventually one simply had to be swept along with it or die.

When he had first come back north, he'd thought he wanted to die. He was weak and ill and bitter, perfectly content to lie in bed and curse fate. But as his health improved, he grew bored with inactivity and began to throw himself into estate business with a fervor. He found he could forget some of the horror of Richard's death if he drove himself constantly, working long hours with his hired men to salve the sheep or repair stone fences, or riding out day after day to survey the farthest reaches of his property. It was on one of those occasions that he'd realized his desire for death had quietly faded.

His nearly debilitating outrage over the indecency of his king's dying was slowly easing too, giving way to a steady, comforting flow of happier memories—Dickon at eighteen, relieved to have proved his valor on the battlefield, gazing with adoration at his older brother, a man who would be king; Dickon at twenty, gently kissing his shy bride, turning on her a look of such warmth and love that it left those assembled feeling awed by the depth of his emotions; Dickon watching his small son at the archery butts, the pride on his face enough to bring tears to the most cynical eyes; Dickon as he was before the years of care and sorrow overtook him. It was becoming easier for Rath to remember him that way.

Now he paced to the end of the balcony and stood lost in thought. There was only one part of his life he had not been able to come to terms with—Marganna.

The deed he wanted to despise her for had simply been the act of a wife driven by unselfish love for her husband. Her only crime had been to put regard for his safety above loyalty to Richard. His years of training had instilled in him the belief that nothing came before loyalty to one's sovereign, but now, whether he liked it or not, a small, determined woman with spice-colored hair had caused him to doubt the worthiness of that concept. In all honesty he knew, had the situation been reversed, he would have moved heaven and earth to save Marganna's life. So how could he fault her for what she'd done?

After leaving Leicester, he hadn't been able to bear the thought of Middleham, so he'd asked Will to bring him back to Rathburn Hall. The first thing he'd seen when he stepped over the threshold was the polished, curving staircase, and he nearly floundered under a wave of remembrance. He could see himself and Marganna on the night of their wedding—she, wildly angry, trying to escape up those stairs; he, elated, threatening to ravish her then and there.

He'd tried to sleep in the bedchamber, but in the wee hours the memories had finally driven him away. He'd moved into a small, seldom-used room on the third floor where he remained.

He'd gone back into their bedroom only one other time. On a gray day when sorrow sat heavily on his shoulders, he had decided to pack Marganna's belongings, thus clearing the room of every trace of her existence making it usable again. When he had thrown open the doors to the wardrobe, the first thing that caught his attention was a dry, withered flower lying atop a folded shawl. It took him a moment to realize what it was: the white rose he had tucked into Marganna's bodice at the dance following the sheep washing. Why had she kept it? Beseiged by conflicting emotions, he'd closed the wardrobe doors and quietly left the room.

He couldn't even escape her outside the house. The curlew's cry, the scent of heather . . . everything brought her to mind.

He supposed the decision had been made long before he stepped out onto the balcony, but something about the sight of his lands unfolding on all sides reaffirmed it. He loved Rathburn Hall and had at last admitted his desire to live there with a family of his own making. More than anything he wanted the pleasure of having his wife with him, to share every aspect of life.

He would plead with Marganna to give him a second chance; he would even find some way to convince her she could be content in Yorkshire. He wanted her to know of a certainty that he loved her beyond reason, beyond life and time and loyalty and honor.

It would soon be twilight, too late to start a journey. Suddenly a broad smile broke over his face, and he strode through the doors back into his parlor. There was no reason to wait until morning to start. Hell, he couldn't sleep in this house anyway.

Just as he reached the hallway, Will Metcalfe came in through the front door. His freckled face lost its anxious expression as he saw Rath looking like his old self for the first time in weeks.

"I've got to talk to you," Will said, slipping off his cloak.

"Then you'll have to do it while I pack," Rath said over his shoulder, vaulting up the stairs. "I'm on my way to get Marganna. Jesus Christ and all the saints, why have I waited so long!"

Marganna was saddened by the changes made at Middleham since it had become Crown property. Many rooms stood empty, though a few were filled with chests and crates that held the possessions of former residents. It seemed too silent, somehow forlorn.

Most of the familiar faces were gone, of course, but there were still a few people she knew. Pickering, the castle steward, greeted her warmly and at her inquiry assured her that although he did not know what the new king had planned for Middleham, he was certain so splendid a castle would not be allowed to fall into disuse and ruin.

Marganna had meant to stop only briefly to collect the belongings she had left, but once inside its sheltering walls, she felt reluctant to leave. Now that she was so close to Rath she had begun to lose her courage. What if he wouldn't listen to her? Or worse, what if he listened, coldly polite, and sent her away again? She needed time to prepare herself, to plan exactly what she would say to him.

Thus, when Pickering extended an invitation for supper and a night's lodging, she accepted gratefully. She would ride out to Rathburn Hall tomorrow.

To Marganna's pleased surprise, Pickering called Lilibeth, her former maid, to assist her to her old bedchamber. The two women hugged joyously, with Lilibeth explaining tearfully that she hadn't known what else to do but stay on at Middleham, hoping someday Lady Rathburn would come for her. It was quickly decided that when Marganna left the castle on the morrow, Lilibeth would go with her.

Following a pleasant dinner, Marganna retired to her bedchamber to enjoy a leisurely bath by the fire. Afterward, dressed in a linen nightshift and bed robe, she stood on the thick fur rug and gazed around her. It seemed so natural to be back in this room with its bed hangings of hunter's green and the whimsical tapestries on the walls.

Unexpectedly she thought of seeing Rath the next day and shivered in apprehension. Knowing of no better way to calm herself and compose her thoughts, she took up the small harp that once belonged to her grandfather.

With a smile, she stroked the instrument's ancient wood, smoothed and burnished by generations of loving hands; tentatively she drew her fingers across the strings, feeling the familiar response to the delicate fragment of music. Sitting in a chair she'd brought close to the fire, she made a little ceremony of tuning the harp, then began to play. Soft strains of music filled the room, and when her tenseness had faded, she sang the song once requested of her by a king.

"Ah, what is love? It is a pretty thing,
As sweet unto a shepherd as a king;

"And sweeter, too,
For kings have cares that wait upon a crown,
And cares can make the sweetest love to frown;
Ah, then, ah, then,
If country loves such sweet desires do gain,
What lady would not love a shepherd swain?"

"So this is where you're hiding. I've been looking for you!"

The soothing strains of the pastorale ended in a series of discordant notes as Marganna's fingers slipped on the harp strings. She stiffened in surprise as she felt two warm hands drop onto her shoulders.

"You don't know how close I came to setting out on my own journey. Thank God Will arrived with the message you were here."

With a low cry, Marganna got to her feet, laying aside the harp as she turned toward her husband.

"Rath," she whispered, her breathing constricted, refusing to raise her cowardly eyes higher than the lacing of the white shirt he wore beneath black velvet. Here she was standing in front of him at last, but with no thought yet of the words she would need to say to win him back.

He seemed to tower over her in the dimly lighted room. The need to speak warred with her fear of saying the wrong thing; finally, with every ounce of courage she could summon, she lifted her eyes to look at his face. His hair was still as black as the dark side of a midnight moon, and his eyes were the same heart-stopping green . . . but, dear God, he looked so tired! Tired and worn, with the look of someone who hasn't slept well for a long time. Seeing the shadow of exhaustion lying upon him, Marganna sensed the desolation he had known and grieved for him, for the pain he had suffered. Filled with despair, she stared at him, both hands moving to cover her mouth in an unsuccessful attempt to hold back wrenching sobs that could no longer be silenced.

Rath drew her into his embrace, one hand cradling her head against his chest. "I never meant to hurt you this way, sweetheart," he muttered, stroking her hair. "I'm a God-damned fool!"

For some reason, his declaration only made her cry harder, her hot tears soaking his shirt and bringing moisture to his own eyes.

When she pushed away to look at him through tear-drowned eyes, his jaw tightened. He should be explaining, apologizing, begging her to forgive him. He had rehearsed what he would say over and over as he'd ridden to Middleham. Where were the words now?

He had not expected to be so intimidated by her beauty. Every rational thought had flown the instant he'd stepped through the door and seen her there by the fire. As it so often did, Middleham had presented another of its sweet domestic pictures, but this one had been so soul stirring, and he was shattered.

He had never seen her look lovelier than she did now, standing there in her simple nightclothes, her cinnamon hair unbound and curling around her shoulders, eyes and mouth vulnerable in her sorrow. There were a hundred things he wanted to tell her, but the words would not form.

"Rath, I . . . I don't know what to say to you," she cried suddenly. "I'm so afraid I will speak the wrong words."

"You?" he gasped. "*You* don't know what to say? But . . ."

He wrapped his arms around her in a fierce hug.

"Believe me when I tell you I've been worried about what to say to you too, sweetheart," he murmured. "I practiced my speech all the way across the moor." He put his face close to hers. "But I've just realized something."

"What is that?"

"If for some reason, we did not have the chance to talk this out—if we had only a brief moment to express everything we needed and wanted each other to know—I think there is one phrase that would suffice." His hands came up to cup her face tenderly, his thumbs brushing away the tears that still seeped through her tangled lashes. "I love you, Marganna. I love you more than life."

Indeed, everything he felt was contained in those few words—his guilt, his grief, his penitence.

"Oh, God, I love you too," she whispered, feeling as though her soul had been unburdened.

His mouth was warm as his lips moved in light caresses over hers, welcoming her back into his arms and heart. Her lips parted, opening in soft wonder.

"I missed you, love," he growled from his throat as his kisses trembled against her eyelids, her temples, along the high cheekbones, and down to her mouth again. Without moving away, she echoed his words, causing his kiss to deepen and become less tentative.

Marganna's hands had been caught between them. Now they slid upward to his chest, her fingers spreading wide to explore the rapid beating of his heart. With feathery strokes they continued on, brushing over his shoulders and up the back of his neck, to weave themselves into his thick hair.

She stood on tiptoe to thrust her body higher, more closely into his shielding embrace. She rested her face against his neck, against bronzed skin that smelled of summer sunshine, and murmured, "Rath, I don't ever want to sleep alone again!"

His pulse went mad.

"Oh, sweetheart! I have lain awake nights wanting you

so damned badly I ached. Those were the times I cursed myself most of all."

"Shh," she chided softly. "No more talk of blaming . . . remember?"

"Then what shall we talk about? If we don't keep busy with talk, I very much fear I might be tempted to . . ." He broke off with a crooked smile.

"I have an idea," she said wickedly, her finger tracing the contours of his ear. "Would I be too brazen if I asked you to show me how a Yorkshireman keeps his wife warm during the long, cold winter?"

He held her at arm's length, his burning look so intense it was nearly a scowl. "I'd like nothing more," he replied, "but, Marganna, I won't . . . I can't . . . make love to you if you aren't going to stay with me."

"But I . . ."

He gave her a small shake. "No, listen to me, please." Feeling suddenly shy, he pulled her to him again and spoke the words into her hair. "When we came north in the beginning, you were my prisoner, but somewhere along the way, things changed so drastically that I now find myself completely at your mercy." He drew a deep breath. "I won't make it worse for myself than it already is. I can't risk more painful memories if you aren't going to stay."

"I came here determined to convince you we belong together," she cried. "Nothing is going to make me leave you again. Not even you!"

The kiss they shared then bore no relation to their earlier ones. Never meant to be reverent or forgiving, this kiss simmered and seethed and burst into flame, threatening to consume them. It sent tongues of fiery need flickering through their bodies, and heated their blood so it boiled and raged.

Clinging together they sank to their knees in the deep, soft thickness of the fur rug. With urgent fingers, Rath stripped the dressing robe from her shoulders and cast it aside. She helped him shrug out of his doublet; her trembling hands tore at the laces on his shirt.

She knew she would never grow tired of the feel of his skin beneath her hands. She loved its warmth, its firmness, the sensual haze of dark hair that felt so exciting to her sensitive fingertips. She kissed the hollow of his throat, his jaw, the dimples that scored his lean cheeks.

Rath pulled her tightly against him, holding her so that one of his corded thighs intruded between hers; he lowered his ardent mouth to kiss and tease her breasts as they tightened and strained against the thin fabric of her shift.

Experiencing an overpowering need to be even closer, they tore away their remaining clothing, and then Rath was gently forcing her down into the sumptuous luxury of the fur. Nothing had ever stirred her as much as the feel of his hard, unyielding body boldly pressing her deep into the cloudlike softness beneath her.

Their combined breathing was harsh and ragged; the only other sounds were their murmured comments and small cries of pleasure. Arousal had been swift and incendiary; release was nearly as sudden, and its effect far more devastating.

Together they had fanned the fire into an inferno, a blaze they feared would destroy them because they had been so powerless to halt it. Like ashes in a hot wind, they spiraled upward, swirling and dancing among the flames, soaring to rarified heights only to explode and fall in a shower of brilliant sparks, finally released to drift slowly, languidly back to the embers from which they sprang.

Lying close together, they watched the reflection of the fire burn in each other's eyes. Peacefully they realized that, instead of being scorched and scarred by the raging heat, they had been cleansed, their wounds cauterized, their love regenerated.

Some time in the night Rath was awakened by the chill creeping into the room. The fire had burned low, and outside a cold autumn wind was flinging icy rain against the window. He kissed Marganna's bare shoulder and she stirred, murmuring in her sleep. He smiled, brushing a strand of russet hair from her cheek.

"Come, love, wake up. It's time to get into bed."

She turned her face to give him a sleepy smile. "I love you," she whispered.

"And I thank God you do," he said solemnly.

He eased her up and onto her feet, leading her toward the curtained bed in the shadowy corner. Halfway across the room she stopped and cried, "Oh, Rath, look at that moon! Isn't it beautiful?"

She ran to the window to look out, and he seized the coverlet from the bed and followed. Just as they had done at other times and in other places, he sat on the window seat and pulled her onto his lap, wrapping the coverlet around both of them.

The moon was a pale, silver disk, partly obscured by ragged clouds buffeted wildly by the raging wind. Below them the sluggish light was dimly reflected in the choppy waters of the moat.

Leaning close to the cold glass Rath asked, "Do you remember the vows we made that day we tossed the pendant and badge into the moat?"

"I do." Her eyes met his.

"Can we abide by them now, after all that has happened?"

Her face was very still. "I'm not certain. I mean . . . well, I've discovered something important in the past weeks. There are just some parts of myself I am not willing to give up."

"What do you mean?"

"Well, I once promised to forget my ties to the Tudor family, but I'm no longer willing to do that."

She felt his shoulder stiffen beneath her hand; swallowing deeply, she went on. "I don't mean Henry Tudor. He will always remain a paradox to me. He is both the cold-blooded monster who murdered Richard and the forgiving cousin who saved my husband's life. How can I deal with a truth such as that? 'Tis best not to think on it too often, I suppose. At any rate, it would seem Henry is much like other men, a complicated mixture of good and bad."

She let her hand drop to her lap where she studied it intently.

"But as I said, it isn't Henry who concerns me. I would never ask your tolerance of him, but, Rath, I am the result of my ancestry. I can't deny it . . . I won't deny it. I refuse to think of my mother as an enemy, or my grandmother. And that harp over there, the one I brought with me?"

He followed her gaze, nodding.

"It belonged to my grandfather, Owen Tudor." Her chin went up in the familiar way. "I never knew him, but I'm told he was a courageous old rebel, even if he did fight for the house of Lancaster."

"I understand, love," Rath said quietly. "And you are quite right. A family is a precious possession."

"And if I ever have children, I want to be able to tell them stories of their great-grandfather."

"Don't look so fierce, sweetheart. I have no objection whatsoever, as long as I am free to tell them stories of Richard."

"Naturally." She grinned suddenly. "I may have a story or two of my own, you know."

He dropped a kiss on her forehead. "So," he teased, "we are to have children, are we?"

Her eyes began to glow. "There are a great many rooms at Rathburn Hall," she reminded him demurely.

He shifted her closer and kissed her slowly and thoroughly. In the darkness, his white teeth gleamed as he favored her with a broad smile. "For the first time in months, Marganna, I'm beginning to see how very sweet our life together can be. We'll make Rathburn Hall the home neither of us had when we were growing up, and we will fill it with children and noise and love."

"And our offspring will write plays to be presented in the garden."

"So long as their mother agrees to dress as Will Scarlett," he murmured against her ear.

"And we will go on picnics to the gill, and you can show your sons how to build a pirates' raft from willow saplings."

"Only if we take along the nursemaid, so that you and I can slip away and observe tradition by . . . well, you know."

His lips grazed her chin.

"I will teach the girls to play the harp, and you can teach the boys to play the lute."

"And together we can teach them the ballad of the North Country man."

He kissed each corner of her mouth.

"And our sons will never have to train to be knights," she declared firmly. "And our daughters will never know what it is to send a loved one away to battle. Promise me, Rath!"

"I swear it, my love. By all the saints!"

His mouth covered hers sweetly, tenderly, telling her more clearly than words that he was honor bound to keep his oath.

He stood up and lifted her in his arms, the coverlet trailing to the floor.

"Rath," she whispered, hiding her face in the hollow of his shoulder, "I never slept with Henry Tudor."

"I know," he replied.

She lifted her face and met his steady gaze.

"But I would have, if it had been the only way."

"I know that, too." Briefly he rested his cheek against her hair. "But those are things we are not going to talk about now," he reminded her. "Mayhap someday . . . but not now."

"Let's go to bed, then. I want to get an early start in the morning. I am anxious to go home to Rathburn Hall."

For a moment Rath stood looking out the window. "You know, someday in the distant future someone is going to find the pendant or the boar badge we tossed into the moat. Isn't it a shame they will never know the story behind them?"

"Yes," she agreed. "I wish everyone could know our story."

"They'd never believe it." He laughed and carried her away to bed.

The next morning Marganna stood in the courtyard waiting for Rath, who was overseeing the loading of her belongings onto a packhorse. She was excited and a little nervous about going back to Rathburn Hall. She knew Rath still harbored some doubt about taking her to live in such isolation; he worried that she might not be able to withstand the Yorkshire winters.

She smiled to herself. She knew she had changed, and she looked forward to convincing him of the fact.

She glanced up to see her husband striding across the courtyard toward her, his handsome face lighted in a loving smile. With a rush of emotion she realized he was the one person who could fulfill every dream she had ever nurtured. She was no longer the lonely child who stood at the convent gates wishing for someone to whom she could belong.

She belonged to Rath. She had found her home.

Author's Note

Middleham Castle keeps its lonely watch in the north of England just as it has done for 800 years.

At first glance it seems forsaken—a desolate tangle of stones looking nothing like the mighty fortress of a king-maker or the favored residence of a tragic sovereign. The lute and viol are silent, the ballad singer and bard gone.

But the broken bases of huge, fluted columns attest to the one-time magnificence of the keep with its splendid great hall and a chapel whose height soared upward for three storys. A certain strength is still evident in the thick foundations and forbidding ramparts, though now the remains of glory are choked with grass, and wild buttercups bloom between the stones.

If there is a stirring of emotion anywhere within those scarred walls, it is in the southwest tower, where cascades of green vines, Nature's lifeblood, flow down from the gaping wounds above. There is something there . . . a faint echo of merry laughter? The soft sigh of a sleeping child? The sensitive listener pauses, but all too often the modern world intrudes and the moment is lost. The visitor leaves Middleham thinking the ruined castle has yielded up few of its secrets.

Ah, but at night when the shattered battlements are bathed in the pale firelight of a Yorkshire moon or illuminated by the strange glow of a midsummer night in the north, Middleham lives again. Its ghostly halls are peopled with the spirits of those who loved, hated, lived, and died there.

The wind sweeps down from the moors to shriek

through roofless chambers or whisper along crumbling walkways. When the wind is untamed, it becomes the cry of a wild-eyed queen grieving for her dead child. When it is gentle, it seems to be the voice of a weary king seeking answers to somber questions posed by destiny.

Middleham Castle stands as a testament to the misdeeds of man . . . the untruths, the greediness, the betrayals. Ironically it also remains a symbol of loyalty, of pledges made and kept, of devotion to duty, and of concern for one's fellow man.

But the real essence of this lonely northern keep has to do with love . . . for there was an abundance of that emotion at Middleham—love of commonfolk for their master, love of parents for their child, love of man for a woman . . .

Love. Ageless, timeless, enduring. Love. The reason for life.

Richard III was the last English king to die in battle, as well as the only English monarch with no tomb to honor his memory. Even now, 500 years after his death, he is the central figure in a controversy that seems never ending. There are those who prefer to think of him as the ultimate villain, the cold-blooded murderer of the innocent princes in the Tower; many others contend he was potentially England's greatest king, a tragic man purposely misrepresented by the historians and writers in Tudor employ who left, strangely enough, the only surviving accounts.

Richard has always been one of our personal heroes, and for this reason we decided to use his story as the background setting for a historical romance. Because of the nature of a romance novel, it was not possible, nor was it our intention, to attempt to vindicate Richard. Briefly, in the only words of defense we will offer here, we suggest as others have that scholars truly interested in the mystery of the princes' alleged death look more closely at Henry Tudor. Why would Richard, if he could so easily summon the ruthlessness necessary to slay his two nephews, fail to recognize that their deaths left at least eleven other heirs to the throne? After Richard's own death, it was Tudor himself who began, quietly and efficiently, to eliminate them all.

Even though Henry managed to maintain the crown until his death in 1509, his reign was an uneasy one, marred by insurrections and misery. He ruled as a tyrant, imposing heavy fines and taxes on his subjects and, by his extreme frugality, built a huge treasury to be turned over to his son, Henry VIII. The more glowing accounts of his kingship were, again, basically written by those in his own employ.

This book was meant merely to offer our version of one theory concerning the fate of Ned and Dickon, the young princes. There is no real proof the boys were ever murdered, or if they were, who actually murdered them, despite the accounts printed faithfully, albeit erroneously, in history books decade after decade. There is some belief the elder boy did suffer from a degenerative bone disease, and it is interesting to note that in later years, the "pretenders" who came forward never claimed to be Edward but, instead, his younger brother.

Please excuse the liberties taken in the writing of this book, primarily with Marganna's ancestry. Only one of the sources we used credited Katherine and Owen Tudor with a daughter; that account provided us with the idea for Marganna's mother. Marganna herself, as well as Rath and the inhabitants of Middleham Castle, are simply products of our imaginations.

Though we created Richard's secret visit to Yorkshire for our own purposes, we did so because there is a period of time during late July of 1485 when his movements were unaccounted for. We felt that had such a journey been possible, he would have taken pleasure in even a brief return to the home he loved so much.

Although we were aware the pastorale sung by Marganna in Chapter 17 actually dated from the sixteenth century, we chose to use it because it expressed Richard's situation so perfectly.

And finally, while there is no proof that Lady Stanley joined her son in Leicester following his victory, her ambitious nature was such that it seemed logical to place her at the scene.

There are two excellent works of fiction we found both fascinating and moving, which we would like to recommend to any reader interested in learning more about Richard III. They are *The Broken Sword,* by Rhoda Edwards (New York: Doubleday and Company, Inc., 1976) and *We Speak No Treason,* by Rosemary Hawley Jarman (Boston: Little, Brown and Company, 1971).

Paul Murray Kendall is probably the best known of Richard's modern-day biographers, and the following is a quote from his book, *Richard the Third* (New York: W. W. Norton and Company, Inc., 1956):

"He was thirty-two years old, had reigned two years, one month, twenty-eight days. The only language, it turned out, in which he had been able to communicate himself successfully to the world was the terse idiom of courage, and the chief subject he had been given to express was violence. It had begun for him as a child in violence and it had ended in violence; the brief span between had been a tale of action and hard service with small joy and much affliction of spirit."

P.S. Incidentally, a boar badge—such as the one Rath used in pledging his loyalty to Marganna—was actually found in the moat at Middleham Castle and is on display at the Yorkshire Museum, York, England.

SCOTNEY ST. JAMES

SCOTNEY ST. JAMES is a pseudonym for the writing team of Lynda Varner and Charlotte Hoy. Friends since high school, both reside in the Flint Hills of Kansas, albeit twenty-five miles apart. Charlotte and husband Clint live on the high prairie in an old schoolhouse, while Lynda and husband Don have a farm in the foothills.

The two always considered writing, but it was not until after their children were grown—Charlotte has two sons and two daughters, Lynda a son and daughter—that they co-authored their first novel.

Sharing a love for books and travel, they were inspired on a trip to the British Isles to write a historical romance, and now their goal is to write only about special places they have actually visited. Scotland is a favorite setting, but castle ruins on the English moors or the lake country of Canada also appeal to them. Charlotte and Lynda are returning to Britain for a stay that is certain to provide a wealth of ideas for future projects.